Love at the Gates of Hell

STELLA ROSSI

Cover Design: KeyVei

Editing: Sarah Pesce of Lopt and Cropt Editing

ISBNs: 979-8-9990826-1-9 (pbk), 979-8-9990826-0-2 (hrd), B0DWY3BSV3 (ebook)

This book is for those who have ever felt like they've had to dim their light and for my friend Bridget who I miss very much.

No use in running from what you're becoming/Don't keep it inside/She's a wild, wild woman

Your Smith
"Wild Wild Woman"

AUTHOR'S NOTE

Content Warnings:

This book contains graphic sex scenes, violence (hand-to-hand combat, gun violence, magic-inflicted violence, off-page recollections of abduction), murder, excessive cursing, off-page parent death, talk of grief, and a lot of talk of ritual sacrifice/virgin sacrifices!

ONE

BENEDETTA

WHEN BENEDETTA RUSSO DREAMT of her death, which she did often due to the circumstances of her birth, she dreamt of a warm breeze and a gentle caress, a blinding white light and her mother's voice welcoming her into the afterlife.

She did not dream of a small, cramped bedroom with boarded windows and an iron chain shackling her to an old radiator as it spit hot water on her skin.

She had hoped for a little bit more glory in her passing.

A hero's death. Or at least a hell of a fight.

She sank back against the wall, her knees drawn up to her chest as she let her head thud against the peeling wallpaper. She was starving. A half-eaten sandwich lay on a paper plate on the floor beside her. She was weighing the consequences of finishing it, knowing it was laced with something to keep her foggy and confused. All her meals had been since she'd been tossed into the room. Each plate nearly the same so she couldn't tell what was lunch or dinner or breakfast. So, she couldn't track the passing of time. Or the time of day. Even when she pressed her ear to the boarded-up window, she couldn't hear anything, not even the white noise of traffic.

The cuffs on her ankles and wrists rubbed raw. Her very bones felt tender.

Without the shackles, Benedetta had a chance to make it out of here.

As it was, the iron was depleting her strength more and more with every passing day.

How many days *had* it been? Two? Three? A week?

Even now she could feel her eyelids begin to droop, the effects of her meal beginning to seep into her skin. She tried to widen her eyes, her hand tapping at her cheek, anything to keep her body and brain alert as movement in the hallway caught her attention. It was too soon for another meal, wasn't it?

As she fought against the sleep she knew was inevitable, a deep and guttural voice barked an order as the bedroom door began to creak open, light spilling into the otherwise dark room.

"Perfect timing little witch," came the drawl. "Now, why don't you hold your arm out so we can draw some of that delicious blood—"

Benedetta could hardly make him out, had never been able to glimpse his face.

But his voice.

She would never forget that voice.

Even as she tumbled back into sleep, his voice haunted her dreams.

TWO

GIDEON

EVERY THIEF HAS A code.

A foundation.

A list of rules to make sure everyone comes home. Safe. Sound. Pockets full.

For the Crawford brothers, it was a mantra from their father.

"You keep your head down and the heat out," he would say, voice marbled from years of drink and smoke. "You protect each other. You don't leave a man behind. And the only thing you gotta concern yourselves with is the target. It don't matter what the hell it is—money, jewels, a mint-condition '71 Chevelle—you bring it home like it's already yours."

Benedetta Russo didn't fit.

She wasn't a prize, for one.

She was a deviation from their norm, a job no one would think to hire them for.

"Something's off," Luke said.

They were standing in front of a rust-eaten shipping container, the number 091820 in large painted white numbers glaring at them from beneath a dim light on the dock, the doors locked with an iron chain. It was tucked away among hundreds of other containers, each of them holding whatever goods were being transported in or out of Philadelphia from other ports. Pier 82 held pretty typical wares, like produce or dry goods.

But this container—this one was special.

Or at least, they hoped.

Gideon grit his teeth, "What, are your Spidey senses tingling?"

Luke smacked at his arm.

"It's her scent."

There was a glimmer of excitement behind his brother's steel-blue eyes, his wire-rimmed frames doing little to hide the red seeping into the whites of them.

Gideon hated that look.

Hated even more how much he'd grown used to it in the past year.

"Retract, Lucas."

His brother waved a hand. "Calm down, grandma. I'm not even hungry."

Before Gideon could remind him of the half-drained security guard they'd left behind, Luke approached the doors to the shipping container, his own gloved hands making careful work of the lock. He caught the chain in his fist before it could clatter to the ground.

A tic worked its way through Gideon's jaw as he watched.

"Simple rescue mission, right?"

"Right," Luke replied.

"And then we're done."

His younger brother lingered by the double doors, his hands gripping at the steel bars. A lot had changed after Chicago. Luke had changed. But when he glanced back at Gideon, his lips curved into a familiar smirk.

"You gotta adapt, brother. Lean into the new."

If 'new' meant this business of becoming glorified private detectives, dealing with panicked mafia dons and clandestine meetings and bulletin boards pinned with strings rivaling that of a goddamn lunatic, Gideon would rather pitch himself into the tumultuous waters of the Delaware.

The call had surprised them both.

He knew they had a reputation among the underground, the other criminal organizations and fronts working the market. They'd worked alongside a few factions over the years, hired for Luke's penchant for locks and safes or Gideon's talent in forgery. Their plans were known for being meticulous, untouchable. But the Caruso crime family worked in an area of pilfered goods that Gideon had up until recently been unfamiliar with.

He was a simple guy. A vault of cash. Some valuables. Tangible shit you could trade and sell. The kind of scores that could let him grow old and fat and happy.

Angelo Torretta and his men had very different goals. They worked in parallel.

Up until three days ago.

When Torretta's only daughter was snatched from her apartment.

A gust of wind rattled the docks and Gideon squared his shoulders.

Benedetta Russo had been living on the wall of their loft for the better part of 72 hours. A grainy screen capture from the hallway of her three story walk-up in Rittenhouse the night she was taken, a timestamp of when the connection to the security cameras cut out, a print out of her teaching schedule at UPenn, the numbers of two ex-boyfriends, a license plate of a sprinter van found speeding down Locust at 3AM...

Any odds and ends that Torretta thought would be helpful.

Little pieces of a life.

It was the vehicle registration that led them to a shell company that led them to Pier 82. He thought it would be harder to find her but they'd connected the dots quickly enough. A relief. Benedetta had been haunting his thoughts, the headshot hanging on the bulletin board a stark reminder of what was at stake if they failed.

She was a future doctorate for fuck's sake. She volunteered at the library for story hour. She was beautiful and vibrant, with a bright, wide smile and startlingly clear eyes.

Eyes that crept into his dreams.

She was the kind of woman Gideon normally wouldn't think twice about because she'd never look his way in a million years. Women with that kind of future hardly did.

He sucked in an unsteady breath as the doors creaked open, metal scraping on itself as Luke stood back to secure them. Gideon hesitated to step forward, his head tilting to the side to inspect the inside. The interior of the container was dark but even as the moonlight filtered in through the open door and his eyes adjusted, he found no sign of their rescue mission.

He crept closer, hand bracing the rim of the doorway.

Had they fucked up? Gotten it wrong?

He should have seen the attack coming.

But the whip of the chain caught him off guard, his body stumbling back to avoid the impact. Gideon barely got himself straightened when what he could only describe as some kind of hysterical shout echoed off the metal walls. It was all he could do to brace himself for impact as a body collided against his. A woman's body.

Benedetta Russo, in the flesh.

Fully ready to knock him on his ass with what looked to be another thick iron chain shackled to both of her wrists.

"Wait," he said, wrapping his arms around her waist. "Wait, *hold on*—"

"Get your hands off of me," she spat out, wriggling in his hold.

She kicked her legs, her heel making contact with his shin and he grunted.

"You know you actually attacked *me*—"

"I am not letting you just take me again, you're gonna have to kill me this time—"

There was a crack in her voice even as she thrashed against him.

"Will you just stop for one goddamn minute?" he bit out. "I'm not going to hurt you."

He braced her back tightly against his chest, somehow managing to keep her arms at her sides despite her best effort. She had a surprising amount of strength, and more energy than he would have expected. If she wasn't barefoot, she might have had a shot at breaking free. But he had the height and weight difference to keep her steady.

"Do you hear me?" he said, voice rough against her ear. "I am not going to hurt you."

Her chest was heaving, her hands were clenched at her sides, but she stilled.

"Good," he said, setting her feet down on the ground. "I'm gonna let you go and you're going to stop trying to kill me, okay?"

She nodded.

"Can you promise me?" he asked. "No more murder attempts."

She let out a breath. "No more murder attempts. I promise."

"Thank you," Gideon replied, letting her go.

She lurched away from him, unsteady on her feet, as if that show of force was all she had left in her. She was dressed in what looked like pajamas—a pair of satin sleep shorts and an old, oversized T-shirt with "LEGALIZE MARINARA" emblazoned across the chest, the design something that would make him laugh at any other time.

A more appropriate time.

The difference between the polished headshot and the scene before him was stark. Her chestnut hair hung in tangled curls around her shoulders, wavy bangs matted to her forehead in the stifling August heat. Her pale skin was knicked with cuts and bruises. But even covered in what was clearly a layer of grime and dried blood, he still found her beautiful.

Feral, alarmingly stealthy, and beautiful.

"Well, this is shaping up to be some rescue."

Gideon turned toward the entrance of the shipping container to find his brother bent over, hands on his knees, laughing his ass off. He leveled Luke with a glare as he straightened the sleeves of his suit jacket. Why couldn't Benedetta have jump-attacked that idiot instead?

"Rescue?" Benedetta repeated, eyeing them dubiously. Then, "Wait, you two?"

Something about that tone felt like an insult.

"I know you were too busy trying to strangle me with that thing," he said, gesturing to the chains around her wrists, very much ignoring his brother. "But we're here to get you home. Your father sent us."

"Oh, you've gotta be fucking kidding me."

He paused. "What?"

A snort of laughter passed through his brother's nose.

"It's probably his fault I'm in this thing," she continued, waving her hand, the chains rattling against each other. "And he hires a vampire to find me? Never mind that I'm—"

But she cut herself off, an irritated groan finishing her sentence.

"Wait, how'd you—" Gideon started.

"He's *all* death," she cut in tartly. "Besides, I know who you are. You're the Crawford brothers."

"Seems our reputations precede us," Luke mused, body leaning against the metal wall.

"Pretty-boy thieves in pretty suits," she shrugged and that was definitely an insult in her tone.

He was beginning to miss the Benedetta he had imagined when she was still a headshot on his wall. But they had a job to finish and it was crucial they got the hell out of there. The pier was patrolled not only by security, but by whoever it was who put Benedetta in this box. Two swarming entities Gideon would rather avoid if they could.

They'd managed thus far to do this relatively unbothered.

Recent attack not included.

"Well, what are you two waiting for?" she asked, holding her wrists out expectantly.

"Coming right up, princess," Gideon muttered.

He cut Luke a look as he plucked his picking kit from the inside pocket of his suit jacket. A look he hoped conveyed how irritating this evening had become. How much he wanted to kick his brother's ass for getting them involved in this.

Luke, however, looked delighted as he approached Benedetta.

But she yanked her wrist back just as he reached for her.

"Careful," she warned. "The iron—"

His brother seemed to understand what she was alluding to and showed her his gloved hands with a hapless shrug. Gideon's brow furrowed as he recalled one of the bits of vampire lore he'd learned over the course of the last year. Something in the mineral was dangerous to vampires. Vampires and other creatures he'd thought belonged only in fairy tales until his brother pulled him into a whole new world.

The entire shipping container was made of steel.

Iron lived in steel.

He looked back at Benedetta, eyes narrowing.

Perhaps Torretta wasn't entirely truthful.

"This whole thing is a prison," Gideon said. "What *are* you?"

"Wouldn't you like to know," she said, a gleam behind her eyes.

But Luke was already picking through the lock at her left wrist, leaving Gideon to work at her right. He couldn't make out much in the darkness but he could see the marks on her skin from where the shackles rubbed raw. And although she was putting on a good front, he could see her hands trembling as they made quick work of the locks. The brothers caught them before they could fall and quietly laid them down. They'd spent too much time as it was in here and he didn't need them making any extra noise.

Benedetta let out a gasp as she was freed, her body swaying a little upon release. She reached out a hand toward the metal wall but seemed to think better of it, instead taking a deep breath. Gideon found himself reaching for her.

"I'm okay," she said, waving him off.

He hoped she was telling the truth because suddenly there was a rumbling of something outside. They'd come this far without having to get physical, each step of their plan perfectly orchestrated to keep that shit to a minimum. The least amount of damage possible had always been one of their rules. He cursed under his breath as he exchanged another look with his brother.

"Well, what do we have here?" came a lazy drawl.

Gideon tucked Benedetta behind him as he stepped out of the shipping container to see two vampires approach, looking incredibly out of place in cowboy hats and oversized belt buckles. Fangs out, eyes blood-red with matching veins simmering beneath the surface. Real ugly mother-fuckers.

"I don't know, boys," Gideon replied, irritated. "What do we have here?"

"Trespassin', it looks like," the one replied, a bolo tie hanging from his neck.

"Good thing we haven't eaten dinner yet," the other one smirked from beneath his cowboy hat.

"Dude, if I ever sound that corny, I give you full permission to stake me."

Luke had come up beside him, their bodies managing to block Benedetta from the vampires in front of them. She seemed woozy, as if her energy was depleting by the second. She winced as the lights of the dock hit her face and then stiffened when she saw the two vampires. He didn't miss the way her jaw clenched nor the bruising that lingered along her arms and legs. Whatever happened, they'd done a number on her. His increasing frustration over the night was slowly morphing into a kind of righteous anger he didn't feel too often.

"Believe me," Gideon said, "you won't even have to ask."

Bolo tie stepped forward, his teeth bared. "You can't think you're walkin' off this dock with our girl here."

"Buddy, we're gonna do whatever the fuck we want," Gideon said.

Which was likely the wrong thing to say to two bloodthirsty vampires because in a flash of a moment, they lunged forward. Gideon ducked a punch from Bolo tie before it could land, pivoting to the side as the other went for Luke and Benedetta. But he had to trust Luke could handle it because Bolo tie was pissed and his teeth were a little too close for comfort.

Gideon and Luke were adept fighters. They honed their skills as two kids growing up in a part of Philly that often forced them to defend themselves. Gideon even found himself in the boxing ring for a little while, earning cash on fights put together by Frank and his men. He didn't like losing, and that pushed him to win every bet made against him.

He landed a punch in the vampire's gut before he reached into the pocket of his suit jacket, grabbing not for his gun but for the new weapon he'd started packing after Chicago. The moment you realize vampires are real, suddenly they're fucking everywhere. Before his opponent could swing again, Gideon plunged the wooden stake into his chest and watched as he seemed to burn up from the inside out, his body exploding into a cloud of ash.

"You brought a stake?" Luke asked before he knocked the other vampire back with a headbutt. "You can't just carry those things around!"

"Kinda seems like I can, considering," Gideon countered.

"Prick."

The vampire that he wasn't related to wavered in his spot for a second before pivoting to where their new friend lingered by the doors of the shipping container, lunging for her with a grunt. The wall was doing some heavy lifting to keep her upright, but she tried to straighten. Before either of the brothers could reach her, the vampire grabbed at the dingy T-shirt she was wearing and pulled her close to him, her legs limp beneath his grasp. She struggled, her hands reaching up to push against the vampire's face as she tried to break his hold. Then suddenly, a bright flash of light filled the dock and the vampire's head exploded in a mixture of blood and ash, the rest of his body following suit shortly after. Little bits of glass littered the ground, lamps surrounding them exploding along with the vampire.

How in the hell did she do that?

"Holy shit," Luke muttered.

Dazed, she wiped the blood from her face, leaving traces of ash behind on her skin before she sunk back against the wall of the shipping container. A trickle of blood pooled at her nostril, and she looked down at her hand, her fingertips tinged black.

Gideon crossed toward her, reaching to help her stand straight.

"I'm fine," she grumbled, a statement Gideon was obliged to ignore at this point. "They kept me out of the sun on purpose so I'd—"

But before she could finish her sentence, or explain what the hell she meant, she slumped over. She would have dropped to the ground if it weren't for Gideon catching her in his arms. He let out a curse as he held her, watching as her eyes fluttered, her lips parting as if she was desperate for the air.

"I need sunlight," she breathed before her body went slack.

Sunlight?

She needed *sunlight?*

It was three o'clock in the morning.

Gideon hovered in the doorway of his own bedroom, arms crossed against his chest as Cleo rifled through his dresser. Benedetta had barely stirred on the drive back to their loft, and was still comatose as she lay in the middle of Gideon's bed. He had brought her to his bedroom on instinct, not even considering the leather sofa waiting for him in the living room once this night from hell came to an end.

"You cool sacrificin' these?"

Cleo was holding an old T-shirt and a pair of his gym shorts.

He shrugged and waved his hand.

He was too busy cataloging the bruises.

She had marks all up and down her arms and legs. Like she'd been handled. Roughly. More than once. She had a split in her lip and a real shiner on her jaw. And there was a deep purplish blemish on the inside of one of her elbows. He almost wanted to step closer, to inspect that one himself, but she was still out cold and he was a stranger.

They were taking risk enough letting Cleo clean her up.

What she really needed was a doctor.

They had seen the state of her apartment, had seen the photos Torretta's men had taken the morning they realized she was gone. Benedetta had put up a hell of a fight. A fight Gideon knew well after her little stunt at Pier 82. His jaw was starting to ache.

"Torretta's aware," Luke said as he approached from down the hallway. "Said to call him as soon as she wakes up."

"What the hell happened?"

Cleo was holding a damp washcloth in one hand, her eyes dark as she too seemed to be tallying up what had happened to Benedetta. Working in the underground like Gideon and Luke, Cleo was no stranger to the dangers that lurked for most women in the business. The pressures and obstacles they faced to be taken seriously, the men who tried to put them in their place. She looked over toward Gideon and Luke, her jaw set.

Cleo was with them in Chicago. And had, in the past year, become a crucial part of their outfit. She had good insights. She could handle herself. Her penchant for acquiring weapons sans serial codes was an added bonus.

"He wouldn't say," Luke said. "But I think he doesn't know. Not for certain."

Luke paused at the threshold of the bedroom. As if he wasn't allowing himself to step further into the room. There was something off about his brother. Something Luke knew that he wasn't telling Gideon.

"What?" he asked. "Out with it. What is she?"

He had been thinking about the metal prison they'd kept her in, the iron chains… the moment that vampire's head burst into nothing. He'd never seen anything like it.

"I have my suspicions," his brother replied with a wave of his hand.

"What's that mean?" Cleo asked.

"I'm just not sure—" Luke shook his head. "I want to be certain."

"Well, get certain," Cleo said, waving the washcloth in their general direction. "As in get out— *both* of you. She needs to get cleaned up and in some fresh clothes and it sounds like you two have work to do."

Gideon didn't need the reminder.

Nor did he want to be here when Cleo undoubtedly uncovered more bumps and bruises and scrapes under Benedetta's torn clothes. He was already pissed off enough. An emotion he was more than happy to point in his brother's general direction.

With a nod to Cleo, he wrapped his hand around Luke's bicep, ignoring his brother's 'Hey!' as he pulled him into the hallway, letting the door shut behind them.

"What do you need to confirm what you're thinking?" he asked.

Luke shook off Gideon's grip with a disgruntled roll of his eyes.

"I can go to Harker's," his brother replied. "But that's expanding the circle on this. I just don't know who else would have the resources."

Gideon scraped his hand across his face.

Torretta had been clear. The less people involved the better. But with his daughter laying unconscious in Gideon's bed, vampire brains all over the docks of Pier 82, and a desperate cry for sunlight— Gideon wanted to have as much information as possible before they moved forward. In any way.

"Do what you gotta do," he told him. "Keep it vague. Harker's on a need to know basis until we decide otherwise."

"Don't be silly, he knows I'm just a man with a thirst for knowledge," Luke said with a shrug of his shoulders. "Harker will be none the wiser."

Gideon let out a scoff as he turned toward the kitchen.

He needed a drink.

"So, how long are you gonna be pissed at me?"

His brother's question followed him to the bar cart.

"I don't know," Gideon replied, grabbing two lowball glasses and the decanter of whiskey. "You said this would be a simple retrieval—" He pointed in the direction of his bedroom. "She blew a guy up!"

"So she's got a little... something," Luke said, trailing off.

"Next job we pull is my choice," he snapped, even as he poured his brother a drink.

Luke took the offered glass, a familiar expression clouding his features. The same kind of look he had as a kid when he was about to get them into a mess of trouble. His lips twitched as his eyes gleamed.

"You gotta admit, it's interesting," he said. "Daughter of mob boss goes missing. Ends up in a shipping container. Has big magical powers."

"Yeah, it's a fucking riot," Gideon sighed.

"With a big fucking payout," Luke reminded him. "Torretta has deep pockets, but I should have known something was off when I got the number."

Gideon wanted to argue he also couldn't get too preachy. He'd seen the numbers. He'd been there in the initial meeting. Torretta had played it cool, kept it business. Gideon never would have known what was at stake.

"What did Torretta say on the phone?" Gideon asked, elbows resting against the kitchen counter. "Exactly."

"He cursed a lot," Luke said, leaning back against the island, arms crossing against his chest as he leveled Gideon with a look. "Mostly in Italian but I got the gist. Thanked us. Profusely. Said it wasn't safe to transport her anywhere, especially not while she's still unconscious. Asked if we'd be comfortable keeping her here until she wakes up."

"Don't see how we have a choice there."

"Told us to call back with an update in the morning," his brother finished.

"That's it?"

"That's it."

Gideon stared down at the countertop, fingers drumming against the cool surface. They had no idea what she was. He didn't have the knowledge that Luke did. And it seemed Torretta wasn't all that interested in sharing.

Why?

THREE

BENNY

BENNY WAS BACK IN the shipping container.

There was a thudding sound, a deep and heavy knocking rattling the metal walls and she could hardly lift herself up from the heap she had become on the floor. She felt heavy, like her bones had been filled with lead. No. No, no, no, no, no.

The drugs.

Someone had slipped them back into her system.

Fuck— she had been so close. She had been free.

The knocking was growing more insistent, more rhythmic, a beat that felt familiar but that she couldn't place. Until she realized it was in time with her own heart, both growing faster, more desperate.

She lurched forward, trying to pull at the chains wrapped around her wrists.

She needed to get out of here. She needed to run.

A red light started to seep through the cracks in the doors, like blood trailing down an open wound. Every inch of Benny was pleading with her to move, to do *something*. But the more she tried, the harder it became.

Something was holding her here, holding her in place.

The red began to fill the container, every inch of the cold iron glowing.

She knew, intrinsically, that if it reached her, she would be gone forever.

Closer, closer…

She cried out, for something, for anyone.

Her hands pressed into the floor, fingers spread wide, light emanating from her skin.

The doors burst open and a scream pulled itself from her throat just as something grabbed her—

No, not grabbed.

Held.

"Whoa, hey," a voice said. "Come on, Russo, wake up—"

Benny jolted awake, her eyes blinking open to a bright wash of sunlight filling her vision. Her heart beat roughly in her chest, a rapid thumping as she tried to orient herself, to quell the impending panic at waking up somewhere she didn't recognize. Again. But when her eye sight adjusted to the welcome light filling the bedroom, she found a pair of striking hazel eyes studying her, concern clear in his familiar features.

"Hey, you're alright," he said softly. "You're safe."

She remembered that voice and the way it vibrated against her skin when he held her in the shipping container. The way he repeated "I am not going to hurt you," right against the nape of her neck.

It was that Crawford brother. Gideon.

The one she basically tried to murder.

She stiffened, embarrassment washing over her in a warm flush. She must have been having a nightmare. A nightmare loud enough that he heard her. And here he was, his body crowding hers on the bed, hands bracing her shoulders, looking at her like she was a problem he didn't know how to solve.

Jesus fucking Christ, could she not catch a break?

It was bad enough she got herself taken.

She didn't need to suddenly become some damsel in distress about it.

"I'm fine," she managed after a moment, voice curt. "You can let me go now."

He cleared his throat and pushed himself up from the bed, "Yeah, sure, I guess next time I'll just let you fall out of the bed."

"Some knight in shining armor you are."

Well, he certainly looked like one.

He was more attractive than she expected. Certainly more so here than in the dull light of the shipping container, her mind too preoccupied with escaping and surviving and generally causing as much damage as she could until she learned she was actually being rescued. She remembered his suit, much like the one he was wearing now, and a strong jaw even as her fist collided against it. A strength in his arms as he held her. A roughness to his voice.

But here, in the bright morning sunlight, he was handsome in a way that brought an irritating flush to her skin. Especially in stark contrast to Benny's unruly state, her body bruised like an overripe peach. He was tall, fit— she knew that from experience now, she realized, and there was a slope to his nose she really liked.

"Oh, you have no idea, princess," he said as he stalked toward the door. Then, with hardly a glance back in her direction he added, "I made coffee. But you'll have to actually get up to drink it. We don't do room service here."

A very small part of her wanted to throw a pillow directly at his pretty, stupid face.

Instead, Benny waited until he was gone and then buried herself beneath the covers. Coffee was an incredibly good reason to get out of bed. But she needed a moment. She needed to get her bearings. It wasn't the first time in the last couple of days she had woken up somewhere new, but at least this time she wasn't chained to a radiator or tossed into a shipping container. The king-sized bed was soft and comfortable and almost *too much* compared to the last few nights she spent sleeping on the floor.

How long had she been out? How long had it been since she was taken? When she woke in the shipping container, she felt clear headed. The drugs they had been slipping into her food must have worn off. Surely that meant significant time had passed?

Sunlight slipped through the open windows.

Benny could feel the heat of it seeping into her skin.

It was the best remedy she could ask for given the circumstances.

Slowly she pulled back the comforter, her muscles shaking with the effort it took to push herself into a sitting position. She almost missed that she was dressed in someone else's clothing, the change taking a moment to register in her very tired brain. A plain white tee shirt and a pair of gym shorts, both belonging to someone taller, broader. She could only hazard a guess they belonged to the Crawford she punched in the face.

But they felt soft, and clean.

She felt clean.

The blood and the dirt that had begun to feel like a new layer of skin was gone. But it only made the bumps and bruises littering her arms and legs all the more evident. She didn't have to wonder about their originations— it was the struggle when they pulled her from her bed, how hard she landed when they tossed her into the back of the van, the chains that kept her shackled to the radiator.

Her body suddenly seemed foreign to her, all marked up and tender to the touch.

Gooseflesh broke out across her skin.

She had spent who knew how long drugged up in a tiny, dingy room, her body unable to feel much of anything. Until now. And it was all bubbling right under the surface.

Her bare feet were cold against the hardwood floors, her steps light as she ventured out of the bedroom and down a short hallway, the scent of that fresh coffee beckoning her toward the kitchen. She raked her fingers through her hair, trying to smooth away what she was sure was a rat's nest after everything that happened. What she really needed was a shower, and maybe a toothbrush?

She breathed into the palm of her hand and cringed. Definitely a toothbrush.

But coffee would do. Answers, too.

She just wasn't sure what kind of answers she'd get from the Crawford brothers.

Not if they were working for her father.

Benny couldn't recall much after the vampire attacked, her memory muddled as she fell in and out of consciousness, her eyes too heavy to even open. But she remembered being tucked into the backseat of a car, the low terse voice that pleaded with her to "stay awake, Jesus Christ" and muttered "this is not what I signed up for" as they drove off to wherever she was now.

Certainly not a five star review on that rescue.

"We were wondering when you were gonna wake up."

She found the one with the glasses, Luke, digging around in a cabinet. He wore a suit similar to his brother's, but his shirt was unbuttoned at the collar and his sleeves were rolled up to his elbows, his suit jacket tossed onto the kitchen counter. He was lean, almost lanky if it weren't for the obvious muscle beneath that white dress shirt. A collection of flash tattoos littered his forearms, the designs nonsensical. A frying pan with a cracked egg. A skeleton wearing a beret with a mustache. A pin-up-style mermaid. On his knuckles in an old-style font were the words "BODY" and "SOUL" in black ink. His dark brown hair was carefully styled and parted down the side. Not a strand out of place.

There was a large butterfly inked at the hollow of his throat, wings spanning wide, the colors a beautiful blend of blues and blacks.

She could see the resemblance between them so clearly.

The dark hair, the similar lines of their jaws, their mouths.

But Gideon looked more clean cut, more buttoned up.

His features darker, Luke's brighter. And while Luke's skin had the porcelain pallor that came with being a vampire, Gideon's skin was tan, sun-kissed. Like he was warmer all around.

Except maybe not in personality.

"How long was I out?" she asked through a yawn.

Something smelled burnt.

She hoped it wasn't the coffee.

"Oh, lemme see," he said, glancing down at his watch. "Almost forty-eight hours."

She reared back.

"Jesus," she muttered. "My father must be losing his shit."

He chuckled as he leaned further into the cabinet. After a moment, he shouted, "Gid— I found it!" before looking back to Benny. "He's been checking in. He's gonna wanna know you're awake."

Benny waved a hand.

"He can wait a little bit longer."

"I don't think so," Gideon replied from behind her, as he crossed the living room from who knows where. He was carrying a tool chest. "You were a simple catch and release, not a babysitting job. We'll be sending you back to Daddy as soon as we get the word."

Like she was a goddamn fish.

But she had no interest in being sent to the compound upstate. Her life was here, in Philadelphia. It was not under her father's overprotective thumb.

Gideon gave her a wide clearance as he passed by her, settling the tool chest on the kitchen island's stone countertop. With two clicks, he popped the top open and pulled out a screwdriver that he promptly tossed to Luke. She didn't even see the vampire turn around, but watched mildly impressed as he caught it in one hand and turned back to half tuck himself into the cabinet. Like they could communicate without even speaking.

"You mentioned coffee?" she said, then, still watching Luke curiously.

She had lived a blissfully vampire free existence until just recently.

And now she was standing in one's kitchen.

"Over there," Gideon said with a jerk of his head. "Mugs in the cabinet."

"I hope you made enough for me to drown myself in it," she said, squeezing past them both. "Forty-eight hours of sleep somehow *not* enough, apparently."

"You've had a hell of a week," Luke said.

She paused.

"A…week?"

The night she was taken, she was prepping for the last week of summer sessions and the start of her final fall semester. Dozens of papers to grade, her thesis to get in order… If she was really gone a week, she was already behind. And her father wanted her to sequester herself up in Hudson?

Absolutely fucking not.

"Took us a couple of days to track you down," he told her. "But the last few, those are on you. I've never seen someone so knocked out."

She lingered by the coffee pot, hands gripping at the edge of the counter.

"What happened?" she asked, trying to sound casual.

Gideon huffed an aggravated breath.

"How far back do you wanna go?" he asked. "The nightmare that just busted a fuse in the microwave? Or the vampire brains splattered all over the docks? How much do you remember?"

"I definitely did not forget about the brains," she said with a grimace. Then, with a jolt of panic, "Wait— what about your microwave?"

He scrubbed a hand over his face.

He looked tired.

She could see a bruise purpling at the line of his jaw and she hoped that it hadn't been from her. She didn't know— she could hardly hear the voices outside of the shipping container, had no idea what was coming for her. Just the scent of a vampire and well, she'd had enough of those for a lifetime.

Though the one rummaging around in his kitchen cabinet seemed friendly enough.

"Whatever magic you've got, princess, it sure as shit doesn't like electricity," Gideon said, gesturing to his brother in the cabinet. Right beside the microwave. "You had this whole place flickering the moment you started shouting."

That explains the burning smell.

"Couldn't that just be faulty wiring?" she challenged, bristling at the nickname.

"Sure," he offered her, waving his hand in a tone that felt offensive. "Philly apartments can go either way. But you did this the other night. You popped three lights along with that vampire's head."

Benny didn't know how to respond. Her magic had never manifested itself like that before. It felt protective, innate in a way that surprised her. But it had been a hell of a drain on her energy. Enough to knock her clear out once the adrenaline wore off.

But he didn't need to know any of that.

"Well, I'm sure my father will buy you a new one," she said, busying herself with a mug and coffee. Black. No milk or sugar. "I bet he's paying you both a pretty penny for finding me."

"Not enough," he muttered, crossing his arms against his chest.

Good, she thought, her lips curling into a smirk. Let him be annoyed by her. It would make this whole saving her life thing a bit more palatable.

"Well, it's busted," Luke sighed. He pulled himself out of the cabinet, wiping his hands on the legs of his suit pants. "Fuse is completely fried."

Benny took a long sip from her coffee.

"Great," Gideon said. "That's great."

"It *is* great," Luke exclaimed with a clap on his brother's shoulder. "None of the texts talk about a Strega's powers behaving this way. Feels like we've made a discovery, brother."

She tried not to give him a reaction.

She had known it was likely impossible given everything that happened at the pier, but she had held onto this little wild hope that the truth of what she was would remain a secret. That the Crawfords wouldn't be able to figure it out. She was merely a fairy tale, after all. But her father had damned that all to hell from the moment he hired a vampire to track her down.

"You know."

"Yeah, well, I'm not an idiot." Luke rolled his eyes. "The moment you started crying about the sun—"

"Crying? I wasn't—" She felt the back of her neck warm.

"And your blood," he continued, his bright blue eyes darkening briefly.

"Lucas," Gideon warned.

"It was like I could taste it," he said. "Those marks on your arm, they're from blood transfusions, right?"

"What is he talking about?"

But Gideon was following the accusation, his eyes lingering on the inside of her elbow, where a deep bruise was forming from irritated veins. She twisted her arm, her hand reaching to cover the spot. He met her eyes with a furrowed brow.

Benny didn't want to answer.

Because the annoyance behind Gideon's eyes had turned into something so much worse. Pity. And she didn't want that from him. She didn't want that from anyone.

"Benedetta's blood is big on the black market," Luke said. He was only slightly taller than his brother, a fraction of an inch. But she felt the full measure of his height compared to her own 5'4" stature. "Strega witches are fucking mythological legend. Blessed by a goddess with the power of the sun. Honestly, I thought you were just some kind of vampire fantasy."

Gideon leveled her with a look.

"What exactly does that mean?"

Benny sighed.

"Vampires believe that if they drink the blood of a Strega, they can walk in the sun."

"What?"

"It's true, isn't it?" Luke asked, seemingly giddy at the news. It was hard to ignore the gleam behind his eyes, the way they glimmered red.

"Yes," she said stiffly. Somebody did his homework. "But I—I'm not some kind of blood bank. You even think of making a move, and I will happily blow you up too."

Maybe.

If she could harness whatever that was from the other night on the docks.

"He's not going to touch you," Gideon said sternly, his eyes traveling to his brother.

Something unspoken passed between them, something that settled her nerves.

"Of course not," Luke scoffed. "I'm not a monster."

Benny didn't know whether to laugh at that response or what. Thirty years keeping her abilities a secret, thirty years trying to figure out how to manage her power and keep herself safe, and it only took a couple of days for everything to spiral out of control.

Was she supposed to trust the two of them to keep her safe now?

Were they her only path to answers?

She blew out a frustrated breath.

"So, what now?" she asked.

Gideon stared at her for a moment, his eyes searching hers. They were pretty, his eyes, though it pained her to admit it. Hazel with flecks of green. Long dark lashes. Why were men always blessed with such long lashes?

"We've got a phone call to make," he said. "But we're gonna need to know everything you remember from the last couple of days. You think you can handle that?"

There was an edge to his tone that made Benny's skin tingle.

"Sure thing, boss," she said. "But maybe we can work our way backwards. I'd love to know who had the privilege of getting me dressed and whose clothes I'm wearing."

Luke chuckled.

"Those are Gideon's," he said with a wicked grin. "You're in his bed, too."

"Cleo got you cleaned up," Gideon said quickly. "Luke and I weren't in the room."

"And who's Cleo?" she asked, crossing her arms against her chest.

"Cleo runs our weapons," he said, his eyes not hiding the trip they were taking up and down her body. Like zeroing in on her arm had triggered something, his eyes darkening when he tracked the bruises down her legs. Still, she felt her stomach flip all the same. "You good?"

"I'm fine," she replied tersely. "I'm alive."

That was bullshit. But it would do for now. Until she knew what was ahead of her.

She pushed herself up onto the counter, legs dangling over the side.

"There were five of them, I think," she began. She could feel a slight tremor in her hands, but she tried to ignore it, instead wrapping them around the ceramic mug steaming with her coffee. "They came in the middle of the night. I was asleep. I didn't even know what was happening until they were already…dragging me from my bed."

It had been so surreal, to wake up already in a struggle, as if her body was trying to save her before she was even aware. She took a long sip from her coffee, the hot liquid soothing her throat. For all that was hazy, this part wasn't.

She remembered every painstaking moment.

"Did you recognize any of them?" Luke asked.

"No," she said, shaking her head. "They were all wearing ski masks. And by the time they got me into the van, I was pretty out of it. They used this potion, and it wasn't like I was paralyzed but my whole body felt heavy. I couldn't move. I definitely couldn't use my magic."

She swallowed, her throat feeling thick.

But neither brother pushed her as the silence wore on.

"I woke up in this little room," she said after a long moment. "Chained to a radiator."

Her eyes flickered to her legs, to the cut on the top of her left foot, a scrape from the chain that had begun to scab. She shifted in her seat.

From that point on, they had kept her in the dark. Literally and figuratively. Without direct sunlight, her magic grew weaker and weaker as the days passed. The drugs they'd slipped into her food made her mostly comatose. It made her easy, pliable, defenseless.

"The transfusions started pretty quickly," she continued. "They kept me hydrated, made sure I had just enough food in my system, but otherwise they left me alone. I have no idea where I was, or if I was even still in the city. All the windows were boarded, and it was quiet. Like, nothing was beyond those walls. But there was this guy, whoever it was, he was definitely the one in charge. He'd do the transfusions himself sometimes. I never got a good look at him."

Gideon made a little noise, like a grunt.

"And the shipping container?" he asked.

"I don't know." She shrugged. She was still figuring that out herself. "He wanted me moved from where I was. I heard him say something about a truck route—"

"How often were they drugging you?" Luke asked.

She frowned.

"All the time?" she offered as if it was up for debate. She rubbed at her temples. She was suddenly so tired. "Except when they moved me to the shipping container. That time they just knocked me out completely. I guess they didn't want to take the chance of anything happening. I had only been awake for a couple of hours when you two showed up."

"Putting you to sleep like that must've given you back at least some of your energy," Luke said thoughtfully. "For that little fireworks show."

"I—" Benny paused. She didn't want to admit to them how unusual that was. She shook her head. Instead she asked, "What day is it?"

"What's the last date you remember?" Gideon asked.

"The 14h."

"It's the 20th," he replied tersely.

She groaned.

"I am so fucked," she said. "I owe like sixty kids their finals."

Gideon and Luke exchanged a long look.

"You should get yourself cleaned up," Gideon said, filling in the heavy silence that lingered in the room. "Cleo's on the way with your things. We'll get in contact with your father and go from there."

"Great," she said, letting her heels knock against the cabinet doors. "Anyone got a spare toothbrush?"

FOUR

BENNY

STEAM FILLED THE SHOWER, the hot water cascading down Benny's back as she pressed her hands against the slick tile. She hovered there for a second, leaning against the wall, letting the heat work out the kinks in her muscles. It was like a little bit of the filth and pain of the last few days was circling the drain. A wince passed through her lips as she reached for the shampoo bottle on the ledge.

She really did feel like she was one giant bruise.

The combination of sandalwood and eucalyptus smelled faintly familiar as she scraped her fingers against her scalp. But before her brain could make the connection, the bathroom door burst open and she nearly fell out of her skin.

"Benedetta?" The voice was bright and sing-songy. "Don't mind me, babe! Just droppin' off your clothes."

But when she didn't hear the click of the door closing, Benny pulled back the shower curtain just enough to peek out into the bathroom.

A striking woman with deep red hair and smooth fair skin perched on the edge of the vanity's counter, one long leg crossed over the other. She twirled at a strand of hair, and Benny could see a faint scar along the crown of her head that ended just before her brow. She had friendly brown eyes and a smile Benny could only describe as dazzling. Sprawled out on the counter in a pair of black denim jeans and a white tank top, she looked a little like an off-duty model.

Cleo, she presumed.

Benny's clothes were in a neatly folded pile on the toilet seat beside her.

"Just dropping off clothes?" Benny asked, brushing back soap from falling into her eyes.

"You caught me," she laughed, hands up in mock surrender. "But I'm a real curious bitch, and you were, like, completely out of it the other night."

The corner of Benny's mouth twitched as she resumed her shower.

"Anyway, it's nice to see you standin' on your own two feet! You're taller than I expected," Cleo continued from the other side of the shower curtain. "You were like a limp little rag doll in Gideon's arms."

Benny grimaced. Had Gideon had to carry her from the pier?

She was rich in embarrassment this morning.

"I heard I have you to thank for cleaning me up," she said, ignoring the visual of those arms carrying her. "I really appreciate it. I'm sure it's not a normal part of your usual…" She paused, fumbling for the right word. "Business?"

"It sure wasn't," Cleo replied. "But we've grown accustomed to some unusual jobs recently. The world's become a lot bigger for us since Luke's change."

Change. An almost quaint way to refer to a vampire transformation.

"You doin' alright, Benedetta? Maybe that's a dumb question considerin' but—"

Benny could immediately tell her yes, she was fine. She had said as much to the Crawford brothers. But she wasn't sure she could lie to the woman who saw every bump and every bruise. She worked the conditioner through her hair, two points to the Crawford brothers for not going with a two-in-one shampoo situation, before pressing into her temples for a moment. She had never been very good about talking about her feelings.

"It's just been a weird couple of days, I guess."

There was a bright shock of laughter from the woman on the other side of the shower curtain. "Weird undersells it. Have you even seen the true crime puzzle board out there?"

"The...what?"

The other woman blew out a raspberry.

"You've been on the wall out there for days," Cleo said. "I know your class schedule, your coffee shop, the name of that little old lady that lives next door to you— Agnes is a gem, by the way. Very chatty. Makes incredible cinnamon buns."

Benny did love those cinnamon buns.

"You should try her sourdough," she said, suddenly feeling incredibly hungry.

Maybe she should have asked for breakfast instead of just coffee.

"Don't tempt me with a good time," the red head mused.

She couldn't help but laugh.

"I think I am figuring out how I feel," Benny said, then. "But at least I'm capable of functioning like a real person now. I don't do well if I'm out of the sun for too long."

Like she was some kind of houseplant.

A bruised, coffee guzzling houseplant.

"Oh yeah," Cleo said. "You're a... oh, what did Lucas call it? A light witch? You know, I saw a tarot reader once at some festival when I was younger. She told me I'd never have a fulfilling relationship with a man until I sorted out my daddy issues but my daddy is dead so I think I'm probably screwed. Do you read too?"

"Sometimes," she said, caught off guard by Cleo's openness. "Every witch has a speciality, somewhere they naturally lean. I read but it's not something I'm very good at. It's not intuitive to me. Stregas can straddle a couple of lines. Healing, energy transference, it all kind of depends. Only vampires call us light witches. Because of how we benefit them."

How *she* would benefit them.

She was the only Strega she knew. Alive, anyway. Her knowledge about herself was unfortunately kind of limited. She lost a bit of the lore when her mother died. She picked up what she could from her father and from the historians that worked with the Caruso family, but even they looked at her like some kind of zoo exhibit.

A rare Strega witch.

And considering the way some of the world's darker creatures liked to harvest her blood for their own benefit, it was better to keep her true abilities a secret.

"There's energy everywhere," she continued. "In everything. My magic allows me to control that. To pluck the light from even the darkest room…"

She thought again about what happened on the docks. Maybe it was more than that now.

"I'm like… the magical equivalent of a microwave."

She laughed in spite of herself.

She would replace the Crawford's broken appliance herself.

"Oh!" Cleo let out a quiet snort. "That makes enough sense."

Benny sighed as she turned off the water.

"I can count on one hand the amount of people who knew what I was before this," she said. She wrapped herself in the soft white towel left for her before stepping out of the shower. "And suddenly now, that number is so much higher."

Her father had to know this would be the outcome of hiring someone on the outside to find her. Only the most senior members of the Caruso family knew her secret, and the penalty for betraying that secret was so high— She hadn't even told her own coven. The two women in the world who knew her best. She'd wanted to a million times over. She hated hiding this part of her. But the risk was too great.

As evidenced by the last few days.

Her brow furrowed as she considered what that meant. Someone in the family was responsible. The betrayal of it all sinking in. The ones that would hurt them the most when they found out who it was that sold her out. The men most trusted by her father. Strategic advisors and consigliere. It had to be one of their men. It was the only path that felt logical in Benny's brain. Who else knew?

"Well, you can trust us," Cleo said, unknowingly snapping Benny from her thoughts. "I know you kind of had a rough start with those two out there, but I promise you, they're honest."

She raised an eyebrow.

"A good thief is actually more honest than you think."

Benny worked another towel through her hair as she considered Cleo. This was the woman who ran weapons for the Crawford brothers? She was tall and lean, with a perfect button nose and cheekbones that made her look like she'd be more comfortable on a beauty pageant stage than shooting a gun. Even the easy drawl of her voice felt charming.

But maybe that was her advantage.

"How did you…"

"End up with the dumbass brothers?"

Benny laughed.

"I was in the wrong place at the right time," Cleo said. "There was this big score in Chicago that needed my expertise, and Gideon and Lucas, they got into some trouble with a woman."

Maybe her poker face wasn't as good as Benny thought because Cleo grinned.

"Nothing like you're thinking," she told her with a shake of her head. "She's not a woman, anyway. Not a *human*, I mean. Hell, I didn't even know vampires were real until I was caught up in this whole big—"

Cleo sighed, cutting herself off.

"Anyway, they figured they'd head back here after Lucas adjusted, and I had some connections we could work with." Cleo shrugged. "It's worked out."

"Aren't you guys technically wanted for like a ton of stuff?"

"You bet." Cleo grinned as she hopped off the vanity's counter. "Now, while I have already seen a good portion of your cute little tush after getting you out of those ratty clothes, I'm gonna give you your privacy while you finish getting ready. I just grabbed whatever I could find that matched. I tried to find your phone, but I think whoever took you might have it."

Benny frowned. Between flaking on her summer session and the hundreds of student emails she'd have to sort through, she knew her group chat with Olivia and Imani was probably out of control. She never missed a Friday esbat with her coven. And Jamie... well, she could only imagine how he was reacting, especially working so closely with her father. She groaned inwardly.

"If you need anything, let me know, okay?"

She nodded, grateful to the other woman.

"Thank you, Cleo," she managed. "For getting my things and for—well, you know."

The red head winked. "No big deal, Benedetta."

"Oh, no, please call me Benny," she almost groaned. Only her father really called her by her full name. "Benedetta is such a mouthful."

"You got it," Cleo replied, her hand turning on the doorknob. She turned back to look at Benny one more time. "Hey," she said, voice soft. "It's fun to give them a hard time, but I trust those two with my life. You're safe here. You're safe with them."

Those words hung in the air long after Cleo left Benny alone in the bathroom.

She hoped they were true.

She ran the side of her fist against the mirror, wiping at the condensation. She took a good, long look at herself and sighed. She looked about as shitty as she felt. There was a dark bruise at the line of her clavicle from some impact she wished she could remember, and her skin was paler than usual, a sallow tinge beneath the surface. Her brown eyes seemed so dark in comparison to the rest of her pallid features. She pressed the pads of her fingers gingerly against her cheek bones as she continued her inspection.

So *what* she looked like shit.

She was alive.

Which was enough for her at the moment.

Her brown hair hung in damp ringlets around her face, and she worked her fingers through them. They'd dry however they wanted to without any of her usual products. But the shower had done her a world of good, as did fresh, clean clothes. Cleo had managed to grab her favorite pair of vintage jeans and the bra she didn't hate. She futzed with the collar of her T-shirt, well-worn concert merch she bought two summers ago after a show at The Fillmore, tucking in the front and then tugging it back out again. What was she worried about? They had certainly seen her look worse.

She took a deep breath. She held it for a moment, her eyes squeezing shut as she tried to center herself. Then, with a heavy exhale, she made her way back into the main room of the loft.

She was met with an oddly domestic scene.

Cleo was at the stove, humming along to a song coming from a small speaker on the counter as she flipped a grilled cheese, her shoulders shimmying to the beat. Luke was reading a book in the living room, his feet propped up on the arm of the sofa as he flipped to another page. Gideon sat at the kitchen island, a towel spread out before him, his gun laying in neatly organized parts. He paused only to take a long sip from his coffee mug.

It was calmer than she expected. It even reminded her a little bit of being back at her childhood home. Gun cleaning and all.

Benny hadn't really taken a good look at it earlier, too disoriented by waking up in another place that was not her home, but the loft was really something.

Exposed brick with tall ceilings and steel rafters, wide-plank hardwood floors, and windows that were nearly two stories high. They didn't seem very vampire-friendly. But Luke looked as comfortable as anything while flipping through a musty-looking old book in full view of the sunlight. She wondered if the windows were tinted for his benefit.

The furniture was worn leather sofas and dark woods, and there was a punching bag tucked in the far corner, boxing gloves hanging from a hook in the brick wall.

The true crime puzzle board Cleo mentioned was right beside it.

She had half a mind to stalk over towards it, see all of the pieces of her they'd managed to comb together while looking for her.

"Wheels up in ten," Gideon said when she crossed into the kitchen. He was perched on the edge of a stool, his suit jacket hanging on the back, his face steady in concentration as he carefully worked a brush tip through the barrel of his gun. But he let his gaze drift up toward her for a moment, a scowl forming on his face as he took her in. Like everything about this was a chore for him. "We've got a decent ride ahead of us."

"Did you talk to my father directly?"

"As a matter of fact, we did," Luke replied, not bothering to look up from whatever page had him so enamored. She tilted her head to read the spine, her brow raising as she saw *A History of Witchcraft* emblazoned in a faded embossed font. He really did like to do his homework. "We agreed on a specific location. Just us. Just him."

Benny sighed in relief.

"I wonder if he knows..." she said.

"Which one of his men sold you out?" Gideon asked, finishing her thought.

Hearing it again out loud made her feel sick.

"If he doesn't, he'll find out soon enough," he continued with a quick rise of his shoulders. "Your disappearance is going to cause a real problem with whoever kidnapped you. And that's going to come down hard on the guy who made it possible."

"He'll probably run," Luke mused from his spot on the sofa.

"And if your dad is as scary as people say he is, I can't imagine that guy is gonna live for very long," Cleo said.

Benny leaned against the kitchen counter as she squeezed at the bridge of her nose.

A flurry of questions were battling in her brain at the moment. Who would sell her out and risk the wrath of her father? She knew the reality of who Angelo Torretta was. She knew what he had to do to ensure he remained in his position in the Caruso family. Maybe she had grown too desensitized to it all, but these men had raised her. She considered them uncles and brothers and friends.

But there was a price for everyone.

"You said my phone was gone," she said, turning toward Cleo. "Did anything else look out of place? Or like it was missing?"

The redhead twirled the spatula between her fingers as she considered the question.

"Hard to say," she said as she turned off the burner. "Your computer was still there. Nothin' looked like it was missin' from the bookshelves. Your bedroom took the brunt of it but there's a trail from the bedroom to the front door. Your dad mentioned the door was unlocked when he and his men got there. So whoever took you either picked the lock or had a key. You have a cute place, by the way. I love that wallpaper you have in the hallway."

Benny couldn't help her smile at the compliment. She had spent six hours trying to get that wallpaper level.

"The coffee table in the living room is an old trunk," she said then, raking her fingers through damp hair. "There's an old lock, like a really old brass thing. You didn't happen to notice if that was broken, did you?"

Cleo shook her head. "Still intact," she said. "You think they took somethin' else?"

Until she knew for sure what was going on, Benny couldn't be sure what was at risk. But she found herself worrying more about the sentimental things in her home, the thesis work on her laptop, the parts of her she'd be devastated to lose. Her mother's jewelry she had tucked away in her closet, the altar she had painstakingly curated over the course of her adult life in the living room, the generations old grimoire tucked away in the old steamer trunk.

"Maybe." She sighed. "I don't know."

Cleo slid the grilled cheese onto a large plate and used the spatula to cut diagonally down the center. Benny's stomach ached at the sight of it, and she realized she couldn't remember the last time she had eaten. She couldn't remember her last meal before the shipping container and if she'd been knocked out the last couple of days, it had been at least three days since she'd eaten anything substantial. But the redhead seemed to understand exactly that as she slid the plate toward her with a knowing look.

"Talk to me," she said. "What's got you worried?"

"I just picked a real shit time to get abducted," she replied. "I've got an inbox filled with papers I need to grade for this summer session I'm teaching and I'm like a week out from fall semester and every single day counts when it comes to dissertation research—and yeah, there's a three-hundred-year-old grimoire in that trunk in my living room and it's the only tangible thing I have that connects me to the other Stregas in my family and if someone were to get their hands on it—"

She had to stop. She was beginning to spiral.

"Yeah, I wouldn't worry too much about those papers, princess," Gideon said with a wave of his hand. "I called Penn the other day."

Benny coughed over her first bite.

"You *what?*"

"You had an accident," he replied with a little shrug of his shoulders as he carefully ran a cloth over the slide of his gun, barely taking his eyes off his project. But he looked pleased with himself, a ghost of a smile playing at his lips. "Even faxed over a doctor's note. You might have to fake a limp once you're back to *really* sell it, but your professor said she'd handle it."

"Wow, you're really a full service kind of rescue service," she said, recovering with another bite of her grilled cheese. "I guess my father's getting his money's worth."

"We'll see about that," was all Gideon said in response.

"Benedetta Russo is a fifth-year PhD candidate at the University of Pennsylvania," Luke read from his spot on the couch, his nose now buried in his phone. "Her research interests focus on mythology and folklore, particularly passed on through oral storytelling, and how the two have influenced an understanding of gender and femininity as it pertains to magic and ritual. She's currently teaching Summer Session II, English 159, Gender and Society."

Benny cupped her chin in her hand as she listened to Luke rattle off the distilled version of the last four years of her life, wondering briefly if she shouldn't work a bit more on the phrasing for her Penn candidate page. But her eyes drifted over toward Gideon, watching as he very carefully smoothed his hands over the barrel of his gun, everything neatly put back into place, looking content with his work. There was something about how meticulous he was about it, how methodical, how expertly his hands worked.

"You actually talked to Dr. Malhotra?" she asked, tearing her eyes away from his hands.

He looked up as he wiped off his hands on a cloth, a slow grin spreading across his face. His eyes lit up, and Benny found herself a little breathless. Even at her own expense, she found she liked that smile. "She seemed really surprised when I told her I was your boyfriend. You never talk about your personal life, apparently. I wonder why."

She groaned before taking a huge bite from her grilled cheese.

Big enough to choke on it, hopefully.

"I can do another sweep of your place," Cleo said. "Grab your laptop and grab your grimoire thing?"

"Really?" she asked, looking up. "No, you shouldn't have to do that, I'm sure it's fine—"

"It's no sweat, Ben," Cleo replied with a bright smile.

"Be careful when you decide to go, keep us in the loop alright?" Gideon said as he rose from his spot. Then, to Benny. "Come on. It's time to go."

Cleo glanced down at Benny's half-eaten sandwich.

"Take that to go. Looks like you're gonna need that energy of yours."

FIVE

LUKE

"WHAT ARE YOU DOING?"

Luke's fingers hovered at the dial of the car's radio as he craned his neck to look at his brother in the driver's seat. Few things were consistent from score to score—they wouldn't be nearly as successful as they were if they couldn't adapt. But in their world, one thing always remained true: Gideon was the driver. It didn't matter what the circumstances were. Not even a bullet wound had stopped him that one time in Las Vegas.

Except that wasn't the case the other night.

Gideon slid into the backseat, a passed-out Benedetta Russo cradled in his arms, and let Cleo navigate the ride back to the loft, not even yelling at her as she almost stalled out on the manual transmission of the 1970 Mustang Fastback he cherished so much.

A situation both intriguing and amusing.

Although it didn't stop Gideon from tearing into Luke the entire drive home.

"Dude, we are not playing this easy listening crap the entire ride," Luke said, his eyes nearly rolling to the back of his head.

"What do you know about music?" Gideon argued, smacking at Luke's hand.

"Jesus, you're testy," he said, sinking back into his seat.

"Am I?" Gideon asked. "You think there might be a reason, Lucas?"

"You said you wouldn't be mad anymore—"

"Mad about what? You're getting paid for this little rescue, aren't you?"

Luke shifted in his seat, his eyes catching Benny's in the rearview mirror, the bright afternoon sun flickering across her features. Rescue didn't seem like the right word, considering she nearly knocked Gideon's head off before either of them could see it coming. Really made him question his vampire senses. He had no doubt she would have figured out a way to break free from her chains whether or not they showed up. He had seen the hints of her power.

The blow-up-a-guy's-face kind of power.

They didn't write about that in the magic books.

They didn't write much about Stregas at all, to be honest. He hadn't been kidding when he called her a fantasy. He had only heard about the witches they called "day bringers" in passing, in the wistful kind of way one would talk about winning the lottery or meeting a celebrity. The book he swiped from Harker's library didn't offer much, either. Just enough to give him confirmation, enough to trick her into admitting what she was.

But he had to admit, he wasn't so sure he'd have passed on Angelo Torretta's offer if he had known exactly what—no, *who*—they were supposed to find.

Understanding the magic that lived in the world had been one of the more pleasant surprises of his second life.

The past year had been a whirlwind.

Learning the truth about vampires while becoming one was a real mind fuck. In the throes of his human death, bleeding out on the marble floors of the bank, Luke had wondered aloud if he was going to come out of the transformation looking like Nosferatu. But Tefi, the dangerous yet alluring woman who had tricked them all into taking the job in the first place, had merely laughed and told him that keeping his beauty was one of the blessings of vampirism, that it would be preserved in perpetuity.

That he would be exposed to all sorts of delicious things once he turned.

Not that it would have mattered. Tefi had ensured he would say yes whether he wanted to or not. Regardless of the blessings. Because Gideon was on his own, in the middle of a shoot-out with a gang of the undead, and Luke was the only one who could help him. The stab wound to his stomach didn't leave him much of a shot at survival without Tefi's help.

But Gideon would never know that. He couldn't know the choice Luke had made. He couldn't know that leaving with Tefi had been the one thing he could do to ensure his brother's safety.

So here he was, twenty-eight years old plus one and some change.

"Believe it or not, princess, not everything is about money."

Benny let out a snort of laughter.

"That's cute coming from a bank robber."

"You know banks are only a small part of the business," Luke offered. "Most don't even keep cash in their vaults, anymore—"

"Operating a job with only half the details is dangerous," Gideon interrupted briskly, his eyes staring into the rearview mirror. "Your father risked our lives. He lied to us. We're lucky it only ended up with some vampire guts and a few broken light bulbs."

The back seat was quiet for a moment.

"Wouldn't you do the same for someone you love?"

The question felt like an accusation.

Gideon didn't respond but Luke knew exactly what he was thinking about. How hard it was to let what happened in Chicago go. His brother had always been steadfast about the rules, about what it would take to get the job done with the least interference. The least risk. Losing Luke in Chicago had intensified that, ten fold.

"Where are we going?" Benny asked after a moment.

"A truck stop off the highway," Luke said. "Another thirty miles."

They had worked out a halfway point between them both. Something smack-dab in the middle of their loft in Fishtown and Angelo Torretta's compound in upstate New York. It was out of the way enough to help with any eyes that might be lingering on Benny's whereabouts. But it wasn't the most economical route out of Philly; in fact, it took them further out into the state than necessary, and the tension that filled the car was enough to make Luke go a little nutty with cabin fever. One of the "blessings" he was gifted with upon his transformation was enhanced hearing. Which meant a long car ride with two sets of heartbeats belonging to two cranky individuals.

He should have brought headphones.

"Great," she said, the word clipped. "Think we can drive faster than my grandmother? She's dead and I still think she'd manage to get us over sixty-five miles per hour."

"Relax, princess," Gideon said. "Pretty soon we'll drop you off with Daddy, and you'll never have to see us again."

Luke could have sworn he could hear Benny's eyes roll.

A moment later, the radio switched stations of its own accord. The volume turned up as the dial moved toward another station. Static filled the car as the pointer cruised along the slider picking up bits and pieces of other channels until it settled on one playing an old 80's power ballad. Luke turned in his seat to find Benny's fingers moving in a gentle pattern, a small smirk on the woman's mouth.

"If we've got another thirty miles, I'm picking the station."

Gideon's grip on the steering wheel tightened and Luke couldn't help but sink back into his seat, an amused grin settling on his features. This was going to be fun.

Whiskey Winnie's was an I-84 institution, hardly just a truck stop. The three-story neon pin-up girl that welcomed customers inside could be seen from miles off the interstate, and it tended to attract curious tourists just as much as the bikers and truckers who stopped off for an overcooked burger and a break from their routes. The beer was watered down. The floors were sticky. The bar stools were replaced regularly thanks to rowdy weekend nights. And there was always some jerkoff with a guitar singing for tips. But it was discreet in the way a piece-of-shit bar could be. And the bartender knew the Crawfords enough to give them the back room when they arrived. Which was for the best because their pristine black suits stood out like a sore thumb in a bar filled with flannel and denim.

He wasn't surprised to see that Torretta was already there when they arrived.

The head of the Caruso crime family was a massive man.

Although he wasn't much taller than Luke, he was denser, broader— like he could stop a guy cold, full cartoon-style. He was dressed in an expertly tailored gray suit. Black dress shirt and matching tie. Signet ring on his pinky finger. He didn't look much like his daughter at all, except for their eyes. They shared the same deep brown eyes, wide and steady and clear. Even in the confusion of the shipping container, Benny's gaze was always clear. But Torretta's weathered skin and slicked back salt-and-pepper hair made him look like an old crooner on stage at a Las Vegas casino.

He was old school, through and through.

Luke was man enough to admit he was a little scared of him. A respectable amount considering the man's influence and power. Being a vampire didn't make Luke entirely invincible.

Not to a man like Angelo Torretta.

He was almost surprised to see the old man soften when Benny walked in behind them.

"Hey, kid," Torretta greeted softly.

Benny hovered in the doorway, her hands wringing against each other. Luke remembered what she said in the shipping container, the blasé response she had to alerting her father that she was awake. There was something there. A tension he recognized. He knew what it was like to have a father work in the underground but he had no idea what it was like to have a father this powerful.

A long moment passed and then, "Hi, babbo."

She rushed past them in a blur, wrapping her arms around his massive shoulders.

Luke watched their embrace with a weird sort of pang in the pit of his stomach. He was fourteen when his dad died. A heist that went sideways. With their mother fuck knows where in the world, it was always just him and Gideon. Frank Markos stepped in where he could—helped cover a few grocery bills, got them work when they needed it (which they always did). Luke figured that the guilt of losing a man with kids nagged at him. But when things were hard (which they always were in the beginning), the brothers relied on each other first and foremost.

"You okay?" Torretta asked, his hands bracing Benny's shoulders. "Look at you. *Madone*, I'm gonna kill that fuck who took you."

The corner of Benny's mouth twitched. "Any guesses?"

"A few," he admitted, shaking his head. "We're working through it."

"How did you know?" she asked.

Torretta hesitated, a resigned look flashing across his face. "The security cameras. When the connection went down and I couldn't get a hold of you, we knew something must have happened."

Benny took a step back, her fingers flexing at her side.

"I thought we already had this conversation."

Luke could have sworn he saw flickers of light in her palms.

"Don't you think you can give your old man a pass?"

"At invading my privacy?"

"Jesus Christ, Benny," Torretta huffed. "I got a man trying to kidnap my kid, and you're gonna yell at me about this shit? You won't accept a bodyguard, you've scared half my men watching guard— can you blame me?"

Benny opened her mouth to speak but seemed to think better of it, her lips pressing into a tight line as she crossed her arms against her chest.

Luke had wondered why someone like Benny didn't have more protection. The only daughter of a powerful crime lord moseying around Philly without a watch dog seemed like an unnecessary risk. A risk that clearly landed them right here. But he certainly wasn't going to add that train of thought to the conversation.

He liked his head right where it was.

Gideon cleared his throat.

"When we spoke on the phone, you asked if we had any more information on who owns the shipping container," he said, his hands slipping into the pockets of his suit pants.

"It's a dummy LLC," Luke jumped in, knowing this was his part of the gig. "Registered to another independent proprietor that leads to a name belonging to a guy who died over sixty years ago. Some accountant from Reno."

"Which could mean vampire," Gideon added.

"At the very least, we know he's got a couple working for him," Luke continued.

"A couple less, now," his brother said and he did not miss the glimmer of satisfaction in his brother's eyes.

Torretta reached for his daughter's arm.

"What's the name?" he asked, his eyes focused on the dark bruises and needle marks on her inner elbow. "We've been careful with Benny, her true nature— it attracts some sick fucks out there. Only my most trusted men know."

"Does Hal Moran ring any bells?" Luke asked. "We did a search, but nothing of value came up. No spending, no real estate..."

It had been a hell of a dead end. No relatives. No wards or inheritances. Even the man's cause of death didn't scream vampire. Plus, they were pretty fucking far from Nevada.

Torretta blinked, his head shaking. "Never heard that name in my life. That sound familiar to you, Ben?"

"No, but whoever he is," she said, gently pulling her arm back from her father. "He's got a real crusty group of dirtbags to do his bidding. They're obsessed with him. They call him 'Master' like he's some kind of cult leader."

"How much blood did they take?" Torretta asked.

Luke could hear the soft thumping of his brother's heart grow more intense. His eyes turned curious as he watched Gideon watch Benny, his attention on the witch rapt.

"I don't know," she said, wringing her hands again. "A couple of pints? It's hard to remember. I was pretty... knocked out there by the end."

Torretta's fist hit the desk, paperwork sliding to the floor.

"I'll find it," he muttered. "You know what it's like when Strega blood hits the market."

Luke didn't know. But it seemed their new friend did, her skin paling at the mere mention of it. He knew the market was vast, selling and trading things he'd never assumed were real or even possible, but he'd never dabbled in it himself. He wondered how much he still had to learn about what was available to vampires, what was lurking still in the shadows. A part of him wanted to ask Tefi, to reach out to his old sire for more insight—but he knew she was always more trouble than she was worth.

"Can you trace it from there?" Gideon asked. "Find the supplier?"

"The way we move product?" Torretta began. "We know every distributor between here and California. We should be able to trace it. But it'll take time. Benny, I need you safe until then."

"Until what?" she asked, exasperated. "I mean what exactly am I supposed to do while you play detective? Sit in some safe house? I am a semester away from my thesis defense. I'm the head of my coven, I can't just disappear."

"You shouldn't even have a coven," Torretta snapped. "You shouldn't be practicing at all. It's not safe."

"We are *not* having this argument again," she said, throwing her hands in the air. "Is that really what you want me to be? A witch who denies her magic? I might as well let them kill me then."

Torretta's face twisted into something cold.

"Watch your tone, Benedetta."

"I am not some delicate thing! I am not going to hide," she told him, voice steady despite the way her heart rate ticked higher and higher.

Then, as if she remembered herself, her voice softened. "What happened to Mom isn't going to happen to me."

"They know where you live," her father replied and Luke could hear the quiet desperation in his tone. "They know where you work. They ransacked your entire lab at school."

Benny stilled.

"What? When?" she said. "Is everyone— was anyone there when it happened?"

"Last night. A janitor." At Benny's stricken face, her father's shoulders softened. "No, he's fine, Ben. He didn't see anything," the man said quickly. "But you can't just act like nothin' happened."

"Don't do that," she said stiffly. "Don't tell me how to feel about this. Don't try and force me to behave how you think I should. This happened to *me*, not you."

Torretta stiffened.

Luke knew Benny's point hit him hard.

"You gotta work with me, kid," her father said, after a moment passed. "You need someone to have your back. At least until we get to the bottom of this."

Benny rubbed her hands across her face.

"Fine," she said, with a shrug.

A beat passed.

"You two," Torretta said, turning toward the brothers.

Gideon's eyes snapped from Benny to Torretta.

Luke had wondered if it would come to this.

The man obviously cared for his daughter, would have likely continued to try and convince her to hide out for much longer if he could. Asking the Crawfords made sense given how involved they already were. But would Gideon be on the same wavelength?

People were messy.

Each job was a risk. Each outcome had to be worth it.

People were *never* worth it.

"You want her to stay with us," Gideon said.

"More than that," Torretta said, squaring his shoulders. "I got work on my end, weeding out if one of my guys is responsible for this. But I'll pay you double what I promised if you can keep Benny out of harm's way while doing a little bit more digging."

"Double?"

Luke didn't like to show his hand. But that was more than Houston and Seattle combined, and that had given them a lot of time and freedom before having to figure out the next job. Not that the time and freedom had stopped them from taking the Chicago job.

It was funny how things worked out.

"You need more?" Torretta asked. "I'll triple it."

"*Babbo*—"

"You think the asshole who took you is just happy to let you go, Benedetta?" Torretta asked. "He won't stop at the lab. And I clearly can't trust my guys enough to keep you safe."

"But you trust them?" Benny asked, gesturing toward Luke and Gideon.

"Think about our options."

There was a silence that filled the room. It wasn't a half-bad plan. Luke and Gideon were used to working in the shadows. They had a dozen identities. It was how they had evaded most run-ins with the cops. The loft was secure, and they had the resources. It was one of the reasons Torretta had sought them out in the first place. They were a small organization, and had proven themselves with more complex jobs before. Torretta had promised them an obscene amount of money even then. What would it cost them to babysit a witch for a couple more days?

But Luke wasn't going to be the one to agree to this. He couldn't be. Not after getting them involved in the first place. No, if anyone was going to make the decision here, he was going to let it be Gideon.

He didn't have to wait long for his brother to make a decision.

"We'll do it," Gideon said.

So much for avoiding trouble.

"But you need to be straight with us every step of the way," Gideon continued sharply. "No more keeping secrets. If we're going to be responsible for your daughter's safety, I don't want another surprise coming our way. Do you understand?"

Torretta looked at Gideon with a sharp glance and Luke straightened, on the off chance Torretta wasn't pleased with his brother's tone. But the old man nodded, his hand resting on Benny's shoulder. The witch merely crossed her arms against her chest, watching her father curiously.

"Understood," Torretta nodded.

Six

GIDEON

GIDEON HAD LOST HIS mind.

That was the only explanation he had for agreeing to bring Benedetta back to the loft. For agreeing to help look into the people responsible for her abduction. For agreeing to keep her safe.

He wasn't a bodyguard.

He certainly wasn't a private detective.

Gideon Crawford was a professional thief. One of the goddamn best.

But double the original offer— it was a lot of money. Early retirement kind of money. Even if the timeline in which this job would be over was to be determined. It was an offer that seemed insane to pass up.

Gideon shook his head, refocusing on the laptop in front of him. An article about last night's break-in at Penn was on the screen in front of him. Torretta had told the truth when he said no one was hurt, but he certainly downplayed the level of destruction. The small classroom that a handful of PhD candidates in Benedetta's cohort were sharing had been ransacked. Furniture destroyed, computers trashed, windows broken.

It was a low blow.

They had to know she wouldn't go back to campus but they destroyed it anyway. Another safe haven gone after what they did to her apartment.

His eyes drifted toward Benedetta.

She was sitting in the window seat on the far side of the living room, her socked feet kicked up and resting on the wall, a book propped up in her lap. It was that old, dusty thing that Luke brought back from Harker's the other night, the book that helped his brother prove his theory about Benedetta. *A History of Witchcraft.* She was muttering something under her breath, a pen laced through her fingers, as she flipped back and forth through a couple of pages.

He debated sharing the article with her, to show her what happened.

But then he wasn't all that interested in seeing a repeat of the horror that had flickered across her features when her father broke the news.

A lock of hair fell into her face and she brushed it back, tucking the strand into her braid. She looked like the Benedetta he had imagined, foolishly, before he knew what she was capable of. The wanna-be professor. The nerdy, quiet academic her father had described her as. He supposed that version of her might be in there, somewhere, along with the violence and attitude and impressive vocabulary of curse words in Italian he'd overheard during one final heated argument with her father the day before. Her attempts at persuading her father that she didn't "need two overgrown babysitters" hadn't gone well. There was an over-accentuated conversation in Italian (that Gideon didn't understand) filled with lots of hand gestures (that he did) before Benedetta finally agreed that she would stay with the Crawford brothers. But only on the condition that her father tell her as soon as he found out who had betrayed them.

"Jesus, who wrote this?" she grumbled.

"Are you angry at the very old book?" Luke asked.

His brother was laying on the leather sofa, body stiff and still like a corpse, his eyes closed and his hands clasped against his chest. He typically slept during the day. Or at least, well into it. Stumbling into his bed from wherever he went during the night. Which wasn't unlike his life before his transformation. Only that Gideon no longer joined his nights out, nor did he want to know the details.

"I'm not angry," she replied with a roll of her eyes. "I'm just wondering how this got through peer review with not a single footnote. The amount of general assumptions and proselytizing in this is ridiculous."

"If it makes you feel any better," Luke said through a thick yawn. "I think the guy is probably long dead."

"Well, his spirit lives on in most men in academia," Benedetta sighed. She shifted so that her legs were hanging over the side of the ledge, her palms resting on either side of her. "Where'd you find this, anyway?"

"A friend," was all Luke said. "An old friend with an old library."

"Cryptic," she noted. "Cool. That's gonna make this house arrest real fun."

Gideon's fingers flexed over his keyboard.

"You can always take your father up on one of his numerous offers," he said. "Let us get back to our lives while you hide away in some safe house."

"And deny you the pleasure of my company?" she said, a glimmer behind her eyes. "Absolutely not, Crawford. Not when you've spent so much time with my pretty picture up on the wall over there."

The pin board was still hanging on the wall beside his punching bag, her Penn headshot smack dab in the center of it. He didn't know why he hadn't taken it down yet, why he let it still follow him around the loft. Maybe it was also why he had said yes so quickly to Torretta's offer. His own curiosity at who she was, beyond the headshot and volunteer work and mean right hook.

As much as she tried to come off as some spoiled mafia princess, there was something more there. Something he'd seen behind her eyes when she first came to, her eyes raking over him in the morning light steeping into the bedroom. Like she was assessing how much she could trust him. Well, if this was going to work, he was going to have to get her there and fast.

"You hungry?" Luke asked suddenly.

Gideon let out a huff of breath, glad for the interruption.

"You don't eat," he replied.

"Some things just don't leave you," Luke said. "Like the craving for a half-and-half milkshake from Betty's."

"How do you even—" But Gideon cut himself off, actually not wanting to know the answer to the question percolating in his brain. "You know what, never mind."

"Besides, we've been cooped up in here all day." Luke pulled himself up to a sitting position, his head peeking at Benedetta over the back of the sofa. "How do you feel about milkshakes?"

"Very strongly," she said. "But I'm a mint chocolate chip girl, myself."

Luke smiled widely. "Oh, I think you and I are going to get along great."

They approached the turn for Betty's, a '50s train-car diner with metal paneling and neon accents a couple of blocks from the loft. It took up prime real estate on a full corner, and Gideon knew the owner had been holding out for years from one of the city developers. But it had the best coffee in the neighborhood and waitresses that at least eavesdropped respectfully, so it had gotten a lot of service from the Crawford brothers.

The tiny parking lot was quiet. It was just after the dinner rush, and they quickly found a spot in the front. He couldn't help the laugh that bubbled in his throat as Luke sprinted from the car, his suit jacket covering his head like he was dashing through a downpour, his hands enveloped in leather gloves to protect the rest of his exposed skin. It felt foolish to drive a couple of blocks in the city, but between Luke's general issue with the still lingering daylight and trying to keep Benedetta off the streets as much as possible, it seemed the only way.

God forbid Luke order take-out.

"You know a very large umbrella would probably look more distinguished," Benedetta said as she climbed the few stairs to the entrance.

"I thought he was going to ram into that one biker back at the bar yesterday."

"He doesn't typically handle the daytime stuff," Gideon replied as he followed her, his hand reaching for the door before she could grab it. "But you're special."

Benedetta didn't respond to his sarcasm, a glare settling on her features instead as she ducked under his arm to head inside. Gideon followed, immediately getting hit with the smell of fresh coffee and pie. Maybe he was hungrier than he thought.

"Hiya, boys," one of the waitresses called from behind the counter. He could never remember her name. "Sit anywhere ya like, and I'll bring over some coffee."

"None for me, Jackie," Luke said, shaking his head as he chose a booth with the blinds drawn.

"Milkshake?" she questioned, with a knowing smile.

"Can you bring me the extra?"

"Sure thing, honey."

Gideon's eyes scanned Betty's. There was a mother with her young daughter in a booth on the opposite end of the diner and an older man sitting at the counter, face buried in a newspaper and a mug of coffee steaming in his hand. A television was mounted on the wall behind the counter, the news playing with captions.

"Regulars?" Benedetta asked as she slid in on one side of the booth.

"Often enough," Gideon said as he settled in across from her.

"Usually the night shift," Luke added with a smile as he plopped down next to Gideon, jostling him slightly as he got himself comfortable.

Jackie returned with menus and two cups of black coffee.

"I'll be back in a second with the shake," she said. "You take your time."

Gideon's usual order was a turkey club and fries. He didn't plan on deviating from that so he didn't bother opening his menu. Instead, he watched as Benedetta opened hers, her eyes scanning the dozen pages, her fingers tapping on the Formica tabletop. She was wearing a band T-shirt and worn-in jeans that hugged every curve of her long legs, and he knew that if he ever passed by her in the wild, he'd never be able to guess what she was really capable of. It was hard to wrap his head around. The secrets people kept. The way he'd been unearthing so many of them since Luke turned and his whole perspective on the world changed overnight.

"We should talk about this little arrangement of ours," he said, clearing his throat. "Figure some shit out."

Benedetta looked up curiously as she folded her arms on the table in front of her. "Like what?" she asked primly, her brows raised.

"You should take stock of what Cleo grabbed from your place," he said. "We have no idea how long this is going to take and if you need something, you should let us know."

"Like my retinol."

"Your what?" Gideon's brow furrowed.

"Skincare, brother," Luke said with a wave of his hand.

"Is that essential?"

"You're talking to a thirty year old woman, Crawford."

"It's hard to tell, sometimes," he told her, resting his forearm on the table.

She propped her chin up with her palm, a wide smile stretching across her mouth. "I know I have this wonderful youthful energy, so I'm going to take that as a compliment."

There was something disarming about that smile, the way it made her dark eyes glimmer, the way it twisted something up inside of him.

"Unless you're with us, you're staying in the loft," he plowed ahead, fingers drumming on the formica. "We can't risk you getting hurt or abducted *again*, so our place is gonna be your new home and we're gonna be your new best friends."

"Well aren't I a *very* lucky girl."

Gideon sighed, "Is there an off switch on this? Or are you going to be a giant pain in the ass this whole time?"

"Varying levels of ass pain," she replied brightly. "Depending on my mood."

"The trouble I have with that is I can't tell if you're going to be worse the happier you are or the sadder—"

"Well, that's the fun of it."

Before Gideon could respond, Jackie returned with Luke's milkshake, and they all gave their orders. Turkey club for Gideon. A side of fries for Luke. A short stack of pancakes, a side of bacon, and a mint chocolate chip milkshake for Benedetta. Jackie hovered at the table for a second, eyeing Benedetta with a soft glance before she gathered up the menus and disappeared behind the swinging doors that led into the kitchen.

"Okay, let's act like grown-ups now," Luke said once they were alone. "I am going to fling myself into the sun if you two don't stop this funny little banter. You're ruining this milkshake for me."

Benedetta glanced at Gideon, "Is your brother always this dramatic or has it increased since he's become one of the living dead?"

Luke slurped at his straw in a way that did not scream grown-up. "I have always been like this and can we be quiet on the dead thing? There are children present."

One child, who likely did not share his brother's elevated hearing.

"Are you a kid-friendly vampire?" Benedetta whispered, leaning forward.

"I'd kill at your story hour," he replied.

She squeezed her eyes shut and it seemed she was trying to keep her composure, a smile twitching at her lips. "You might want to consider a better word choice."

Luke let out a burst of laughter.

Gideon was going to open his mouth to say something, but he couldn't help but become distracted by her wrists. They had been rubbed raw when they found her but some of that bruising looked like it was beginning to fade. Even the mark on her jaw was already yellowing. He didn't know why he was so surprised. He'd seen wounds heal on his brother in a matter of minutes.

But Benedetta wasn't a vampire.

"You're healing."

She looked up, eyes blinking, surprised.

"Yeah, I figured as soon as I kinda got back to normal," she said, with a small shrug. "I mean, I'm not, like, immortal or anything. But Stregas heal faster than a typical person, or even a typical witch, I guess."

"What do you mean, a *typical witch*?" Gideon asked, his voice quiet. Would he ever catch up on what was out there in the world? "What kind of other witches are there?"

"Oh, loads," Benedetta replied. "Healers, hedge witches, Seers—"

Luke shifted in his seat as he dug a spoon into his milkshake.

"Witches all have their own unique talents," she continued. "My grandmother had the gift of Sight. She had visions all the time. And my mom..."

Benedetta frowned as she picked at a corner of her placemat.

"She was incredible in a million different ways, but she was a kitchen witch. When she cooked for you, it was like she could share a little bit of her magic with you. She could soothe your soul."

Gideon felt all of those past tenses more than just heard them. And he saw something pained, furrowed in the space between her brows.

"My coven," she said, clearing her throat. "Olivia's really good with potion work and she's never without her cards and Imani— she's like my mom. She's got a bakery in Northern Liberties. Her croissants will make you see God."

"And you?" he asked.

"I don't know," she said. "Stregas can Heal, and we can play with energy but I've never felt a strong calling in any direction until..."

When she didn't continue, Gideon leaned forward slightly.

"Until?"

Something like guilt flashed across her face.

"That night on the dock was the first time I've ever used my magic defensively," she said as she leaned back, her palms pressed against the edge of the table as her fingers flexed. "I'm not even sure how it happened."

Gideon could feel his brother's eyes on him.

They had both been shocked by what they saw that night, the way she destroyed that vampire with such ease. It had been one thing when they both thought that was something she did purposefully. But knowing how new this was definitely presented some challenges.

Was it something she could control?

"I don't know any other Stregas who've ever turned their light into something..." She paused as she seemed to search for the word.

"Explosive?" Luke ventured, the corner of his mouth twitching.

"I guess."

"Do you think you could do it again?" Gideon asked.

She seemed unsure of how to answer.

"Do you know what I think?" Luke started, cutting his elbow into Gideon's side. "Seems like something you could work out in a ring."

Gideon couldn't imagine anything worse than getting into a boxing ring with Benedetta. "Oh, no, that's—"

"Wait, yeah," Benedetta cut in, looking back and forth between them. "Can we? I want to be able to figure this out. Maybe that could work."

"Sure," he said, surprised by her response. "We can give it a go."

"Do you think that's why you were taken?" Luke asked suddenly. "They knew how special you were?"

"We have to stop throwing that word around," she said. "I'm just... on the endangered species list."

"What do you mean?" Gideon asked, not liking the way that sounded.

"Stregas don't tend to live out their golden years," Benedetta said carefully. "Our average life expectancy is shit. A vampire can pick a Strega out of a crowd pretty easily. We're hunted. It's why my father is so upset I practice. My mom died when I was a kid, and he still blames himself."

"Vampires?"

Benedetta nodded.

"Is that what you think this was?" Luke asked. "A hunt?"

"Could be," she said, shrugging. "My blood can get you thousands on the black market. It's pretty easy money. Keep me alive just enough—"

She paused, seeming to talk herself out of that scenario. Which Gideon was grateful for. The idea of her being used as some kind of blood bank made him feel uneasy. There was a lot of gray to his moral code, but that kind of shit was always off limits. The Crawford brothers didn't work in people.

"But I think it was more than that," she said, fingers resuming the small tears she made at her placemat. "The way they talked about me, there seemed to be an end. There are rituals I've read about. Spells you can do that call for a witch's blood. And some that need Strega blood specifically. That could be a good place to—"

She cut herself off again, her eyes catching something behind him.

Gideon turned in his seat to follow her gaze and noticed a breaking news bulletin interrupting the weather report. "FIFTH MISSING TEEN" flashed on the chyron. His brow furrowed as he looked back at Benedetta. He didn't like the look on her face one bit.

"Hey, Jackie," he called out. "You think you can turn on the volume?"

The waitress popped her head out from the kitchen.

"Sure thing, doll."

"—and the search continues for sixteen-year-old Abigail Milligan who went missing over the weekend after she was seen cheerleading at the Central High School football game on Friday night," the news anchor said. "Local authorities believe that this matches four similar missing persons cases in the city. Each one reports a teenager disappearing one week apart—"

"Shit," Benedetta muttered. "Shit, shit, shit."

"What?" Luke asked, in between slurps of his milkshake.

"One week apart," she repeated, her fingers pressing against her bottom lip, and it took Gideon an embarrassingly long time to tear his gaze away from her mouth. "This is maybe a little crazy, but rituals are no different from a science experiment. Everything needs to be done exactly. Five kidnappings, all exactly five weeks apart."

"You think that's related to you?" Gideon asked, gesturing back toward the television, not sure he bought into her theory.

"I did this paper early on in grad school on the societal response to sacrifice. Particularly the impact it had on virginity as a construct, and I'd bet you *everything* my father said he's going to pay you that all of those kids are virgins."

She made a face.

"It's bullshit," she continued, raking her fingers through her hair, pulling at her braid. "Virgin blood is *bullshit*. It's a mistranslation. Most of these texts call for the blood of *innocents*, not virgins, but men can hardly tell the fucking difference, I guess. So, for all of that to be happening at the same time I'm snatched from my bed? Yeah, I think there's a connection."

Gideon sat for a moment, unsure of what to say. What had the agreement been? Keep Benedetta safe. Do a little bit more digging. But with the way Benedetta was fidgeting in her seat, she wanted to do a hell of a lot more than just dig. She wanted to act.

He could see it written all over her face. And he found he couldn't blame her.

But could he join her? Let himself run head on into whatever supernatural shit she got roped into? It was wildly out of his wheelhouse. And while his brother had the luxury of an immortal life, Gideon was squarely human. With human strength. Human mortality.

Human fears.

"You think you can call up that old friend?" she asked.

"Abso-fucking-lutely," Luke said, seemingly excited by this whole idea.

She sighed, sinking back into the booth. "I need a very strong drink."

SEVEN

GIDEON

"Do your vampires know you're a neighbor?"

"Is there a real sentence in there somewhere?"

Laughter filled the loft, the sound soft and surprising as Gideon dropped his keys onto the console table by the front door. Benedetta had ordered herself three dirty martinis with extra olives while they were at Betty's, politely flagging down Jackie every time she finished a glass and apologizing for each new request. It was actually pretty fucking endearing. But he hadn't been sure when or even if he should stop her.

She was a grown woman.

She could drink herself into a stupor if she wanted.

But the volume of her voice increased a few decibels with every drink, and he wanted Betty's to remain the nice and anonymous refuge it was for them. So after leaving Jackie with a forty-five percent tip, Gideon found himself putting Benedetta in the backseat of the car a second time this week—though this was a far more pleasant experience. She wasn't unconscious, and he could make do with an arm slung low around her waist to guide her while she quizzed Luke on his vampire abilities.

Could he eat garlic? Yes. Could he turn into a bat? No. What about silver? Not the best color for his complexion but hardly as damaging to him as it was to werewolves.

That last one had brought a goofy grin to Benedetta's face. And Gideon wasn't sure what he was more affected by, the way her face lit up with her smile or the press of her body against his as they crossed the parking lot. Neither of them were going to do him any good.

"Wait." Benedetta flopped herself down on the sofa, her lean body stretched horizontally across the cushions as her legs hung over the arm, feet swinging, more laughter bubbling in her throat. He could get used to that sound. "You know what I mean."

"Strangely, I do," Luke replied.

"Well?"

"I do not make it a habit of exposing my fangs to everyone in the lobby."

Benedetta peered up at Luke with a discerning glance.

"Couldn't you just hypnotize them to forget, anyway?"

"Benny, that Bela Lugosi shit isn't real," Luke sighed, his hand rubbing at the butterfly tattoo that adorned his neck.

"You are *stomping* all over my preconceived vampire notions," she replied, her hand waving as she spoke. "No shape-shifting, no hypnosis."

"How do you know so little about vampires?" Luke asked.

"Well, Luke, when you've been told your entire life that they want to eat you and harvest your blood, you tend to avoid them." She flung her arms out at her sides dramatically. "My father doesn't work with vampires all that often, and if he does, he's certainly not bringing them home for a family dinner, so I only know what I've read about in books, and there's no, like, perfect compendium out there. Most texts are super contradictory."

Gideon laughed inwardly. Only an academic could still work words like "compendium" and "preconceived" into drunken conversation.

Luke's smile stretched wide across his face.

"Fine, professor," he said with a nod of his head. "Ask me anything."

Benedetta beamed, a hint of wickedness flashing behind her eyes.

"Can you fly?"

Luke stared at her for a moment before narrowing his eyes.

"Shouldn't I be asking *you* that question?" he asked.

"So that's a no," she said, rolling her eyes. "God, vampires are so boring."

"Well, I don't see you showing off your little explosions to everyone you meet," his brother countered as he leaned against the back of the sofa. He peered down at Benedetta, his arms crossed against his chest.

A little sigh passed through her lips, and there was something about the sound that forced Gideon to walk toward the bar cart near the kitchen. He'd abstained at the diner because he was driving, but after the last couple of days, he deserved a damn drink.

"Well, that's not fair," she replied. "I didn't even know I could do that until the other day. And I don't really think that's a great conversation starter. *'Hi, did you know I can make your brain blow up?'*"

Luke just fixed her with a look awfully similar to the one she gave him previously.

"Fine, okay, you caught me," she said. Gideon couldn't see her from where he stood, but he could have sworn he heard a pout in her tone. "But I choose to be a boring old witch. On *purpose*."

"Good," Gideon said as he shrugged off his suit jacket. He draped it carefully on the back of a stool at the kitchen island before rolling up the sleeves of his dress shirt. "Boring in this case keeps you both alive and makes my job a hell of a lot easier, so we should keep it that way."

"Ah, so you're boring too," she replied.

Benedetta pulled herself up to a kneeling position, her arms crossed against the back of the sofa, her chin resting on her hands. Her brown eyes were a little glassy but curious as they assessed him.

Luke snorted as he pushed off from the sofa. "An understatement."

Gideon's eyes lifted to the ceiling as he sighed. "Okay, yes, we are all boring," he said, cursing this entire asinine conversation as he poured himself two fingers of whiskey. "We can resume this assessment tomorrow while we wait for Harker to get back to the city. Until then some of us should get some rest."

"You know my night is only beginning, brother," Luke said with a smirk. "I will see you both tomorrow."

He shared a long look with Gideon before he crossed back toward the front door. Gideon knew he'd run off, doing whatever it was Luke did in the middle of the night while the human world was sleeping. Which meant Gideon was on his own with their intoxicated charge. He took a long sip from his glass, nearly draining the contents, the smoky flavor lingering in his throat.

At least she seemed to be a happy drunk.

He could work with that.

"Goodnight, Benny!" Luke called out as he closed the door behind him.

Benedetta called out her goodnight in a sing-songy voice before he heard two distinct thuds on the hardwood floors as she kicked off her sneakers. His brow furrowed, watching as she pulled herself off of the couch and rounded toward where he stood by the kitchen island, her steps a little wobbly. She wore yellow striped socks on her feet, the legs of her jeans half tucked into them.

"I'm not ready for bed," she said. But her body didn't seem to agree as a yawn passed through her lips, her arms stretching over her head. The hem of her T-shirt lifted to reveal just a sliver of her skin. He drained the rest of his glass. "What are you drinking?"

"Nothing, now," he said, though he had half a mind to reach for the decanter again and pour himself another drink. "You need the rest, Russo."

She shook her head, her curls whipping around her face. She had pulled her braid free, her hair in a halo of messy curls.

"I've had enough sleep," she said with a wave of her hand. "Pour me a glass?"

Her movements were a little heavy, all of them big and exaggerated. It was one of the few signs that she wasn't as sober as her words made her sound. And he had to admit, he found the whole thing a little amusing. She was funny like this. Unguarded.

"You know you're gonna have a hell of a hangover tomorrow, right?"

"Well, I've very recently lived through worse," she told him smartly. "And that is precisely why I would like to drink myself into oblivion, so please, help me get shitfaced."

"And here I thought you were already there."

"Hm, well, I can still see shapes, so no."

He hesitated for a moment, his eyes scanning her face for some of that earlier brightness from the car ride home. He was worried her happy drunk was about to curtail into a sad one. But there was an expectant look on her face, her chin jutting up slightly. Like she wouldn't take no for an answer. He poured them both two fingers of whiskey each.

"Have at it, princess," he said, handing her the glass.

She offered him another one of those bright smiles as she took the drink from him and he felt a tug of something he didn't expect in his chest.

If she kept smiling like that, he'd be happy to keep saying yes.

"To being especially difficult to deal with tomorrow," she said, some of that wickedness creeping back into her gaze as she held out her glass in a toast.

Gideon choked back a laugh as he clinked his tumbler against hers.

"I've come to expect nothing less," he said.

She glanced down at the amber liquid, hesitating for only a second before she took a sip. A grimace worked its way through her features before she shrugged her shoulders and took another one. She really was a woman on a mission. He could almost admire it. He'd had his fair share of wallowing in a drink or two over the years.

"Wow, this is disgusting."

"This is Macallan," he said, exasperated.

"It tastes like death," she replied merrily, turning away from him.

"And what, those olive juice martinis were top-shelf?"

He couldn't help but follow after her, watching as Benedetta flopped herself down on the sofa again. She sure was making herself at home for a woman who seemingly wanted nothing to do with the idea just a couple of days ago. Still, there was a part of him that was happy that she was coming around. Even if seeing this kind of familiarity from her in his home tugged at something he wasn't quite ready to name.

"Are you insulting Jackie's bartending skills?" she asked.

He sighed as he perched on the arm of the sofa.

"I thought you said you weren't going to be difficult until tomorrow."

"No, no, you misheard," she said. "I said '*especially*' difficult. This is just standard level stuff, Crawford."

He shook his head, his fingers pinching the bridge of his nose.

"Christ, I should really put you to bed."

She sputtered into her drink, and he couldn't help but like the pink he saw creep into her skin. She coughed as she turned back to look at him, her fingers brushing against her bottom lip. A funny little smile tugged at the corners of her mouth.

"You love being in charge, don't you?"

That felt like a trick question.

"I'm just doing what was asked of me, Russo," he said. "Keeping you safe includes not letting you drink yourself to death."

"You're not gonna get rid of me that easily," she mused.

"Clearly," he said, fingers ghosting the bruise on his jaw absently.

Her eyes tracked the movement, her features softening.

"I'm sorry," she said. "If I had known it was you—"

"You might have swung harder?"

"No," she said quietly, though there was something light in her tone, her cheeks warming again. "I just think I'm starting to see the benefit of having you around."

"Is that right?" he asked.

"My own personal hero," she mused.

He let out a breath. "Don't do that," he said. "That's nothing close to what I am."

"Right, right," she nodded. "Big bad bank robber. Wanted felon. Yadda, yadda."

"You don't know anything about me," he told her, though there wasn't a bite to his words but a plea. "The things I've done…"

"Some of us didn't have a head start on the reconnaissance work," she told him, her head tilting back toward the damned pin board. "But we're roommates now, Crawford. I'll figure you out soon enough."

"That sounds a little threatening."

The laugh that passed through her lips was as delicious as any whiskey he'd ever tasted. A thought so sudden, it nearly knocked him back. But he pushed it away, tamped it down. That was not what this was. Or could be.

But then she shifted to her knees, drawing herself up to meet his height, her body only inches from where he was perched on the arm of the sofa. And just as it had every other time he had her this close, his heartbeat started to quicken in his chest. He watched as she tilted her head, considering him with those deep brown eyes.

"I can heal it," she said, peering up at him. "If you want."

It barely stung, he thought. He shook his head. He didn't mind it so much.

"Show me another kind of magic," he said before he could stop himself.

Her face lit up and any regret he had fizzled away. She sank back down onto the sofa, folding her legs beneath her body before patting the seat beside her. "Come here."

He hesitated for only a moment before he slid down next to her, her feet pressing against the outside of his thigh. She wriggled a little in her seat as she flexed her wrists and Gideon wondered what he'd gotten himself into, what rabbit she was going to pull out of a hat. But she merely held her hands up in front of her, fingers wiggling gently, and suddenly little flickers of light began to glow in the air in front of them, a warmth filling the room. Like the muggy heat of the August night had seeped into the loft. He blinked, letting his eyes adjust, like his brain couldn't wrap itself around what could suddenly just appear.

"Fireflies," Benedetta said, waving her hand, the lights moving in a fluid wave. "That's what my mom used to call them when I was a kid. It's just energy, really. The air is thick with it."

The lights shifted into something more solid, like a glowing orb, and she reached out, her hand curving around the shape. She let it rest in her palm and Gideon could feel its heat. He turned to look at her and found her aglow, her skin glimmering in the reflection of the light, her eyes bright and clear and delighted. He could see now, why she was so fervent about her practice, why she'd choose death over the lack of her magic.

She raised her eyes to meet his and for a moment, this was all there was between them. Until she closed her hand into a fist and the light snuffed out, Benedetta still staring at him in the sudden darkness.

"Why'd you say yes?" she asked.

Gideon didn't allow himself to consider another answer. "A job is a job."

She pressed her lips into a line as she nodded her head.

"Yeah, of course. Double the offer."

"It's a lot of money," he said quietly.

"I bet." She drained what was left in her glass and slid it onto the coffee table as another yawn escaped her lips. "You're right. I should get some sleep."

"Good idea," he said as he got to his feet.

But she didn't budge from the sofa. Instead, she grabbed one of the throw pillows and curled herself up on her side, her fists drawn up to her chin as she closed her eyes. Her voice was soft when she murmured, "Goodnight."

Gideon frowned. "What are you doing?"

"Going to bed."

"Wrong bed, Russo."

"Walking is too much. I'm *really* comfortable here."

He chuckled quietly. "Bullshit."

This was a sitting sofa. Not really a sleeping one. And it was absolutely responsible for the current crick in Gideon's neck. But he wasn't going to tell her that.

Benedetta's eyes fluttered open as he crouched down beside her, all warm and soft and drowsy. Something else was there too. Something more vulnerable than he expected to see from her, and he didn't quite know what to make of it.

What would have happened if he *had* seen her in the wild? If they had been strangers. Their lives different. If they had stumbled upon each other during a late-night coffee at Betty's or even the art museum. She seemed like the type to hang around at the Rodin. Would he have tried to talk to her?

When was the last time he allowed himself to do that?

Gideon never considered himself much of a coward, but when it came to women, he had a hard time with relationships. With committing to anything longer than a one-night stand or a short fling. But his line of business didn't lend itself to being a decent partner. Hell, his parents' marriage was a goddamn nightmare from start to finish.

By the time his mother walked out, she couldn't even stand to be in the same room as his father. Even as young as he was, he could see it. He could feel it.

He wasn't sure he could take the risk.

"You said yes and now I have your room," she said, frowning.

"You definitely don't want Luke's," he grinned. "Come on, let's get you into a real bed."

"But what about you?" she asked as she pushed herself up to a sitting position, her hair falling across her shoulder as she leaned on the palm of her hand.

"What about me?"

"This couch sucks."

He barked out a surprised laugh. "That's not for you to worry about."

"You don't have to be so nice, you know," she said. "I'm a big girl. We can share."

Gideon stiffened.

"I'm fine out here," he said again, more sternly.

The idea of sleeping beside Benedetta was like a shock of electricity through his body. Another feeling he had to shove back down to wherever annoying place it came from. Because absolutely the fuck not. He knew better. He pulled himself back, sitting on the edge of the coffee table across from her, both their empty glasses resting beside him.

"Now, come on," he said, voice gentler as he reached for her.

She took his offered hand with only a moment of hesitation, and he was careful to keep her steady as she got to her feet.

"Okay, okay," she grumbled. She rubbed her hand across her face ruefully. "You gotta quit this whole knight in shining armor thing whenever I'm about to fall over."

He couldn't help but laugh.

"That's just part of the job."

"Yeah, yeah, you've made that clear," she said with a glare that held no real malice as she slipped past him and began to make her way back toward the bedroom. "Goodnight, Gideon."

He didn't think he'd ever heard his name before on her lips.

He didn't think he'd like the sound so much.

"Goodnight, princess."

EIGHT

BENNY

"THIS DOESN'T LOOK LIKE a library to me."

Benny climbed out of the backseat of the car, her eyes taking in their new location with interest. It was a small Italianate style building nestled in between a few other shops in a quieter part of Philly's Northern Liberties, no more than a couple of blocks from Imani's bakery. She had likely walked by a dozen times and had never really noticed the tea shop before.

The sun had begun to set, the sky darkening to hues of deep purple and magenta, and Benny could feel a pleasant chill start to creep into the air. It had been an achingly hot day, the August air humid and sticky. Which hadn't helped with the dull hangover she'd been nursing since she woke up, her marathon of martinis hitting her pretty hard. The aspirin left on the bedside table had helped, but she was regretting her obvious quest to Blackout City. The allure of drowning out everything that had happened in the last few days with gin had seemed incredibly appealing at the time.

But parts of the night felt a little hazy in her memory.

She was worried she might have said something stupid when she was alone with Gideon. Or worse, something flirtatious. Choosing to engage in anything with the man hired to protect you did not seem like a very smart life choice. But it was starting to feel frenetic sharing the same square footage with him, catching sight of him wherever she was, living in his bedroom, sleeping in his sheets.

This field trip was a good distraction.

An appeal to the academic side of her.

Though she was still hung up on her life just somehow pausing, as if she could be plucked from her day to day with no consequences. No phone, no work, no teaching. She wasn't sure what the rules were on contacting her friends, on trying to somehow grasp at some facet of her life.

Benny felt like she was suspended in some kind of stasis.

"That's the beauty of Mathilde's," Luke said.

Her eyes flickered to the sign hanging above the entrance, the black metal with neat gold script, as she followed the two brothers across the quiet street. There was only a dim light coming from the inside, and she could see that the shop had closed about an hour ago from the sign on the front door. That didn't stop Gideon from rapping his knuckles against the window as he checked the watch on his wrist.

"Is Cleo on her way?" he asked.

"Should be here soon," Luke replied.

"How do you know this guy again?" Benny asked.

Luke and Gideon exchanged a glance that left her extra curious.

"He tried to kill me once," Luke said. "It was just a misunderstanding."

"I seem to remember it being very clear why," Gideon replied.

"We were all working off of missing information at the time," Luke countered.

Benny's nose wrinkled as she looked back and forth between the two brothers. She had a million questions she wanted to ask. But the light brightened inside the shop, and suddenly the front door swung open.

"I didn't realize you were bringing me a gift!"

Standing in the open door, illuminated by the lamp light behind him, was a tall, black man with long locs down his back. He looked forty, maybe, with a lopsided grin and piercing dark eyes. He had a lovely Irish brogue with a warm tone. He did not immediately scream four hundred-and fifty-year-old demon-hunting vampire, but Benny wasn't exactly sure what she'd expected.

Maybe more leather?

Certainly not a knit sweater vest and pleated trousers.

Still, she knew he was dangerous. All vampires were. How she'd become entwined with so many in such a short amount of time, she had no idea. What could you call a person knowingly entering in to a lion's den?

"Harker," Gideon warned.

"Kidding, kidding," Harker replied, waving his hand, his smile bright and infectious. "You know I've gone veggie."

"Pig's blood," Luke said to Benny with a wink.

"Semantics," Harker said as he ushered them inside.

The interior of Mathilde's Tea House smelled faintly of peppermint and vanilla. The wallpaper had an intricately designed floral stripe that matched nicely with the vintage hexagon tile and marble-topped bistro tables. Floor-to-ceiling shelves behind the cash wrap held hundreds of flavors of tea, all neatly tucked away in their own squares.

"Wow," she found herself saying, her eyes catching sight of the ceramic teapot collection in another corner of the room. "This place is really cute."

Harker beamed and something in Benny's nerves settled.

"It's a fun little thing to do during the day," he said.

"You know what would be fun? Getting to work," Gideon said as he leveled them all with a look, his hands resting on his hips. "Russo here thinks she might have an insight into the prick who kidnapped her, and the sooner we figure this shit out, the sooner it's over with."

The sooner he wouldn't have to deal with playing bodyguard felt like the unspoken sentence, and Benny tried to not let that bother her. What did Gideon say last night? "A job is a job." She would be smart to remember that.

"That's right," Harker said, taking a step toward Benny. "Do you know I've never once stumbled across a little day bringer in all my years?"

Thirty years of secrecy, and now suddenly everyone knew.

"Well, today's your lucky day," she offered.

"Quite," the demon hunter replied. "Now follow me."

Harker approached the wall on the far side of the counter, and with a short sequence of taps, a hidden door gently swung open. Benny's eyes widened as the door opened to reveal a wood-paneled hallway. Luke followed Harker inside, and Benny eagerly stepped in after him with Gideon close behind her. That warm, soft scent that lingered in the sheets of her new bed hit her and she realized stupidly it was the scent of the shampoo. Gideon's shampoo.

She pressed her lips together, her teeth digging into the skin.

It was like she was wrapped up in his scent.

She had a brief vision of a flurry of light and getting tucked into bed.

"Mind your step, love," Harker called back as he jiggled a skeleton key in the lock. "It can feel a bit cramped going down."

Harker pulled a thin metal cord once the door opened, and a dim light turned on. As Harker and Luke descended down the staircase, Benny was hit with thick, heavy energy in the air. A blanket of magic surrounding the entrance of the basement. She almost took a step back but strong hands curved around her shoulders, keeping her steady. And then she remembered what she said the night before, the knight in shining armor line and briefly wanted to die.

"Whoa," Gideon said. "You good?"

He was close enough that she could feel his breath at the nape of her neck.

Her eyes fluttered shut for a moment.

"Hm?" Benny felt her skin warm. "Oh, yeah. There's just a lot of magic down there."

He stepped back, his hands quickly dropping from her shoulders.

"You can *feel* magic?"

She turned, a smile working its way across her face. He could, too, if he opened himself up to it. "It's like this faint pressure," she told him, leaning her head as if she was telling him a secret. Maybe she was. "Like the air is just a little bit thicker. Does that make sense?"

He stared at her for a moment, his eyes considering her carefully. This close, she could see the depth of his hazel eyes, the little flecks of green that seemed to shine even in the dim light of the corridor. The corner of his mouth twitched.

"Yeah, I think it does."

The basement was larger than she expected. The ceilings were higher. Each and every available service was covered in books, talismans, and antique boxes that surely held items she'd be eager to sit with if she had the time. Walls of built-in shelving were crammed full of books she knew her thesis advisor would lose his mind over if he had the chance to see them. A floor-to-ceiling glass cabinet held weapons Benny had only really read about in fantasy novels.

There was a *mace*, for crying out loud.

Rosemary lingered in the air, no doubt part of a warding spell that Benny was sure came in handy. She found herself drawn to an altar set up on a long wooden table, an intricate black lace cloth setting the stage for crystals and candles. She loved knowing that a tea shop was just above, the customers likely having no idea what happened beneath the floorboards.

It was the beauty of the magic.

She immediately felt as if she could spend hours here, digging through whatever it was Harker had to offer. It made her long for her grimoire, to run her fingers along the pages, to feel a connection to the witches in her life she'd lost, their written words. So many gone because of what they were. It was strange how the emotion swelled through her as she followed Harker and Luke toward the center of the room.

It was why she was so hell bent on practicing with her coven. Why she constantly put herself at risk of being outed. She couldn't imagine her life without her magic. It was all she had left of her mother.

"I did a little digging before you lot arrived," Harker said, standing across from Benny, his hands splayed across the table by a stack of books, gold rings stacked on nearly every finger, the color shining against his dark skin. "There are a few rituals that call for Strega blood. And frankly, I'm not sure what I'd rather we be up against."

"We?" Gideon asked.

"Oh, so I do all the research and then can't join in on any of the fun?"

"Our ideas of fun are very different."

"I was a hunter long before I was a vampire, love. I can't help it."

"How did you manage?" Benny asked.

She found herself fascinated by the sheer testament of his will. Gideon and Luke had explained who Harker was, how much he had helped Luke in his transition in the last year. A demon hunter vampire who swore off of harming humans! It was a conundrum, and one that she knew didn't happen very often. She wondered if Luke and Harker realized how strange it was that they were so different from the rest of their species. How special they were. So much of what she thought she knew about vampires was suddenly being turned up on its head.

"Not entirely well in the beginning," Harker replied. "The first few decades were a blur of blood lust and self-hatred. But I come from a long line of hunters, and to see myself outlive so many of them—I knew I needed to carry on."

"Lucky us," Luke quipped.

Benny watched as the younger Crawford plucked a book from the top of the pile, the title etched in gold, some of the letters faded over time in a language she had never been able to master. But she knew this book. She had cited it as a source in a recent journal publication about ritual and sacrifice, although she had only photos and other academic journals to go off of. Most professors in the field assumed it had been lost to time, no one able to account for it.

But here it was. Sitting right in front of her.

The Hierónymos Codex, or the Devil's Bible.

She was twittering with excitement. And nerves. And a whole mess of emotions she wasn't sure she could keep at bay. This was tangible proof of ancient magics long considered to be left to history. It was in better condition than it had any right to be considering it was hundreds of years old. But she assumed there was some magic in that as well.

But beneath her excitement lay a deep uneasiness.

Like her body was calling out to warn her.

"*How* do you have this?" she asked. "It's been missing for more than a century."

"Missing?" Harker mused, a gleam behind his eye.

"The amount of libraries looking for this," Benny breathed. "And it's here."

"And thank goodness it is, darling," Harker said. "Because I think this is it."

"What?" Gideon asked, looking between them both. "What are we missing?"

"Uh, something really fucking ugly by the looks of this," Luke said, his finger pointing at a page midway through the book, right where Harker had marked the page with a ribbon. "What is this?"

The worn vellum was slightly faded with age and the diagram had lost some of its coloring, but the outline of the beast was still clear. It looked almost right out of a mythology book, a manticore come to life, though it stood on two legs instead of four. It had human-like arms instead of that of a lion's, and the hands curved into long, gnarled talons. And although so much of its body was lion-like with thick fur, its face resembled a bull with four large horns adorning its head. A long tail wrapped around its legs while two large wings stemmed from its back.

Harker stepped forward to lift the page carefully, showcasing the image of a human man directly behind it and then back again to the beast.

A transformation.

"There have been many men over the years who crave more power than they were born with," Harker said. "And that need can warp the mind. It can turn the desperate into demons. Literally. They think it's ascension, but the gods don't tend to agree. They do their best to mitigate what comes from hell—which is, of course, one of the delightful reasons Lucas and I are confined to the darkness."

Benny could feel Gideon tense beside her.

"The gods favor some more than others," Harker said amiably.

"What's a gift from a god but a curse anyway," Benny muttered, thinking of her own power.

"This book in particular is a collection of sorts," the demon hunter continued. "A compendium of men who have gotten what they wished for—or, well, not quite exactly, but it's a bit like finding a djinn, isn't it? You don't really know what you're going to get."

"Great," Gideon said, stepping back from the table with a flourish. "So we've got a guy running around, fuck knows who, planning to what? Kill a bunch of virgins, use *her* blood, and turn into a fucking dragon?"

"Maybe," Harker said. "There's also a possibility he's preparing a sacrifice for the Devil in order to command a portion of his army here on Earth. A fresh heart from a Strega is a rare find."

"The *Devil?* The actual Devil?" Gideon asked.

"You're standing in a room with vampires, and you're skeptical that Lucifer exists?"

"Yeah, well, I'm still wrapping my head around a few things, alright, Harker?"

"Right." Luke leaned both his palms down on the table, hovering over the Codex as he looked up at everyone. "So, what do we do to stop it—stop... any of it happening?"

Benny looked at Luke with a bemused smile. Their task had been to keep her safe. Help suss out why she was taken while her father dealt with whoever it was that sold her out. But by no means did she assume they'd participate in whatever this was— she wasn't even sure she wanted to, her blood be damned.

"This isn't your fight, you know," she said. "This isn't your responsibility."

"And it's yours?" Gideon asked, hitching a brow.

She swallowed. She wanted to tell them that yes, it was. It was her blood, after all. She was the last Strega. But she didn't say anything. Because if she had to, if she was going to figure out how to stop this from happening, how to keep herself safe— she really didn't want to do this alone.

"I've never encountered a true ascension," Harker said, somewhat giddy. "It sounds like it could be a good time."

"So it's settled," Luke said, glancing back down at the book. "What's our first step?"

"Well, I think I'd love it if we could keep my heart where it currently is," she offered.

"Nothing is going to happen to your heart," Gideon said firmly.

He was leaning against a bookcase behind them, his arms crossed against his chest, and their eyes caught for a moment. There was a flicker of something there in his. Something angry. He was duty-bound now to protect her if he wanted her father's payout. And it was hurtling them toward danger.

"Virgins and blood are not the only things the ritual calls for," Harker said before turning his attention back to Benny. "There are steps that lead to this transformation. We're going to have to figure out what's left on his list before the ritual completes. Benny, is there anything you can remember that might help?"

Benny brushed her hair back from her face, shifting to the other foot as she played the last few days back over in her head. She leaned forward, reaching for the Codex. She felt a little thrill just having the book in her hands, like it spoke to some base part of her. Magic worked best with a balance of both light and dark. But the darkness had a way of sinking its claws into a witch if they weren't careful. She sucked in a breath as she pushed the feeling away, turning the pages back to the beginning of this particular section.

"A ritual doesn't work unless all the pieces are in place," she said. "The missing kids still feel like a lead. There's a timing to everything."

Her eyes scanned the first page, scanning over the entry until she saw the phases of the moon drawn out on the very bottom of the page.

"A blood moon," Benny breathed. "But that's—"

"Three weeks from now," Harker nodded.

"We better get you and Gid in the ring and fast," Luke said.

The demon hunter raised a brow.

"I might be able to harness my magic in a more... offensive kind of way," she offered. "We think Gideon might be able to help me figure that out."

"Interesting," Harker replied with a look in Gideon's direction. "I would like to see that."

"You and me both," he muttered.

NINE

CLEO

CLEO WAS BEING FOLLOWED.

She was almost positive that the blacked-out SUV behind her was going to make every single move she did. If she switched lanes, then a few moments later it did too. If she made a left, or a right— oh look at that. There it was.

She wasn't loving this little surprise in her evening.

Especially considering she was due to meet the others at the tea house. The secrets Harker kept beneath the floorboards had to remain as they were. The basement was a crucial meeting spot and an incredible resource as they all adjusted to this new world in the time since Luke's transition. Even the most basic of jobs had them all thinking a little bit differently now that they knew what went bump in the night. Their rules had to shift. Plus, it was Harker's home. Which meant something to her. He had become just as much a friend as he was an ally over the course of the last year.

Cleo was going to have to take a detour. She reached her hand out to feel around for her phone on the passenger seat, the device just an inch out of her grasp. She leaned slightly to the right, careful to keep herself steady on the road. She didn't want them to think she knew.

Not yet.

"Pick up," she grumbled.

"Where are you?"

There was a slight irritation to Luke's voice, a petulance that Cleo came to expect from the younger Crawford brother when he didn't get his way. Cleo was supposed to be at Mathilde's twenty minutes ago.

Well, she wasn't exactly thrilled about this change of plans, either.

She let her eyes flicker to the rearview mirror.

There was enough traffic on the road around them, which would buy her some time.

"About to get on 79," she said.

"What? Out of the city? Cleo, what are you doing?"

She smiled at the new inflection to his tone, the hint of concern.

"I'm being followed," she said. "Last five miles at least."

"Fuck—"

She had an idea formulating in her head and enough fire power in the glove compartment to protect herself from most things. The problem, of course, was that she didn't know exactly what she was up against. And she hated going into a fight without that kind of knowledge. Especially when the difference between an alive man and an undead one was so extreme. Not to mention the leather-bound grimoire she had stashed in the back of the Jeep along with Benny's laptop. She couldn't risk whoever it was behind her getting their hands on either of those things.

"Which mile marker?" Luke asked.

"No." Cleo shook her head. "You're not meeting me."

"Don't be stupid," he scoffed. "You're not handling this alone."

"You have no idea what could be in the car behind me."

"Exactly, dumbass," he said. "This whole thing is bigger than we could have ever expected."

She heard muffled voices in the background. Noises that sounded a hell of a lot like Gideon and Benny, the two of them bickering over something she couldn't quite make out.

"Lead them to the quarry. We'll be there as soon as we can."

She sighed.

This was not the night she had in mind. She was going to make herself some tea in the shop, she was going to curl up in the corner of the basement in one of the more comfortable chairs, and watch as Gideon and Luke bickered over how to manage their Benedetta Russo problem. She'd get to try out a new brew combination from Harker and maybe sneak a day-old scone or croissant, or both. The bickering was just an added bonus.

Well, the night was still young.

She dropped the phone back onto the passenger seat and turned up the dial on the radio. An old pop song was playing, and she found herself singing along, using the steering wheel as a drum as she kept driving, navigating to the exact spot Luke had instructed. Was it weird to be headed to a deserted rock quarry on the outskirts of the city?

Sure was.

But she'd probably done weirder in the last year.

Actually, she'd definitely done weirder.

It came with the job, working with the Crawford brothers.

Cleo hadn't been lying when she told Benny that the boys were trustworthy. They were stubborn and egotistical and more brilliant than she'd ever admit to their faces but they had their moments of being good, too. Good enough for her to join up with, anyway.

Not that she was so good on her own.

She shouted along to the chorus of the song, her head bopping slightly to the music. No, she wasn't exactly what anyone would call "good" but maybe that was why they worked so well together. They were the unwanted, the abandoned, the ones who were left to figure it out on their own. And they'd done a hell of a job so far.

Surviving a vampire attack had a way of bonding people.

So, they could handle watching over one witch, right?

She actually liked Benny. She liked knowing there was going to be more feminine energy in the loft for however long this whole thing lasted. Benny's interactions with the brothers were amusing, especially how quickly she seemed to grate on Gideon's nerves—always a plus in

Cleo's mind. He needed someone to put him in his place from time to time. She even had a bet going with Luke on when things were going to finally come to a head.

Plus, she saw something in the witch that Cleo felt a kinship with.

A longing for something.

She turned on her blinker, prepping for the exit.

Just as she expected, the SUV behind her did the same.

Her fingers tapped against the steering wheel, the song switching into another one. She hummed, her hands turning with the wheel as she pulled onto the dirt path. The quarry was empty, a few abandoned cars on the left side, and an old bulldozer down in the partially dug-out valley. It was dark, only the lights from the nearby highway offering any kind of illumination outside of her own headlights.

It was a hell of a place to pick as a meeting point.

She hated the palpable relief she felt knowing that Luke and Gideon were on their way. Especially when more SUVs than she expected turned into the quarry behind her. Three of them altogether, all exact copies. She cursed under her breath when she realized how stupid she'd been to have missed them. Maybe the obviousness of tailing her had been on purpose.

Something she fell for easily.

Her mother told her once she was always gunning for a fight.

Well, maybe she was right.

She did her best to channel something resembling calm as she got out of the car, one hand firmly on the gun strapped into the holster underneath her jacket and the other adjusting the smaller pistol she tucked into the waist of her jeans. It was impossible not to hear her father's voice in the back of her head during moments like this, his slow Appalachian lilt reminding her how crucial it was to always have backup. How important it was to always expect the worst.

"What a quaint little meeting spot," came a scratchy voice.

Half a dozen men were ambling out of their own vehicles, all of them carrying, only some of them human. She'd gotten better at tracking vampires, learning the tricks and tells, the way some of the older ones tried to mimic modern dress and speak, the way others forgot to pretend to breathe. Sometimes she got close enough to know their hearts were quiet. Nothing beating beneath the surface. Though it was still hard for her to wrap her head around.

All that time alongside Luke, and if she placed her hand on his chest, what would she feel? Anything?

She wasn't sure she could live a life without that sound, that little drumbeat ticking in her ribcage. She liked knowing she was mortal. She wanted to see the end of things. She had earned that.

"Well, if I'd have known about our little date tonight, I might have gone for something with a bit more ambiance," she said, leaning back against the side of the car, arms crossed against her chest as she dug the heel of her boot in the dirt.

"This will do just fine."

The man who was speaking was clearly human, an average-sized white guy dressed like he was about to offer to file her taxes. It was intriguing. Frankly, everything about what happened to Benny seemed like a bizarre little mystery she was dying to understand. Humans and vampires working together to find a witch? She'd learned in the last year how rare it was to see humans and vampires working together, period. Luke living a somewhat similar version of his human life was an apparently unexpected choice. A choice looked down upon by other vampires.

But she'd never known Luke to give a shit about what anyone else thought.

"What's *this*?" Cleo asked, using air quotes around the word.

"You're gonna give us back the witch."

She furrowed her brows.

"Which witch exactly?"

"Don't do that," he said before he spit into the dirt. "Don't play dumb. You think we don't know who you are, *Cleo St. James*? You don't think we knew the moment you waltzed into Benedetta Russo's apartment? We know *everything* there is to know about you, red."

A breeze whipped through the quarry, her hair batting around her face. She brushed it back, wondering if he was bluffing or not, and trying to figure out how to know that without taking his bait. Because that's what it was, after all. But she knew better than to give a man what he wanted. She had learned that the hard way more than once.

A tall, brown vampire with long black hair tied back in a low ponytail stepped forward, his eyes darkening into a blood red.

"It's alright, Mack," the vampire said. "I've got ways of making her talk."

"You do that," Cleo said, cocking her gun. "And you'll get a wooden bullet straight through your heart."

"You wanna see who's faster?" the vampire taunted before baring his fangs, a wicked grin flashing across his face. "I bet you I know who wins."

She was almost willing to take that bet when she heard the crunching of gravel and another car pulling into the quarry. The midnight blue Mustang pulled in at a fast clip and swerved to the side before hitting the breaks. Gideon loved a showy entrance.

The corner of her mouth curved into a smirk as she held her gun steady.

Luke climbed out of the passenger side, amusement flickering across his face.

"Six on one. Wow."

He approached the group with long and confident strides. Cleo had always found Luke to be incredibly cocky, a real know-it-all. His new-found immortality only made it worse. However when his eyes traveled to her, there was a silent question there. Was she okay? Her nod was slight but clear enough, and Luke returned the gesture before turning toward the men. He stopped just in the middle of the standoff, separating Cleo from the rest of them. Another car door slam found Gideon lining up his shot from the hood of the car while Benny lingered beside him.

"Cleo, I feel like I'd take this as a compliment," Luke continued.

"Believe me, I'm gonna be bragging about this for weeks."

"You can laugh, red," Mack said. "But you did exactly as I asked."

"Well, would you look at that?" Cleo said, before turning toward Benny. She gave the other woman a little wriggle of her eyebrows. "Hey Benny, these ugly creeps want you to go back with them. What do you think? Do you wanna go?"

"Not a fucking chance," Benny replied with an attitude Cleo respected.

"Alright, looks like that's settled," Luke said with a clap of his hands.

Mack let out a huff of breath.

"We haven't settled shit," he replied. "Let's go."

He gave a low whistle, and suddenly it was Go time, like she was in a bad Western.

"See, this is why I prefer to shoot first if we're not going to have a *plan*," Gideon groaned as he reached for Benny, his arm guiding her back. "Get behind me."

"I am not going to just stand here," she argued, pushing past him. "Not when I can help."

Gideon let out an exasperated breath as he followed after her.

"By doing what? Some magic move you have no control over?"

"No, Crawford," she said smoothly. "By getting my hands on that gun in your waistband."

A flash of something flickered across her face and Gideon blinked.

"Jesus Christ, what do you have, a death wish?" he asked, though he reached behind him to give her exactly what she asked for.

"Oh, yeah, you got me. Sucks for the guy who signed up to keep me safe, huh?"

"Yeah, I'm beginning to regret that decision," he said dryly. "You know how to use this thing?"

"I'm Angelo Torretta's daughter," Benny said, as if that answered the question.

Cleo supposed it did.

The whole interaction would have made her laugh if she wasn't suddenly trying to make sure a vampire wasn't about to bite her head off. Luke had taken on two men, leaving her with this scrawny-looking white guy wearing a hoodie. It was August. Did vampires not sweat?

She staggered back, her body hitting the side of her car as she slammed the butt of her gun into his cheekbone. It was instinctive but not the best move. She found a quick kill was the only way with a vampire. They had far more resilience. At least she had come prepared with a clip of wooden bullets.

Still, she felt no honor in scrambling back to her feet and essentially fleeing to the other side of her car, trying to drive as much space between them as possible. But she knew her strengths, and one-on-one brawls were not one of them. The vampire followed after her, a hiss passing through his lips as he lunged across the hood of her car. She dropped to her knees and pointed her gun at him with both hands. She was going to have dirt smeared into her jeans.

"Sorry, dude," she said as she fired a shot directly into the center of his chest.

She watched as his body began to immolate from the inside out, like the edges of a newspaper after being lit with a match. The bullet lodged in his heart lingered there in the air, hovering in the ash before both the bullet and the ash fell to the ground, and subsequently covered her windshield.

"Aw man, I just got a car wash."

Ten

Gideon

Well, the whole night went to shit real fast.

Someone fired. Gideon couldn't be sure who, but a bullet whizzed right past his head, leaving him with a faint ringing in his right ear. Dust and gravel kicked up all around them and he could hardly make out who was who in the ensuing madness. Someone swung at him. He dodged it, and was able to land a heavy blow into the other man's neck. Not exactly where he'd hoped to aim but it would do. He heard a faint grunt and then a hiss.

Vampire.

Great.

He was an ugly sucker, veins popping bright red under pale skin, eyes like pools of blood. It was the same vampire with the ponytail he saw approach Cleo as they were pulling into the quarry. The hit came fast, right into Gideon's gut, and he staggered back. It was like blunt force with a fucking brick. He wasn't sure he'd ever get used to their strength. He clutched at his side as he tried to dodge another hit. The success was short-lived as the vampire lunged, pushing into Gideon's shoulders and taking him down into the gravel. There was that ringing again.

Fuck, this was gonna hurt in the morning.

They wrestled, Gideon struggling against the sheer force of him as he scraped at the ground, gathering dirt into his palm. He swung hard, letting the dust and gravel do their job as they hit the vampire square in the eyes. It gave him the briefest of moments to grab his gun and aim a bullet directly at his forehead.

The vampire went flying back.

Gideon didn't waste any time as he staggered back to his feet.

He blinked and Luke came into his vision, his brother whaling into another vampire, sending him soaring through the air just as Cleo took a shot at another one from behind her car. But what he couldn't see was the whereabouts of the goddamn witch he was supposed to be protecting. She'd fought him tooth and nail to come to the quarry instead of staying behind with Harker where it would be safe, and he was regretting ever letting her get into his car.

But he found it was hard to say no to her.

"Come now, pretty girl," a scratchy voice hissed. "Don't make it so hard—"

Benny.

Mack, the one who talked a lot, had her hands behind her back, a tight hold on her wrists. Gideon could see the gun on the ground at her feet and he cursed under his breath. How did she get so far from him? She had just been there, right beside him, hovering so close Gideon could hardly think straight. Let alone formulate a fucking plan. A seemingly recurring problem since they'd found her. It was hard to imagine it had only been a week since she'd walked into their lives.

And now goddamn gunshots were ricocheting off goddamn quarry walls.

But Benny didn't look scared. She had dug her heels into the earth, her chin raised high as Mack tried to yank her back toward one of the SUVs. Gideon managed to catch her attention, his brow furrowing in a confusing mixture of concern and aggravation. She stared back and for a fleeting moment, fear flashed across her features. But just as quickly it was gone.

Not so fucking fast, buddy, he thought.

He swung his arm left and took out both front tires, one-two shot, his gaze never leaving her.

That was when a small burst of light filled the space between them. The man let out a yelp of pain, and she slammed her heel back onto his ankle with a sickening crack, taking the opportunity to pull herself free from his hold. Gideon was already crossing toward her, relief coursing through him.

"Benny—" Gideon reached for her, his hand curving around her shoulder.

"I'm okay," she said, brushing dirt from her chin.

"What the fuck were you thinking?" he snapped, the words stumbling from his lips without thinking. "I told you to stay behind me."

"I can take care of myself," she bit out as she picked the gun up from the ground. "I don't need you to play bodyguard."

"If that were the case, we wouldn't be in this situation would we?"

The look on her face was scathing and he felt a fleeting stab of regret.

"Hey, a little help here?" Luke shouted.

A wooden stake came barreling at his face, and Gideon caught it just in time to sink it through the chest of a very poorly dressed vampire coming at his right side. By the time it burst into ash, Benny was gone. Again. Gideon bit back a groan as he trudged along after her, his eyes scanning the quarry. Suddenly an engine revved, and Gideon realized one of the SUVs was taking off. Two of them were making a run for it, Mack and the vampire he shot in the forehead. It was just a regular bullet, nothing wooden. He hadn't been able to switch out the clip before everyone started shooting.

He really hated not having a plan.

Cleo and Luke stood side by side, their guns aimed directly at the back tires.

But the SUV was too far too fast and their shots hit the dirt.

"Fuck," Luke muttered. "We could've gotten one of them to talk."

"We still can," Benny said, tucking his gun in the waistband of her jeans.

"What? How?" Cleo asked.

"The half dead guy over there," she said, gesturing to one of the men propped up against a large boulder, a gunshot wound staining his shoulder a deep red.

"Can he even talk?" Gideon asked.

Cleo nudged him with the toe of her boot.

He moaned but said nothing, the blood loss leaving him nearly comatose.

"He doesn't need to," Benny said as she approached him. "I can speak for him."

But before Gideon could ask what she meant, she was kneeling on the ground in front of him, resting back on the heels of her sneakers. She considered the man for a second, her face screwed up in concentration as she flexed the fingers on both her hands.

"Luke, can you hold him down?" she asked.

His brother stepped forward, his eyes sparing Gideon the briefest of glances, but he did exactly what Benny asked, pressing the man's uninjured shoulder firmly against the boulder, locking him in place.

"Once I'm in," she said, looking back at them all, "We'll get the truth."

"How will we know?" Cleo asked.

She offered them a wonky smile, and it cut right through Gideon. "Your blood never lies."

She leaned forward and pushed two fingers into the gunshot wound in the man's shoulder. Gideon couldn't help but grimace at the strangled cry that emitted from the man's throat, watching as he struggled against Luke's grasp. With her face screwed up in concentration, Benny used the man's blood to draw something on her left forearm, four symbols Gideon didn't recognize. She repeated the process with her other hand, her other forearm filled with four new symbols.

He was transfixed.

They were all watching with bated breath, the quarry silent save for the man's whimpers. Benny's forehead wrinkled as she considered him, like she felt sorry for him, but it lasted only a moment before she closed her eyes and held her arms out in front of her body, palms facing up. All at once, a small wisp of light appeared in the center of each palm. Her lips spoke words Gideon didn't understand in a language he didn't know, and the light seemed to sink back into her skin, the symbols on her arms starting to glow.

The man's whimpers stopped. His eyes opened, and they were glowing the same bright white light that was just hovering in her palms.

"Holy fuck," Luke breathed.

"Master is gonna be real pissed," Benny said in a strange tone. "He wants the witch."

Gideon hadn't expected this to be the result, and frankly had no idea how to go about an interrogation this way, but he didn't seem to have much of a choice. He ran his tongue over his teeth as he crouched down across from Benny, his eyes meeting his brother's, the two of them sharing the same brow raise.

They were a long fucking way from bank robberies.

"Right, so—" he began, considering how to phrase this question without sounding like a total asshole. "Can you tell us about this 'Master' of yours?"

"He is a powerful man. With abilities that deserve loyalty and our respect."

Gideon sighed. "Sure, yeah."

"Why does he want Benny?" Luke asked.

"The witch is crucial to the ritual. He needs her blood in order to complete the final step of the transformation. To become *Halmanthoran*."

It was fucking unnerving to see Benny speaking in a voice so unlike her own. So flat, so devoid of the attitude he'd already become so used to. But this was finally getting them somewhere, wasn't it? Even if nothing made any goddamn sense to him.

"What else does he need for the ritual? How many more steps are there?"

"Master has to bathe in untouched blood," she said.

A look of disgust flashed across Luke's face.

"The kids," he said, looking at Gideon. "Benny's right about the sacrifices."

"And then there are the offerings," she continued. "The sacrifice for the blood moon. The Strega to appease Hell. The stone heart of the sun to give *Halmanthoran* life."

"The stone heart of the sun?" Cleo repeated.

"The stone heart of the sun is a jewel that burns so bright it can boil oceans."

There was a hazy smile that lingered on her face, an empty gesture as it didn't reach her eyes. But it lasted only a moment before Benny began to cough. Her body doubled over, her hands flat on the ground as the man seemed to crumble, Luke hardly needing to hold him back. Gideon reached for her, but she waved him off, shaking her head.

"I'm sorry," she said, wiping at her mouth with the back of her hand. She righted herself slowly as she tried to catch her breath. "I lost him."

She coughed again, and Gideon swore he saw blood drip from her lips.

Benny rested back on her heels, her chest heaving in and out.

"The spell doesn't work if the host is too weak. Did we get anything?"

"We got a hell of a lot more than we had," Luke said.

"Yeah?"

Cleo blew out a breath. "That was insane."

"Blood magic," the witch replied with a grimace. "It works but it's gross."

What the hell was blood magic? And when did Benny learn it?

Gideon rose to his feet, taking a moment to wipe the dirt from his trousers before he reached his hand out for Benny to take. She looked up at him, and in a flash, it was like all her initial anger came bubbling back to the surface. Still, she placed her hand in his, and he helped her to her feet. There was a brief moment her hand lingered in his before she pulled away from him and stepped back, putting distance between them.

Distance he needed.

"Okay, what do we do with the almost-dead guy?" Cleo asked, staring down at the slumped -over man with a grimace.

"Oh, I can handle that." Luke grinned.

And in a flash, Gideon watched as his brother's familiar features contorted into his second face. The one Gideon had struggled with in the beginning. The obvious proof that the brother he knew was something else entirely now. His skin paled while his veins grew brighter, his pupils growing larger as the whites of his eyes turned red. It was the face of the monster within the body, the blood rush of the vampire coming to the surface and leaving his brother behind. He chose not to watch as Luke descended upon the man, the pathetic whimpers enough to paint the picture.

"You and me, we need to have a conversation about what happens in situations like these," he said instead to Benny. "You could have gotten yourself really fucking hurt."

"Is this what you want to do right now?" she asked. "*Lecture* me?"

"I am trying to keep you alive," he said. "So stop being a brat."

"Jesus Christ, would you two just chill out?" Luke wiped at his mouth. "I can't have a goddamn meal in peace with you two."

"Shut up, Lucas," Gideon snapped.

Luke sighed before he resumed feeding, Cleo turning away from the scene.

"Come on," Gideon grit out as he wrapped his hand around Benny's wrist.

"Hey—*what* are you doing?"

He bit back a grunt of frustration as he led them both back toward the Mustang, Benny marching alongside him with heat behind her eyes.

"You know, you're being a real dick," she muttered as they rounded the hood of the car. Gideon fished for his keys in his pocket with his free hand, his jaw tightening at the insult. "I was perfectly fine out there."

"None of us were perfectly fine," he snapped. "That was an ambush."

He could hardly look at her as he dropped her wrist, focusing on popping open the trunk. He was mad for a million different reasons, and he was trying to figure out which one of those was Benny's fault as he tucked his gun back in his holster. He had a duffle bag tossed in the back, among other various things that came in handy in a pinch, most of them illegal in one way or another. But he found what he was looking for in a side pocket of the duffle bag, yanking out a clean towel.

"This isn't the kind of situation where you can just run off guns blazing," he said, voice rough as he reached for her right arm. She tensed beneath his touch but she didn't budge, her eyes tracking every movement he made. Gideon tried to be gentle as he wiped away the blood but it was beginning to dry on her skin. "Those were hired men. They don't give a fuck about who they hurt. Do you understand?"

"So, I'm supposed to do what?"

He moved on to her left arm, flipping the towel to the clean side before carefully wiping away the remains of whoever the fuck that was lying dead in the quarry behind them.

"You listen to me," he said, irritated. "Stay back when I tell you to stay back."

"They want *me*, Gideon," she said, and he hated the way her voice cracked when she said his name. "I will not just sit here and watch as everyone else tries to fight this for me. I don't care if you're being paid— I can't watch—"

"So, your plan is to just put us all in harm's way instead?"

He stepped back when he was finished, balling up the towel in his fist, trying to ignore the stricken look on her face. The way her lips parted as if she was going to say something before she thought better of it, her jaw tensing instead.

"I was so fucking focused on finding you out there," he continued, unable to stop himself. All of his focus for the last week has been on Benedetta. "You are a goddamn distraction. And that's the kind of shit that'll get me killed. All of us killed. And then who's going to keep you safe?"

He could feel the heavy thump of his heart beating rapidly in his chest, the same kind of ache that was twisting up his insides. He was gonna have a hell of a bruise in the morning. And he knew he was taking out some of his anger at the attack on her, but Jesus Christ, it could have gone so sideways. They were lucky. They were really fucking lucky. And he needed her to know that. He needed her to get on the same page and fast. Because Gideon knew this wasn't the last time they were going to see those men.

They weren't going to give her up without a fight.

Well, neither was he.

But if Gideon was hoping for some kind of acquiescence, some kind of agreement, he was shit out of luck. Benny reached for the gun and held it out for him and as he took it from her, she was storming past him and pulling open the passenger side door to the Mustang. Without even bothering to look back at him, she slid inside and slammed the door shut. The car rattled with the impact, and all he could do was let out a weary sigh.

"Well, good luck with that, brother." Luke laughed as he led Cleo to her Jeep. "I'm gonna go in the happy car tonight."

"Fucking hell," Gideon muttered under his breath.

It was going to be a long ride home.

ELEVEN

BENNY

BENNY COULDN'T SLEEP.

After what felt like an eternity of tossing and turning and burrowing underneath the comforter until she was nearly at the foot of the bed, she finally gave up and flung the covers off her body. The loft was quiet. Though not nearly as quiet as the rest of the ride home from the quarry had been. Benny had plopped herself in the passenger seat of Gideon's precious Mustang while he stewed beside her, neither of them saying a word to each other. But she had zero interest in attempting to continue their previous conversation.

It was Grade A Brat behavior.

Unbecoming of a grown ass woman, that was for sure.

But Gideon deserved it. Maybe.

Except he was right. It *was* an ambush. It was all she could think about as she tried to sleep. If anything had happened to Cleo... She would have been responsible. This was all happening because of Benny. Because of her blood. Which was exactly why she couldn't just stand by and watch everyone else go to bat for her. She wouldn't become a bystander in the fight for her own life.

She needed Gideon to understand that.

If he could just stop acting like such a sanctimonious prick...

Except for the moments he wasn't.

The aspirin on the nightstand. How gentle he was in scraping the dried blood off of her arms. The way he handed her his pistol without a second thought, even when he wanted her as far away from the fight as possible. Which somehow made her even more annoyed. Pick a goddamn lane. Her brain couldn't handle the whiplash.

She wrapped her arms around her body, wishing Cleo had thought to grab her something less embarrassing to wear to bed and not her matching Skateboarding Kitten pajama set. She sighed. The whole reason Cleo got tailed at all was because she had risked getting Benny her things from her apartment. So she was gonna have to be grateful for what she got.

And she was.

Both the grimoire and her laptop were now safely tucked away in the loft.

Benny stretched, a yawn passing through her lips as she made her way into the main room. It was dark, save for what seemed to be headlights streaming in through the windows, the shadows shifting with the highway traffic.

Shadows that splayed across a sleeping Gideon's form, his body strewn across the leather sofa, a pillow tucked beneath his head. She stopped in her tracks when she noticed him, tilting her head as she caught sight of the book laying across his chest, one hand still pressed to the binding, the other hanging off the edge of the cushion. It was that fucking book, *A History of Witchcraft.* She felt a soft breath pass through her lips. It was the first time she'd seen him out of a suit. His gray sweatpants stretched across his thighs, and the white T-shirt he wore had allowed just the hint of a tattoo on his chest to peek through. She pivoted toward the kitchen, feeling as if she had just intruded on a version of Gideon he didn't like most people to see.

Especially when he was sleeping on a couch so that she could have his bedroom.

Had she asked him last night to share?

She groaned inwardly at the recollection.

Benny would get her glass of water and then go back to bed and not at all lay there thinking about what that tattoo was or the way his T-shirt fit a little too snug across his broad chest. Which of course created another problem for Benny. Because as she lingered in front of the cabinets, she couldn't remember which one held the glasses. She bit down on her bottom lip as she gingerly opened each cabinet door, trying to figure out which one had what she was looking for.

Plates. Bowls. Lucky Charms cereal?

"Are you trying to case the joint?"

Benny jumped, accidentally slamming the cabinet shut. She winced at the sound as she slowly turned around. Gideon was sitting up now, one elbow resting on his knee as he raked a hand over his face. His dark hair was a little mussed from sleep, and his eyes were heavy. But there was a glimmer of amusement behind them.

Was that a smile?

"Sorry," she winced. "I didn't mean to wake you."

"I'm a light sleeper," he said before yawning. "Glasses are on the right."

"Right. Thanks."

And Benny found exactly that in a small cabinet beside the refrigerator. A perfectly smart place to put them and not at all a cabinet she had checked. She grabbed two glasses from off the shelf and filled them with water from the filter as Gideon slowly padded his way barefoot across the living room. She wasn't blind. Gideon Crawford looked good in those perfectly tailored suits of his. Too good, really. But this? This half-asleep, soft version of him? Leaning against the island, watching her beneath those heavy-lidded eyes?

Absolute trouble.

But his movements were jerkier than normal, she noticed. Almost heavy and lumbering.

"Couldn't sleep?" he asked, his hand pressing against the countertop.

She shook her head.

"Weird day."

His laughter was such a pleasant surprise after how they'd left things, she almost missed the wince lingering there, the way his weight shifted as he held onto the counter. Her smile faded as she moved toward him, guilt and concern prickling her skin. Had something happened at the quarry?

"You're hurt," she said. "Where?"

He waved his free hand, "No, it's nothing."

"You're holding onto the counter for dear life," she said. "Can I—I can fix it, you know. If you want."

This laugh was more of a choke as he shifted, letting his body rest against the island, as if he was no longer putting on airs on her account. She stepped back, her fingers pressing against her bottom lip as she let her eyes trail up and down his form. She couldn't see too much obvious bruising, save for a shallow cut on his cheekbone but there was a lot of surface covered by clothing. Not like she could just ask him to strip down so she could play nurse.

The thought alone made her feel briefly insane.

"I'm fine," he said, shaking his head. "I'm sure it'll feel better in the morning."

"You're hurt because of me. The least I can do is try and—"

"I'm hurt because I let a vampire sucker punch me," he cut in. "Not because of anything you did."

And yet, she still felt in her bones that it was all her fault.

"Gideon," she started, her voice soft. She reached for his hand, her eyes catching the fresh cuts across his knuckles, the redness around them. His skin was warm against her fingertips and his fingers flexed beneath her touch. She felt the ghost of his thumb grazing her own, so gentle she wondered if she imagined it. "Let me do this for you. Please."

He stared at her, his throat bobbing as he seemed to mull it over.

Then, "How does 'this' even work?"

"It's magic, Crawford. I don't think I could explain it to you if I tried."

The sheer skepticism settling into his features made her laugh.

"Can I see?" she asked.

He hesitated for only a moment before he pulled up the hem of his T-shirt, just high enough to expose the large, mottled bruise on the left side of his abdomen. A very toned, tanned abdomen that led into a deep V beneath the waistband of the sweatpants slung low on his hips.

"Right," she said, nodding her head.

She flexed her fingers at her sides, wondering what had gotten into her. She'd seen plenty of men shirtless before. He wasn't even fully shirtless. He was a few inches of exposed skin level of shirtless. What was this? The Regency era? An old timey movie where a woman could knock a man out with a sliver of her ankle?

"I—I have to touch you to do this, Gideon. Is that okay?"

His eyes fluttered shut and Benny was about to rescind her offer when—

"Yes," he said. "Please."

Please.

She breathed in as she took another step toward him, her hand hovering near his abdomen. Healing magic could be clinical. All the Healers her father employed were hardly precious about their work. But right now, here, Benny touched him with tenderness. He had gotten hurt to protect her, to keep her from being taken again. How could she not want to fix that?

She could feel his gaze on her, his body tensing as her palm hovered near his skin. She needed to feel the wound first, to see what it was that needed mending. Her ability to heal allowed her to almost see beneath the surface, to feel what needed fixing. A faint glow emitted from her hand, the light illuminating the bruising, showing Benny just how bad the impact had been. Her face screwed up in concern as she tried to bite back her gasp. She could feel the way his body was struggling.

"You should have told me," she said, as she pressed her hand now firmly against the bruise. "I can't believe you're even standing up straight."

"I didn't think it was that bad," he huffed with a terse chuckle.

"Okay, tough guy."

He let out a soft grunt as she pushed into the bruise, her magic beginning its work. She felt terrible, knowing she was responsible for this. Knowing he was sitting with this while she spent the entire car ride icing him out.

She was an absolute idiot.

"Listen, Gideon, about earlier—"

"No, that's on me," he said firmly, interrupting her. "I'm sorry."

"What?"

"I shouldn't have yelled at you like that."

Her brows furrowed as she considered him, her lips twitching as she realized he was being sincere. Gideon Crawford was *apologizing* to her.

"This isn't really…" He trailed off with a sigh, shifting his body almost further into her touch as her magic continued to spread throughout the wound. She found she didn't mind it. Being this close to him. "I don't know what the hell I'm doing here. This supernatural shit is not where I excel. I don't like feeling one step behind. And from the moment we found you, I've been scrambling to try and keep up."

He shook his head, his free hand raking through his already sleep-mussed hair. She was hit with a sudden instinct to brush her fingers through it. "When Luke and I work, I'm the one who takes the lead. That responsibility, making sure things go smoothly, that's on me. I thrive on that. It works. But I haven't been in control since—"

There was something stopping him from finishing that statement but Benny knew.

"Me."

The look on his face told her all she needed to know.

"I didn't ask for this, you know."

A week ago she was scheduling out her final fall semester, making sure she had all her advisors lined up and her thesis work in a good place, and now she wasn't even sure she'd be given the opportunity to finish the program, something she'd spent the last four years working on. But maybe she had been too optimistic to think she'd get this far anyway.

She'd always been living on borrowed time.

"I know," he replied and there was a softness to his tone she didn't realize she needed until she heard it. "But we're not gonna get through this if we don't figure out a way to work together. I need you to trust me, Benny."

Not Russo. Not princess.

She liked the way her nickname sounded on his lips.

Like at the quarry when he thought she was hurt, the urgency in his voice. Right after he shot out Mack's tires. A move that had given her the opportunity to save herself.

"I do," she said, and she meant it. Somehow she did. "But I can't be passive in this."

"I know," he breathed.

Her magic began to cool, an icy chill passing from her hand into his abdomen to soothe the muscle. His body twitched at the change in temperature and his free hand wrapped around her wrist. Perhaps instinctively because the moment she stared down at where he held her, his grip loosened and his hand fell slack at his side.

"Just try to dial it back on the death wishes, will ya?"

But she could only nod, her eyes fixed on his hand, wondering why he'd reached for her at all and wishing she wasn't also hoping he'd touch her like that again.

The chill of her magic turned warm and she watched as the bruising faded, the blood vessels healed, and his wound turned into clear, unblemished skin. She let out a breath, relieved to find no sign of the original mark, her fingers grazing against the smooth expanse in brief awe.

She pulled herself back, a little woozy from the magic. Or from the proximity. Both, maybe. But her hand was tingling and she rubbed at her palm as she steadied herself. She hadn't done that in a while. Hadn't had much reason to go around healing people pre-abduction.

"That's it?" he asked, surprise flickering across his features.

He brushed his hand across where the bruise had been and it did something to Benny to see him touch himself. A weird little laugh passed through her lips as she brushed her hair behind her ears. She was thankful it was so dark and Gideon couldn't see the flush likely creeping into her cheeks.

She needed to get a hold of herself.

"That's it."

"Thank you, Benny," he said. "I feel good. Better."

"I wish I could say no more vampire fights," she told him, throwing out her hands "But—"

"I know," he said. "Next time we'll have a plan. No guns blazing bullshit."

"I'm sorry I ran off."

"Are you?" he asked and there was something playful to his tone.

She bit back a smile. "No, but I am sorry for being a distraction."

He smiled, wide and bright, and a warmth reached his eyes. She liked seeing him like this. It made her stomach flip. Jesus Christ. They weren't even touching anymore.

She really wanted him to touch her again.

The realization was so sudden, Benny wasn't sure how to handle it.

"I don't think you're sorry about that, either, princess."

He held her gaze for a moment before his eyes flickered to her jaw.

"Why haven't you healed yourself?" he asked, his thumb brushing the softest stroke against her chin. "It kills me to look at it. To see everything they've done to you."

Her lips parted at the touch, a faint breath passing through them. It was like he had heard her thoughts. Like she had compelled him to touch her. It felt even better than she thought it would.

"I can't," she said. "It's the balance. I already cheat death healing the way I do naturally, so a Healer's magic can't help me. Even my own."

"And earlier?" he asked. "That blood magic, it scared the hell out of me and it seemed to do a number on you."

She could still taste that man's blood on her tongue.

"It's dark magic," she admitted. "A Caruso family favorite during interrogations. I don't, I mean that's not something I just do on a random Saturday night. But I didn't think we had any other option."

"No, it was good," he said, though his brow furrowed. "It helped, I mean. We at least have a starting point now."

She ran her tongue across her bottom lip as she considered him.

"I know you think I'm reckless," she started. "But I'm— Gideon, I'm just trying to not act as terrified as I feel. If I think about everything that's happened for too long, I'll lose it."

He frowned.

"I'm not going to let anything else happen to you, Benny."

"You can't promise me that."

"Watch me."

He said it with such confidence, she almost believed him. And she could have argued with him, God knew they were good at that. But she didn't want to, not after the last couple of days— after seeing the damage he took to keep her safe. He would try. She could feel it.

And maybe that was enough.

To have someone just try.

"*Real* tough guy," she said, letting herself smile big.

Gideon shook his head, a huff of laugher passing through his lips. "You're a real pain in my ass, you know that?"

"That was part of the agreement, I think."

"Oh, was that right?"

They were nearly on top of each other now, bodies all but pressing against each other. Benny wasn't too sure of herself at 3 o'clock in the morning, of what decisions she should or should not be making. But she now knew she wanted something she was sure she probably shouldn't have.

And Gideon—

The way he was looking at her. Like he could see all there was.

When had anyone ever looked at her that way?

It inched her closer and closer to making a very bad decision when the door to the loft opened and Luke surprised them both. She all but jumped back, her heart beating so rapidly in her chest she was sure that Luke could hear it from all the way across the room. In fact, she was certain of it.

"Shit," Luke managed, his hands coming up to shield his face. "I didn't think—shoot, I hope you're both decent over there—I'm sorry, I'm just gonna keep walking like this, not looking, not thinking about it, definitely not thinking about it—"

"Lucas," Gideon bit out.

"Nope, I'm good, brother," he said. "See you in the morning!"

Luke's bedroom door clicked, and Gideon let out a long breath, his fingers pinching the bridge of his nose.

"You should go to bed."

"Yeah," she nodded, already turning back toward the bedroom, her hand running over her face. Someone needed to put her out of her misery here. "Goodnight, Gideon."

What had she been thinking? In what world did kissing the man hired to keep you safe feel like a good decision? It was just too much time spent together. That's all.

"Thank you, Benny," he said. "For taking care of me."

She felt her skin flush at the sincerity in his voice.

"Someone's gotta make sure you don't die from internal bleeding," she said, twisting to throw him a playful look.

He pushed himself off of the counter, that grin splayed across his features twisting her right up inside. "Nice pajamas, by the way."

TWELVE

THE WAREHOUSE

"TELL ME."

There was silence from the two men that knelt before him, heads bowed underneath their hoods, eyes trained on the floors beneath their feet. It was a heavy silence, a quiet that almost reverberated off the warehouse walls surrounding them. A syncopated rhythm matching the steady heartbeats from the men who surrounded them, all in matching dark hooded robes. Well, some of them. Others had their own kind of silence within their rib cages. But they were waiting all the same.

Just like he could. He was a patient man. He had waited fifteen years, after all.

But he needed to hear it. He needed them to carry the weight of their failure.

"The witch evades us still, Master," the man on the left said, his hands raw and blistered as if they had been held in a fire. "The brothers are protecting her."

His face remained passive but he felt the fury beating within his veins. "The Crawford brothers."

"Yes, Master," the other one replied, the vampire. "And another one. A woman."

He drew his dagger from his inner pocket, the handle made of an opal that glittered in the morning sunlight that streamed through the warehouse skylights. He toyed with the tip of it, letting it twirl around his fingertip until he could feel it cut through his skin. But no blood appeared. The virgin sacrifices, the bath of the untouched blood, it had done its job.

He was due for the next step. Eager for it.

He stepped closer to them, until the polished toes of his leather brogues reached their kneecaps.

"And what will you do to rectify this mistake?"

He was met with silence again.

"Answer me."

His voice became a low boom, enough to cause a shudder among the rest.

"We will f-find her," the first one said. "We will bring her to you, Master."

He had his doubts. He was promised an easy catch. A catch that had been in motion for years. Angelo Torretta employing the Crawford brothers did pose a problem. One he did not foresee. But no bother. He knew well enough how to handle them.

He would just have to do it himself.

"Very well."

The dagger sank into the vampire's shoulder, cutting into the sinew and twisting. He would heal, he knew. But he could still feel the pain. He could still bleed. And he needed the reminder. They all did.

THIRTEEN

GIDEON

"WAKE UP, BROTHER."

Gideon grunted as the pillow hit him in the face, his hands capturing the offending weapon in his arms. He didn't need to wake up. He hadn't fallen asleep. He hadn't slept a fucking wink. His body and his brain had come to a crossroads. Why grant him the gift of sleep when they could just torment him instead?

He had flown a little too close to the sun, his body buzzing with Benny's magic running through his veins. He could still feel the press of her hand against his skin, the way her fingers lingered, every moment of her touch driving him absolutely mad. So much so he leaned right into it, unable to stop himself. Had she magicked him in some other way?

Put him under another kind of spell?

"What are you doing out here?"

"Fuck off," Gideon groaned, turning his body into the couch, all but smothering his own face into the pillow.

"You didn't actually bang on the counter, did you?"

"Why don't you go out for a walk in the sunshine?"

"I'm out a hundred bucks because of you."

Gideon sighed as he pushed himself up to a sitting position.

"Pray tell, Lucas," he said, running his hands through his hair, trying to smooth out what he was sure was a mess of bedhead. He braced himself for pain that never came. He still couldn't wrap his head around how easily she had healed him. "Why would that be?"

"Cleo called it."

He grinned from his perch on the edge of the coffee table.

"Called what?" Gideon asked, though he had an idea of the answer already.

"You see, I told her you wouldn't," Luke said, as he took his glasses off his face, holding them up to the sunlight before wiping them clean on his handkerchief. "That you, of all people, wouldn't risk the payout. You've been dead set against this little rescue mission since I took it, so I couldn't imagine you'd become so wrapped up in our little witch that'd you'd risk everything we've got riding on this just so you can get laid."

Gideon really hoped Benny was still sleeping because the walls in the loft were thin and this was not a conversation he wanted her to hear. This wasn't a conversation he even wanted to have. He leaned forward to smack his brother's glasses out of his hands before he stood up, grateful for the renewed energy he felt in his body. Luke fumbled to catch them as a laugh burst from his chest.

"You like her," his brother said, surprised.

"I do not want to have this conversation with you."

"Too bad," Luke continued, following him into the kitchen. "Because this isn't part of the job, Gideon. And it's messy enough as it is, so you've gotta squash this shit before it goes any further."

It hadn't gone anywhere.

He knew Luke was right. They both understood the trouble with getting emotionally invested. Trouble he knew Benedetta Russo was going to bring them from the moment the door to the shipping container opened. But that didn't stop him from agreeing to take it all one step further, by agreeing to become her bodyguard for better or for worse.

She sparked something in him that he hadn't felt in a long time. He liked it. Liked her. Liked those stupid fucking pajamas, and the way she always had something to say, and the ferocity in which she wanted to fight regardless of her fears.

How could he not want to keep her close? Keep her safe?

But he knew that was all that could come of it.

Because she deserved better than him.

His life wasn't like hers. She was about to add 'Dr.' to her name and he had a rap sheet a mile long, a mug shot in three different states. Just a couple more weeks and then they could return to the admittedly weird normal they'd created for themselves since Chicago. And he could say goodbye to Benedetta Russo.

He almost laughed in spite of himself.

"Gideon?"

He blinked, and saw Luke staring at him expectantly.

"Nothing happened last night," he said, reaching for the coffee maker. He desperately needed a strong cup of coffee. "And nothing will."

"Good," Luke said, clapping him on his shoulder roughly. "Cleo and Harker are on their way."

"Jesus Christ," Gideon muttered. "It's not even nine o'clock. Don't you bloodsuckers need to sleep during the day?"

"We've got some maniac trying to become a demon from hell, and we have no idea who we're looking for," Luke told him pointedly. "We've got a lot of work to do."

"I need a map of the county."

The brothers turned to find Benny standing in the hallway. She was fully dressed and recently showered by the looks of her hair, her curls still damp as they grazed her shoulders, leaving wet stains on the white T-shirt she wore, this one with "TROPHY HUSBAND" written across the chest in a strong serif font. Why did he have to find that so stupidly funny? Gideon focused on grabbing coffee mugs from the cabinet, not at all thinking about the denim cutoffs she was wearing and the way they hugged her hips.

Or how close he had been to kissing her last night.

"A map?" he asked.

"I think I can get us closer to the ritual," she said, her nose wrinkling. "I just need to see if I'm right."

"I'll call Harker," Luke said.

He crossed to the other side of the loft with a pointed look in his brother's direction as he pulled his phone from the inner pocket of his suit jacket. Gideon watched after him, wondering if he was going to be using that elevated hearing of his to eavesdrop. Gideon's privacy had become supremely lacking in the last year, wreaking havoc on his already pathetic dating life. When the beep of the coffee maker snapped him out of a particularly uncomfortable memory, he realized Benny was looking at him curiously.

"You sleep okay?" he asked.

"Good enough," she said, offering him a small half smile. "You?"

"Good enough," he mimicked. "It's a lot easier to sleep when your insides aren't all torn up."

She waved her hand.

"It was nothing," she told him.

Magic came with a price. He had heard Harker say that last night. It wasn't nothing. But he didn't know what to say next. How to relay how much it had meant to him for her to even offer, to worry over him the way she did. How it felt to have someone take care of him in that way.

"Benny—" he started at the same time she said, "Gideon—"

He laughed as he gestured for her to go, pouring her a cup of black coffee. She reached for the mug with a sheepish smile, their fingers grazing against each other with the exchange, and Gideon would have loved to shove his brother off the roof of the building at this point.

"I've been thinking a lot about last night," she started.

Gideon swallowed, the hot liquid of his coffee burning his throat.

"About what we have to do, and how there's even a 'we' at all," she continued, her hand waving. "I don't want you or Luke or anyone to feel obligated to do this with me—"

"I don't," he said, perhaps more firmly than he intended. He relaxed his shoulders. "I'm on board. We all are."

She looked at him, smiling.

"I imagine no one makes you do anything you don't want to do," she said.

Not typically.

He had a feeling Benny could.

"I don't make it a habit," he told her.

Her smile widened. "Thank you. That's all. I know a 'job is a job' and everything but I just— I want to make sure you know how thankful I am. For all of it. All of this."

A job is a job.

He had said that to her the other night. When she looked up at him with those doe brown eyes, drunk as hell, making magic glitter in the air around him. It hadn't been true then and it wasn't true now.

"It's good to diversify the resume," he said, with a little shrug.

"Sure, I imagine 'saving city from demon' is right up there alongside 'heist' and 'breaking and entering' on the list."

"Not nearly as high as you'd think," he told her.

"No, of course not," she said, leaning her hip against the counter, the hem of her T-shirt riding up slightly on the one side, enough to showcase the tiniest sliver of smooth skin. "What's a little hero behavior among criminals? I've gotta stop acquiring such morally grey individuals as friends."

Friends.

Gideon choked out a laugh.

He could be friends with Benny. That could be enough.

Telling her how he really felt would be a disaster, anyway. There was no indication she felt the same way. No concept in which the two of them would make sense beyond the insane situation they currently found themselves in. If they survived. A small nagging part of him needed to make sure he didn't ignore that part. The surviving part.

Luke was right.

He had to focus.

The kitchen island had become their ground zero, the countertop covered in old books, candles, and parchment that smelled an awful lot like the inside of a gym bag. In the center lay a large map of the county, the edges curled from where it had been rolled up. Gideon watched as Benny all but draped herself over the counter, her knees carefully positioned on a kitchen stool for leverage as she drew a spot with a thick black marker at a point on the map. He refused to let his eyes stray from the map, refused to let them rake over the slope of her back as she shifted, the way her hair spilled from its braid, the way her face screwed up in concentration, her bottom lip caught between her teeth.

He knew what it was like now to have her close, to feel the touch of her hands. He scraped his hand against his jaw. He had to get it together.

"Okay, so, Abigail Milligan was last seen at Central High, and they said James Rivera never came home from his job at the bakery here—" She scanned the map, drawing out the word as she found the next point. "And then there's Connor Crosby who never got on the bus here—" Another mark. "Lizzie Wells was taken from Saylor Grove—" One more. "And Nina Cho—"

Her brow furrowed as she looked down at the map.

"Nina Cho was babysitting," Cleo said from beside her, leaning forward to point at a far spot on the map. "The corner of Somerset and Helen."

"Right." Benny reached for the spot to make her last mark. "Thanks."

Harker leaned forward, his finger hovering over each black "X" as he walked around the edge of the island. He shook his head, a faint chuckle passing through his lips as he stopped on the other side of Benny.

"Of course," he said.

Luke came around the other side, lingering beside Cleo, studying the map.

"What exactly are we looking at?"

Gideon was the only one on the other side of the island now, and he couldn't help but glance at the others standing across from him, the way each of them held different emotions. Harker was impressed, a rare reaction from the demon hunter. Cleo and Luke shared vaguely confused looks. And Benny? She looked pissed. Like all the rage she'd been holding was ready to burst. Which left a heavy feeling in his gut.

He glanced back down at the map and felt a moment of realization. "It's a pentagram," he said, surprising himself.

And the others, apparently.

"Bravo, Gideon," Harker said with a smirk.

"Isn't that a little on the nose?" Luke scoffed.

"The pentagram is sacred," Benny said. "To use it for this purpose feels rotten."

"Darling, this is one of our best leads yet," Harker said, plucking another marker from the island. He connected each 'X' with a line, formulating the exact shape Gideon had remembered reading about in the witch book. The book he had fallen asleep reading the night before, trying to not only understand a little bit more about Benny and her power, but what bothered her so much about how it was written. The center of the star covered a part of Philly Gideon didn't spend much time in, Hunting Park. But there was one thing that stood out. "We might have just figured out the location of the ritual."

The man at the quarry had said they would unlock the gates of hell.

Gideon plugged in the location into the laptop beside him. "A church?"

"I don't know, brother." Luke grinned. "Being forced to sit through mass always felt a little bit like torture when we were kids."

"Can you guys even go inside churches?" Cleo asked, turning to Luke. "Or will you burst into a little confetti bomb of ash?"

Luke opened his mouth to say something, closed it, and then opened it again.

"I actually have no idea," he said. "Harker?"

"There will be no confetti bombs of ash," the demon hunter replied. "As long as we stay clear of the holy water and the crucifixes, we ought to be just fine. And even then, it's a bit of a pinch, a burn—we'd heal."

"Okay, but that shit still hurts," Luke countered.

"Touché," Harker said.

"I'll do some research," Luke said, then. "See what we can dig up on Our Lady of Perpetual Help. If there's a gate to hell hidden in a church, some weird shit has probably happened there before, right?"

"Try and find the blueprints," Gideon said as he stared down at the map.

"And the kids?" Benny asked, worry creeping into her features.

"The text isn't entirely clear on their purpose," Harker said carefully. "Each kidnapping has been exactly a week apart but we're still a few weeks off from the blood moon. From my experience? I'm not sure there are still children to find. But I will see what I can find through my contacts."

There was a heavy lull.

Gideon had a feeling Harker was being incredibly kind in his response.

"Hunting Park, huh?" Luke said, interrupting the silence as he glanced back down at the map, his finger tapping against the paper. "Feels like a weird place for a gate to Hell."

"Rumor is there's one in Orlando," Harker said with a shrug.

"Tell me it's underneath Cinderella's castle," Cleo said.

"See, now that wouldn't surprise me." Luke chuckled.

Something was nagging at Gideon as he thought more about the previous night.

"Halmanthoran," Gideon said slowly, sounding out the word. He let out a huff of breath as it suddenly clicked. "Hal Moran."

Luke snorted.

"You're fucking kidding me," he said.

Gideon shrugged. "I mean, everything else we dug up has led us to jack shit."

"Great," Cleo said, punctuating the word with both hands. "We've got Benny. We've got the ritual location. The only other thing I can think of is the—"

"The stone heart of the sun," Luke finished for her.

"Whatever the hell that is," Cleo chimed in.

"Oh!" Benny shifted on the stool, her bare legs swinging on either side now as she drummed her fingers at the countertop. They tapped a steady rhythm as she spoke, "I actually think I know someone who can help us with that one. But that means making a phone call."

Gideon and Luke exchanged a glance.

"Who?" Gideon asked.

"A witch from my coven," she said. "Liv is the best gemologist I know. If anyone knows what the stone heart of the sun is, it's Liv."

Luke fixed her with a stare, "And you trust her?"

"The bonds of coven witches are sacrosanct," she said. "A betrayal like that, it's a curse. If Olivia or Imani were responsible, I would know. I would trust those women with my life."

"Well then, be my guest," Luke said, tossing her his cell phone.

Fourteen

Benny

Benny was crying.

Full snot, red faced crying.

She hadn't expected the burst of emotion when Olivia Hsu and Imani Egan arrived at the loft but it was there all the same and she was wiping at her face as her sisters wrapped their arms around her in a tight squeeze. So tight she could hardly breathe but what did it matter when she was with her coven again? Maybe she had compartmentalized too hard, so focused on trying to solve the equation of her abduction that she hadn't processed what had actually happened.

The people she had almost lost.

"Oh my God, are you kidding me?" Olivia exclaimed, wiping at her face. They were all crying it seems. "I thought you died, Benny. I thought you were abducted and brutally murdered and about to become the topic of some horrible true crime podcast—"

"We would have known," Imani reminded her gently, using the pads of her fingers to brush back her own tears. "When a coven loses a witch—"

"We lose a part of ourselves," Olivia sniffled. "I know, Imani. I know."

The blood pact.

When covens come together, each witch bonds themselves to the rest. A ritual of blood magic that weaves their power together, strengthens each of their abilities, bolsters the magic of the group as a whole. It's incredibly special. It also becomes its own living, breathing thing.

If Benny had died, Olivia and Imani would have felt it.

"Jesus, Benny, what the hell happened?" Olivia asked, her eyes widening as she seemed to take in her less than stellar appearance.

Although her injuries were nearly healed, there was still enough evidence of what had happened to her. Pinkish-red lines on her wrists, cuts on her knuckles, the yellow-tinged bruise on her jaw. She pressed her lips together in a thin line as she stepped back, trying to curve in her elbow where the bruising was still much more obvious from the blood transfusions. She suddenly felt so self-conscious of how much her body was marked. Of what had been done to her.

"You look like shit," Imani said, her honey colored eyes tracing every inch of her. "It's been almost two weeks since we've last seen you and you call us out of the blue to some fancy loft in Fishtown?"

"I know, I'm so sorry," Benny said, not nearly as graceful as her friend as she ran the back of her hand across her nose. "I wanted to tell you both but it's been— I don't know, confusing and my phone is gone and if I didn't have Liv's extension at school— It's been a chaotic few days."

"You could say that again," Cleo said from the kitchen as she flipped through the pages of the Codex, making notes on a legal pad.

Imani turned, looking past Benny to see the others lingering in the kitchen, the four of them all trying very hard not to blatantly stare while they pretended to continue researching. As if they hadn't just been watching her in horror as she hiccuped her sobs away. She really hated crying in front of other people. That was a level of vulnerability she had reserved for only a few after her mother died.

"Okay, yeah, we're gonna need a full run down," Olivia said, crossing her arms against her chest. "What happened to you, where we are—"

"Why there are vampires here—"

Benny did not miss the disdain in Imani's voice even as Olivia's face lit up.

"Okay, okay," Benny said, maneuvering them both away from the front door and toward the living room. "We have to talk."

"We sure do," Olivia replied as she sank down on the sofa. "What is going on? Are you alright?"

"I'm alright." For all intents and purposes that was mostly true. "But I was—well, I was actually abducted."

"Oh, for God's sake!"

"Hold on, hold on," Benny said, reaching for Imani's hand. "There's something I have to tell you both."

"Benny, if this is about your father, we already know," Imani said.

Benny perched herself on the edge of the coffee table, "You do?"

"Come on." Olivia rolled her eyes. "You told us he works in the antiquing business. Except every single time I've ever met him he's wearing thousand-dollar suits and he pays for everything in cash and no offense... but you're Italian so I just put the pieces together..."

"I wasn't actually lying about the antiques," Benny said, running her hand over her face. "It's just...they're not normal antiques. I mean, you know, they're not smuggling Stonehill sideboards. They're a lot more like..."

She gestured toward the kitchen island.

"Thousand-year-old artifacts that I thought were essentially lost to time until this very moment?" Olivia finished with a curious tilt of her head.

"Something like that," Benny said.

"Well, that does explain a few things," Imani said thoughtfully, before sitting down beside Olivia, her long leg crossing over the other. "Would you care to fill in the rest?"

"Imani," Olivia whispered with an elbow nudge.

"Well, we've been worried sick," Imani snapped.

"Yeah, so the thing is," Benny started, her fingers pulling at her braid absently. "My dad isn't why I was taken. I mean he might know who did it. We think someone he knows is responsible but..."

She blew out a breath. *It's now or never, Benny.*

"I was taken because I'm a Strega. One could say the… last Strega."
Olivia blinked.

Imani's back straightened, her eyes widening.

"Stregas aren't real," Olivia said slowly.

"They're mythology," Imani insisted. "Folktales."

Benny pressed the heels of her palms into her eyes.

"Not quite," she muttered. "Not yet."

"What does that mean?" Olivia asked, stricken.

Benny shook her head.

There was so much to explain, she wasn't sure where to start. How to start. Benny, Olivia, and Imani had been practicing together since they were eighteen years old. Undergrads. Baby witches. They were inseparable. Even now, twelve years later, Benny considered them both family.

She had lied to them the entire time.

"Someone wants my blood," she said. "For some ritualistic bullshit. They took me with the intention of keeping me locked up until it was time and if it weren't for them--"

She tilted her head in the direction of the others, her eyes falling to Gideon. She was surprised to find that he was watching her, a quiet intensity behind his eyes. She found herself comforted by it, almost. Maybe a little frazzled, too. Especially when she thought about how just a few hours ago, the two of them had been standing in that same spot, bodies close, poor decisions lingering on the tip of her tongue.

Friends.

The corner of his mouth twitched, the barest hint of a smile, and he gave her a small nod of encouragement. As if he somehow knew how much she was struggling. She felt her cheeks flush.

"If Gideon and Luke hadn't found me when they did, I'd be one big vampire blood bank," she finished, turning back to her friends. "I know it's a lot. I know I should have told you but I've been keeping this secret my whole life and talking about it is new for me."

"Are you kidding me?" Olivia exclaimed. "I can't believe you just called me out of the blue, from some random phone number to tell me you were kidnapped and now you're telling me that you've been lying to us this whole time?"

Benny jerked back.

"Liv," Imani said, voice firm. "It's alright."

"Like hell it is," Olivia said, her pale skin growing flush with pink. Her skin always turned a little splotchy when she was upset. "This is huge, this is—"

"A very big secret to share," Imani said softly.

She tilted her head as she considered Benny, her mouth curving into a slight smile, as if she was suddenly seeing her up close for the very first time. Imani was her most cynical and most difficult friend. The one who never shied away from telling Benny what she needed to hear, no matter how hard. She was the one Benny had been most worried about.

"I wish you would have told us sooner," Imani continued. "But I understand."

Olivia's brow furrowed, her hands twitching in her lap.

"Fine," she said, shrugging her shoulders. "I suppose in light of recent events, I can give you a bit of a break. But no more secrets, okay?"

Benny sighed, the relief coursing through her.

"I've wanted to tell you both for so long. Believe me, hiding so much of myself sucks," she said. "Practicing at all is a constant fight with my dad. If he had it his way, I don't think I'd have any power at all."

"That is only something a person without magic would ever think," Imani sighed. "As if it's that easy."

A beat passed and then Olivia poked at Benny's knee.

"Okay, so now that the secret's out," she said. "Can you explain to us what's going on with the Codex? And the hot Scooby Doo gang over there?"

Luke's burst of laughter devolved into a poorly disguised coughing fit and Benny watched as Gideon whacked him on the shoulder with a roll of his eyes. She couldn't help but find something endearing about those

Crawford brothers. The personas they put on while they're working versus the way they were in the comfort of their own home. The way she might have liked both versions.

"Well, the Codex is helping us parse out the steps of the ritual," she said. "We're sort of on a race against the clock to stop some guy we don't know before he turns into a demon from hell."

A snort of laughter passed through Olivia's lips.

But when Benny's brows merely furrowed in response, Olivia's eyes grew wide.

"Wait, for real?" she asked, soft features lighting up. "We're trying to stop a legitimate demon transformation from taking place?"

"We?" Benny repeated, trying to stuff her hope back into her throat.

"Darling, if you think for even one second we wouldn't help," Imani sighed.

"It's just—" Benny paused. "This is really dangerous."

"And you don't do dangerous shit without your coven," Olivia argued. "We have always worked best as a team. And that's not going to stop just because—" She gestured with her hand. "Strega or not. We do this together."

Benny didn't know what to say.

"Besides, if you think I'm not gonna want to get my little fingers on that Codex, you are out of your mind, Benedetta Russo," Olivia exclaimed.

FIFTEEN

BENNY

THE SUN HAD BEGUN to set, the pinks and oranges of the sky filtering in through the windows of the loft. The county map had been tacked up beside the pin board that still featured Benny's face, a large black cross crudely drawn in the center of the pentacle to mark the spot of the ritual. They had been in the loft the entire day, going through old texts Harker brought from his library, trying to decipher as many details as they could about the ritual.

The man from the quarry had created just as many new questions with his answers.

She could still feel an inkling of him inside her and the fervor in which he served whoever it was responsible for her abduction. *His Master.* It was a level of devotion she could find impressive.

If not for the whole demon worship aspect of it all.

She hiked her leg up onto the seat of her stool and rested her chin on her knee as she carefully flipped through the pages of her family grimoire. The book was over a hundred years old, preserved with a spell to protect its pages from age or destruction. It marked multiple generations of Russo witches, nearly all of them Stregas, and all of them dead.

Except for Benny.

It was a lonely existence. Her father could never understand what it was like. To be alone with your magic. How could she not crave the sisterhood of a coven?

Benny ran her fingers across the pages, following the different handwritings, and she wondered if this had happened before, if one of her ancestors had suffered the same fate that the Crawford brothers had saved her from. *Momentarily*, she reminded herself.

But most of the deaths recorded in the appendix were brutal, quick, and random.

She lingered over her mother's name, the date written beside it in fifteen year old Benny's handwriting. A loopy, delicate scribble. The grimoire had become her sole responsibility following her mother's death. Marking Sophia's passing had been her first ink spilled in the pages.

"Anything?" Imani asked from her beside her.

Benny glanced over her shoulder as Imani stretched in her seat, long limbs raising above her head. Her long, dark brown hair was in twists, half of it tied up in a messy knot, the rest tossed over one side of her shoulder as she poured over an old manuscript Harker brought with him. Imani had modeled her way through culinary school, using the money from her photoshoots to pay for supplies and tuition. She was infamous for coming to dinner dates or Friday esbats with Benny and Olivia still in her photoshoot make-up and hair.

The bakery she opened two years ago was hardly as glamorous.

Not that Imani needed to be all dolled up. She was naturally stunning, all high cheek bones and pouty lips and midnight black skin. Even now, bare faced in a sundress, she was beautiful. Which both helped and hindered her more direct way of communicating, luring people in with her beauty and terrifying them with her attitude. Benny loved it. Had from the moment she sat down beside Imani in a Women's Studies class freshman year.

"I don't think so," she sighed. "Just a bunch of depressing family history. You?"

While Olivia was pouring over JSTOR articles for any signs of the "stone heart of the sun" problem, the others were trying to understand what level of sacrifice the ritual called for— how much of Benny's blood did Hal Moran need?

It was something Benny had been trying to tune out.

"Nothing I'd particularly like to share," she said, tapping long fingers against the counter.

"Sounds promising," Benny grumbled.

"Benny, love, you know as well as I do what a ritual like this calls for," Harker said gently from across the kitchen island.

He was right.

Any kind of out they were looking for was likely for naught.

"Then why the transfusions?" Cleo asked from her perch on the kitchen counter.

"I'm sure keeping Benny captive wasn't cheap. So, why not profit?," Luke shrugged. "Hey, Olivia, can you pass the naan?"

"How do you eat?" Olivia asked even as she passed the tinfoil wrapped package. She looked at Benny with a sheepish smile. "I'm sorry, is that rude? I just... I mean, you're—"

"Dead?" Luke grinned before shoving an entire slice of garlic naan in his mouth.

"Blood is our only essential," Harker said. "But we all imbibe from time to time."

"I haven't been dead long enough to not miss food," Luke said.

The island was scattered with takeout containers from an Indian place down the block. But Benny had lost her appetite, trying not to think of the amount of blood she'd lost while taken, trying not to worry about whose hands it might be in. She had never seen firsthand what Strega blood did to a vampire, but she had heard the stories. Knowing her blood might be on some black market, fueling that kind of violence? Making her abductor thousands of dollars?

She suddenly felt a little sick.

"I just have so many questions," Olivia said, fascinated. "That I, of course, will not ask. But I will think about them. Just so you know."

"Some of us will hear them," Imani said dryly.

"I admire your self-control," Luke said. "Benny here can probably answer every single one. She put me through a hell of a round of Vampire Jeopardy the other night."

"You still never told me if you can fly or not," Benny replied, relieved for the distraction.

"Neither did you," Luke retorted.

"I'm not sure you could handle the extent of what we can do," Imani said with a gleam behind her honey brown eyes.

Luke seemed extremely excited by that statement.

"You should both come to the shop," Harker said to Olivia and Imani.

"Like in the old freaky library part?" Olivia said, perking up in her stool.

Perhaps Benny's condensed storytelling on the events of the last week had simplified a thing or two. She hadn't even mentioned what happened with Gideon in the kitchen. Too many sets of supernatural ears. Honestly, Benny still didn't know how to feel about it. About him. About how badly she had wanted him in that moment. How hard it had been to fall asleep, thinking of him just a room away.

Harker sighed. "We can't think of a better name?"

"You've leaned in too hard, buddy," Gideon said, before he took a swig of his beer. He was standing to Benny's other side, hip resting against the counter, the sleeves of his dress shirt rolled up to his elbows. "Liven up the joint and it might get a new nickname."

"Oh, oh," Olivia said suddenly as her fingers flew across the keys of Gideon's laptop. "I think I found it. The ruby. It's here in town. I knew it sounded familiar, but I wanted to check just to be sure, and I was, of course, correct."

Benny couldn't help her smile, she knew her friend was the right person to call. The only daughter of Chinese immigrants, Benny met Olivia during freshman orientation, the two of them assigned to the same pod. They had bonded quickly when they realized they were both in the same major. Benny could see the power in her almost immediately. And when Olivia learned that her assigned roommate was a secret kleptomaniac who snatched things with a reckless abandon, including Olivia's underwear, Benny let her crash in her single until they could find a double together the following year.

Benny was even there when Olivia broke the news to her parents that the Dr. before her name would be in Feminist Studies and not medicine. They applied to Penn's program together.

"The 25th anniversary Penn Museum Fundraising Gala will be taking place September 5th at eight o'clock in the evening at the Ritz-Carlton Philadelphia," Olivia read off the screen as she tucked her hair behind her ears. "Bid on unique and extraordinary blah blah blah during our silent auction—oh wow, is that an Aston Martin? Okay, sorry, hold on, yeah, here it is."

Olivia took a bite of her food before continuing.

"On display during the gala will be some of the world's most famous jewels. Although they are not up for auction, they are available to view throughout the evening—"

Luke groaned. "So a fucking goldmine."

"Focus, Lucas," Gideon said, smacking his brother's shoulder.

"The Heart of Fire," Olivia said, sighing. "I can't believe it. This thing is apparently cursed, you know that, right? Like dozens of royals have turned up dead after wearing it."

Harker huffed a breath of laughter. "Likely cursed by the people it was stolen from."

Imani's lips twitched.

"How much time do we have?" Cleo asked.

"It's cutting it close to the blood moon," Luke said, leaning back against the counter.

Gideon shrugged. "We've pulled off bigger scores on shorter timelines."

"What's bigger than a priceless cursed stone?" Benny asked as she peered up at him.

"We only had 72 hours to find you, princess," Gideon said with a smug smile.

She fought back a smile of her own, her skin warming.

"The security at the Ritz is a joke," Luke said. "We can run this one quick. Harker, you have connections there, don't you?"

"A few," Harker nodded. "One I've been meaning to see, actually."

"The bartender?" Cleo asked, her eyes lighting up.

The demon hunter grinned, his canines looking extra sharp. "Perhaps, love."

"What do you think, Gid?" Luke asked. "A repeat of Vegas?"

"I'd prefer to not get shot this time," Gideon huffed. "But that could work. We probably need a few extra hands, though, if we want to run a surround."

There was jargon here that seemed unique to Gideon and Luke.

"Is this heist talk?" she asked, raising her brows as the others descended into ideas and plans in the background. "You gonna start another pin board to add to the collection up there?"

"Getting excited, Russo?" he countered.

"Just trying to see if the Crawfords live up to their reputations," she shrugged.

"Still worried your father isn't getting his money's worth?"

Somehow the conversation had become just the two of them, Gideon leaning down toward her, palms pressed against the edge of the counter. There was a heat behind his gaze. Maybe she was just imagining it but there was an edge to his smile that made her want to squirm in her seat. Her tongue ran across her bottom lip as she turned away from him, focusing instead on the grimoire open in front of her.

"I'm exceptionally hard to please," she said primly.

"Don't I know it, princess," he said, voice ghosting against her ear before he straightened.

She pressed her tongue to the roof of her mouth, fighting the shiver that crept into her skin. She had to find a way to get in control of whatever these feelings were. They were sharing walls for God's sake. With a vampire. There was nothing good that could come of anything her body was itching for.

"And what about the demon wannabe?" Olivia asked, continuing a conversation Benny hadn't been paying attention to. "Won't he also be after the ruby?"

"Of course," Luke said. "The question is before the gala or after."

"Not before," Gideon said, shaking his head. "Security will be heaviest during transport. If this guy knows what he's doing, it's gonna be right after. "

Luke blew out a breath he didn't have.

"So during," he said, looking at his brother with a wicked grin.

"During," Gideon nodded.

Cleo let out a little "*Yes*," under her breath, looking giddy at the prospect.

"St. James loves an excuse to flex that BFA," Luke said.

"You would too if you were as good as me, Lucas," the red head replied.

"And if we see him?"

Suddenly all eyes were on Benny.

"Is there a chance we could… run into each other?" she asked, fingers tapping against the cover of the grimoire. "What happens then?"

"What do you want to happen?" Gideon asked.

Benny tugged on her bottom lip with her fingers as her knee bounced on the stool.

She knew the answer.

She knew exactly what she wanted to happen.

Gideon seemed to know too, his eyes darkening.

"I want him dead," she said.

Sixteen

Gideon

He rapped his knuckles against his bedroom door.

It felt funny knocking on a room that had been his up until very recently. Of course it still was, mostly, in name. But in the random hours when Gideon would slip inside for fresh clothing, or some other thing he needed, he would find signs of Benny slowly taking over. Her clothes strewn over an armchair, her grimoire resting on his dresser, even just the energy lingering in the air. It began to feel like he was encroaching on her space.

Enough her space that she had disappeared in the bedroom following dinner and hadn't come back out. Much like the night after they'd returned from Whiskey Winnie's, Benny using his room like her own personal safe haven. She hadn't even said goodbye to Olivia or Imani. Just said she needed a minute and then never returned, leaving the rest of them in the kitchen, wondering if her death threat had been sincere or said in some mixture of nerves and fear and anger.

He had restrained himself from checking in on her all night. He wasn't sure she would welcome the intrusion. Gideon wasn't her babysitter. He was hardly her bodyguard. But the worry still crept in, clinging to his skin, driving him nuts all night he slept on that fucking sofa.

He wasn't supposed to care like this.

Not about Benny.

"Come on, Russo," he said, voice rough as he knocked. "Training starts today."

Not like he wanted it to.

That was another level of proximity he wasn't sure he could handle. But if they were going to run a jewel heist in the middle of a charity gala, and there was even a slight chance they came across the asshole who took her, then making sure Benny had real control of her power was crucial. How he was going to swing that, he had no idea.

This felt more like something Harker should handle.

The door opened and Gideon found Benny laying back on the bed, her legs dangling over the edge, one hand flung out to the side while the other covered her eyes.

She must've magicked the door open.

"What are you doing?" he asked, forearm resting on the doorjamb as he leaned into the room.

"Moping."

"Yeah? How's that going for you?"

She removed her hand from her eyes and turned to look at him.

"It would be going better if I was left alone."

"No can do, princess," he said, doing his best to avoid the long line of her bare legs and the fact that she was wearing what seemed to be a pair of his boxer shorts. "We are on a short timeline and you are still working with magic you can't control."

"Who made you the magical Mister Miyagi?"

"You did," he told her, fighting his smile. "When you begged me to teach you."

She turned onto her side and propped herself up on her elbow.

"Was that what I did?" she asked, eyes glittering. "I begged?"

He was having a hard time formulating a response, his eyes tracking the curves of her body, the way his boxer shorts hiked up her thigh, the brazen look behind her eyes as she teased him. He pushed himself off the door and stepped further into the bedroom, the door creaking shut behind him. He glanced back briefly. More magic. The little bits of it she seemed to do with zero effort at all.

"You don't have much time to get your shit together," he said, swallowing down all the other words he wanted to say. "And the sociopath after you isn't going to just give up. So if you really want him dead, don't you think you ought to figure this out?"

She groaned.

"You're no fun at all," she said, flopping down on her back again.

Gideon sighed as he crossed the room, the edge of the bed sinking beneath his weight as he sat down beside her, their knees lining up in a neat row.

"You could channel some of this energy into punching, you know."

"I don't know what you're talking about."

"You're a shitty liar, Russo."

"And you're a shitty Mr. Miyagi."

"You want the guy dead, it's not gonna happen while you're hiding in here."

Benny didn't respond in words, just a little irritated groan. He leaned back, letting his back hit the mattress, his hands clasped against his chest. He turned his head to look at her properly, taking in the slight bump at the bridge of her nose, the curve of her cheekbone. Like he wanted to categorize every detail of her features.

"You hit a wall last night," he said. "You wanna talk about it?"

Benny stared up at the ceiling.

"Are you my therapist now?"

"I seem to remember a conversation the other night," he started. "About us working together on this. Which means you don't have to hide out here. You don't have to hide whatever it is you're feeling."

She closed her eyes.

"I feel so many things I'm worried I'm actually going to combust."

She rubbed her hands over her face, letting them linger there for a moment before she let her arms relax at her sides. He watched every

movement, took note of every little breath. But Gideon didn't say anything, he didn't move. He just waited for her to be ready.

Because he wanted to know. He wanted to know everything she was
feeling.

All of it.

"I'm just so mad," she said after a moment. "I'm embarrassed. I've
spent practically my entire life learning how to keep myself safe, and I
couldn't do it when it counted. And now...now there are kids holed up
somewhere that are going to die because of me. Maybe they're already
dead. You heard Harker."

"Benny, this is not your fault."

She blew out a frustrated breath in response.

"Isn't it?" she said. "I'm it, Gideon. I'm the only one left."

His jaw tensed at the phrasing. The pressure and guilt she must be
feeling. Before he could stop himself, he reached for her hand. Her fingers
flexed beneath his touch as she turned to look at him, soft brown eyes
wide and round, and it was like he could see every flicker of emotion she
was feeling.

The whole world of it.

He fought the sudden feeling of wanting to be in that world.

Beyond just this moment, this arrangement they had.

"We're going to figure this out," he told her.

Even if he wasn't sure how.

"He already has my blood," she said quietly. "My *blood*. I keep trying
to ignore it. Focus on everything we have to do but it keeps creeping up,
and the rage I feel, I don't know what to do with it."

"You use it," he told her. "I've seen what you can do, Benny."

She frowned.

"I don't know if I'm strong enough."

She said it so quietly, it startled him. From the moment Benedetta
Russo had shattered the idealized version of herself that he'd created in
his head, the moment she become a real, living person in his life, she'd
had this air of confidence and bravado that he hadn't expected. This

self-assured attitude. This way of getting right under his skin. She had confided in him the other night that it was a way to deal with her fear. But to hear her say shit like this? To not know how brave and strong she was?

"The bruise on my jaw says otherwise," he said.

A faint smile ghosted her lips, her cheeks reddening slightly.

"Imagine how good it'll feel when it's the asshole responsible for all of this."

"You know, for a big, bad bank robber, you're not bad at this."

"Wow, not bad," he replied, failing to hide his smile. "I'll take it."

She squeezed his hand. "Thank you."

"You're welcome," he said, before pushing himself up from the bed. "Now get your ass out of this bed, get on something you can sweat in, and meet me outside in five minutes. We have work to do."

Benny rolled her eyes.

"Okay, okay," she said. Then, "Think I can borrow a T-shirt?"

He threw her a look as he reached the door.

"You're already wearing my shorts."

She grinned.

"All my stuff is in the laundry. Should I just walk around naked?"

He swallowed, thankful his back was to her, as he passed into the hallway.

"Definitely not."

"Let's go again."

Gideon held up his hands, keeping himself steady as Benny swung.

Her fist connected with a satisfying amount of force, her wrapped knuckles scratching his wrapped palms. In the last hour, they'd gone through half a dozen punches and jabs, Gideon working through a few combinations with her. She was a quick study, and more capable than he expected.

He should have known better. She had a habit of surprising him.

"Good," he nodded. "I'm going to come at you now."

"And do what?" she asked between breaths, brushing a stray curl back from her forehead, her hair damp with sweat. She had tossed it into a ponytail at the start of their session but it was coming loose now, tendrils framing her face.

He stepped into her space, forcing her a step back, her sneakered feet sinking into the foam mat he'd dragged upstairs to the rooftop. The sun was beginning to set over the horizon, the heat cooling in the evening air. No one else had access to the roof and it was a relatively safe space to train. Plus, it was out of Luke's earshot. He'd had enough of his brother's inquiring looks whenever Gideon and Benny were in the same space.

Which was always, considering their predicament. These annoying, messy little feelings he was dealing with were hard enough on him as it was. Especially now, as he tried not to let his eyes linger on the way his clothes looked on her body. She had rolled the waistband of the boxers a few times and knotted his T-shirt tight around her abdomen. It was the least amount of clothing he'd seen her in and he was about ready to fling himself over the side of the building when she looked up at him, waiting on his next instruction with an adorable look of concentration on her face.

Adorable? He was in so much fucking trouble.

"Just focus on me, princess," he said, taking another step toward her, crowding her body with his. "Sometimes the most simple reaction is the best. Someone like me might underestimate you—I might come right into your space and try and intimidate you and end up leaving myself wide open—"

He mimicked grabbing for her shoulder.

"So you can get me here," he continued, gesturing to her leg. "A snap kick, kind of like what you did at the quarry but—"

She didn't need him to finish, her leg coming up quick to his groin.

He grabbed at her ankle, ready for her, and swept her back. She landed in a small heap on the mat with a startled "Ah!" as Gideon dropped down to a squat. His eyes did a quick scan to make sure she was alright before he grinned.

"You didn't think I was going to just let you kick me, did you?"

She narrowed her eyes, brushing her hair off her face.

Then, without warning, she lunged at him, knocking him off his feet and flat onto his back. She was straddling him, her hands pressing his shoulders into the mat as she peered down, her ponytail falling over her shoulder. She was breathing heavily, her chest heaving, a wry little grin on her face.

"And this move?" she asked, self-satisfaction dripping from her smile.

"Feral," he breathed, his hands flat on the mat, fingers itching to press into the soft skin of her thighs. "It'll work better if you can use your magic with it."

She sank against him, her head hanging low and it took everything in him not to just wrap his arms around her.

"I'm *trying*," she said. "But I don't actually want to hurt you."

Well, that was a win. He propped himself up on his elbows.

"Was it fear?" he asked. "Anger?"

She looked up at him, her brow furrowing.

"Which one is better?"

"Anger," he said, almost immediately.

"Why?"

Because the idea of her feeling any more fear than she already did made his heart ache. It had been hard enough watching her break down into tears when her friends arrived. And anger seemed like a healthier alternative, at least until she could summon the magic without needing either. If that was possible. What the fuck did he know about magic? Other than the incomprehensible way he felt about Benny in such a short amount of time. That felt a little bit like magic to Gideon.

"It's a lot more fun to make you mad."

Benny huffed a breath as she pulled herself off of him, settling in on the mat, drawing her legs up to her chin. She wrapped her arms around her calves and leveled Gideon with a look he couldn't read.

"I think it was both," she said, after a moment. "Maybe. The docks felt different. Like I was completely out of control of my body. But when that guy grabbed me at the quarry, I was just pissed."

"You were in control," he said, recalling the moment he found her with Mack, and the resolution he saw on her face.

"I saw you," she said. "You had just lectured me about staying behind and the moment I go off on my own, this idiot grabs me and I was just…"

"So you were pissed at me," he laughed. "We can definitely work with that."

"I wanted to prove you wrong," she admitted, her nose wrinkling. "I wanted to show you that I could control it."

"You did." God, he loved when she scrunched up her face like that. "Do you think you can do that again?"

She grinned, "Prove you wrong? How much indignity can you suffer?"

He laughed, knowing he had walked directly into that. But he liked seeing her smile. And this *was* progress. He pulled himself up to sit, watching as the sky darkened overhead, the shadows of the sunset creating a warmth in her skin. He pulled up the hem of his T-shirt to wipe at his face.

"Let's try again tomorrow," he said, before reaching for one of her hands.

He was careful as he pulled at the velcro, unwrapping the fabric tied around her fingers. She tilted her head as she watched him, another stray curl falling from her hair tie and he wondered briefly what it would feel like between his fingers.

"When did you start boxing?" she asked, and something in her voice made him steal a glance. She was staring down at their hands, at his fingers pressing gently into her wrist as he used his other hand to unwrap her palm.

"Eighteen," he said looking back down, thinking about his first fight and the money he'd been able to bring home that night. It had kept the electricity on. "Went pretty hard for a few years, made some money on fights… But it helped. I needed the release."

"Release from what?"

He moved on to the other hand, not quite sure how to answer.

"A lot of things," he said instead. "Luke was a handful and money was tight. It was probably the safest choice I could have made at the time."

"What about your parents?"

"My mom fucked off when I was a kid and my dad—"

Fifteen years and this was still really fucking hard.

"He died that year," he said finally, letting her go, the wraps balled up in his fists. "So it was just me and Luke."

"Oh, I didn't know," she said, immediately reaching for him again, her hand resting on his forearm. "I am so sorry."

He was hesitant to meet her gaze, to see the pity that usually came with this reveal. Gideon and Luke had managed a real life for themselves, however gray it was in the grand scheme of things. They'd paid their dues with Frank, they'd worked hard to get out of the two bedroom twin row house in Oxford Circle. He was proud of what they'd built. Proud that it was done on a foundation their father secured for them.

But when he looked up, all he saw in her eyes was a warmth and a compassion that would have shocked the hell out of him a week ago. He scrubbed his hand across his face, unsure of what to do with himself. Or the fact that she was still touching him.

"It was a long time ago."

"Time has never made it easier for me," she said. "I still think about my mom all the time. Wonder if she'd be proud or disappointed or completely horrified at the choices I've made…"

"Horrified?" Gideon mused.

Benny waved her hand, a question she wasn't going to answer.

"I don't mind it, though," she continued. "Living with the grief. I like thinking about her, and missing her. It's all that love, you know? It's gotta go somewhere."

He hadn't thought of grief in that way before, of love manifesting itself in a different way after death. He was still fighting with some resentment. Of what he needed to give up. But his father couldn't have known. And so what was the point of holding that against him?

He wondered if what happened to her mother helped shape her grief.

Eamond Crawford went into every job knowing it was a risk. The boys had always known that something could happen to their father. Hell, he knew it now. *Especially* now, with Benny to keep safe.

Benny's mother was taken from her.

"Sounds like good therapy."

He watched as Benny smiled, the way it lit up her face even as the sky darkened around them. "Exceptionally good," she said, squeezing his arm. "I should probably schedule a session. I bet you she'd have some really good insight for me right now."

"Right this minute?"

"Very much so," she sighed.

Gideon pressed his tongue to the roof of his mouth. He wanted to touch her so badly he was staring to lose his resolve. But what would that accomplish? They were just starting to find their footing with one another. He didn't want to do anything to complicate that further.

He pushed himself up to stand before offering her a hand. When she took it, she had this look on her face, another expression he couldn't read. She steadied herself, her hand pressing against his shoulder as she straightened. She was so close. He could smell his shampoo on her hair, the sweat on her skin…

Jesus Christ he needed to step away from her.

"Go shower," he said, moving to start cleaning up the roof. "I'll figure out dinner and see if we've got anymore news from Harker."

"Hopefully the dryer is done," she said, stretching her arms above her head, his T-shirt riding up on her abdomen. "Otherwise I'm raiding your closet again."

He tried to bite back his smile.

"We've got to get you more clothes," he sighed.

Seventeen

Luke

Luke had always been the wild card.

He was the one who needed to be reined in, reminded of the plan, convinced that there was a track to stick to when things started to get a little chaotic. Luke had a short fuse and a problem with impulse control. He got into trouble a lot when he was a kid, and if he wasn't careful, it was easy to fall back into bad habits. Especially now, especially after Chicago. Because vampires took what they wanted. It was a heady concept for someone like Luke.

Gideon had spent much of their adult lives—hell, much of their lives in total—keeping Luke on track. They had both learned how to adapt at a fairly young age, but it was Gideon who kept them in line. When their dad died, it was Gideon who gave up a baseball scholarship to make sure Luke finished high school, working in a chop shop owned by Frank Markos to make sure he could pay rent and keep them both fed, boxing in some piece-of-shit gym to win the fights Frank wanted him to.

Now, the rules had reversed.

Now, it was Luke ensuring Gideon stayed on track.

Which should have been frustrating. It should have pissed Luke off. All that time following the Eamond Crawford mantra of "Keep your head down and the heat out," and at the first sign of a pretty witch in distress,

Gideon became some lovesick teenager mooning over Benny whenever he thought no one was paying attention.

But there was actually something kind of liberating about it.

To not be the problem this time.

"I'm impressed," Luke said from his spot holed up at the island, his legs kicked up onto the countertop. He was swirling a finger of whiskey around in a glass, his eyes locked onto his brother, intrigued by the vein that seemed to pulse in his neck. "I would have thought something would have happened by now."

They had settled into something of a routine these last few days. Once they knew they had a concrete timeline in the charity gala, the Crawford brothers had gotten to work. Accessing blueprints, securing tickets, working their way into the security company hired to take care of the event.

The last three days had been busy.

But not so busy that Gideon didn't find time to train Benny.

They spent every evening up on the roof, tossing each other onto the mat.

"Don't be gross," Gideon said, his hands braced against the counter, his eyes watching as Benny paced the length of the living room and back again, her voice quiet, the Italian growing more and more aggressive with each step.

"Listen, brother," Luke started, holding his hands out in mock surrender, "far be it for me to lecture you on women—"

"Great, don't."

"I just want to make sure you're going into this with clear eyes."

Gideon's eyes narrowed in Luke's direction.

"What is that supposed to mean?"

Luke kicked his legs down from the island, his palms resting flat against the counter as he held his brother's pointed stare.

"What happens when this is all over?" he asked. "We slay a demon, save the girl. What exactly comes next? You think we just go back to robbing banks while you date Angelo Torretta's daughter?"

His brother seemed to want to say something, his eyes darkening as he leaned forward on the island. But he said nothing, instead taking a step back and walking toward the bar cart. He reached for the decanter of whiskey and gave himself a generous pour. Luke couldn't remember the last time he had seen him this way.

Even when Luke was struggling with adjusting to his second life, Gideon seemed to have a plan. He was a problem solver. He always had been. It was an easy role for him to fall into.

"There's just something about her," he said, so quietly Luke might not have heard him if he didn't have enhanced hearing. "But you're right. I don't know what happens next. I don't even know if we can survive this, Luke. If I survive this. I'm not exactly Buffy the fucking vampire slayer."

Luke had no intention of letting his brother think anything less than survival was possible, even if he, too, was a little nervous about what had fallen to their feet. Tefi had told him things when he turned, made grand promises about his destiny and his role in this new world. But Tefi was unpredictable and usually full of shit. So, did Luke think they could pull this off?

He still hadn't decided.

But they didn't half-ass anything. And they weren't going to start now.

"Well, not with that attitude," he scoffed.

Gideon rolled his eyes, his glass hovering at his mouth as he struggled to stop himself from laughing. "You're a real piece of work, you know that?"

"Says the asshole who kicked everyone out of the loft," Luke countered.

When Benny disappeared into the bedroom the other night, and the chance of her returning grew slimmer and slimmer, Gideon had called it for the night. Had all but kicked everyone out of the loft with a promise to reconvene in a couple of days. It was the friendliest "get the fuck out" he'd ever seen.

"We needed a break," his brother countered. "My eyes were starting to cross. Those books smell like actual fucking death."

"Well, if legend is to be believed, the Devil's Bible is actually written on human skin," he said, adjusting his glasses. "They do this weird ritual to thin out the—"

"Jesus Christ, Luke."

"What?" he asked. "I was just reading—"

"I want to know so much less than what you're saying to me right now."

He shrugged. "Your loss, brother."

Gideon huffed a breath, his head shaking with a little laugh.

But his brother's attention reverted quickly to the wandering witch behind them just as Luke heard the voice on the phone go silent. A heavy sigh accompanied the footsteps that echoed off the hardwood floors. When he spun around in the kitchen stool to find Benny approaching, he was surprised to see her face twisted up in a mixture of disgust and something else. Embarrassment?

He took note of her hands as she returned the phone to Gideon.

They were shaking.

It took everything he had inside him to suppress the urge he had to pounce on that. Her blood was ringing through her body, buzzing with every little bit of anxiety he could see radiating off of her. It was an inconvenient aspect of his abilities. Of her own. Like it was unnatural for them to be around each other.

"Everything okay?" he asked, swallowing his urges down.

"Yeah," she grit out, looking up at him with a nod of her chin.

Gideon cleared his throat and looked to Benny with a knowing raise of his brows. Luke watched curiously as a sort of wordless conversation seemed to pass between them. He finished the last sip of his whiskey to hide his smile.

"They found him."

She ran her hand across her face, her fingers pressing into her temple. Something flickered behind her eyes, something heavy. She plucked Gideon's glass from his hand, downing what was left in the tumbler in one gulp.

"God, how do you two drink this garbage?" she grimaced.

"It grows on you," Luke shrugged.

"Like a fungus," she muttered, shaking her shoulders.

Gideon was watching her intently, his brows furrowed.

"Who is it, Benny?"

She ran her tongue across her teeth, like she was trying to get the taste out of her mouth. She was twitchier than usual. Even her heartbeat was thumping like crazy. Luke was incredibly intrigued, leaning forward to rest his elbows on his thighs as he watched her. He wasn't used to this side of her. He was used to the confident, offbeat Benny.

The one who always had something to say.

"Just some guy," she said, tapping her hand on the counter.

Luke and Gideon exchanged a long glance.

"Just some guy," Gideon repeated.

"A lot of yelling over there for some guy," Luke added.

Benny closed her eyes as she sucked in a breath.

"It's not important," she said tersely. "I just... need to get up there."

"And do what?" Luke asked, leaning back in the stool, crossing his arms against his chest. "Help daddy with a little interrogation?"

"Yes," she snapped. "I'm owed that, aren't I?"

Luke would never deny her that. And frankly, he would be lying if he said he had no interest in seeing whatever was about to unfold. But there was something she wasn't sharing, he could feel it.

"We'll take you wherever you need to be, princess," Gideon said. "If you chill out on the light show."

Benny's hands were glowing.

Luke could feel the heat emanating from her magic. He watched as she held up her hands in front of her, a dazed look on her face. She let out a huff of breath, almost a slight laugh, as she shook her head.

"I guess anger really is a good motivator," she breathed.

"Jesus, Ben," Gideon said. "Who is this guy?"

She sighed and her hands dimmed, the light and heat dissipating just as quickly as they had appeared. "A huge mistake," she said, shaking her head. "We met through my dad, he runs with some of the trade guys. We— I mean, it was nothing, really. A couple of dates? We only... you know, the details aren't important. I just don't know *how* he knew. I never told him. Unless he—"

"Found out from someone else?" Luke suggested. "Knew before you met?"

"Any of those options suck," Benny said, sinking into the stool beside him. "I never told my dad. He has this rule... Men under his employment aren't allowed within ten feet of me. So him finding out this way, it just kills me."

Luke blew out a breath he didn't have and watched as his brother processed all of this information. Watched as Gideon propped himself against the island, his fist curled so tightly his knuckles turned white. He wouldn't look at Luke, wouldn't let his brother see the emotion swirling behind his eyes. But Luke knew. He could hear it in his heartbeat.

"When do you want to leave?" Gideon asked tersely.

Benny lifted her head to look at Gideon, a mixture of shame and regret all over her face.

Luke frowned. He didn't think Benny had anything to feel ashamed about. It wasn't her fault some douchebag she used to date sold her out.

"Whenever we can," she said. She chewed on her bottom lip. "If that's alright."

Gideon nodded, "Fine. Wheels up in fifteen."

Luke leaned back into the stool.

This was going to be a hell of a visit to the Caruso Family compound.

EIGHTEEN

BENNY

THEY DROVE THROUGH THE night, alone on the highway, mist clinging to the windows of the car as moisture seemed to hover in the air around them. It was nearly three and a half hours to Hudson, to the home where Benny spent most of her childhood. She was curled up in the backseat, her legs tucked underneath her body, her head resting on her palm as she stared out the window. What would they be walking into? Would her father have Christian there? Would he be somewhere else?

Would the interrogation have already begun?

Benny had known who her father was for a long time.

What he was.

Her mother's death had made it sort of impossible for him to keep his secret, because her murder consumed him, like an unclaimed vengeance that would have eaten him alive had she not stepped in. Had Benny not reminded him that he wasn't alone. She was there too.

And she missed her mom just as much as he did.

Her father hadn't kept secrets from her after that. He wanted her to be aware of the dangers that lurked, the burden her kind had to bear in return for the power they were gifted.

But her actual abilities weren't his focus. He resented her power. Though he was never explicit, she could feel it. She could see it whenever she was pouring over the grimoire, doing what she could to teach herself in her mother's absence. His grief created an aversion to magic, and especially to what Benny was capable of. How he managed to continue his own work in the field, she had no idea.

It hardened him.

It made him almost fanatical in instructing Benny on the business.

Her father wanted to make sure she understood the inner workings of the Caruso family, of the way goods passed through their hands, how they decided what to move and what to keep. He wanted her to know where all of their privilege had come from, the work that went into keeping it alive.

She hated to admit it, but she had found herself intrigued by it.

And that was exactly why she dove into academia. To separate herself from that world. To focus on her magic and her schooling and to find a community in which she could thrive away from that darkness.

She knew who her father was.

She just didn't know exactly who *she* was yet. What version of her would come out.

But when the car turned down the long gravel drive, the path softly lit by oil lanterns, and the main house came into view, all she felt was a yearning for her home. The old Tudor manor, with ivy creeping along its brick, was dark save for a light on in the room she knew to be her father's study. The sun was barely beginning to rise, and the sky was burning into shades of orange and pink. She couldn't remember the last time she'd properly visited, so much of her focus on school and her thesis and teaching.

The car pulled into park and Benny felt Gideon's focus shift toward her.

He looked at her through the rearview mirror, his brow a little wrinkled, concern in his eyes. There was a depth to them more recently, a softness that made her feel a little tingling of hope deep in her belly. Like there could be something more. God, she wanted more. Even if that felt insane to want. Even if she knew their circumstances made those wants feel insignificant.

She still wanted it. She wanted him.

But he had been quiet on the drive, letting Luke pick the music, hardly saying a word to either of them. She couldn't understand the shift. They had been training on the roof when her father had called, Gideon intent on helping her harness her power, working with her so closely these last few days it was as if they had found new ground with each other. And now…

"You ready?" Luke asked, startling her from her thoughts.

She nodded.

The light above the front door turned on, and by the time Benny had crossed the driveway, her father had met her in the front yard. It was strange to see him dressed so casually. But she couldn't help the swell of emotion she felt when she saw the UPenn sweatshirt he was wearing. He seemed anxious, though. Restless.

No. Uneasy.

As if he was waiting to be chastised. As if this was somehow his fault. Neither of them said anything at first, only wrapped their arms around each other. She knew deep down this was on her. She had made a reckless choice with Christian and now she was paying for it.

That wasn't on him.

Benny hugged him tightly, smelling his familiar cologne, the hint of a cigar. Bourbon.

"You doing okay, kid?" her dad asked, his broad hands wrapped around her shoulders as he held her back a step and took a solid look at her. His one hand moved to lift her chin. "You look good. A little thin, though. Jesus, Benedetta, are these boys feeding you? Are you sleeping?"

"Babbo, please," Benny replied, flustered, waving her hands. "I'm okay. They're taking good care of me, considering the circumstances, and we've made a lot of progress. We haven't been attacked in what?" She glanced back at the Crawford brothers and offered them a rueful smile. "A couple of days?"

Angelo narrowed his eyes. "Attacked?"

"Babbo—"

"So you found this Moran guy?" Angelo turned his attention to the brothers.

"Yeah, about that," Luke said, his hands tucked into his suit pants. "We should talk."

"Inside," Gideon said, gesturing to the brightening sky.

"Right, yeah, come on." Angelo gestured for them to follow.

But Benny lingered in the drive, letting her head tilt back toward the approaching sunrise. Her father used to joke that she was a little solar light when she was a child, the way she would lay in the grass and soak up the sun. She would close her eyes and let its heat sink into her skin. Much like she was doing now. No matter how many years passed, how many thousands of mornings, she still felt humbled when she stepped into the daylight.

She had been so close to losing this.

She could feel her skin prickle with fury.

Would she be able to remain calm when she saw Christian? Would she be able to control herself?

Should she?

A gentle touch brushed across her shoulders, a tingling fluttering down her spine. She felt her breath catch when she opened her eyes to find Gideon beside her. A warmth that could rival the sun seemed to linger in his gaze. There it was. There was that softness.

She wondered if he had any idea the effect he had on her.

"Hey," she said. "I just needed a minute."

"A recharge?" he said, seemingly amused at his own little joke, the quiet chuckle that followed diffusing the fury lingering inside her. Like he knew she needed a break. "So, how many embarrassing childhood photos will I find when we go inside?"

Benny rolled her eyes as she turned to follow him toward the house.

"You know I went to Catholic school," she said casually.

"Did you wear a uniform?"

She smiled.

"I also had braces for, like, five years," she conceded.

"Jackpot."

The house felt so quiet.

When her mother died, friends and family and wives of his men came calling, filling the refrigerator with lasagna and stuffed shells and homemade key lime pies (Benny's favorite). There were weekly cookouts over the summer, jam-packed Thanksgivings and Christmases. Angelo created a pseudo-family for Benny, and the house was always bustling. But now it felt empty. She wondered briefly if her father had sent everyone home for her arrival, if he was still unsure of who he could trust. Which brought an ache to her chest. To think of her father struggling with who he could turn to while Benny was gone. Their relationship had grown so complicated after her mother's death, neither of them knowing how to be together without her there to make them whole. But she couldn't fight the guilt that hit her, knowing how alone he had been these last few weeks.

But after granting Luke an invitation into the Torretta home and stepping through the threshold into the foyer, she could hear the creak of the old hardwood floors and faint footsteps coming from the study.

"There she is!"

The relief she felt was palpable and a wide smile appeared on her face when she saw her godfather come around the corner.

Jimmy Antonella was her father's cousin and his right-hand man. His underboss, to get technical. He reminded her a lot of her father. Except he was a little leaner, a little taller, and had these incredibly kind green eyes. He had always been sweet to Benny, teaching her how to ride a bike when she was a kid and how to tell the difference between a good fake and the real deal when she was a little bit older.

"Hey, Jimmy," she greeted, giving the older man a kiss on the cheek.

"Hey, Pat," he yelled, his head turned toward the living room. "Benny's home."

She noticed that his knuckles were a little raw, a little bruised.

There was a quiet curse and a thud before another man came from the living room. He had clearly just woken up, his eyes tired and his movements a little slow. Pasquale De Vito, her father's most trusted advisor and consigliere, was the kind of man who was all gruff. He was stern and dry and an old friend of the family whose children had grown up with Benny. They shared nearly every holiday together. He was on the shorter side, with thinning hair, and, despite scowling being his preferred facial emotion, deep smile lines. And of all the men who worked for her father, he had the worst reputation of them all. Which was hard to imagine as a wide yawn stretched across his face.

"Piccola," Pasquale said, a term of endearment she hadn't heard since she was actually a little girl. He pulled her into a giant bear hug. "You have no idea how happy we are to see you."

"What'd ya do?" Jimmy asked, gesturing to the living room. "You fall asleep on the La-Z-Boy?"

"It's six o'clock in the fucking morning," Pasquale countered with a wave of his hand. "At least give me some coffee if we're gonna wait up all night."

"Basta," Angelo sighed. "Jim, Pat—these are those Crawford boys I was tellin' you about. The ones who pulled that score in Vegas. They've been taking care of Benny while we sorted out our little issue."

"The balls on you two for that hotel hit," Jimmy nodded appreciatively.

"Good to see you're out from Frank Markos's shadow," Pasquale added.

Luke smiled, though it bordered on smug, and his shoulders straightened just slightly at the praise. Gideon looked at Benny with a slight roll of his eyes, and she couldn't help but smile. But as the pleasantries were shared, she looked around at this group of men and wondered what was going to be harder to discuss.

The ritual targeting her, or the stupid summer fling she'd had being the one to sell her out?

"Come on," Angelo said after a moment. "We all got a lot to sift through here. Jimmy, put on a pot, will ya?"

"Sure, cugino." Her godfather nodded before he wrapped his arm around Benny's shoulder, guiding her toward the kitchen. He lowered his voice to a conspiratorial tone. "Your zia Gloria left some pastries for you in the fridge."

"Really?" She perked up. That woman was an artist with a pastry shell. "Cannolis for breakfast it is."

While Jimmy busied himself with the coffee maker, Benny grabbed mugs and plates from the cabinet, her body on autopilot. She stared at the mismatched collection they'd acquired over the years, an oversized "PROUD PARENT OF AN HONOR ROLL STUDENT" mug with a little chip in the handle making her smile. She reached for that one along with a few others, including her very favorite *Wizard of Oz* mug.

Her father squeezed her shoulder as he leaned against the counter beside her.

"I wish you would've told me," he said, his voice quiet.

It took her a moment before she understood what he was referring to, but when she realized he was talking about Christian, she froze. She could only imagine how Christian spun their relationship. He hadn't exactly taken their break-up super well.

She swallowed.

"It wasn't—" She paused, struggling to figure out what to say. "I mean, we weren't…"

Her father looked at her, his eyebrows knitting together in concern.

"It was just a stupid fling," she said, finally. "It barely lasted a couple of months."

Her shoulders sagged.

"If I had known that he was going to do this…"

"This is not your fault," Angelo told her sternly.

The coffee machine beeped, drawing them both out of the conversation. She took the escape, attempting to pour the coffee, but Jimmy shooed her away, a soft look on his worn face. It felt a hell of a lot like pity, though, and she hated that. Even as she crossed toward the kitchen table, sinking down in the same seat she'd sat in every night as a kid for dinner, she didn't want anyone in this room to feel pity for her.

And when Gideon's eyes lifted to meet hers, from where he sat across from her, she was relieved to see something different behind his. Even if it was a rage she hadn't quite expected, his hazel eyes darker than she'd ever seen them. She frowned.

"Benny, you still take your coffee black?"

Jimmy hovered by the table with two coffee mugs in his hand.

"Yeah," she said, offering him a smile. She gestured to Gideon. "He does too."

Which was a thing she hadn't realized she knew until just that second. But she ignored the flush in her skin as Jimmy placed both mugs on the table in their respective directions. Luke chuckled softly beside her.

"What about me?" he challenged.

"You don't drink coffee," she said, narrowing her eyes back. "You drink English Breakfast and, like, questionable amounts of orange juice."

She had spent a grand total of two weeks at the loft, and she already knew more about their habits than she thought she would. And one of those days she was essentially passed out. But you tend to get to know a person quickly when you spend every waking moment with them. She drew her knees up to her chest, the heels of her feet hanging on to the edge of her seat.

Luke grinned.

"Just checking. Anyway, I'm fine, honestly. I fed before we left."

Jimmy returned to the table with his own mug of coffee and one more for Angelo, her father's nearly white from all the milk he liked. Pasquale huffed a breath.

"What do you think, I'm your maid?" Jimmy scoffed.

"You brought everyone else's!"

"These kids drove all night to be here," Jimmy said. "And Angelo's been up since last night. Benny was abducted, Pat. Were you abducted?"

"Fuckin' Christ, fine, I'll get my own damn coffee," Pasquale grumbled.

"Bring the cannolis too," Jimmy called out.

"So, you wanna tell me what you found out?" Angelo said, looking between Gideon and Luke. "Because I've heard a lot of shit tonight from that fuckin' snake that's hard to keep straight."

"Is he still alive?" Benny asked.

Her father didn't say anything for a moment, his eyes drifting to Jimmy.

"He's alive," Pasquale said as he crossed back toward them with his coffee. "Barely."

"Keeps sayin' this was all inevitable," Jimmy said.

"I don't know about 'inevitable' but—" Luke shifted in his seat, drawing his ankle onto his knee as he tapped his fingers on the tabletop. "—what we've learned definitely leads me to believe all of this was premeditated."

Angelo raised an expectant brow.

"A ritual," Gideon explained, his eyes still focused on Benny. "Using Benny's blood to become some kind of demon."

"An ascension?" Pasquale asked, before blowing out a breath. "Fuckin' Christ."

"Why are you saying that like you're familiar with them?" Benny asked.

"Kid, we've been around a long time," Jimmy replied. "Lotta power-obsessed men out there with shit for brains who think this is gonna give them what they want."

"So, somebody got to d'Aviano," her father said. "Or he's been yakkin' it up about your abilities, Ben, and someone got real fucking lucky."

Benny couldn't help the flush of embarrassment.

"I never told him," she said. "I have no idea how he knows."

"It doesn't matter," her father replied. "What matters is we find out who's responsible. We'll break him. Just need a little bit more time to talk."

"I want to see him."

They all turned to look at Benny.

She sat up in her chair, face resolute.

"I want to see him," she repeated.

"Benny—" her father started.

"No," she said firmly. "If anyone is going to get him to talk, it's me. I don't care what you do to him but you leave him conscious. I'm not going to sit this one out."

"I wouldn't expect anything less," came a voice from the other end of the kitchen.

Benny looked up to find Jamie Locantore lingering in the passthrough, a wide grin on his face. She was up and out of her seat in a flash, her arms thrown around his shoulders as he hugged her tightly. God, it felt good to see him. Jamie was Pasquale's oldest son, and Benny's closest childhood friend. For a long time, her only friend. One of the few who was allowed to know her secret.

"Holy shit, Ben," he breathed. "You have no idea how good it feels to see you."

She blinked back tears, laughing at herself as she stepped back from his arms. She had never considered herself much of a crier. But seeing the people she loved these last few days brought out emotions that felt impossible to ignore. It had been a hell of a couple weeks. And she couldn't stop thinking about how much she had almost lost.

"I didn't know you'd be here," she said, brushing at her nose with the back of her hand.

His blond hair was ruffled with sleep, making him look younger than his thirty-one years. But he'd always had a boyish quality to him, with his bright blue eyes and freckled skin and wide mouth. He was very out of place among the more grizzled men who worked for her father but he was an incredibly strong Healer. Working for the Caruso family had always been his plan.

"Dad let me know you'd get in early." He reached to brush at a tear on her cheek. "I didn't want to miss you. You alright?"

She nodded.

"James, you hungry?" Jimmy called. "Gloria made some pastries."

"Oh, that woman is magic in the kitchen," he said, tossing Benny a wink.

Luke cocked his head to the side as they came back toward the table, something glimmering behind his wire-rimmed glasses as he met Benny's gaze. Something delighted. Her brows hitched as Jamie pulled up another chair, putting himself between Gideon and his father.

Gideon hardly glanced up from his coffee.

"Gideon, Luke," Angelo started. "This is James, Pat's kid. He's our best Healer on staff."

The men all shook hands, the table looking so extremely overwhelmed with testosterone Benny had half a mind to leave them and take a nap upstairs in her childhood bedroom.

"What did I interrupt?" Jamie asked, looking around the table.

"Benny wants to interrogate the man who sold her out," Luke said, tossing her a look.

"And Dad doesn't think I should," she said pointedly.

"I never said that," Angelo sighed, running a large hand over his face. "I just— I want to make sure you're ready for this. For what you might encounter."

Benny shook her head, her jaw tensing. After everything she'd been through, all the work she'd done to try and get control of her abilities...this was her right. She felt it.

"You have no idea how ready I am."

Nineteen

Cleo

Cleo was half asleep, sunlight leaking through the blackout curtains of Harker's guest bedroom when her phone started to vibrate across the pillow. She had been holed up in the apartment above Mathilde's since she had been followed from her own place. She appreciated Harker's generosity and Luke's overprotective streak and Gideon's insistence that she "not be stupid" and try and go back home after the fight at the quarry, but she missed her bed. She missed her linen sheets and her humidifier and her diffuser that let a steady stream of lavender soothe her to sleep.

She fumbled for her phone, her face half planted into the pillow as she cracked open one eye. Luke's name flashed across the screen. She inched her body across the bed, her finger just tapping at the speaker phone before she curled up against the comforter.

"What?"

"Good morning, sleepyhead," came Luke's cheerful voice.

"Why are you awake?" Cleo asked, glancing at the clock.

Although Luke tended to live like a human, he wasn't. And he frequently spent most of the night up and awake and doing whatever it was Luke did while the rest of them were sleeping. It was when the sun rose, when the morning came, that he disappeared to get some rest.

"Why aren't you?"

"Harker and I smoked a joint before bed," she told him, voice still scratchy from sleep.

"I didn't realize that was an option," Luke said thoughtfully. "I didn't think it was possible."

"You can't get drunk but that hasn't stopped you from drinking all my good tequila," she countered.

"Touchè."

She heard a faint curse in the background, no doubt from Gideon.

"Where are you?" she asked, rubbing the sleep from her eyes.

"Hudson," he said. "We got the call from Torretta late last night. They found the shithead who sold Benny out. They've got him holed up in some warehouse in the woods up here, so we're gonna go see him for a little visit."

"How's Benny?"

Cleo felt a pang of solidarity with the witch.

"She's hanging in there," Luke said. "Can you do me a favor?"

"What do you need?"

"If we're gonna do this thing at the gala, I think there's a few things we're gonna need," he said. "I'm sending you a list. I think Huck should have everything."

She felt the quick vibration against the mattress, and she could see the text message pop up on her notifications. She grabbed the phone as she rolled onto her back. Nothing seemed too out of the ordinary, until she reached the crossbow.

Well, there was a first time for everything.

"I can handle it," she said with a yawn.

"Thanks," he said but she could hear the hesitation in his voice. "Cleo?"

"Yes, Luke?"

"Be safe, okay?" he said. "Don't let any of those pricks at the shop rile you up. And if anything feels weird, you know where to go, right?"

"I know," she said, a soft smile tugging at her lips.

They hung up, and she pulled the comforter up over her face as she buried herself beneath the blankets for just a little while longer. Nothing would be particularly hard to put together, but Cleo knew there was a certain level of negotiation she would have to entertain. Which meant a shower and a blowout and enough lip gloss to distract from the fact that she was looking for rifles with scratched-out serial numbers.

But Cleo needed coffee before she embarked on any of those things.

The muted sounds of an old soul song led her to the little kitchen in the apartment where she found Harker drinking tea in a matching set of silk pajamas. It was a modest space for the vampire, filled with thriving plants and incredible art and vintage furniture that probably wasn't vintage when he first found it. She had wondered countless times why he wasn't holed up in some gorgeous row house or at the very least a three-bedroom, but he seemed content in the space. He had told her once that after all the years he'd moved through the world as a vampire, he'd simply seen too much. Which was why he opened Mathilde's.

A calm away from the demon hunting.

The catacombs of supernatural books he kept in the basement was a bit of a bonus.

"Good morning, love," Harker greeted from the table.

"Good morning, Harker," she replied brightly.

"Cleo, darling, this is Teddy," he said with a wicked glint behind his eyes, gesturing to a lean and attractive brown man, wearing nothing more than a silk floral robe at the counter. "Teddy, this is Cleo. We met at the Ritz a few months ago."

"Oh!" She smiled. "Good morning, Teddy!"

"Coffee?" he said, holding up the pot with a bright smile, his teeth very straight and very white. He was cute as hell, with a little dimple in his left cheek and warm brown eyes. Two tiny faint bite marks were just hidden by the neck of his robe. *So much for being vegetarian, Harker.* "I just put on a pot."

"Yes, please," she said, another yawn passing through her lips as she sank into the seat across from Harker. "I've got a few errands to run for the boys today. Do you need anything?"

"For the gala?" he asked. "Take a peek in the basement before you go, love."

"Oh my God," Cleo said. "Thank you, yes, that'll help. You know I hate Huck's."

"All this time, and you haven't found a better connection?"

"It wouldn't matter. Everything worth anything is owned by Markos," she said, rolling her eyes. "It's like he purposefully picks the perviest guys to run his businesses."

"Do you want me to come with you?" Harker asked.

Cleo shook her head.

"No, I'm sure I'll be fine," she said, waving her hand.

Harker looked at her over his nose.

"I've got Missy running the shop," he said. "I'll come with. Even if I just stay in the car. I'd prefer to at least be close by in case any of those little worms gives you a hard time."

"If anyone gives me a hard time, I'm going to take care of it myself," she told him pointedly. "Between you and Luke, I swear."

But by the time Cleo pulled into the back alley beside Schmidt's Shooters Supply, she was actually grateful Harker had bullied his way into her car. She hated the way she had to navigate the world sometimes, knowing what it meant to be a woman in this business. Knowing that she also had to account for some nutcase trying to become a demon who had little cronies at his beck and call to follow her around if they wanted to wasn't all that fun, either.

She raked her hand through her hair, fluffing out the barrel curls she'd pinned earlier and spared a glance at Harker.

"I'll be right behind you, love," he said. "Absolutely gorgeous work on all this, by the way."

The perks of being a pageant queen.

She smiled before she made her way toward the back entrance, the heels of her knee high boots clicking on the sidewalk. A bell chimed as she pulled open the door, and she was relieved to find the place mostly empty. No half-drunk survivalists trying to mansplain their way around an automatic rifle or men with patchy beards and polo shirts hovering near the Glocks breathing all over the cases. But as she made her way further inside, the door behind the counter swung open, and she was surprised to see Frank Markos in the flesh walking from the backroom. He seemed surprised to see her too, but a smile worked its way across his face.

"Cleo St. James," he greeted, voice gruff and scratchy. "Long time no see, kid."

Frank Markos was tall, thin—weedy may be a better word to describe him. His skin was weathered from a little too much sun, and his hair was cropped short into a neat buzzcut. Underneath his tweed blazer was a simple white dress shirt, and although she wasn't certain, she had a feeling he was wearing loafers. It was like a funny trick he played. To look so friendly and so unassuming. Handsome, even, in a way. But Cleo knew what he was capable of. Knew the power he had in this city. Knew that there wasn't really a secret he couldn't overturn if he was curious enough to know.

And she hated how much Luke and Gideon owed to him.

"Mr. Markos," she greeted, putting on that bright and sunshiny smile, letting that Appalachian accent just drip with honey. "How are you?"

"Oh, managing just fine," he replied.

"Where's Huck?" she asked, tilting her head in that dumb little way of hers. "He's usually my go-to guy here."

The bell on the back door rang again, and Cleo hardly needed to look to know that Harker had slinked inside, his body covered by a basic black trench coat, no doubt an umbrella hovering by the door to keep him safe from the sun. Lucky for them the weather was shit enough for the umbrella to make sense, the sky overcast and cloudy.

"Oh, Huck's running an errand," Frank replied, his eyes also tracking where Harker entered. "You know we all wear quite a few hats in this operation."

She laughed, hoping it reached her eyes.

"After this, I'm dropping off dry cleaning," she said, rolling her eyes. "I feel like their mother sometimes."

"Mother?" Frank repeated, amused. "Neither one of those boys looks at you like you're their mother, Red. In fact, I'm often wondering which one of them it is you're attached to. Dragging a woman around in this line of work... what's the fun of it if you're not, you know..."

He smirked, his eyes raising as he considered her, and she hated the way that up and down look made her feel. But she powered through it. Bright eyes, big smile.

"I can assure you, it's more like I'm the annoying kid sister."

A long silence lingered between them.

"If that's what you're calling it these days."

She let out a forced laugh before digging in her pocket for the short-ened list of items she needed to acquire that she couldn't pull from Harker's weapons closet. She was lucky the more unsavory things had come from Harker. She wasn't sure how she'd be able to explain the crossbow. It wasn't exactly bank-robbing typical.

"You think you could help me with some of this?" she asked, sliding the list toward him. Her handwriting was soft and rounded, little hearts dotted over each letter I. It was exactly the vibe she knew worked with men like this. Sweet. Feminine. "We're doing a little audit on our inventory, and there's just a few things we're missing."

He plucked a pair of glasses from his suit jacket and glanced down at the list as he perched the half-moon frames on his nose.

"We should have what you need," he said, before he gestured for her to follow him toward the back room.

TWENTY

BENNY

IT WAS HUMID OUTSIDE, the air sticky with the afternoon heat. Benny was sitting by the pool, her legs wading through the cool water, her palms resting against the pavers. She closed her eyes, letting her head tilt back and her body soak up the sunlight drenching the backyard. She hadn't realized how much she had missed home until she was here, sitting in these achingly familiar places, hearing the wind rustling through the maple trees that lined the edge of their property.

The morning had gone by in a flash.

Breakfast had turned into a full debrief, the Crawford brothers going through the events of the last few weeks. The missing children, the attack at the quarry— even Benny's training with Gideon. The news about her power had started a heated discussion between Benny and her father and her use of blood magic had turned it into a full blown argument. She had desperately needed the fresh air.

She was too old to have this argument with him again and again.

Especially now.

When her very life was a stake.

The door that led to the deck slid open and Benny turned to find Jamie crossing the patio toward her. He was wearing a pair of green khakis and a gray T-shirt, his sneakers scuffed and his hair was still a mess, blond locks falling across his forehead. He looked like every other guy she came across on campus and not at all like a high ranking member of a crime family.

"You're gonna give the old man a heart attack you know," he said as he sank down on the ground beside her, letting his long legs spread out into the grass.

"I just can't do it anymore," she said, kicking her feet through the water. "I don't know how many more times we can fight about this."

"Oh, give him a break, Ben," he said. "He's been worried sick these last few weeks."

"I'm going to throw you in the pool."

"No one is saying this hasn't been hard for you," he told her quickly. "Believe me. I can't tell you the relief I feel seeing you here in front of me right now. He just doesn't know how to fix this. He doesn't have the power you do."

She sighed, waving her hand above the water, creating a little whirlpool with her magic. "Power I am still not sure I can wield."

"You said you were making progress," he said, nudging her body with his foot.

"I am," she said. "I think. I've gotten close."

Little bits of power, but nothing as intense as that night on the docks. But she knew why.

Gideon had become a distraction.

Anger had been her tool thus far, focusing in on her rage in order to mimic what she had done at the docks. But the more time she spent with Gideon, the less anger she felt. The more confused and stupid and smitten instead.

She put her face in her hands.

"I miss school," she said. "I miss the library. I even miss grading papers."

"You do not miss grading papers," Jamie snorted.

She peeked at him through her fingers, "Let me be dramatic."

"I'd never stop you," he told her, pressing his hand to his chest.

Benny pulled her feet out of the pool and tucked her knees under her chin.

"I missed you, Locantore," she said.

"I missed you, too," Jamie said. His eyes wandered up and down her body. A clinical assessment if she ever saw one. "I think your wrists might always look like that. What was it? Iron?"

Her wounds and bruises had healed, her body no longer riddled with the signs of what happened to her. Except for her wrists. The marks where the iron chains rubbed her skin raw never fully healed. Wounds left behind by magic, especially marks left by iron— they had a way of sticking around. She looked down at the thin red scars.

"Yup," she said, shaking her head. "Little mementos, I guess."

"Shit," he muttered. "I'm sorry, Benny."

"It's okay," she told him. "It's a good reminder that I'm still here."

She just hoped she could keep that going. At least for a little while longer.

"You know I think I saw some pie in the fridge," Jamie said.

"What *kind* of pie?"

Jamie got to his feet, his hand extended to help Benny to hers.

"Why don't we find out?"

"If it's key lime I can't make any promises," she said as she straightened.

"If it's key lime I'll make sure to give you your privacy."

She shoved at his shoulder as she turned back toward the house, a laugh bursting from his chest as he staggered a step back. Jamie had an easy way about him, always had. When they were kids he knew exactly the thing to say to make her laugh. When her mother died, he was the only person she wanted to be around.

"You going to stay for dinner?" she asked.

"Ben, I eat here more than you do," he laughed.

Jamie pulled the sliding door back, leaning against the glass as she passed in front of him. The chill of the air conditioning hit her skin and she shivered as her bare feet padded across the hardwood floor. She wondered briefly if she had any hoodies upstairs in her old closet when she saw Gideon at the other end of the hallway, a picture frame in his hands.

"Oh, no," she said. "I hope that's not—"

He turned, the curve of his lips absolutely wicked.

"I didn't know you were a ballerina," he said.

Jamie spared her a glance.

"Is that the—"

"The bee costume," she sighed.

Her friend grinned and clapped her on the shoulder. "Listen, the eyebrows eventually separated."

"You're a menace," she said. "No pie for you."

She was power walking down the hallway as her hand waved in front of her, the frame plucking itself from Gideon's fingers and floating toward her. She met the frame halfway down the hall, her eyes taking in the thirteen year old Benny dressed for her ballet recital. A bumblebee themed costume complete with a stinger off the back of her tutu and a pair of antennae ears tucked into her hair. The partial unibrow and rainbow rubber-band braces certainly completed the picture.

It had been her first recital on point and she remembered being insanely proud of herself. She had to respect that version of her. Even if she could have been a bit more generous with the tweezers.

"You weren't kidding about those braces," Gideon said, his stride slow and purposeful as he walked toward her, his hands stuffed into the pockets of his suit pants.

"It was a very long five years," she groaned, clutching the frame to her chest.

"You were cute," he told her.

He was absolutely on the verge of laughter but she appreciated his restraint.

"I'm gonna go check on the old men," Jamie said with a nod toward Gideon. "Save me a slice, will ya?"

Benny nodded but her attention was monopolized by the man in front of her. It hadn't fully sunk in until now that Gideon was in her home.

Standing here in the hallway where her childhood was immortalized in picture frames— school portraits, prom photos, her first snowstorm in one of those snowsuits where she could hardly move her arms. Photos with her mother.

She hugged the frame more tightly against her chest.

It was a lot to see, a lot of her life to digest.

"How long did you dance?" he asked.

"I never stopped," she said. "There's a studio a few blocks from Betty's that has a Wednesday night ballet class. But I guess it's been a couple of weeks."

His brow furrowed.

"You could still go," he offered, his hand rubbing at the back of his neck. "One of us could take you there, pick you up, you know, if you wanted."

"Really?"

"We could figure it out."

She beamed. "You're being awfully nice to me, Crawford."

"I'm nice," he said, affronted.

"No," she said, shaking her head. "You're not."

But he was kind. In ways he thought no one would notice. The aspirin on her nightstand, the way the fridge was suddenly stocked with her favorite yogurt, the bar cart stocked with gin, vermouth, and olives.

He rolled his eyes but there was a hint of affection there.

She could feel it.

Benny took a step forward, closing the distance between them. She loved the way he smelled. She loved waking up to that scent every morning, loved the moments she spent in the shower, lathering herself up in his shampoo, touching herself to the fantasies that played in her mind, thinking about him even when she knew she shouldn't. She was on the verge of no longer caring about what she should or shouldn't do when it came to Gideon.

She pressed a kiss to his cheek, her lips lingering against his skin, his five o'clock shadow itching in a way that sent a shiver down her spine. His hand curved at her elbow as she leaned against him, his thumb pressing into her skin. Her eyes fluttered shut as her voice ghosted against his ear.

"Thank you for taking such good care of me, Gideon."

It was when she was already walking past him down the hallway that she heard him say, "Always, Benny."

Twenty-One

BENNY

"Are you sure you wanna do this?"

No. Benny wasn't sure at all.

The Caruso family had a warehouse near the manor, a collection of things that were too important not to keep close. It was mostly used for meetings, and it was kept safe under a mixture of warding spells and security systems. After a day of arguing back and forth, Angelo finally relented. But Benny's nerves were starting to get to her. She was pacing back and forth in front of the room where they were keeping Christian, working a path into the concrete floors. Her heart was beating so rapidly in her chest she was certain it was going to explode as her brain played out every imaginable scenario.

She could feel Gideon's eyes on her. But he said nothing as she paced, merely watched as she spiraled. She rubbed at her chest, shaking her head as she spared him a glance.

"No," she told him, the word truthful enough. "But he might be our best bet at finding out who's behind all of this. So I'm going to do it anyway."

"Okay," Gideon said. "We'll do it together."

She stopped in her tracks, her brow knitting together. But when she opened her mouth to say something, he raised his eyebrows as if to challenge her. As if this wasn't a suggestion.

"After everything you've been through recently?" He shook his head before pushing himself from off the wall. "I'm not letting you go in there alone."

"Good," Jamie said from the opposite end of the room.

He had been there when they arrived, his gloved hands covered in blood splatters that told her all she needed to know about how the interrogation was going.

Healers were required during interrogations, if only to be there to help continue the process, letting the body mend just enough for the talks to keep going. It was a particular kind of torture. To be half-fixed.

And when it was one of their own?

Christian had been working for her father for the last couple of years. He was loyal. Had proven himself enough to pass all of their rigorous screening procedures. But maybe Benny's secret was too good to keep to himself, however he learned. She couldn't have felt like a bigger fool.

Having Gideon by her side felt like a relief.

So, she nodded and offered him a grateful smile.

"Thank you."

"Just so you know, I already hate the guy," he said, shrugging.

Jamie snorted. "Wait until you meet him."

She heard a grunt from behind the door and exchanged a look with Gideon. Her father was inside with Jimmy. Luke and Pasquale were in another part of the warehouse, digging through manuscripts and artifacts to see if they could find anything on Halmanthoran while Benny was talking with Christian. Luke was like a kid in a candy store at the prospect. He would have thrived in an academic setting.

Suddenly, the door swung open, and her godfather stepped out into the hallway first. He flexed his hands, a scab from his knuckle freshly cut open. Her father followed after a moment, the door slamming shut behind him, his chest heaving slightly. His hair was a little matted with sweat. There was a level of anger in him she'd only seen a handful of times in her life. Benny stepped toward him, her hand resting on his forearm. He considered her for a moment before his eyes drifted to Gideon behind her. There was a little wrinkle of his brow before he looked back at her with a nod.

"Are you sure you don't want me to come in with you?" he asked.

She knew Christian well enough that he would make any interactions with her father present extremely uncomfortable. She was already anxious about what he had relayed to her father, how he might have talked about her and their relationship. She shook her head.

No, that was absolutely not an option.

"It's alright," she said. "Besides, your hired bodyguard here will keep me safe."

Gideon's eyes flickered to the ceiling as he exhaled.

"We'll be right outside the door," Angelo said. "If you need anything."

"Thank you," she told him, reaching up to kiss her dad on the cheek.

The doorknob felt cool to the touch as she turned it and the heavy metal door creaked open slowly. There was a single hanging lamp in the center of the ceiling but nothing more. Save for the figure sitting in the middle of the room. Tied to a simple wooden chair with zip ties, his head hanging slack against his chest, was Christian d'Aviano.

The light overhead reflected deep shadows across Christian's face, but the damage that had been done to him was clear. His fair skin was bruised and bloodied, and his normally bright blue eyes were black with welts. His lip had been split, blood spilling down his chin, staining the neck of his shirt a deep red.

His body seemed to jolt awake at their presence, and he slowly dragged his head up. The smile that once endeared him to her was plastered across his face, his teeth stained with his own blood. He looked nothing like the man she had once let into her bed. The shame and embarrassment she felt before had started to warp into something new. Something darker.

Here was the person who sold her out.

The man responsible for the scars on her wrists.

"My little witch," he said, his eyes brightening.

Benny hovered in the doorway. Once she crossed this threshold, she knew there would be no turning back. The thrill tempting her right now was the exact reason she had stepped away from her father's business. Had been the reason she had chosen academia, instead.

Gideon's hand ghosted against her lower back, fingers curling in the fabric of her shirt, and it gave her the little push she needed. She could do this. She wanted to do this.

"Christian."

"Did you bring a bodyguard?" He gestured toward Gideon with a nod of his head, amusement flickering behind his eyes. "Or is this a new friend? Wait—no, a boyfriend?"

"You don't get to ask the questions."

"Oh, is it *your* turn to interrogate me?" His grin was toothy and red and vicious. "You know, it didn't go so well for your father. And he doesn't mind getting his hands dirty. What do you think you'll accomplish?"

"I don't mind getting my hands dirty."

There was a wicked glimmer behind Gideon's eyes as he adjusted the cuff of his dress shirt.

Benny took another step toward Christian.

"I think you're going to tell me the truth," she said. "I think you're dying to."

"Is that right?" Christian dragged his eyes from Gideon to fix his stare back on Benny.

"He promised you something," she continued. "He needed my blood and you delivered. You knew the opportunity would put you in his good graces. So, what is it? More money? More power? Were you unhappy with your role here? Did you feel unappreciated?"

The look on Christian's face sent a chill down Benny's spine.

"Do you think you know me, Benedetta?"

She thought she did.

But this— stupidly, she never saw this coming.

"Parts of you," she said, instead. "The things that made me want to leave."

"I scared you, didn't I? Was I too possessive? Too hungry?"

She crossed her arms in front of her chest.

"You were a walking red flag," she muttered.

"Can't blame me for wanting more," he said, somehow shrugging against his bindings. "There's something addictive about a Strega witch. I wish I would have gotten a chance the last time we tried this."

Benny stilled.

"What?"

"Did you think you were the first?" He smiled. "This was a grift, Benedetta. You were a target. The man you were with was Christian d'Aviano. But that's not me."

Gideon cursed quietly under his breath.

"No." She felt a deep sinking in the pit of her stomach. "That can't be right. My father has every man vetted. How could you—"

"Get one over on the infallible Angelo Torretta?"

"How did you find out?" Gideon asked. "About Benny?"

"We've known for a while. Since mommy bit it all those years back." His laugh was menacing. "Well, I guess, it was the other way around, huh? Really put a damper on things."

Benny swallowed, shock rattling her bones.

Her mother was killed fifteen years ago. It was brutal and shocking and the details had always felt fuzzy. Her father never wanted to talk about it. But she knew the vampires responsible were taken care of soon after. The rampage her father had waged was something she would never forget.

"Is it connecting for you, little witch?" Christian said. "Is it starting to make sense?"

"You tried this with my mother," she said quietly.

"A setback." He shrugged. "But we aren't going to let it happen again."

She could feel Gideon's eyes on her but she tried to keep her focus on Christian—or whoever he was now. They had done this to her mother.

Had tried to use her for this stupid ritual. She blinked her eyes shut to calm herself. To take a moment.

"Your blood has come in handy," he continued. "It's a wonderful insurance while we prepare. But Master will find you, and he'll keep you. He's been planning this for a long time."

"And you've just been playing double agent?" Gideon asked.

"It was fun," he said, a flicker of something dark behind his eyes as he stared at Benny. "I've got a special talent for attraction. Seducing you was hardly difficult. You were so eager at first. Maybe I got carried away, but you were such a good fuck—"

She could feel Gideon's movements behind her, knew his intention, but she held out her arm to stop him, her hand pressing against his abdomen. She spared him a small glance, a shake of her head, and he stilled but there was something simmering inside him. The same rage she felt, no doubt.

"I really wish I could say the same," she mused. "At least then I would have gotten something good out of this."

Christian snarled, his eyes darkening. "You lying little bitch—"

There was a sickening crack as Gideon slammed his fist into Christian's face. His head snapped back, the chair shifting with the weight of him and Benny wasn't sure he wasn't going to topple over. But he managed to stay put, his tongue running over the new split in his lip, his nose now looking incredibly broken. Benny didn't have it in her to stop him this time.

"Boyfriend," Christian said as he spit out blood.

Gideon flexed his fist, and Benny could tell he was itching to hit him again.

"When can we kill him?" Gideon said, sparing her a glance.

Christian smirked. "You know, death isn't what it used to be."

He flexed his hands against the arms of the chair, the zip ties cutting into his skin and he didn't so much as wince as the blood began to pool on his forearms. Benny bit back a gasp as they snapped, her head tilting in a sort of morbid fascination at what was happening.

Suddenly the ones around his ankles snapped too.

Gideon moved quickly, placing his body in between Christian and Benny, his arm wrapped around her waist. His other hand held his gun, pointed squarely at the other man's chest. But Benny was too fascinated by what just happened to move behind him.

Was this the gift Christian had been given for selling out Benny? Was he human, still?

Was he ever?

"Is it strength?" she asked. "Or not feeling pain?"

"Oh, Benedetta, I *like* the pain," Christian said as he stood, the audacity of him to take a casual stretch after all of this. "Something you never gave me while we were together."

His eyes started to glow, the blue turning into a bright and blinding gold.

"What the fuck," Gideon muttered, pulling back the safety. "Benny, stay back."

"Oh, come here, little witch," Christian said, his voice growing deeper as he took a step closer toward them. "Show me why you're so special."

He lifted his arm to reach for her as his wrist cracked, each finger twisting and mutating as if they were breaking and reforming in rapid succession. Long claws began to tear through his fingertips, his flesh peeling back in ribbons. Benny's curiosity morphed quickly into fear, and she could feel Gideon's grip on her tighten as they both staggered back. But Christian's pace only quickened as his body seemed to transform in a horrifying cacophony of sounds.

Snap. Click. Snap. Click.

And then, in a flash, he was lunging at them both with a chilling growl.

Gideon didn't hesitate to shoot.

The sound was so loud, it echoed off of the bare walls.

Christian's body lurched back at the impact, his gaze dragging to the bullet wound in the center of his chest, watching as what was left of his shirt darkened with fresh blood. He touched his fingers to the wound, a wicked smile creeping into his new features. His eyes felt rounder, his cheekbones sharper, his skin paling to an almost transparent hue. Even his hair, usually a sandy blond, was pitch white. Like all of the color and life was draining from his body.

His human life.

"I can't wait to take a piece out of you, Benedetta," he growled.

"Jesus, Ben, I thought this guy was human."

"*I thought he was, too*," she grit out.

The door to the room slammed open as Christian lunged again.

"What the fuck—"

Her father burst into the room with Jimmy on his heels, their faces a mirror of shock. But Angelo's words of surprise were cut short as Gideon pushed Benny out of Christian's way, forcing her back just as Christian collided with him, throwing them both to the ground with a loud thud. She stumbled over her feet, her body all but falling into her father's as he rushed for her. She gripped at the sleeve of his shirt as she righted herself.

"Jimmy, shoot—" he instructed.

"Don't," Benny urged. "It won't work!"

And his body was so entangled with Gideon's, it didn't matter how good a shot he was.

The two of them wrestled for the upper hand, Gideon managing a rough right hook before Christian flipped them over, his claws dangerously close to tearing through Gideon's jacket as he slammed him into the floor.

"*No—*" she cried, the light hanging from the ceiling flickering as Benny threw herself from her father's grip, hands tingling with her magic.

Christian looked up, his gold eyes gleaming, amused at her outburst.

She hadn't managed so much as a spark in the last few days with Gideon, the explosive power she felt at the docks, the burning heat she attacked Mack with— it had been a struggle. But now, Benny felt her whole body tingling with an energy that felt unfamiliar. A power she was itching to use.

Was this it?

Christian seemed to have a similar question.

"What will you do, Benedetta?" he asked as he left Gideon on the floor, his body rising to his full height now, his clothing in tatters from where his limbs grew, his skin sallow. "Will you give us a little light show? Give me a fever? You don't have it in you. You hardly know your real power—"

He was goading her.

And it was working.

Because she could feel the heat start to work its way through her veins, her skin growing hot to the touch. Her heartbeat began to thud in double time as the light emitting from her hands grew brighter, enough for Gideon to lift his hand to shield his eyes as he got to his feet. She had thought it was rage. Or pain. Or fear. But it was more than that.

It was Gideon, charging toward a demon to protect her.

It was Benny, doing everything she could to protect him in return.

The room filled with a spectacular light, every ounce of her power striking Christian's heart, like a jolt of lightning as it scattered across his chest. She was struggling to maintain her breath, her hair beginning to stick to her skin as she fed into the magic. The bulb in the light fixture sparked and then shattered. Gideon tugged her backwards to avoid the fallout.

A mighty roar filled the room as it went dark, the only light coming from the open door behind them.

"Fuck," Gideon muttered. "Benny—hey, you okay?"

She blinked.

Had she blacked out?

All she could see was Gideon holding her face in his hands, blood splattered all over him, his eyes a mixture of pride and worry and something else she didn't have the energy to name. He was studying her, making sure she was alright, his hands smoothing back her hair, his thumb grazing against her cheek. She couldn't help but lean into it, to lean into him, his body solid and strong against hers.

"Did I do it?" she asked, trying to slow her breathing.

"You did it," he said.

"Wow, you sure love blowing shit up" came Luke's voice.

They both turned their attention to the open door, the rest of the men hovering in the doorway, the looks on their faces as if they had just seen something absolutely insane happen. Except for Luke, who seemed more amused than anything else. Gideon's hands dropped from her face and she couldn't help but feel all the more empty for it.

"What the fuck just happened?" Angelo asked.

TWENTY-TWO

GIDEON

THE DRIVE BACK TO Torretta's estate was quiet.

Gideon sat beside Benny in the backseat of the car, their bodies covered in a mixture of blood and viscera. He was exhausted, stiff, pain stemming from his shoulders and his side. He pressed at his temple, the skin tender and taut to the touch, his fingers sticky with what looked to be blood. His own, probably, from the gash at his forehead.

It was a hell of a way to spend a Saturday.

But then Benny curled up against him, letting her head rest on his shoulder and he knew he'd take a hundred tackles from some dickhead demon if it kept her from harm's way. He reached up to brush her hair back without thinking, his thumb grazing against her forehead. He knew he shouldn't. He just didn't have it in him to care. It was agonizing not to touch her. Especially now. She drew something out of him he hadn't expected, a deep-seated hope that he had been content to lock away.

Someone who wouldn't flinch at the parts of him that were unsavory. Someone who wouldn't run when things got hard. Someone who saw him. All of him. And still wanted to stick around.

Because tonight, when he thought Christian had his card, Benny made the whole goddamn room light up in an effort to protect him. She ran right into the fray. For him.

She had saved his life.

Benny leaned into his touch, and he dared a glance in her direction, brow furrowing as he noticed her hands. They were wringing in her lap, leaving traces of ash against the fabric of her T-shirt. It was something he had only briefly noticed that night at the docks. The way the tips of her fingers resembled the wick of a candle. Almost like she dipped them in soot. But he had been too absorbed in making sure the strange woman who fainted in his arms was going to last the car ride home to really think too much about it.

It was amazing what could change in just a couple of weeks.

He watched as she flexed her fingers in her lap, her body still rattling with adrenaline. He couldn't help but worry that she was going to slip into some kind of post-traumatic-stress-induced breakdown after what happened. She killed Christian. Or whoever—*whatever*—that fucking guy was. Gideon didn't want to judge. He didn't want to pull a "kick her while she's down" kind of thing, but Jesus fucking *Christ,* what a douchebag. He had gone into the room hating him on principle. But the absolute fucking rage he felt for him now?

Well, he certainly wasn't upset to see the guy-demon-whatever blown up into literal pieces.

Even if this was his second suit to go to shit in the same amount of weeks.

The transformation had been a hell of a shock. Like something out of his worst nightmares. He didn't have a lot of experience with interrogations. That wasn't his line of work. But he knew that they didn't usually result in demon transformations and explosions. So this was definitely competing to be one of the most chaotic days he'd had in a long while. And he'd once taken on a gang of vampires while his brother died in another room.

Gideon reached for her hands, gently stilling their fidgeting.

She looked up, a quiet breath passing through her lips as her eyes met his. There was a softness to her smile, an almost shy quality to it. It was so unlike her that he hardly noticed how tightly she was holding onto his hand.

She had been in complete control in the interrogation room.

It was a side of her he hadn't seen before. He liked it.

The crunch of the gravel underneath the tires seemed to signal something in Benny. She straightened slowly, giving his hand one more squeeze before she leaned toward her father in the driver's seat. She said something in Italian, he assumed, the words almost familiar but not quite.

Torretta nodded silently as they pulled up in front of the house.

If the man had seen the way they were sitting in the backseat, if he had seen how tangled up in each other they had been back at the warehouse, Torretta said nothing. But Gideon remembered the long look the older man had given him before the interrogation. The strict rule Benny had mentioned that the men in his crew were to stay away from her.

Did he count?

He sighed inwardly.

Whatever his feelings for Benny, he was pretty sure Torretta had not been betting on it.

Well, join the fucking club.

Luke twisted in his seat and let out a low whistle as they pulled into the driveway.

"Dude, you look like shit."

"Do I, Lucas? Thank you."

The car doors all slammed shut as they stepped from their respective spots, Torretta very quickly helping Benny from her side of the car. Gideon followed Luke to the Mustang, needing to grab one of his go-bags from the trunk. They had planned to spend a night, tops, at the compound but there was no way any of them were driving back to Philly now.

He kept Benny in his peripheral, finding it hard not to keep an eye on her as she walked into the house with her father. Torretta wrapped his arm around his daughter and tugged her into his side, the two of them talking in low hushed tones as they reached the front door. She turned back to look at Gideon, concern flickering across her features before she followed her father inside.

Luke chuckled as he popped the trunk. "You're so fucked."

"Shut up, Luke."

His younger brother only laughed as he tossed Gideon a leather duffle bag.

"Is that like, demon guts?" his brother said, leaning in closer. Disgust flashed across his face. "Jesus, what is that?"

"I don't know." Gideon sighed. He was trying not to think about it. "I need to shower."

"Benny's got some real shit taste in men, huh?"

Whether Benny's taste extended to Gideon remained to be seen. But he knew what Luke was getting at. "You're very funny."

"Did that guy look familiar to you?" Luke asked, slamming the trunk shut. "I mean, I know the crime circles can run small here, but I feel like we've worked with him before."

They had worked with dozens of men over the years, between the crew that worked for Markos and their own connections. But Gideon would have remembered Christian, he thought. Dick heads like that were hard to forget.

"If we ran a job with him before, I'd remember," he said. "He'd have been on the no fly list."

The *'We're Never Working With These Morons Ever Again'* list.

It was so much longer than the *'Competent People List'* they had.

"Spoken like a true Taurus, brother."

"Oh, no, fuck no," Gideon shook his head. "Don't tell me you're into that shit now."

"What?" Luke asked. "I've been doing a lot of reading on astrological signs recently. You'd be surprised how much it influences some of these rituals—"

"Nope. I'm good."

His brother laughed again as they reached the front door.

"What?"

"Capricorn moon."

"I'm gonna kill you."

"We should do Benny's birth chart."

"Leave Benny's birth chart alone," Gideon said.

"She's a Pisces, isn't she?" Luke wondered aloud. "You know that's not bad—"

The house was quiet as they entered. Benny must've gone upstairs and Torretta's men were still at the warehouse cleaning up. Where that left Torretta, Gideon had no idea. He was fine with not running into the old man. He ran his hand across his face, his body craving a very long, hot shower and about fifteen hours of sleep. But he wanted to find Benny. To make sure she was alright.

To thank her.

For saving his life.

"You."

Torretta lingered in the pass-through to the kitchen, his hand bracing against the jamb.

"Let's talk," he said, gesturing to Gideon.

Luke gave his brother a two-fingered salute before making some comment about catching the rest of the basketball game and took off toward the den. Gideon watched after him, muttering a curse under his breath. *Traitor.*

"Let's talk," Gideon mimicked, following him into the kitchen.

There was a bottle of bourbon and two tumblers on the table. Torretta wordlessly filled them with generous pours, sliding one in Gideon's direction as he sank into a seat at the head of the table. Gideon followed, hanging his suit jacket on the back of his chair before sitting in the chair catty-corner. Even the simple act of bending felt like an effort. But he said nothing, only nodded his thanks as he picked up his glass.

"*Salute,*" Torretta said.

The bourbon was warm, with hints of vanilla and it felt good on Gideon's throat.

"My kid, she's tough," Torretta said after a moment. "But I had no idea she was capable of that kind of magic. That was…"

"I know," Gideon said. "She's been working really hard to get it under control."

Torretta leaned back, tapping the edge of the glass against the table.

"I've been hard on her," he said. "Since her mother died, the idea of someone finding out about her had me all twisted up. I didn't want to lose her, too, you know?"

Gideon understood it, to an extent. She was too precious to lose. But he saw the effects that had on Benny, how fraught her relationship with him was. The way her face fell whenever her father alluded to her magic and how little he cared for her practice.

"But I almost did anyway," Torretta continued. "So where the fuck did that get me?"

"You've still got her," Gideon said. "You've just gotta let her *be*. The person you described when you hired us, that's only part of who she is. She's capable and smart. She's funny. I mean, she really knows how to bust your balls. And when she's practicing her magic, I've never see someone happier in my life. I would never want to take that away from her."

Torretta pursed his lips, his hand swirling the tumbler, sloshing the remaining liquid in the glass as he leaned forward. He rested his forearms on the table, a look that was hard to read flickering across the old man's face, thick brows narrowing. Gideon might've over-stepped. Might've said too much. But he couldn't take it back. He didn't want to.

Everything he said about Benny was true.

"You two have gotten close," Torretta said, finally.

He wanted to say yes. A part of him knew it to be true. They'd spent every single day together since they'd found her on the docks. Day and night in the same space, you get to know someone. The way they take their coffee, their favorite foods, their inability to stay quiet during a movie, the little bits and pieces that made a person whole.

But the way he felt about her…

Did she feel the same? What she'd done for him at the warehouse, wouldn't she do that for everyone? She'd said as much at the quarry, she'd put her life on the line for any of them. As much as he wanted her to be his, what could he give her in return? Not a life above the line.

He drained the rest of his glass.

"I should shower."

Torretta huffed a breath.

"Yeah, you really do look like shit."

Twenty-Three

BENNY

Benny's childhood bedroom was a time capsule to the teenaged version of herself who loved pastels and ballerinas and the lead actor in a high school drama that she watched with alarming regularity during its six-season run. Pale pink walls were covered in faded posters, and the ceiling still had those glow-in-the-dark stars scattered just above the white wrought-iron bed pressed up against the wall. The quilt that covered the queen-sized bed had been hand-stitched by her grandmother, the patchwork a collection of stars and moons in muted versions of all her favorite colors.

A very long and very hot shower had been her intent as she climbed upstairs but she hadn't gotten very far. She was standing at her dresser, staring into the mirror adorned with photos crammed in the frame, stickers reflecting off the glass. Photos of Jamie and Benny from prom, Imani and Olivia on the quad, old Polaroids faded from the years. Benny was a blight in the otherwise sweet bedroom. Her hair matted with blood, her hands streaked with ash, and her clothes covered in the remains of what Christian had become. Or always had been.

She looked down at her hands, surprised to find them steady.

The layer of ash clinging to her skin was a small physical reminder of her magic, the cost of what she had done. The blood on her hands, literal and not. There was always a price. And didn't killing someone come with the biggest price of all? And yet, her conscience felt clear. The ash a powerful reminder of what she could accomplish instead of a price to be paid.

The last few days had been a real whirlwind understanding of the true potential of her abilities. These weren't the kinds of things found in a history book, and her grimoire had never hinted that this was a possibility. She wished she had her mother. She wished she could ask her for advice, to help her understand. To just tell her how much she missed her. How sorry she was that the last thing she ever said to her was in anger. She still couldn't wrap her head around the connection they shared now, their place in this sadistic ritual.

So much had been taken from them both and for what?

To build a man up with power he didn't deserve?

Was that all Christian wanted?

She was never very good with relationships.

Benny thought it was a by-product of being a Strega. The allure of a long-term, monogamous relationship never held much appeal when you were constantly worried about your lifespan. But she'd had various flings over the years, men and women she'd meet on campus or witches from other covens…

But a demon? That was new.

It was hard to believe there was a time that she had been attracted to him. She groaned, her head hanging low. Maybe she'd never had a long-term, monogamous relationship because her taste was garbage. A literal bone-cracking, pain-seeking, demon kind of garbage.

She'd never seen anything like it before.

The transformation had happened so quickly, his attack on her so swift. If it weren't for Gideon… He had thrown himself to the wolves so many times for her. She kept telling herself 'a job is a job.' But that didn't stop her from wanting it to be more. Mean more.

Because she had finally learned how to control her power.

It was Gideon. Protecting Gideon.

The man who used his body as a shield for her with zero hesitation, just like he had at the quarry. The same man that walked into that room with her so she wouldn't have to face Christian by herself. The thought of anyone hurting him…

She could feel her palms heat at the thought.

Benny blinked her eyes shut.

She needed to stop thinking and just get in the damn shower.

But to her surprise, the moment she opened her bedroom door to grab some extra towels from the linen closet, she came face to face with Gideon, a duffle bag swung over his shoulder and his tie loosened around his neck. Her eyes drifted to that little patch of his throat, his shirt unbuttoned, the hint of that tattoo peeking out. She tried not to stare.

Had she somehow summoned him?

"Hi."

"Hey," he replied. "I was… just looking for the bathroom."

"Other side of the hallway," she said, pointing just past him.

Which he knew well enough, having already spent one night here. But she didn't mind. She wanted to see him. She wanted to make sure he was alright, to heal the parts of him that got hurt at her expense.

And maybe he wanted to be here too, because he lingered in the doorway, his eyes working their way up and down her body, in that way he did that first morning. Like he was tracking each and every inch of her to ensure she was all in one piece. Except this time, she felt her skin flush.

Everything was different now.

"You okay?"

His favorite question.

Or maybe it spoke more to how many weird and dangerous situations they had fallen into since knowing each other. Either way, she hardly knew the answer. But it didn't matter. Because he was standing here, on the threshold of her childhood bedroom, and the only thing she could think about was getting him out of that suit.

She leaned against the door jamb as she chewed on the inside of her cheek.

"I'm figuring that out," she told him. She had promised him honesty. She only wished she was brave enough to be fully truthful. "But maybe. I might have a better answer for you tomorrow."

"You don't have to have an answer at all, Benny."

But didn't she?

Wasn't she supposed to know how to feel after killing someone?

He leaned toward her, fingers brushing the hair off of her forehead as he leveled her with a look. Like he somehow knew what was going on in her head.

"Are you hurt?"

She felt a little dizzy, but that wasn't because of any injury. It was his hands on her skin, however fleeting. "I should be the one asking that question, Crawford."

"I don't care about me."

"But I do," she said, her voice cracking in a way she didn't expect. "I care. You can't keep putting yourself in harm's way for my sake, Gideon. You just can't— if something had happened to you tonight, I—"

"What?" he asked, his voice so gentle, his body so close. "What would you have done?"

She blinked back the irritating tears that had sprung to her eyes.

"I'd have burned down the whole warehouse," she said quietly.

A surprised breath passed through his lips.

"Fuck, Benny," he said, voice rough in a way that sent a wave of gooseflesh over her skin. "Come here."

Gideon cupped her face in his hands, his thumb brushing across her bottom lip before he crushed his mouth against hers without a second thought. Benny felt her whole body sigh with relief as her eyes fluttered shut, a soft breath passing from her lips to his. She curled her hands in the lapels of his suit jacket, tugging him backwards into her bedroom, magicking the door shut behind them with a soft click of the lock.

"Love that little trick," he said into her mouth, his hand tangling in her hair as he deepened their kiss.

Her lips parted eagerly for him, a quiet moan caught in her throat as he pulled her flush against him, every plane of his body warm and hard and hers to touch. He was careful as he guided her backwards, her body pressing against the door that led to her bathroom. She could feel the weight of him as his body crowded up against hers, the little thrill that trembled through her as his hands pressed against her hips, fingers digging into the soft skin at the waist of her jeans. He kissed her again, his lips soft and hungry, trailing from her mouth to the column of her throat to the soft spot just behind her ear. She hummed a little at the sensation.

She could hardly think straight.

Not while his hands were slipping under her T-shirt, fingers blazing along her skin.

"Gideon," she breathed.

His hands stilled so quickly she wondered if he was waiting for her to stop him.

"Are you okay?" he asked as he drew back. "Do you want me to stop?"

She shook her head. No. She wanted him to keep going, to keep touching her, kissing her. She wanted him to undo every button, to carry her right to her bed and slip beneath the sheets and show her if his hands were as talented as his mouth. She wanted all of it.

"You have to say it," he urged gently, his fingers tugging at the waist of her jeans.

"Please don't stop."

He sighed as he ran his hands up her sides, slipping his fingers beneath the lace of her bra, pressing his thumbs against the skin just below her breasts. The pressure made her squirm with pleasure.

"Thank Christ," he whispered.

She lifted her arms up as he stripped her of her shirt and tossed it to the floor. He gave her a look that made her feel wicked as he shrugged out of his jacket and loosened his tie further, tossing them both into the small pile forming at their feet. She reached for the buttons of his dress shirt, working through them as he watched her, her fingers leaving traces of ash against the crisp white. She paused, frowning, looking at the marks.

"I don't give a shit about this shirt, Benny."

She laughed in spite of herself as she pushed the shirt from his shoulders. He wore only a white tank top underneath, the fabric stretched across his chest. She ran her fingers down his stomach, feeling the way his muscles contracted beneath her touch. God, she wanted this gone.

He seemed to read her mind, his arms rolling the shirt from the bottom and pulling it up over his head. She could finally see the tattoo on his chest more clearly now, a portrait of a lion resting just above his heart, with gorgeous reds and yellows and oranges in the design. But before she could ask about it, he kissed her again, teeth nipping at her bottom lip.

"We should shower," he mumbled into her mouth.

"We should?"

He pulled back just slightly, a smirk curving at his lips.

"The places I want to touch you, princess," he said, his thumb teasing at her nipple through the lace of her bra. "Your body deserves me at my best."

She ran her tongue across her bottom lip as she reached behind them, her hand twisting at the doorknob. He walked her backwards, leaving her with another rough kiss on her mouth before he turned toward the shower. Her eyes tracked his movements, the way his back muscles ripped as he leaned forward to turn on the water. There was a small "E" tattooed in red on his right shoulder very close to what looked like a scar, a small round mark that looked oddly like a bullet entry point. When he turned back to look at her, water droplets collecting on his skin, his lips quirked devilishly.

"Benny," he said with a tilt of his head. "Take off your clothes."

She let out a breath.

Benny kicked off her sneakers and socks as she undid the fly of her jeans, watching Gideon as he watched her. The way he licked his lips as she pushed the denim down her thighs until she was clad in only her underwear. They didn't match. Cleo hadn't been as cognizant to pick anything that did. But that didn't seem to matter. Not when he was looking at her the way he was. In a way that made her feel more seen than she had ever felt before.

"Everything," he said, voice growing rough.

She almost held her breath as she undid the clasp of her bra, letting it fall to the floor beside her. She saw the look behind his eyes, the way they darkened as she hooked her fingers in the waistband of her underwear and shimmied the fabric down her hips. And when she was fully undressed, fully bare before Gideon, she stepped toward him with her singed fingers and skin stained with blood, and she kissed him.

There was a freedom in this new choice they made. The way she could just kiss him now, as much as she had wanted to before, with all the hope and the want that had been building up inside of her. He groaned as she nipped at his bottom lip, his hands grazing her back as she stepped away from him and into the shower.

The water was hot but felt good, her muscles crying out for the heat. She let the water wash over her hair, running her hands over her head as she turned to find Gideon still standing there, still half dressed, his hand rubbing at his chest.

"Are you going to keep me company or—"

He barked out a low laugh as he undid the belt of his pants, the bathroom soon littered with his clothing as well as hers. She was shameless in her perusal of his body, her eyes tracking every inch of him as he stepped under the shower head, the water dripping down each plane of muscle. His broad chest and strong shoulders, that delicious V at his hips. She spied another tattoo, this one taking up one side of his right thigh. Pharaoh's horses. It was beautiful. She felt her throat tighten at the sight of his cock hanging between his legs, hard and thick, and her eyes lingered on it for maybe a second too long because—

"What are you doing?" he asked, his hands scrubbing the muck off his face.

"Just wondering if you know how to use that thing," she replied as she reached for the shampoo.

Gideon rolled his eyes.

"You're gonna find out soon enough."

Benny accidentally squirted an aggressive amount of shampoo into her palm at the tone of his voice

"Oh no, come here."

A real shit-eating grin spread across his face as he stepped forward, their bodies barely an inch apart. She only cursed their height difference for a moment before she carefully lifted herself up on her toes to lather his hair with the shampoo. His grin felt infectious as she ran her hands through his hair, fingers massaging at his scalp. She watched as his eyes closed, his hands gripping at her waist, holding her steady against him.

She liked how well their bodies fit together.

Satisfied with the lathered-up spikes she'd given him, she used the remaining shampoo for her own hair, but Gideon didn't let her go, instead tugging her closer, watching her with a fondness she wanted to bottle. They had been this close before. Training on the roof or the night he carried her to the car, drunk from too many martinis. But this, this kind of closeness, it was different. It was tender and intimate.

It was also driving her absolutely mad with want.

She could feel every ridge and plane of his body pressed up against her, his cock hard against her belly, and yet he was content to hold her like this while she washed her hair.

"Time to rinse," she said.

He reached up with one hand to cover her eyes before shuffling them slightly backwards, the shower head raining down on both of them. She couldn't help her laughter as they both rinsed out their shampoo, his hand still covering her face. She reached up, fingers curling around his as she peeked out from behind his palm.

"I think you've protected my eyes, thank you."

"Just making sure I'm doing my job."

She felt her skin flush as she reached for the body wash. They had come a hell of a long way since that night. But even then, even in her drunken daze, the truth of her feelings had started to take form, however embarrassed she was of them. She had found that there was more to Gideon than he let on. More than the cocky, clever thief or the man who needed to be in control. And she had been unraveling those parts of him ever since, collecting all of those secret sides of him for herself.

Was it the same for Gideon? Was that was this was?

"Yes, you're a very good bodyguard, Crawford."

He growled as he cupped her chin in his hand.

"That's not what this is, Benny," he said. "This is not a part of the job for me. The way I feel about you—"

She could feel her chest start to tighten, the steady stream of the water working in tandem with the rhythm of her heartbeat, as she looked up to meet Gideon's gaze. He drifted closer, her body pressing up against the tile, her palms flat against the wall as he held her face in his hands. She tilted her chin back, her lips parting—

"I didn't expect to want you so much," he continued, his voice barely a whisper as he held her gaze. "I can't seem to go one fucking minute without wanting to touch you."

"Gideon—"

"Benny, listen to me." His words were like gravel, his thumb grazing against her bottom lip. "I don't want you to misunderstand me. When I kiss you, when I touch you, when I worry about you, it's not because of this job. I don't want it to be. I like you, princess. I like your smart mouth, and your inability to listen to a damn thing I say. I like you so fucking much that it's driving me out of my goddamn mind. But if you're unsure, if you want me to stop—"

"No," she said, shaking her head. "God, no, that's the opposite of what I want."

Something flickered behind his eyes. Something she had seen before.

A genuine warmth and affection that made her stomach flip and her body feel like it was on fire.

She reached for the handle and turned off the water.

"I like you, Gideon Crawford. I like every part of you," she said. "And I very much need you to touch me now."

His lips curved into a smile that made his eyes crinkle, and she reached up, her fingers tracing at the lines. She liked him very much. She liked his smiles and how they transformed his face. She liked how protective he was and how much he went to bat for the people around him. How gentle he was with her when she needed him to be.

Like he knew just what she needed, when she needed it.

She reached up and kissed him—his mouth, his jaw, his nose, every inch of his face until he was laughing again, his arms scooping her up and carrying her carefully out of the shower. He dried her off with a towel before he led her to her bed in all of its teenage pastel glory. She couldn't believe she had him in her bedroom like this. Why hadn't she been cooler as a kid? But he didn't seem to mind. Not when he was laying her on her back, his body drawing over hers, his mouth already making its way down her throat. And then she knew, no matter what happened next, that things would never be the same between them.

TWENTY-FOUR

GIDEON

BENNY WAS LAUGHING.

It was a sweet sound, a little breathless, her fingers tugging at his hair still damp from the shower as he dragged his mouth down her throat. Gideon hadn't exactly expected that to be the first sound she made, but it wasn't the worst reaction, right? He continued his path across her skin, his lips working their way at the soft curve where her neck met her shoulder, and her laughter quieted into a soft hum, a low moan as his teeth nipped at her skin. She dug her nails into his shoulders, the sting echoing through the rest of him, and he relished in the feel of it.

This was the kind of pain he liked.

Her body arched against his as he cupped her breast, fingers finding the soft peak of her nipple, his thumb teasing until it grew hard under his touch, another whimper passing through her lips as he replaced his fingers with his tongue. But it was the friction of bare skin on bare skin, both still slick from the shower, that turned him hard.

Again.

As if he hadn't been since she dragged him into her bedroom.

But there was that laughter again, soft, but still there.

He drew his eyes up, fixing her with a curious glance as he shifted to his side.

"You know, the laughing would be cute if I wasn't working toward different kind of noise," he told her, his finger grazing a steady and slow line from her between her breasts down to her belly button.

"I'm sorry," she said, her body squirming under his touch, her head turning to meet his gaze, her skin just slightly flushed and pink. "I just can't believe I finally have you naked, and I'm staring up at a ballerina kitten poster."

"Finally?" he asked, raising an eyebrow.

"A woman might have thought about it."

"I'm gonna want to know more about that later."

He hadn't given one thought to the posters on the walls, far too consumed with the woman beside him, all lush curves and soft skin and beautiful wide mouth. But his eyes flickered around the room, his lips curving into a smile when he took in their surroundings—the pink walls, the posters and prints framed above the bed, the comforter they were currently laying on top of a sort of pastel celestial thing. And then there was Benedetta Russo, who wore band T-shirts and sneakers.

He leaned in to press a kiss against her stomach, his hand squeezing at the curve of her hip. "If all you can think about is that cat poster, I'm not working hard enough."

"Maybe so," she hummed, her fingers toying with his hair.

It was his turn to laugh, the sound muffled against her skin as he trailed kisses down the soft swell of her belly. His lips lingered at the small patch of curls between her thighs, his breath ghosting against her skin as she let her legs part for him. He bit back a groan, grateful for the invitation. Benny let out a little breath as he draped her leg against his shoulder, his mouth trailing errant kisses along her inner thigh. He teased his thumb against her clit, finding her wet and perfect and so fucking soft as he slid in one finger, then another. She twitched beneath his touch, and he felt his cock mimic the feeling, but all he wanted to do was find out if she was as sweet here as she was everywhere else.

"Fuck, Benny," he breathed. "I can't wait to find out how you taste."

She gasped as his mouth found her once again but this time right at the core of her, his tongue teasing her, taking his time, tasting her slowly. And fuck if he wasn't right. If she wasn't absolutely fucking perfect. If he wasn't eager for the way her legs wrapped around him or the way her hands turned to fists in his hair as he worked his fingers in tandem with his tongue.

"*Oh,*" she said, her voice soft, her hips rising just slightly.

His other hand splayed against her stomach, pressing down to keep her steady beneath him as he crooked his fingers just slightly, enough to draw another low and heady moan from Benny. His eyes flickered up as he worked his tongue deeper inside of her, watching as her back arched, her eyes fluttering shut, a smile working its way across her face. It was blissful, free, relaxed.

Rare emotions considering the last couple of days.

Well, he was going to make sure this lasted.

He drew her clit into his mouth, increasing the pressure of his fingers, and he could feel her body twitch again, her grip in his hair tightening.

"Gideon, oh, I'm—"

But her body finished the sentence her mouth couldn't as she reached her peak. It was in the way her thighs tightened around his shoulders, the little convulsions of pleasure in her body that vibrated against his own, and the muffled scream, the back of her hand pressed up against her mouth to combat the sound. It seemed to undulate through her until she was giggling through unsteady breaths, curling her upper body slightly. But he stayed put, gripping her tightly, savoring the taste of her until she was pliant beneath him. And even then, even as he drew back, he was still invested in tracing every line of her body with his mouth.

His hands smoothed along her thighs as he rested back on his heels. His eyes trailed the length of her body and the way it fit so neatly against his as he positioned himself between her legs. Benny looked up at him from beneath those thick, long lashes and eyes that were so dark and round and warm. But her lips were curling into a smile, her gaze steady as she reached for him and it lit him up from the inside.

"Come here, please."

"Yes?" he replied as he leaned back down, unable to hide his own smile as she wrapped her arms around him. "Can I help you?"

"Do you think," she started, her fingers beginning to trace little shapes against his skin, her tone innocent and questioning, and Gideon knew it wouldn't matter what she asked for, he would do it, "that little go bag of yours has condoms along with whatever three-piece suit you have tucked away in there?"

He stifled his laugh. "As a matter of fact, Benedetta, it does."

He was the kind of guy who liked to be prepared.

She pressed a soft kiss to his jaw as those shapes she was tracing turned into a sharp line down the center of his back, and he could feel his muscles twitch at the sensation. And when her mouth moved to his throat and her teeth nipped at his skin, she lifted her hips just slightly against his. He could feel his cock press at the slick center of her and he bit back another groan.

"You should get one," she said, her voice barely a whisper in his ear. "Or two."

He pressed a kiss to her mouth before he pushed himself up. Who was he to keep the woman waiting? Even if the sudden loss of her warmth left a chill working its way through his skin. He wasn't actually sure where he kept the condoms, somewhere in a side pocket, and after removing an extra round of ammo and a pair of black of gloves, he found them.

Benny was kneeling on the bed when he turned back, resting on her heels, her hair a mass of curls and waves around her face. Her skin was tinged with a little pink, her hips bearing the faint marks of where he'd held her. She was chewing on her bottom lip, her eyes trailing his every movement. He felt a weird tug in his chest, a twist, an ache, and he rubbed at the spot absently as he reached the foot of the bed.

She took the condoms from his hand with a sly smile. "I'll take these, thank you."

They were nearly eye-level with each other, the lift of the bed giving her a bit of a boost, and before he could even question her, she cupped his face in her hands and kissed him. She leaned in, letting her body rest against his, her breasts pressed up against his chest, her hips nearly aligned with his. Gideon's hands found the small of her back, the curve of her ass, the soft flesh as he dug his fingers into her skin.

He wasn't sure he had ever wanted someone so badly before. And when her mouth trailed from his, finding its way down to his chest and then his abdomen, the muscles contracting with every swipe of her tongue, something a little wistful passed through his lips. Like a sigh molded around her name.

"Benny—"

She had wrapped her hand around the base of his cock, her tongue drawing light circles around his shaft, her back arched enough that he had this incredible view of her ass if he watched her. But he could feel his eyes flutter shut as she took him into her mouth and his head tilted back, his throat working over itself. He wrapped her hair around his fist as she let his cock slide in and out and the way she stroked him made his muscles tighten. His hips gave a little twitch, and he moaned, unable to help himself. She felt too good. He ran his tongue over his teeth as he opened his eyes, seeing the way she looked up at him as she took him further, deeper, and he could have died right there.

But she drew back just slightly, and he could hear the tear of the wrapper. And he could hardly contain himself once she rolled it down. Gideon wrapped his arm around her lower waist and moved them both further up the bed until her body was once again beneath his, her legs drawn up against his hips. She was looking up at him with that smile, a little self-satisfied smirk, and she was right.

She had gotten him.

He'd nearly come with just her mouth.

He kissed her, and he could swear he tasted the mixture of them both on his tongue as he pressed his hips down against hers, his cock teasing at her entrance. She moaned into his mouth, her hands pressing into his shoulders as he rocked against her. Benny dragged one hand toward his jaw, her thumb pressing against his bottom lip. He teased her again and another gasp left her lips.

"Gideon," she breathed. "I'm losing my mind."

He smirked. "Is that right, princess?"

She tugged at his hair, drawing his lips against hers.

"I need to feel you inside of me," she said. "Please."

Fuck. He wanted that too. So badly.

"Since you asked so nicely."

He reached between them, both their bodies slick with sweat and sex. He worked his cock against her entrance slowly, inch by inch. She squirmed against him, working her hips to take him deeper, her breath a little whine that made him feel like he was going to lose it right there. But she was tight and warm and felt every bit as good as he thought she would. Gideon knew that sex with someone for the first time could be awkward—hell, he'd had plenty of one-night stands that were less than fulfilling. But this? All the ache and need and pure want?

"You're fucking perfect," he couldn't help but say as he fully sank into her, his words a mess of a groan as he began to buck his hips. "Christ, Benny, the way you feel—"

"I know," she said. "I know, this is—"

But neither of them managed to finish as their mouths found each other again, the kiss growing more intense, a little sloppy, both of them hungry for each other. And for a long moment, it was like they were completely lost in each other, their bodies falling into a rhythm. Like they were becoming acquainted with each other in a completely new way.

Gideon snaked his hand around her back, pulling them both up so that she was in his lap, his hips still rocking with hers as he held her upright. The position gave them both an edge and an incredible friction, and he loved the way she rode him, her hips pressing against him with every rise and fall of her body.

He clutched his hand against her lower back as the other curved at her breast, his thumb toying at the stiff bud of her nipple, and she tilted her head back as a low hum vibrated on her lips, her hair hanging around her shoulders. He kissed her throat, her chest, unable to keep his mouth off of her. A sudden tingle worked its way through his body as she ran her hands along his back, his shoulders, ruffling through his hair, and his name tumbled from her lips so softly.

"What magic is this," he grumbled against her skin.

"It's just me," she whispered. "It's how you make me feel."

It was a warmth and a little vibration, a sizzle of something he couldn't quite grasp. It felt fucking incredible. Was that how he made her feel? He moaned against her skin, letting the magic work through him.

She murmured something and Gideon lifted his head to meet her gaze.

"Use your words, princess."

"Touch me again," she said, her tone pleading. "Please."

The corner of his mouth curved into a smirk as he dragged his hand down, his fingers pressing against her clit, moving in soft circles and the way she clenched against him forced a low groan from the back of his throat. He was nearing his own peak now, just close enough he could feel the sensation working through him in a kind of frenzied buildup. She shifted against him, finding her leverage with his hand, squeezing her thighs around his hips in a way that dragged another heavy breath from him.

"You feel incredible when you do that," he managed roughly. "But you're gonna make me come if you don't stop."

Benny's laughter was light as she whispered, "But that's what I want. Let's see who gets there first."

He grunted as she sucked his earlobe into her mouth, teething at his skin. She might just be the winner. Or maybe he was. It didn't matter. He was lost to every inch of her. He increased his pressure on her clit, his other hand working its way down to the curve of her ass, fingers digging into the flesh as he bucked up into her. He wanted to feel her fall apart on his cock, just like he had his hands and his mouth. It was a fucking privilege.

Benny's body seemed to almost spark as her hips convulsed against his. She was gripping so tightly on his shoulders, he was sure she was going to leave a mark. Which was no different from what he already felt was there, but at this least one would be visible. Her face was buried in his shoulder, her moans and whimpers sending him over the edge. One arm clutched her tightly to him as he felt himself come, his cock twitching inside of her. He could feel the release work through him like a wave of shocks over and over again, and he couldn't remember the last time it had been this intense. His growl turned into a moan as he let it ride through him.

They both lingered there, in each other's arms, bodies too entwined and spent to move for the moment. She rested her forehead against his, and he snuck a kiss, a light one, just barely grazing her lips. She laughed as she brushed her fingers through his hair, seemingly trying to fix whatever had happened to it after the shower.

"I think you won," she whispered.

TWENTY-FIVE

THE WAREHOUSE

THE MOOD IN THE warehouse was precarious and delicate.

He knew that his men were waiting for his reaction. What kind of response would he have after another loss? After all, he had spent the last fifteen years waiting for the precise right moment to arrive in order to complete the ascension. And he had been so incredibly patient. Biding his time. Ensuring nothing would prevent him from achieving the final step. Because the requirements of the ritual had been quite clear, and up until recently, each piece of the puzzle had been within his reach.

Even the stone heart of the sun.

The Heart of Fire.

It had felt like fate—kismet, in fact, when news of the gala reached him. Was this a gift from beyond the gates? Were they speaking to him? Telling him that he was on the right path? He had held fast to this belief, allowing it to empower him as he began to collect. The untouched blood, the Strega, the offerings that would move him beyond the temporary veil of this preternatural invulnerability he was granted. A little gift from below to protect him as the ascension neared.

But now, word came that one of his best soldiers was gone.

Doluviri was a shapeshifter. A rare child of a human and a demon, gifted with the uncanny ability to sway or attract certain things into their favor. A creature so strong, he felt very little pain. The perfect choice to infiltrate the Caruso family. To seduce Benedetta Russo. To ensure that the witch would become easy prey. And Doluviri had played the role of Christian d'Aviano perfectly, picking out each and every delicious weak point in the witch all while keeping her out from underneath her father's thumb.

His death was a loss.

A setback he did not need. And his patience was wearing thin. Thin enough to wear a line in the concrete floors of his office as he paced back and forth. And he was still no closer to having the witch back in the cage where she belonged.

The gala was in just one week, and there was plenty to prepare.

He just had one little problem to deal with.

The Crawford brothers.

TWENTY-SIX

BENNY

IT WAS JUST AFTER three o'clock in the morning when Benny found herself wide awake and tucked beneath Gideon's heavy arm, his body strewn across hers, his breath soft and steady against her skin. She was on her side, back pressed against his front, and the weight of him felt good. So good that she almost tried to will herself back to sleep. But the urge to pee was stronger, and so she shifted very carefully out from his grasp and slid from underneath the covers. She was still naked, and a shiver worked its way through her body as she crossed the bedroom.

She grabbed an old T-shirt from her dresser before moving into the bathroom, her skin flushing as she saw the piles of their clothing littered across the floor, the shower door still open. Her eyes widened as she saw her reflection in the mirror. Her hair was out of control, her curls a maddening mixture of flat and voluminous and sticking up in ways she wasn't sure were possible. She tried to smooth it out, brushing her fingers through it, grimacing in the mirror.

Well. These were the risks that came with frantic post-shower sex.

A thought that brought a funny smile to her face.

She'd never really been with anyone who put her pleasure first.

It was an intoxicating kind of discovery. And although she was still trying to wrap her head around everything that had happened in the last few weeks, Benny knew that the feelings she had developed for Gideon Crawford were real. The kind of ache she could feel in her bones. She had held onto them until she couldn't anymore. She saw who Gideon wanted to be for her. She could love him, she thought.

She could fall right in love with him.

Benny knew deep down that she was the reason her previous relationships never had much depth. Falling in love had never suited her when she knew she was living on borrowed time. She had always been too afraid to hand herself over to someone.

But Gideon felt different.

She wanted him to be different.

Benny wasn't sure she was going to make it, so why couldn't she just have this one good thing?

She winced at the sound of the toilet flushing, then tiptoed back into her bedroom, wiping wet hands on her T-shirt before climbing back into the bed.

Gideon pressed a light kiss to her forehead before wrapping his arm around her, scooping her back up against him. She could feel the easy strength in his grasp despite just how gentle he was being with her. There was something about knowing both versions of him that made her wriggle that much closer to him.

"I didn't mean to wake you."

"You can wake me up any time," he murmured into her hair, voice rough with sleep. The hum of it brought a tingle to her skin. "You alright?"

She sighed, her eyes blinking shut.

"Yeah, I am," she replied. She shifted onto her back. "Which is freaking me out. I shouldn't be, right?"

Gideon pushed himself up onto his elbow. It was dark in the room but her eyes had adjusted, and glimmers of moonlight peeked through the edges of her curtains, allowing her to see the traces of sleep on his face. His soft eyes, and how a flicker of concern passed through them.

"That depends," he said. "Is this freak out about the murder or the sex?"

"Jesus," she groaned. "*Murder?*"

"Oh, good," he said, relieved. "I was hoping it wasn't the sex."

Benny rolled her eyes, "Gideon."

He snuck a small kiss to her nose before he brushed her hair back. "I know this is hard," he said. "This felt different than the docks, didn't it?"

Her nose wrinkled. "I didn't fuck that vampire on the docks."

Gideon twisted his head to the side.

"Sorry," she grimaced. "It's just—"

"It's fine," he said, waving his hand. "The visual was fleeting. But I get it."

"Does it get easier?"

"No. But it shouldn't. If it starts getting easier, you're venturing into serial killer territory."

"Oh, sure, yeah," Benny replied.

"We are constantly weighing the cost, princess and your life has to rank at the top. Someone tries to hurt you, some *thing* comes after you— there can't be any other outcome than you walking out that door with your life."

"It wasn't about me," she said quietly.

He considered her, his features softening.

"Well I'm not gonna complain."

"Should I have told you about him?"

"You don't owe me that," he said. "We've been going a hundred miles per hour the last couple of weeks. We get through this ritual, we'll have all the time in the world to go through our shitty exes."

Benny propped herself up on her elbows.

"How many shitty exes?" she asked.

A smile stretched across his face as he gently nudged her back down.

"Not that many," he assured. "And they were all human as far as I'm aware."

"Boring," she said, matching his smile. That word triggered something. "Wait, where is your brother?"

Gideon's chuckle was low and quiet and she felt it more than heard it.

"He was passed out on the couch when I came upstairs," he said. "But he's been running on fumes for a while."

"Since me?"

He brushed his fingers through her hair, and she briefly wondered just how stupid it still looked until his thumb grazed against her skin, distracting her from the thought completely.

"This shit is like catnip to him. Luke has always been curious by nature. But since he's turned..." he trailed off, brow furrowing slightly. "Finding out there's been a whole world out there we didn't know about—I think he's trying to catch up or something."

Benny wasn't sure she could remember the first time she heard of the Crawford brothers. The infamous bank robbers were sort of always on the board in the Caruso family. Part of an underground who's who. They had a reputation for intricate heists that left the police deeply confused, which made them hard to track and valuable. But she had heard something from her father—about a shootout in Chicago that resulted in one of the brothers turning. And how surprised he'd been when he learned they were still working together. Human and vampire.

"Was the transition hard?" she asked.

Gideon didn't answer, his eyes blinking shut for a moment.

"It was the scariest fucking thing I'd ever experienced," he said, finally. "I didn't understand what was happening until it was too late. The job had seemed routine. It passed all our usual sniff tests, you know? I still don't know what it was that made Luke the target. Things between us got bad for a while after that. I lost him for a little bit."

He started to play with her hair again, fingers brushing against her scalp. Like it soothed him to touch her while he spoke. Benny curled up closer against him.

"But he's all I've got," he continued, voice quiet. "It's always just been us. Even when our dad was alive, he was always on a job. And our mom dipped out when Luke was six. So when he turned, I just had to figure out how to deal with it."

He let out a breath.

"It still kills me a little bit when his face changes."

Benny frowned.

"How old were you?" she asked.

He looked at her, a confused flicker behind his eyes.

"When your mother left," she clarified. "Luke was six. How old were you?"

"I had just turned ten."

"Gideon." Benny sighed, her hand reaching up to cup his face. "You were just a little kid. You shouldn't have had to take on a responsibility like that."

"My dad wasn't exactly a guy who could make his own hours," he replied. "But he provided for us. I just did what I could to handle the rest."

"In the fifth grade."

"It wasn't that bad," he told her, inching his head toward her as his lips brushed against her nose. "We managed, and when we couldn't, we figured it out."

She tried to visualize a ten-year-old Gideon Crawford. She wondered if he still had the same sardonic smile when he was feeling particularly proud of himself or the same wrinkled brow when he was unsure, if his hair still had the same cowlick at the back of his head. If all those years ago, he had completely different aspirations for what his life would have been. Or if it would somehow have always been this. And she felt the ache of it all the same.

"Well, it's not just the two of you anymore," she said.

His brow knit as he considered her.

"You've got Cleo and Harker," she told him before she pressed her lips to his. She let her mouth linger there for just a moment, his lips so soft and full against hers, as she drummed up her courage. "And me. You've got me, Gideon. If you want."

He smiled.

"I do," he said, his hand smoothing at her hip. "I want you in every way."

"I wish you would have told me."

"There were more pressing matters to attend to," Gideon said, fixing her with a roguish grin.

They were still in bed, the hazy morning light drifting in through the curtains. Benny was resting on her heels beside him, her hand pressed against a nasty bruise that had formed overnight on his shoulder. Right where Christian had slammed into him as they were rolling around on the floor of the warehouse. He lay on his back, one arm tucked behind his head, his hair mussed from sleep and his gaze predatory as she let her magic do its work. The sheet was barely covering his hips, his naked body beside her a tempting distraction as she tried to focus.

"Is that right?" She bit back the smile that threatened to overtake her face, her skin warm with the memories of last night, and earlier that morning… "Are there any other bumps and bruises you're hiding from me, Crawford?"

"I got slammed into concrete by a ten foot tall demon," he said. "I think my whole body is one giant bruise."

She frowned as her magic cooled, the bruise beginning to dissipate under her touch. She had been so scared, the thought of anything happening to him almost too much to bear—

"No, hey," he said, pushing himself up to sit. He reached for her, his hand curving at her jaw. "I'm good, princess. Still standing and everything."

Benny leaned into his touch, her eyes fluttering shut for a moment.

"It's amazing what you can do," he told her. "Thank you."

"Well I'd genuinely appreciate it if you stopped throwing yourself into fights with the super strong demonic beings we've been encountering," she said.

"Not sure I can promise that considering our circumstances. But I'll do my best."

She laughed, "No, you won't. I think you like seeing if you can knock 'em around."

The grin that stretched across Gideon's face was almost boyish, his eyes crinkling, the hazel looking particularly green in the bright, natural light.

"It ain't bad for the ego, I'll say that."

Her smile turned into a yawn as she stretched her arms above her head, the old T-shirt she'd grabbed riding up on her waist. She could crawl right back under the covers and sleep another eight hours. Benny had half a mind to make that exact suggestion when Gideon grabbed her and pulled her back down to lay beside him, his legs tangling with hers.

"We should probably get out of this bed," he said, his nose nuzzling against her neck.

She tilted her head back, his mouth warm and soft against her skin, her fingers teasing light strokes down his arm. "Is that what you really want to do?"

"No, baby," he said, the timber of his voice deep enough to make her squirm against him. He hooked his hand underneath her knee, draping her leg over his. "What I want is to stay here in this bed with you and learn every place you like to be touched."

She dug her fingernails into his bicep as his hand dragged up her thigh.

"You've gotten quite a few of them," she said, her breath catching as he squeezed her hip.

"I want them all, Benny," he said, his mouth finding hers again with a rough kiss. "But we've got work to do today. And as much as I've grown to love this room, I'd much rather have you back in my own bed at home."

"Oh, that does sound appealing," she said, though that didn't stop her from pressing herself against him, feeling him hard against her. "Does this mean you're moving back into your room?"

"If you'll have me."

She licked at her lips as she found his gaze, those hazel-green eyes soft and warm.

"It's about damn time."

He barked out a laugh as he rolled her onto her back and the weight of his body felt delicious against her own. She drew her legs up to his hips, a defiant look on her face as she reached between their bodies, her hand wrapping around the length of him. She relished in the soft moan that passed through his lips as she began to stroke him.

"Benny, baby, you're killing me," he groaned, his hips twitching.

"I can play a dirty game, Crawford," she said, her hand warming with her magic. He buried his face in her neck, another soft sound muffled against her skin. "And it's only fair, I've got a little catching up to do after last night—"

"That's not how this works," he said. "You don't have to—"

"I want to," she said, voice soft.

She'd played with magic in the bedroom before, especially with other witches, but this was different. The way her power flowed through her, it felt like she was giving a part of herself to Gideon, letting him feel her in ways she'd never experienced with anyone else before. It was a pleasure akin to rapture, and she wanted nothing more than to share that with him.

Feeling him come undone in her hands was a gift.

"*Baby*," the word a moan as it slipped from his lips, his hips bucking against her hand and she let the energy flow, working his cock over with her magic until he spilled out of her hand and onto her belly. "Fuck, Benny—"

He sank against her and she wrapped her arms around his broad back, fingers brushing through the hair at the nape of his neck. She felt a satisfaction ripple through her, and she pressed a kiss to his temple. She wanted to stay here, just like this, keep them out of the outside fray as long as possible.

"That was," but Gideon couldn't seem to formulate anything more than a lopsided grin as he turned his head to catch her gaze. "Jesus, Benny."

She smiled.

"Should we shower again?"

TWENTY-SEVEN

LUKE

"So, what? Are you two going steady now?"

"Will you shut the fuck up?"

Luke let out a deep laugh as he plucked his glasses from his face. He had thought the big bad Angelo Torretta was going to tell his brother to fuck off, a far more generous forecast considering what he knew the man was capable of. But when Gideon came downstairs this morning, hardly bruised after that dust-up with the demon ex-boyfriend, and Benny trailing behind him with a big dopey smile on her face, it seemed that whatever conversation his brother had with the head of the Caruso family went a lot better than Luke thought it would.

So maybe he *could* go a tiny bit easier on Gideon.

It wasn't like he hadn't noticed the little changes he had seen in his brother over the last couple of weeks, like the protective dumbass caveman thing or the way he doted on Benny when he thought no one was paying attention. It was just outside of his typical character, which was something Luke was having trouble reconciling.

All these years, he'd never seen his brother take to a woman this way.

Not since before their father died. And that was simple, high school shit.

Luke rubbed his glasses against the lapel of his jacket.

"It's cool, brother," he started as he slipped the wire-rimmed frames back on, his eyes squinting against the bright sun ahead of them on the highway. He flipped down his visor, thankful Gideon had the windows tinted on this thing. "I like Benny. She's good for you. She knows exactly how to make that vein pop on your forehead."

Even if being in her vicinity was a constant test of Luke's endurance.

"Sweet of you to say, Lucas."

There was a hint of amusement behind Gideon's eyes, an easiness to his brother he hadn't seen in a long time. Too bad he was about to fuck that right up. He cleared his throat.

"The gala next week. I have a feeling we're going to see an old friend there."

Gideon tossed him a look. His brother had always been good at reading Luke. Too good, probably. "I thought Tefi was in Europe."

"She was."

He had been surprised when he heard from her.

He had thought—no, he had hoped—her disappearance off the continent was going to be permanent. The end of their relationship was tumultuous, violent. It was plain fucked, if Luke was being honest with himself. Which he had a hard time with where Tefi was concerned. He didn't like the hold she had over him. The sort of dull ache he still felt when she was nearby. They say a vampire never really loses the connection to their sire. And no matter where Tefi traveled, whatever country or continent, Luke felt that connection intrinsically. Like it was her blood still flowing through his veins. Like he could still hear her whispering into his ear.

"And what does she want with a charity gala?"

"It's the auction," Luke replied. "There's something on the list she wants."

"Are you sure she's not just saying that?"

"I know her too well not to pick up on her tells," Luke said. "Tefi loves shiny things, don't get me wrong, but I don't think she's after the ruby."

"Well, she better fucking behave," he muttered.

Luke coughed out a laugh.

"You know better than to expect that," he said. "But she won't be a problem."

"Tefi is *always* a problem."

Well, he couldn't exactly argue with that.

The warehouse loomed ahead of them, the afternoon light hazy as they pulled into a small parking lot. Pasquale and Jamie were waiting for them outside, the two involved in some animated conversation that Luke couldn't pick up from within the car but he noted the aggressive hand waving. He wanted to brush that off as a quirk of Benny's family at large but there was something behind the younger man's eyes that piqued his interest.

Something to store in the back of his brain for later.

"Pull up close to the entrance will ya?" Luke asked.

"You don't wanna speed run inside?"

"Funny."

While Benny and Gideon were in the interrogation room yesterday with the ex-demon douchebag, Luke had dove in to the archives of the Caruso family. It held the items and goods they hadn't sold yet, the ones waiting for verification, and the things they didn't want to part with. It was incredible. Filled with priceless heirlooms and ancient texts, probably half a dozen amulets that were cursed... it certainly rivaled Harker's library. But the monster explosion cut his time short and Torretta was more than happy to grant him more access knowing what was at stake.

He thought Benny would come with them, but Torretta had asked her to stay behind.

Gideon parked right beside an overhang and the men approached just as they slammed the car doors shut. Luke adjusted the cuffs of his sleeves, eyes darting back and forth between father and son. Jamie must take after his mother. Tall and fair and pretty. Nothing like the short, grizzled old Pasquale.

"Angelo said you were looking for something?" Jamie asked.

"A book," he said as they ducked inside, the warehouse cool and air conditioned compared to the heavy heat hanging in the outside air. "I should've grabbed it yesterday but what with the *incident*—"

Gideon raised his eyes to the heavens.

The Healer raised a pale brow.

"And you have permission to just take it?"

"Kid, they wouldn't be here if they didn't," Pasquale said.

Jamie said nothing but his face spoke volumes. He didn't trust the Crawfords. Not like Luke gave a shit. They had Benny's trust, and Angelo's. That was enough.

They followed the men down a clear hallway, the warehouse quiet. When they reached the room that led to the archives, the energy in the air changed. He could only imagine the wealth of power behind the large double doors, the money that came with it. It was enough to consider expanding the kind of loot the boys looked for in future gigs.

"You go on in," Pasquale said with a wave. "James and I are here to make sure the boys cleaned up last night. It's a hell of a hard time to get demon blood cleaned up, you know?"

"Tell me about it," Gideon muttered.

Twenty-Eight

Benny

Benny had missed the first day of the fall semester at Penn.

She had missed the second, third, fourth, and fifth days, too.

Olivia had mentioned the other night that they'd shut down their wing in an effort to clean up the destruction left behind by the men who'd taken Benny. It had been the talk of the campus. No one knew why it happened, the investigation still ongoing. Night security had been increased, and curfews enacted for all students and professors. It wasn't exactly the exciting welcome to campus they'd all expected for the new school year.

When Benny had thrown herself into academia, it had been to escape the allure of her father's work. She had found herself slipping into the roll of mafia don with a surprising ease. Even in the interrogation room with Christian, she'd felt a little thrill at the opportunity. It hadn't been fear that had her hesitating at the threshold of the room, it had been the excitement gnawing at her. The last few weeks with the Crawford brothers had only solidified that academia had been an escape.

The blood magic, the power dynamics.

Boxing with Gideon, learning how to harness her power, digging through ancient tomes to stop an ascension. Her life had been upended in ways she could never have imagined. A blissfully quiet, academic life traded for vampires and thieves and demon hunting. How could she be content now in her little corner of the lab?

She had lied to Jamie. She didn't miss school.

Benny wanted to finish her program. She wanted to defend her thesis. The completion of the last five years of her life's work was important to her. But the future she had envisioned for herself didn't seem right anymore. It was a life without risk. A life worried about a death that would come whether she hid herself or not.

She didn't know what was next— if there was a next at all.

If she would survive the ritual.

But she knew that if that was all the time she had left, she wasn't going to hide herself anymore. She wasn't going to bury herself down deep in an effort to protect herself. She was going to keep learning how to fight. She was going to go down swinging.

"You know, I shoulda given this to you fifteen years ago—"

Her father's voice snapped her from her thoughts, and Benny looked up, startled by the admission. Angelo was standing with his back to her, his shoulders hunched, his fingers grazing the spine of a leather-bound book on his bookshelf. He let them linger there for a moment, and she was almost certain that his hand was shaking. She frowned, sitting up a bit straighter in the leather chair she had been curled up in since Gideon had left with Luke to go to the warehouse.

"Babbo, what are you talking about?"

Her father slowly pulled the book from the stack, his head bowed as he turned toward her. It didn't have any words etched on the binding, and the brown leather cover was plain, only a single wisp of gold embossed where a title would be. She pressed her lips together as he walked toward her, a look of guilt flashing across his weathered features.

"This was your mother's," he said. "A journal she kept."

Benny reached for the book tentatively with both hands.

"Mom kept journals?" she asked, eyes focused on the soft and worn spots on the edge of the cover, like her mother had left her fingerprints in the leather for her to find. She traced her fingers around them, unable to flip the cover open.

"Notes, really," he said, his large hand coming up to rub at his jaw. "Stuff to do with her magic. Things she didn't think had a place in the grimoire."

"What do you mean?" Benny looked up, startled. "We're supposed to write everything in the grimoire. That book is all we have."

Angelo sank into the chair beside her, his hands resting against his chest.

"Your mother was different, Ben," he said. "That power you got, it scared the shit out of her."

It used to scare Benny, too.

But that was beginning to change.

"I still don't understand," she said, shaking her head, both her hands gripping the book. Her confusion was beginning to morph into a kind of resentment. "You've had this the whole time? Why didn't you say anything? Why would you keep this from me?"

"I don't know," he replied. "I kept thinking I had a good reason. That I was protecting you. Maybe in a way I couldn't protect her—"

His voice faltered for a moment, and Benny felt her chest tighten.

"But I think that was a mistake," he continued with a huff of breath. "I think I was the one that scared you. Maybe her too. I was so goddamn worried about what could happen to you. To both of you. And it didn't even fucking matter."

"Dad." Benny leaned forward, her hand reaching for his. "None of this is your fault. Not what happened to me, and not what happened to Mom."

He squeezed her hand tightly.

"That's not true, Benny," he said sadly. "Look at who I am."

She scoffed. "That's not fair."

But wasn't it? Hadn't she held this against him herself?

"I'm always a target," he told her. "That's the nature of this business. And what I do, what I have to do to make sure we retain what we've got—it makes everyone around me a target too. That's how they found out about your mother."

Benny sucked in a breath.

Her father never talked about her mother like this. Her death was always off the table. She thought back to what Christian said, about her mother's part in the ritual. Did her father know? Had he been keeping that from her too?

"We came across this shipment," Angelo said, his eyes focused on her hand wrapped in his. "A pile of cargo came in from the UK, a transfer to the Met for some kind of display. We had a tip that there was something in that shipment, something we knew we'd get a lot of bids for. And we got lucky, kid. The value coulda paid every one of our guys for a year. But apparently we weren't the only ones after it. And he had a pack of vampires who were real fucking feral types."

She swallowed.

Was this who they were looking for?

"A few of them followed us, tried to track where we kept the cargo." Angelo sighed. "And I led them right to her. Like a wrapped fucking present under the Christmas tree."

Benny remembered what Luke said. How he could sense her blood.

"What happened?"

"They took her," he said as if he still couldn't believe it after all these years. "That was the reason she never came home, Benny. They grabbed her right from the hospital. A random fucking Tuesday. She called to tell me she was on her way home and then—well, she never made it."

She would never forget the night her mother died. The way Benny stupidly fought with her about things that felt so meaningless now. But she also remembered the rampage her father went on trying to find her. The blood bath he left in his wake.

She felt that fury now. For a hundred different reasons.

"But you sent a vampire to find me," she said, suddenly. "How could you trust that Luke wasn't going to do the same thing? You didn't even warn him about what I was. Do you know what could have happened?"

"Of course," Angelo said, affronted. "Jesus Christ, Ben. Give me a bit more credit. The Crawford boys are just like their old man, vampire or not. They've got the same code. And once I met them, I knew I'd made the right decision."

Benny's brows knit together.

"You knew their dad?"

He nodded. "Eamond Crawford was a decent man. Smart as a goddamn whip with a safe. I don't think there's a lock he couldn't pick, to be honest. We tried to get him to come work for us a couple of times, but he was loyal. To a fucking fault."

There was a trace of something in her father's tone. Something dark.

"Gideon hasn't really mentioned—" She paused. There hadn't exactly been a ton of time for them to trade all of their family trauma. Even if they had seemed to be making a decent headway in the last couple of days. "I mean, I know he passed, but I don't know what happened. Do you?"

"I don't remember much. Your mother—" He stopped himself, rubbing at the nape of his neck. "Well, it happened around the same time. Just a job gone bad."

Benny chewed on the inside of her cheek.

"It was during a blood moon," she said, finally meeting her father's gaze.

His heavy brows drew together.

"What are you talkin' about?"

"I had hoped he was lying," she said. "That Christian was just saying it to upset me. But when Mom died, it was right before a blood moon. Just like now. I looked this morning."

He sighed, leaning back into his chair. "I wasn't sure. I never—well, I didn't take the time to really find out. I was like a crazed fucking maniac. I wanted to turn every single one of those bloodsuckers into ash. But I should have dug deeper. Maybe we wouldn't be here now if I had."

Benny stiffened. She was beginning to feel similarly.

"Well, we are," she said, knowing that sounded harsher than she intended. "And unless there's something in this book that shows us how to time travel, all we can do is figure out how to deal with it."

Angelo closed his eyes.

"I'm sorry, kiddo," he said. "All I've ever wanted was to keep you safe."

Benny stood up from the chair, the book tucked in one hand as she looked down at her father. It was hard to hold on to the anger she felt bubbling beneath the surface. Because she knew. She knew how much he loved her. But she spent so much of her life worried about her fate, and so much of that came from him.

"I think it's time to go back to Philly," she said.

Angelo looked at her for a moment before he nodded and rose from his seat.

"There's one more thing," he told her before crossing toward a large mahogany desk near the window. She watched as he reached into one of his side drawers and pulled out a small jewelry bag, a crushed black velvet with satin strings. "This drawer has been locked for years, you know. I lost the key sometime around the funeral, and I'll tell you I'm good with a lock pick. But I've never been able to get through this one. Not without taking a sledgehammer to the whole thing. And this morning, it just fucking clicked open."

He huffed a breath, the disbelief etched into his features.

"But it was always meant to be yours," he said, the bag laying in the palm of his hand.

"What is it?" she asked.

"It was your mother's," he said, offering her a slight smile. "You'll remember. She wore it every day. She said it was meant for you. When you were ready."

Benny's nose wrinkled as she took the velvet satchel from her father, fingers pulling at the satin ties, her eyes stinging with fresh tears. She knew, the memory flooding back to her. The thin gold chain. The round pendant and the small peridot, all in gold, all etched with perfect precision. Aurora. The goddess of the Dawn. Riding in her chariot, her hand outstretched as the peridot rested in her palm, like she was bestowing it upon the sun as a gift.

She clutched it in her hand, looking up at her father through blurry tears.

"What happened to Mom isn't going to happen to me," she told him. "I promise."

TWENTY-NINE

LUKE

THE DRIVE BACK TO Philly had taken longer than expected.

An accident on I-95 had set them back another hour and by the time they arrived at the loft, even Luke was too tired to carry on with his usual nighttime activities. He had retreated back to his bedroom and fell into a deep sleep for near half the day. Much to the mutual relief of everyone in the loft. Luke had no interest in overhearing anything that might happen behind closed doors now that Gideon was sleeping in his own room again.

Vampires required rest but Luke had been running himself a bit too hard.

When Angelo Torretta had first called them, he had no idea the job would spiral like this. A search and rescue— sure. Not a typical gig but easy enough. Safekeeping? Why not. Playing bodyguard and private detective? A little beyond their typical scope but they were smart and well-trained. Prevent a demon ascension?

It was absolutely fucking insane.

But he loved every minute of it.

It was the conflict in his head every minute of the day. The good and the bad of his human death, the whole wide world he'd never expected to exist seducing him almost immediately. With Tefi as his guide, it was hard not to become enamored.

It was easy to let it consume him.

But now he was wide awake, rejuvenated and downright giddy at his discovery. It was a needle in a haystack kind of find. Hardly bigger than his palm, tucked deep in an old filing carton, a box of goods they had plucked from an occult shop in Baltimore that had been tossed aside for an upcoming audit by the Caruso men.

But written on the inside cover were the words '*recordum mutationis*' in faint chicken scratch. A record of a change. Or something to that effect. Luke hadn't ever been all that good in school. He was too restless, too distracted. He had passed most of his classes by the skin of his teeth, and a little bit of extra homework help from Gideon. But he had always been pretty good at picking up languages. He learned Spanish while running errands for Frank, and bits of Latin and Aramaic and Ancient Greek while dicking around in Harker's library, pouring through the texts and doing a hell of a lot of research.

The words scribbled in Latin definitely piqued his interest.

Which is why he was staring so intently at Harker as the demon hunter flipped through the diary, eager to see if the book was what he hoped it was.

"You really don't have anything else you could be doing right now?"

"Nope," Luke replied brightly.

"Yeah, not true, babe," Cleo called out from the living room.

"Didn't you say something about finalizing the schedule?" Gideon asked from the opposite end of the kitchen island. He was staring down at the hotel floor plan spread out on the counter, a thick black marker in his hand as he marked their entry points. Luke scoffed. As if Gideon would ensure the minute-by-minute play to anyone else.

"Or you could sort through the ammo you made me pick up for you," Cleo added. "Considering I had to deal with Frank and all his creeps to get it."

Luke twisted around in his stool, his eyes narrowing at Cleo.

"You said it went well."

"It did," she shrugged. "But that's because I know how to play him. Doesn't make him any less of a woman-hating weirdo."

He frowned.

Frank Markos wasn't much of a charmer, that Luke knew. But if he had made Cleo feel uncomfortable in any way—well, just the thought of it was making his skin itch. He also didn't love the idea that this felt like new information to him. He knew Huck was a problem. But Cleo had met Frank before, had been dealing with him in one way or another since she signed on to work with Gideon and then Luke full-time.

When Luke took off with Tefi, Gideon was recovering from a brutal fight with a vampire gang and Cleo had blown her way out of a safe with a homemade bomb. From what he heard through the grapevine during those first few months, Cleo and Gideon went way underground. Hard to continue behaving like normal after that kind of run-in, harder still to go their own separate ways. Luke knew he'd left his brother in the lurch. They had worked together for so long, their communication was almost wordless.

But Luke was changed. Made entirely new.

He had to learn how to adjust, and he couldn't do it with his brother looking over his shoulder.

Gideon and Cleo did the same thing. She stepped up. Gideon could rely on her in a different way, the two of them developing their own shorthand. And soon Luke was getting word through various channels that Gideon was back in action and Cleo was right there with him. It had surprised the hell out of him. He couldn't deny there was a small part of him that wondered if their relationship was more than professional.

Despite that, he also felt relief.

Like it alleviated some of the guilt he felt by leaving in the first place.

"Yeah, I'm gonna wanna talk about that more," he told her.

She merely rolled her eyes in reply before she went back to loading up the clips sitting on the coffee table in front of her, boxes of ammo stacked neatly on each side.

Luke wasn't sure he'd have a place when he returned to work with his brother. He didn't want to impose on whatever dynamic they'd created. But when he realized Gideon and Cleo behaved more like siblings than lovers, a very small part of Luke was pleased as all hell.

And they became a very easy trio.

"Alright, I think we've got something," Harker said, drawing Luke back around.

"Tell me," he said, though he now felt a little bit more distracted than before.

"Judging by the binding, I'd wager this dates back maybe a hundred and fifty years," Harker said, finally making eye contact, his dark eyes glimmering briefly. His locs were piled up on top of his head in a loose bun, and he was fiddling with a chain hanging around his neck. "The Latin is a bit baffling—like it's all in a personal short hand."

"And? Anything that might help us with the ritual?"

"The entries seem to follow a lot of what we already know," Harker said, before he shuffled to a few pages toward the end. "But there is something here I haven't seen before, and if it's true, we're in for a bit of trouble."

"Oh, cool," Gideon said dryly. "Because we've had a really easy fucking go of it so far—"

"What is it?" Luke asked..

"There's a bit here where he writes about this stage before the ritual officially takes place," Harker started, holding the diary out for Luke to see. "*Immunis sum.* Immune. Essentially, he's saying that he was... invincible until the blood moon took place. He could not be harmed."

"Could not be harmed," Luke repeated.

"That thing the bloke said to you in the quarry," Harker said. "About bathing in untouched blood? I think that's it."

"Okay, but not... literally, right?" Cleo asked.

Harker grimaced.

"Well, no one's had any fucking luck tracking down those kids," Gideon muttered.

"Whoever it is we're looking for," Harker started, "we can't kill him. Not yet."

The mood wasn't exactly light, but in that moment, there was a heavy lull that settled over the group. Five kids. All gone, if this diary was to be believed. It was only a few days until the ritual. If it were Luke, he'd want immunity as long as he could before the ritual took place.

He raked his fingers through his hair as he shifted back on the stool.

"There are a lot of tight squeezes here," Luke said to his brother.

"I know." Gideon sighed.

"We can play keep-away," he replied. "We just gotta hold on until the moon rises."

"Where's Benny?" Harker asked.

"In the bedroom," Gideon said, gesturing behind him. He rubbed at the back of his neck. "She's got some research of her own she's investigating."

"What does that mean?" Luke asked.

"That's for Benny to share," he said. "Not me."

Luke didn't like that. He didn't like being in the dark.

"Perhaps we make a little visit to our usual haunts," Harker suggested, catching Luke's eye. "See if we can't drum up a little gossip. A man puts together an ascension ritual, he's sure to reach out to some of the more unsavory channels."

It was hard to believe that just six months ago, Harker was more likely to stake him than take him out to a vampire bar for a feed and reconnaissance. Tefi had amassed a lot of enemies over the decades, and while Luke was with her, they became his enemies too. It was the connection between a sire and a vampire. It was also the protectiveness that lived within Luke whether he was vampire or human. But in the short time they were together, he had to figure out his own allies, his own way of navigating the supernatural world.

Convincing Harker he wasn't the same kind of trouble Tefi was had been a process.

But Gideon had been able to vouch for him.

Luke shrugged. "I could always use a drink."

"Why does that not sound like you're gonna order a mai tai?" Cleo asked.

Thirty

CLEO

A GENTLE NUDGE BRUSHED against Cleo's shoulder, and she shifted, her cheek pressing into a soft down pillow. She could hear her name being whispered, the deep voice amused as that gentle touch moved from her shoulder to her forehead, fingers brushing back her hair. A yawn passed through her lips even as her eyes willed themselves shut a little bit longer. She had been wrapped up in a dream she wasn't ready to leave. She never could remember them when she woke, and this one seemed important. It was lingering in the back of her mind—a wall, maybe, or a large door. Intricate carvings. A bright white light. A deep voice speaking a language she couldn't understand.

"I think you're drooling," came a familiar voice.

Her nose wrinkled as she batted away Luke's hand.

"I was having a very good dream," she groaned.

She blinked open her eyes to find herself in a bedroom, Luke crouching beside her, a bright glint behind his blue eyes as his lips curved into a smirk. "How good?"

Cleo pushed herself up to a sitting position, her hand brushing her hair out of her face, strands sticking to her skin. "You're disgusting, you know that?"

He gave a hearty chuckle as he straightened. His hair was disheveled, strands of dark hair hanging in his eyes. He looked tired but satiated. It was intimate, almost. For Cleo to see Luke this way. His suit jacket was gone, the sleeves of his shirt rolled up to reveal strong forearms and those stupid tattoos scattered across his skin. Drunken dares. Spontaneous flash designs. A red outlined "E" she knew he shared with Gideon. Her eyes lingered on the colorful swallow at his inner wrist and the pulse point there. She suddenly found herself wanting to press her fingers to the spot.

"What time is it?" she asked.

"Early," he said as he crossed to the other side of the bed, the mattress sinking beneath his weight as he settled down beside her. He kicked off his shoes and crossed one ankle over the other. "I just got in."

"Why am I in your bed?"

"You were passed out on the couch," he said. "Felt cruel to make you sleep on that thing."

"Were you out with Harker?"

He leaned his head back against the headboard, his hands clasped at the nape of his neck as his eyes closed. Her eyes lingered on the colorful butterfly at the base of his throat, the bright orange and the striking blue of the wings. That one would always be her favorite.

"We hit up a club," he said. "Found some chatty miscreants. Had a little fun. I'd consider the night a success."

She grimaced as a million different scenarios flashed through her mind. It was hard to reconcile the version of Luke she knew with the version she didn't. And there *was* a version she didn't know. She wasn't naive. What he did in the night, what he did when the rest of the human world was sleeping—whatever it was that kept him going, Luke kept that to himself. Maybe Gideon had seen that part of him, but never Cleo.

She didn't know how to deal with the fact that a part of her wanted to.

A morbid curiosity, but it was small enough she could keep it at bay.

She had seen him feed before, like the man at the quarry. But it had been someone trying to kill them, and maybe Cleo could excuse that in her head. She had her code just like the brothers had theirs. Someone tries to hurt her? They're fair game. Someone tries to hurt someone she loves? They're already dead. But what did Luke's moral code look like as a vampire?

Was he like Harker? Were there… women or men he slept with? Consensual feedings? She wasn't sure she was ready to think much more about that.

"Are we good?" he asked.

She blinked, her skin feeling warm as she turned and met his gaze.

"With what?"

"With the ammo," he said.

"Oh… yeah," she said, nodding. "We're really good. We've got plenty of backup."

"Good," he said, repeating the word again.

She could sense something else from his tone. Hesitation? Concern? She frowned.

"Lucas," she started, twisting her body to face him. "You really think we're going to need all of this? It's a charity dinner."

"It's not the dinner I'm worried about," he said, shrugging his shoulders. "It's what comes after. It's been a weird couple of weeks, and I'd rather not be unprepared."

Cleo couldn't argue with that.

"Well, I'll let you get some rest then," she said, pushing herself up.

"Wait—" Luke reached for her, his hand grazing against her arm, his skin cold to the touch. "I want to know what happened. With Frank."

She turned back to look at him, a smile curling at her lips when she noticed that familiar concern flicker across his features. Luke Crawford. Ever protective.

"I'm fine."

"Of course you are," he replied, rolling his eyes. "But I still want to know."

She hesitated for a moment before she matched his expression with an eye roll of her own and sank back down on the bed beside him. He spread his arm across the back of the headboard, his body turning toward hers as she settled in. There was something about seeing him sprawled out like this, in his bed, that felt dangerous for Cleo.

"I didn't think I'd have to actually deal with him," she said. "You know Huck practically lives there. But he sent him on an errand, I guess. So it was just me and Frank. And Harker."

Relief flashed across his features so fast she wondered if she imagined it.

"He was just being kind of weird," she continued. "About you. About Gideon. He's always seemed like a grade-A creep, no offense, but it was like he'd really amped it up. He thinks, you know, we—"

She was reluctant to actually relay the next bit.

"We what?" Luke prodded, brow knitting together behind his glasses.

"He just made a comment about our relationship…" She waved her hand. "Not that we— oh, fuck it, you know what I mean."

"Cleo." Luke leaned toward her, voice stern but warm. "Tell me what he said, exactly."

"He asked which one of you I was attached to. Apparently I'm not enough on my own. I need to be sleeping with one of you to be here."

And if Cleo had wanted to see the more feral side of him before, the wicked glimmer of red that seeped into his eyes at her words sparked something in her she hadn't expected. But it was just a moment. A flash of rage. And she swallowed, watching as it all faded back to normal, wondering why her heart was thumping so rapidly in her chest.

She tried to calm it down. She knew Luke could hear it.

And she didn't want him to know just how much that affected her.

"Frank has always been a means to an end," Luke muttered darkly as he got to his feet. "Maybe we've just reached that point sooner than I thought."

She frowned.

"Luke—"

"No one should ever speak to you that way."

"You're not going to do something stupid, are you?" she asked, suddenly worried.

The corner of his mouth twitched.

"Isn't that my baseline?"

"Lucas."

She reached for him, her hand wrapping around his wrist. Could she feel a faint thumping? A slight beat beneath her fingers? She couldn't be sure. Maybe it was her own. She always felt this way when she was this close to Luke. From before Chicago and even more so afterwards. But it wasn't something she could think about. Especially not now.

"Don't worry," he said. "One problem at a time."

The problems seemed to be piling up.

"Wait a second, what?" Cleo asked, her hand curving around her coffee mug, her eyes peering down at the caramel-colored liquid as if the caffeine had somehow betrayed her. She was exhausted, her skin felt dry, and her hair was in desperate need of a wash. The fact that she was wearing her clothes from the night before didn't help. She tugged at the hair tie holding up her messy bun. "I'm sorry, I don't think I heard you correctly."

Gideon leaned against the island, his hands pressed flat against the counter.

"Tefi is going to be at the gala," he repeated, offering her a wonky smile. Like he was *thisclose* to losing his mind. Gideon was always about ready to start a fight in an empty house, but there was something special about Tefi that riled him up.

"What the hell?" she muttered. "I thought she was in Switzerland or something."

"Well, she's back," he said, throwing up his hands.

Cleo had never had the pleasure of meeting Tefi.

The night everything went to hell in Chicago, Cleo had been trapped in a bank vault, trying to work her way out from the inside. It had been a nightmare from start to finish, and by the time she finally freed herself, thanks to a very crude and desperately made explosive, Luke was gone. With Tefi. Like they were some kind of undead Bonnie and Clyde.

It would be another six months before she saw Luke again.

And while she laid low with Gideon and learned how to be a proper thief, she worried about the younger Crawford brother. Maybe needlessly. Luke could strut sitting down. But it didn't stop her from wondering.

It was hell enough knowing that all the things that went bump in the night were real.

"So, what?" she asked, looking up at Gideon. "Is she gonna be an issue?"

The elder Crawford brother rolled his eyes.

"Of course she is," he said. "You get Luke and Tefi in a room together, and it's chaos."

"Is any part of trying to steal a jewel in plain sight not chaos?" Benny asked sweetly, her hand wrapped around her mug. She was sitting at the island beside Cleo, her skateboarding kitten pajamas rumpled, a few of the buttons misaligned.

Cleo pressed her lips together.

Gideon and Benny had come back from Hudson attached at the hip. It was incredibly satisfying for Cleo when Luke pressed a one hundred dollar bill into the palm of her hand. She was happy for Gideon. After everything they'd been through together, everything he'd done for her, she wanted Gideon to have something good.

She watched as he pressed a kiss to Benny's forehead.

"Tefi is one of a kind, princess."

An understatement for sure.

Luke hadn't been altogether too interested in relaying the details of their relationship. Just that whatever it had been was over. Of course Cleo wanted to know. She was curious to a fault. But she had also knew Luke well enough to let it lie. Still, Tefi had become a sort of phantom in their lives. She was responsible for Luke's transformation and for catapulting them into the world of the undead and supernatural. But at least she kept her distance.

As far as Cleo knew, anyway.

"Let's just hope we can get in and get out without too much trouble," she said.

"Don't jinx us, St. James," came Luke's voice.

He had slept for maybe an hour, tops, and yet he looked refreshed and recharged. Cleo grumbled as she took in the still wet hair from his shower, the freshly pressed suit. A boyish kind of smile stretched across his face, reaching the bright blue of his eyes.

It was easy to forget how quickly he could transform when he looked like this.

"Good night?" Gideon asked, raising his brows.

Luke nodded. "Informative, brother."

"Oh no," Cleo said, twisting in her seat. "What does that mean?"

"You would be surprised what you can get out of a couple of blood-drunk vampires at four o'clock in the morning," he said before a yawn passed through his lips. He raked his hand through his hair, smoothing it back, putting himself into place. "Our guy's been recruiting."

"You never bring good news," Gideon muttered.

Luke's smile widened into a grin.

"Okay, what does that mean?" Cleo asked. "Recruiting who?"

"Word is he's *pissed* about losing his demon buddy," Luke said, pulling up a stool on the opposite side of Cleo. "And he's looking for a replacement. There's some interest from a dark coven. A couple of witches who are very into the serving Lucifer thing."

Gideon sighed, the sound deep and heavy, and Cleo could feel it in her bones.

"Interesting," was all Benny said, her face screwed up in thought.

"You got some kinda witch network you could tap into?" Gideon asked.

The witch nodded, her fingers toying with a necklace Cleo hadn't seen before.

"I'll reach out to Liv and Imani," she said, reaching for her laptop.

"Anything else you might want to share with the class?" Luke asked suddenly.

Benny looked up from her computer, her eyes curious.

"What do you mean?"

"That little book you've been nose deep in since yesterday," Luke said.

"Lucas—" Gideon said but the younger Crawford held up a hand.

"Just want to make sure we're all on the same page here," he said. "Because I've been working my ass off these last few weeks figuring out how to keep you safe, Benny. So if this is something that could help us, I want to know."

Cleo looked back and forth between them both, twisting in her stool.

"It's my mother's," Benny said, drawing her knees up to her chin, her bare legs no longer holding any signs of what had happened to her, her bruising all gone. "Apparently there were things going on with her magic she didn't feel comfortable writing about in the grimoire."

"Really? Like what?" Cleo asked.

"She blew up the toaster once," Benny said, her brown eyes soft and a oddly wistful. "Said she felt like she couldn't contain her energy. That there was... too much of it."

Gideon's hand curved around the nape of her neck and Benny closed her eyes.

"I've been trying to figure out if she was realizing it too," she continued. "If she knew the potential. Some of these journal entries... I feel like I could have written them myself."

Luke watched her intently, his fingers drumming against the countertop.

"I think there's still a level I haven't reached yet," Benny said. "I think it scared the hell out of my mom but if I can figure it out, maybe we can use it to our advantage."

"A nuclear option," Luke said.

"A nuclear option."

Thirty-One

Benny

"Dirty ass Devil worshippers."

Benny laughed as Gideon sputtered into his coffee, a bemused expression settling onto his features. But Olivia powered on, swinging her legs over the arm of the sofa, her bright pink sneakers falling to the floor as she kicked them off. She was on a roll now.

"It's amateur shit," she continued. "It's *basic*. We're going to spend our time worshipping a *man*? Absolutely the fuck not. It's all 'dost thou want to live deliciously' but no one tells you it's only gonna happen if you bend your will to his every whim. Who has the time?"

"It is excruciatingly heteronormative," Imani agreed.

"I bet you it's that same group that still sells white sage at all the holiday markets," Olivia said.

Cleo plucked a pin from between her lips to ask, "White sage?"

The dress code for the upcoming charity gala was black tie and with Benny going as a guest, she needed something far beyond the denim and T-shirts Cleo had grabbed for her at her apartment. But the last time she'd been to an event that formal, it was her cousin's wedding and she was a bridesmaid. She still shuddered to think about all the ruffles.

Cleo was generous enough to bring over a few options from her pageant days.

Benny was currently all pinned up in a beautiful red silk gown that was a little too long in the leg and a little too generous in the bust. But it was the most simple of the offerings and made her feel a little bit like a Bond girl. The look on Gideon's face when she stepped out of the bedroom, the heat behind his eyes, it was enough for her to want to order the dress in a hundred colors.

"It's a closed practice," Imani explained as she rifled through Cleo's sewing kit. The bakery was closed on Mondays and she was intent on putting together protection poppets for the gala. "And it's sacred to the indigenous population. But a lot of these capitalist hags will do anything to make a few dollars at their little tents on Cherry Street."

"We are amped up today, I see," Benny said, lifting up one arm as Cleo pulled in the bust on one side. "I am liking the energy."

"This is what happens when we find out you were fucking a demon," Olivia said, flopping onto her back. "Am I allowed to ask questions in present company?"

Benny felt her skin flush as Gideon looped around the island with his hands raised.

"Ask all the questions you want," he said. "I've got an errand to run."

"You'll be safe?" she asked as he drew closer.

"I'll be safe," he confirmed, his fingers ghosting her jaw as he kissed her.

It wasn't two seconds after the door to the loft closed that Imani approached Olivia with a slow swagger, her hand curving at Olivia's jaw with an exaggerated swing of her arm. Olivia lifted herself onto her elbows with a dramatic gasp and Imani planted a cute little kiss right on her mouth.

"You are children," Benny said.

"And you are required to tell us everything," Imani said.

"The dirty, nasty details," Olivia added.

"As someone who has never once remotely considered Gideon in a sexual manner, I'm not entirely sure I can handle this," Cleo laughed.

"Really?" Olivia asked. "I mean I'm a lesbian and even I get it a little bit. It's those pretty eyes of his, you know? He looks at Benny like he's starving. Why can't a woman to look at me like she's starving?"

Benny sucked in a breath as Cleo tugged at the waist of the dress, making another pin.

"No he doesn't."

"Yes, he does," the red head said thoughtfully. "He has since y'all came back from Winnie's. I bet Luke a hundred dollars you two were going to hook up before this was all over."

"I'm so glad my love life has been such a passion project for you all."

But Benny could hardly contain the smile that had bloomed across her face. It felt precious, this thing that had developed between them. Something she wanted to protect and cherish.

"Spill it, Benedetta," Imani said. "The last guy couldn't even make you come."

"*And* he was a demon," Olivia chimed in. "Lest we've forgotten in the last few minutes."

"Gideon does not have either of those afflictions," Benny said. "He's very... *intentional* about making sure I get there. Preferably more than once."

"Oh, thank Hecate," Imani said.

"I love being right," Cleo mused.

She crouched down to start pinning the hem, the difference in their height giving her more than a few inches to mark. Benny was going to have pull out her highest heels in an effort to cut back on the amount of length Cleo would have to trim. She pressed her tongue to the inside of her cheek— she did have a gold pair of slingbacks she had a feeling Gideon would love.

"You've got a ridiculous look on your face," Olivia laughed. "You smitten little freak."

Smitten was just one word for it.

She only hoped they'd get a real chance.

They were just one day out from the charity gala and Benny would be lying if she said she wasn't a little nervous about what was to come. Each day that passed, each day that brought them closer and closer to the Blood Moon, Benny's body seemed to hum in anticipation. It was driving her a little bit mad, the fear and nerves and thrills mixing into something she could name. It was coursing through her veins even now, as Gideon hovered behind her, his hands steady on her shoulders. The boxing dummy swayed in front of them with her last round, little singe holes marking where each fist had landed a punch.

"That's it, princess," he said, voice warm on her ear. "You got every hit."

She brushed her hair off of her face, her breath coming in staggered bursts.

"Now let's focus less on the up close and personal," he continued, dropping his hands from her shoulders. He lifted the one hundred pound boxing dummy with ease, carrying it a few yards away from where Benny stood. "Because if you can hit them before they even see you that would be great for me, personally."

"Gid—"

"Benny, we have no idea what we're going to be up against," he said, adjusting the dummy until it was facing her once again. "My only goal is to keep you out of harm's way as much as I can."

She knew there was no use in arguing. Especially when she knew he was right. Benny may have power but she wasn't a vampire. If she let one get too close—

Gideon jogged back to where she stood, his T-shirt clinging to his skin in the muggy evening air. The sky was readying itself for an impending storm, the clouds thick and grey in the sky. She watched as he lifted the hem of his shirt to wipe at the sweat across his brow, his abs constricting with the movement. She pressed her tongue to the roof of her mouth as she drew her eyes away from him, focusing instead of the dummy in front of them.

"Just one hit, Ben," he said. "That's all it takes."

She nodded, her hands drawing up in front of her, fingers splayed as she focused her magic on the dummy in front of her, picturing the blast of power in an effort to call it to the surface. A flash of lightning illuminated the sky as Benny watched her skin start to glow from within. She had done this before, at the warehouse with Christian, had sent a burst of magic in his direction with little thought beyond saving Gideon's life. She could do that again.

A crack of thunder shook the sky.

The training dummy went up into flames.

"Oh, no," she said, wincing.

Gideon's shoulders shook, his hand rubbing at the nape of his neck as the rubber started to smoke and melt. His laughter was low and easy and she couldn't help but watch him and the way his eyes crinkled. It had to be one of her favorite things about him, maybe one of her favorite things in the whole world.

But still, there was a full fire hazard happening on the roof.

"You're absolutely fucking terrifying," he said, awe in his voice.

Benny grimaced as the dummy's face began to ooze.

She didn't want to be held responsible for a building wide fire alarm.

"Wait, maybe I can—" Benny focused her magic again, informing it to reverse itself or put itself out, and with a little extra effort on her part, the flames dissipated and the ruined husk of the dummy remained. "Okay, there we go."

"Well, he's looked better," Gideon mused.

Another flash of lightning slowly followed by an echoing thunder.

"Should we call it?" he asked, eyes glancing up toward the sky.

"I don't know," she said. "I still feel—"

"What?"

"I'm just anxious, maybe," she said, shrugging her shoulders. "I have all this energy built up inside of me, like my body knows the ritual is coming. I'm beginning to have this fear that this was meant to happen. That maybe this is my fate."

"No," Gideon said, shaking his head. "No, that's bullshit."

The thunder came more quickly now.

"Is it? How do I know this isn't going to end the same way it did for my mother?"

"Because you have me, Benny," he said. "And I keep my promises."

She started to unravel the wraps tied around her hands just for something to focus on that wasn't the frustration and concern evident in Gideon's face.

"I told you that you can't make me a promise like that."

He took over for her, hands deftly working the wraps off of her hands. She loved the way his hands felt on her, how gentle they could be when she needed them to be, how rough when she wanted that too. She didn't want to think about the ritual anymore. She didn't want to think about the gala or the Blood Moon or the man who took her.

"Baby, just tell me what you need," he said quietly.

She didn't know.

More time, maybe. More of this.

Then, the answer was clear.

"You."

Benny lifted herself onto her toes, her hands twisting in the fabric of his T-shirt for leverage as she pressed her mouth to his. He only hesitated a moment before his body relaxed into hers, his hands smoothing across her waist. He knew what she was doing but he was going to let her and she wanted him all the more for it. Benny dragged her hands across his chest toward his shoulders, fingers digging into the hard muscle. He lifted her up around his waist, his hands cupping her ass as he led her toward one of the lounge chairs.

The sky felt as if it were about to open right up but neither of them seemed to care.

Gideon kept her in his lap as he sank down on the chair, his fingers brushing the hair that came loose from her braid off of her face. Benny pulled back, eyes scanning his face, seeing the heat behind his gaze, the way his eyes darkened for her. She cupped his jaw in her hand, her thumb pressing against his bottom lip. His mouth was so lush and full. He nipped at her finger before sucking it into his mouth and her breath caught in her throat, her thighs tightening against his waist.

"I want more time," she said softly, before kissing him again.

"Right now, princess, we have all the time in the world."

"Then let's go slow," she breathed, her hips rocking against his.

"I'll give you anything you want, Benny."

And when he kissed her again, the heavens opened wide, rain soaking the earth.

Thirty-Two

Gideon

"You look like you're about to strangle yourself."

"Extremely helpful, Lucas," Gideon grumbled.

He was struggling with his bowtie, fingers fumbling with the fabric. He frowned at his reflection in the mirror before he yanked at the black silk to start over, the two ends hanging around his shirt collar limply. He didn't know what his problem was. This wasn't his first black-tie event, and he knew how to tie a goddamn bowtie.

There was just too much at stake, and for the first time in a long time, Gideon was doubting the efficacy of his plan. There were too many variables. Too many unknowns. He didn't know how to account for magic he didn't understand. They had no idea who their wannabe demon was or what he looked like, and knowing they were going to likely be in the same room at the gala was annoying the shit out of him. He didn't like to go into a plan without knowing every single possibility.

Then there was Benny.

He'd never run a job with someone he was intimate with before.

It was an unspoken rule between the brothers. The risk was too great, the rewards too important. Of course, he'd never take a job to play bodyguard, either.

Yet here he was, breaking all his rules for Benny.

Luke hovering in the doorway of his bedroom with a dumb fucking smug smile on his face certainly didn't help. His younger brother was already dressed, fully leaning into his persona for the evening. A burnout college kid with a part time job in catering. No glasses, no slicked-back hair. He looked young like this.

Young enough for Gideon to remember he'd never see his brother grow old.

Gideon sighed in surrender, his palms resting against his dresser as he caught his brother's eyes in the mirror. "Do you remember how to tie these things?"

"I remember Dad teaching us before your senior prom," Luke replied as he stepped into the room. Gideon turned toward him and watched as Luke narrowed his eyes on the bowtie, adjusting it so that one end was a bit longer than the other. "You were sweating bullets because you were taking Jess March, and you didn't want one of those pre-made ones from the rental place. I think it was the first time I ever saw you really nervous. Not like I didn't get it. Jess was so cool."

"I was cool."

Luke paused, his eyes flickering up as his brow raised. "Sure."

Gideon ignored that, his chin pressed into his chest as he tried to watch Luke's hand movements.

"Anyway, whatever happened to her?" Luke asked as he resumed, working one loop over the other, his long fingers making quick work of the task.

"I don't know. She went to college? She's probably married at this point. It's not like I kept in touch with her after Dad—" He stopped himself. Neither of them needed to think about that. "You know we had other shit going on."

Luke didn't say anything for a moment as he tugged at both ends of the loop.

"There you go, Bond."

He stepped back and clapped Gideon on the shoulder before settling in beside him, the two of them staring at their reflections in the mirror. Luke in his white dress shirt and black slacks with matching black tie, his hair falling in his eyes. Gideon in his tuxedo, freshly shaved, fidgeting with his cufflinks. They had both been surprised when it turned out Luke still had a reflection. But it wasn't like either of them had any understanding of what was fact and what was fiction about something they'd only just learned existed. He wondered what the eighteen-year-old version of himself would think if he could see them now, preparing for one of the biggest jobs they'd ever planned.

A heist with bigger stakes than any job they'd ever done before.

How the hell had they gotten to this point?

Vampires and witches and cursed fucking rubies.

Luke rolled his eyes. "Stop worrying."

"I'm not worrying."

"I can hear your heartbeat, dumbass."

Gideon ignored that too, taking one final glance at himself in the mirror before ducking out into the hallway. A little worrying had to be good, it kept him honest. But a part of him couldn't shake what Benny said on the roof, about how her life might be up for the taking regardless of what they achieve tonight.

"Are you two bozos ready?"

Cleo was perched on the kitchen island, her heels tapping against the cabinets as she leaned back on the palms of her hands. She was dressed in the exact same outfit as Luke, her red hair tied back in a complicated looking braid. She raised her brows expectantly as they came into the kitchen.

"We're ready," Gideon nodded. "Where's Benny?"

"Hold on—" And he could hear her voice came from the other end of the hallway, a frustrated edge to her voice and then a bang. "Whoops— I'm almost done!"

Gideon looked down at the watch on his wrist.

If they didn't leave now, they'd fuck the whole plan. They had a twenty-minute window after the doors opened before they were too late to arrive. The viewing schedule for the gems was tight, and they needed as much leverage as possible. They couldn't fall behind their schedule.

But when she finally appeared, Gideon's heart seemed to plummet to his stomach.

He rubbed his hand against the tightness growing in his chest as Benny adjusted the skirt of her gown. He had seen her in the dress the other day while Cleo helped with the tailoring and he had thought she looked good then. But this? The red silk twirled around her bare legs, revealing a thigh high slit on the one side and there was a sleeve that seemed to slip off her shoulder on purpose. That was going to distract him all night, he knew.

She looked up at him with an apprehensive smile, her chestnut curls smoothed out and hanging around her shoulders, her lips painted in a red that seemed to match her dress.

She was the most beautiful thing he had ever seen.

"Am I late?"

He shook his head.

"We will be if we don't go right now," Luke said, amusement dripping from his tone.

"Right," Gideon said. "You and Cleo take the Jeep, we'll meet you there. Olivia, Imani, and Harker are already en route."

"Let's do it, brother."

THIRTY-THREE

THE HEIST - PHASE ONE

8:13pm

"ALRIGHT, YOU GUYS KNOW the drill. I wanna see big smiles tonight. They're trying to save the arts or something before this planet goes tits-up. I don't wanna see a single empty water glass. And if they ask you for anything, just say yes. Tickets were $1350 a pop, and I don't want some Karen giving us a hard time because she got tap instead of sparkling, okay?"

The cater manager looked at her team expectantly, her brows raised in a pleading "don't fuck this up" kind of way before she clapped her hands and went back to the clipboard tucked under her arm.

Luke huffed an amused breath as his eyes scanned the rest of the servers lined up in the kitchen, all of them wearing the same ill-fitting white dress shirts, black slacks, a long black apron, and a matching black tie. Some of them were even wearing Crocs. Jesus Christ.

He leaned over toward Cleo, his shoulder nudging against hers.

"You ready to relive your youth?"

Cleo snorted.

"This isn't a Martinsburg truck stop, babe," she said, her eyes glancing down at the watch strapped to her wrist. "This is rich people shit. It's gonna be a cakewalk compared to drunk truckers."

She tilted her head thoughtfully, and Luke's eyes lingered on the curve of her neck.

"Probably the same amount of grabby hands, though."

"What?" he said, snapping from his daze.

"Hey, you two—"

The cater manager approached them, her eyes deep in her clipboard.

"Looks like we're down a couple of servers," she said, before tilting her head back to look up at Cleo and Luke. "You think you can handle taking that back section near the stage?"

Luke smiled.

Those servers got a decent little payoff to skip out on the event courtesy of the Crawford brothers' petty cash.

"Sure thing, Laura. Whatever you need."

8:21pm

Olivia was nearly buzzing with excitement as she ducked her way through the crowd in the Grand Ballroom. The gowns, the champagne on little sterling silver trays, the fourteen-piece band playing some kind of springy jazz from the stage. It was a level of luxury she had never experienced before. Hell, the fanciest event she'd ever been to was her senior prom. The theme was Under the Stars. It was on a boat, and it was actually a total nightmare. Who thought trapping a bunch of teenagers on a boat in the middle of the river was a good idea? But still, the fanciest party in her life up until this moment.

She checked her watch.

The silent auction was due to start soon, and while she was still wrapping her head around the Aston Martin just sitting out in the hotel lobby, she knew she had one very important job for the evening. She couldn't get distracted by hundred-thousand-dollar cars and luxury vacations, and honestly, how on earth was all this for an art museum?

No. No. She had to focus.

Which was why she was currently making her way across the ballroom, doing her best to keep her vibe as chill as possible. But as she approached the row of clear display cases near the stage area, Olivia found herself getting a little clammy. And not only because she was low-key excited to see the stunning sapphires and rubies and diamond up close and personal, but because at the crux of all of this was a plan to try and stop some random power-obsessed guy from becoming a freaking demon.

Her life really was extremely different from what it was a couple of weeks ago.

A tall white woman in a stunning pink suit was hovering near one of the display cases. She had long blond hair and striking blue eyes and an earbud in her ear that Olivia noticed almost immediately. Bingo.

"Wow, this is incredible," Olivia said, peering into the display case nearest them both. A pair of oversized emerald earrings with diamond accents sat in a little velvet bed under a small light. "Is this your job for the night? Getting to hang out with all this amazing jewelry? I can't believe some of the pieces you have on display. I'm geeking out a little bit!"

The woman smiled in return and she had little dimples in both her cheeks.

"Me and a whole army of security detail," she said with a slight wink as she gestured to an array of men and women dressed in all black, all stationed closely to the various display cases. One man in particular looked incredibly familiar to Olivia, and she couldn't help but smile. Harker hardly paid them attention, save for a little twitch at the corner of his mouth. "Do you know what you're looking at here? Or should I go into my spiel?"

"I would love for you to tell me everything you know."

8:30pm

Harker glanced down at his watch as the band took a break, the cymbals from the drum set reverberating slightly as footsteps clicked across the stage. The silent auction was about to begin, and a woman in an emerald-green gown and a man in a black tuxedo were at the microphones going into a clearly pre-written speech welcoming everyone to the event, the witty banter and repartee scrolling along a teleprompter in the back of the ballroom. It wasn't exactly a night at the Apollo, but the crowd seemed into it, some scattered laughter following each pause.

One bright laugh in particular caught his attention, and Harker looked up to find Olivia still deep in conversation with the woman from the museum who was handling the jewelry for the evening. She was a Research Director in the Gems and Minerals department, and the responsibility for the jewels rested in her hands. Which was exactly why Olivia was talking her ear off about gemology and history.

But he didn't think they'd be standing this close to each other.

He smirked just as a crackle of white noise hit his eardrum. He pressed his finger to the earbud he wore, the one that connected to the radio all the security detail shared. A broken voice alerted them it was time to rotate. Security would swap off on the half hour, each of the men and women assigned to support the museum working a different area of the display.

Which meant he knew exactly when he'd be tasked with watching over the Heart of Fire.

8:36pm

"What about you two, how long have you been together?"

Gideon had his glass halfway to his lips when the question was sprung on them by the older woman sitting across the table. They had made it through the beginning of dinner, through the inane welcome speech by the museum committee. He had half hoped they'd be able to bypass most of the small talk but it was hard to avoid the curiosity of some of the other guests at the table. He was sure they were all familiar with each other. The charity circuit. But before he could say a word, Benny gave him a knowing look, her hand squeezing his thigh underneath the tablecloth. He swallowed as he took a long sip from the champagne glass, the bubbles hitting the back of his throat.

"Oh, not that long," she said, with a bright and airy smile. "But it feels like we've known each other a whole lifetime, you know?"

The older woman chuckled.

"Just wait until you've gotten as old as us," she replied with a playful roll of her eyes, gesturing to the older man sitting beside her. Gideon guessed they were in their seventies, maybe. And frankly, they didn't look as sick of each other as she made it sound. "It really will feel like a lifetime."

"I don't know, I think I'd be a pretty lucky man to get to that point."

One glance at Benny, and he could see the way her skin flushed.

"Excuse us, actually," he said, pushing his chair back. "I think I promised my girl here something from the auction. We should make our rounds."

He helped Benny up from the table, his hand curving around hers as they stepped away from the table. That damned slit in her dress pulled his focus, his eyes focusing on the soft smooth skin of her thigh. Gideon was going to have a hard fucking time concentrating if this was his view for the night. He cleared his throat.

"*My girl?*" Benny mused as they reached one of the auction tables.

He grinned. "Just playing to the character, princess."

"And who exactly are we this evening?" she asked, tilting her chin at him playfully. His eyes scanned her face, taking in her blood red lips, the way her skin seemed to glow in the low light of the ballroom.

"Not married," he said, turning his attention back to the table of auction items. A cruise through the Arctic. A long weekend in the very hotel they were standing in. A date with some rich fuck in attendance. "But definitely in love. Honeymoon stage. Like we can't get enough of each other."

She let out a low sigh.

"Honestly not sure I can swing that."

"A glass of champagne?"

He turned to find Cleo standing before them holding a tray filled with glasses, a big shit-eating grin on her face. Gideon eyed her with a knowing look. Her grin went to more of a polite smile, but there was still an amused flicker behind her eyes. Benny stepped forward, unable to stifle her laughter, but the sound was so nice Gideon couldn't bring himself to say anything. Instead, he watched as she reached for a glass, her free hand hovering near the apron tied around Cleo's waist. If he wasn't specifically looking for it, he was certain he'd have missed the tiny spark emitting from her fingers and the Latin that dripped from her lips.

8:42pm

A finger snapped furiously in Cleo's direction.

She almost ignored it until she remembered where she was.

A man in his mid-forties was staring at her expectantly, waving his empty glass in her direction. No one at the table seemed to have the good sense to be embarrassed about this. Still, a job was a job—and this one had a payout they needed to see through. So, Cleo put on her best smile as she tucked her serving tray under her arm.

"Hi, what can I help you with?"

"Can't you see I need another drink?" he asked. "Whiskey, neat."

It wasn't exactly her job to run drink requests to the bartender, but the overwhelmed catering manager Laura seemed two shakes short of a breakdown, so Cleo nodded silently and grabbed the empty glass from the guy's hand.

"Of course," she said.

"And none of that well shit. Top shelf only."

"Yes, I'll be right back."

But just as she spun on her heel, Cleo found herself face to face with a guest in a black gown and almost accidentally tossed the glass right in her face.

"Shoot, sorry," Cleo said, taking a step back. "I didn't see you there."

"It's alright," the woman replied, her voice soft and her accent hard to place.

She was incredibly striking. With black hair pinned up and her brown skin giving off a subtle glow, Cleo found herself wishing she wasn't dressed in her too-big-for-her cater waiter uniform. Something about her seemed familiar, though.

"I was in your way, I'm sure," the woman continued. She looked past Cleo's shoulder to the table behind her, a flicker of something behind her brown eyes. "Was that man giving you a hard time just now?"

Cleo glanced back at the offender sitting at the table. He pointed to his watch.

She shrugged. "Nothing I can't handle. I really should go, though."

"Please, don't let me stop you," the woman said with a smile.

9:01pm

"Make your moves, boys."

"Come on, Pete," came an irritated female voice.

"Sorry, Beth," the voice over the earbud coughed. "Time to rotate."

Harker rolled his eyes as he shifted from across the area in the back of the ballroom where the jewelry was on display. He had been dutifully standing nearby an acrylic display case with a diamond-encrusted tiara that he learned was from a South African mine. Nothing like protecting some blood diamonds while a party goes on to support the very museum likely responsible for its theft. It was truly alarming in its dissonance.

Still, Harker was ready for the next phase as he settled himself beside the display case where the Heart of Fire ruby lay. It was a curious thing to finally see it up close. It was a standard emerald-cut hanging from a simple gold chain. There was a smattering of smaller diamonds surrounding it in a sort of floral design.

Honestly, it was fine?

Certainly nothing he thought would impress the Devil himself.

But then what did he know?

The Devil got his kicks in ways Harker was sure he'd never comprehend.

9:08pm

Imani slinked through the tables in the Grand Ballroom, her eyes scanning the guests. She took note of the Armani suits, the couture gowns, the Rolex watches and the Schiaparelli accessories. She knew this crowd. She'd worked this crowd. At fashion shows and industry parties, modeling agencies and Michelin star dinners with designers and photographers.

She hated this crowd.

It had been a means to an end, an opportunity to pay for school, a way to keep her mother taken care of. But she didn't have to work this crowd. No. Her job tonight was to scry.

If there were other witches in this room she would feel them. If they were in this hotel, she'd find them. If some ratty ass Devil worshipping coven was in a two block radius, she would do her damndest to make sure they didn't interfere.

9:13pm

"Well, fancy seein' you here, kid," came a familiar voice.

Luke wasn't sure why he was so surprised to see Frank Markos staring down at him. This event was a legitimate score for all the big-time hitters. He knew they weren't going to be the only ones making a hit out of the gala. But he had hoped they wouldn't run into anyone they were too familiar with. Still, if it was anyone, at least it was Frank. He'd been a decent enough ally to them since they'd gone out on their own.

The older man had his hands in his pockets as he watched Luke gather a few more empty glasses and plates into a bucket. He wore an expertly tailored black tux, and he was rocking back on his shiny patent leather shoes with an amused smile on his face. Most of the guests had cleared the tables; the dance floor was packed, and the auction tables were filled with guests making last-minute bids. They had enough space that Frank recognizing Luke wouldn't have the worst consequences. He hoped.

"Working?" Luke asked.

"Not as hard as you," Frank replied with a wriggle of his brows. "You pull the short straw tonight?"

"Something like that."

"Where's your brother?"

"Working his end," he said, his eyes scanning the room until they landed on Gideon. He was with Benny back by an auction table, lingering close to the dance floor. They were playing the part of the happily in love couple pretty fucking well, it looked like.

Frank followed his gaze, that amused expression turning to curiosity in a flash.

"Oh, you definitely pulled the short straw."

"Yeah, well, it'll all have the same outcome if we're lucky," Luke replied. "Let's just hope we're on different ends of it, yeah?"

"I think there's enough to go around. I mean, you know the value of what's in this room tonight?"

Luke laughed, knowing full well exactly how much. And he couldn't touch any of it.

"I do," he replied.

Something glimmered behind Frank's eyes. "Listen, kid. You know you're always welcome back, right? The pot we're taking home tonight is gonna be a real game changer. It's the kinda thing that could change your life."

Luke could see the excitement behind his words and he hated how much it intrigued him. But still, there were more important things at play. And if he was honest with himself, the last few days made him wonder if playing thief was all he had to offer. He shook his head, raking his hair back with his free hand.

"We'll see, Frank," he said.

THIRTY-FOUR

THE HEIST - PHASE TWO

9:15pm

GIDEON GAZED AT BENNY as she checked the gold watch around her slim wrist, her eyes raising to meet his with a shy smile. They were inching closer to the next part of the plan, and he could see her nerves starting to settle in. It was really the first time all night he saw any sign of apprehension in Benny, and he was impressed with how hard she was trying to hold it all together. He reached for her, his hand curving lightly around her elbow. He couldn't help but step closer toward her, his other hand brushing back a lock of her hair. It gave him a little thrill to be so intimate with her in public, to actually hold her like this. But fuck if he didn't like how easy it was, how natural it felt.

"You good?" he asked.

"Yeah," she said, her hands reaching up to fuss with the lapels of his jacket, her fingers smoothing at the satin. "Just a little nervous."

He nodded, knowing exactly the kind of jitters going through her system. How nerve-wracking his first big job was. How worried he was he'd fail Luke, fail Frank. And now, here they were, trying to work through the biggest job of their lives.

"One step at a time," he said. "Nerves are good. Just don't let them overwhelm you."

The corner of her mouth quirked. "You really are good at this, you know."

"He's a certified fucking therapist," Luke muttered quietly, his appearance sudden.

Gideon rolled his eyes but didn't make any movement toward his brother, instead keeping his gaze trained on Benny. Luke picked up an empty glass from the auction table, his shoulder nearly brushing against Gideon's. Close enough they could whisper and still hear each other.

"What's going on?" he asked, matching his brother's tone.

"We're good," Luke said, and Gideon felt an immediate wave of relief. "But I just ran into Frank."

Benny fixed him with a knitted brow.

"Shit, okay," Gideon replied. "Of course."

"Of course," Luke repeated. "Just keep an eye out, okay?"

Gideon nodded and watched out of the corner of his eye as Luke made his way back toward the kitchen. When they were alone again, he sighed and checked his watch. A couple more minutes. Frank didn't have to be a problem. They just had to hope they'd steer clear of each other.

"Everything okay?" Benny asked.

"Yeah, Luke just ran into an old friend," Gideon replied. "You ready?"

9:18pm

Olivia stole a quick glance at her watch as she approached the bar. She was definitely going to need something stronger than champagne. She had spent almost an hour bothering the hell out of the nice, gorgeous woman from the museum, asking her all sorts of ridiculous questions before she finally drummed up the courage to see if she wanted to get a drink. Much to her surprise, the woman said yes, and Olivia made a brief note to reconsider her typical dating approach.

Her name was Maggie and she was absolutely out of Olivia's league, but hell if it wasn't a fun little twist to her initial role in the evening's plans. She didn't think a scam to steal priceless jewelry was the kind of meet-cute that resulted in a healthy and long-lasting relationship, but a drink was a drink.

They gave their drink orders to the bartender—a martini with a twist for Olivia, and a gin and tonic for Maggie—and then let themselves settle against the bar for a little people-watching while they waited. A woman in a gorgeous black gown lingered at the other end of the bar, dark curls pinned up to expose the low cut of the back of her dress as she leaned in toward the other bartender.

"Are you sure you're okay to take a break?" Olivia asked, tearing her eyes away from the stranger.

"That's what they get for leaving me alone the whole night," Maggie said with a shrug. "Plus, I'm right here. What could happen?"

"Totally, right," she said, with a wave of her hand.

She tried to ignore the inching guilt she felt. So, instead, she went back to people-watching. Her eyes caught a flash of red silk, and she couldn't help her smile as she watched Gideon lead her best friend out onto the dance floor.

"God, what a night," Maggie exclaimed. "Did you see the Aston Martin in the lobby?"

Olivia barked out a laugh.

"Right? How do you think they even got it inside?"

9:24pm

The band was playing an old soul song, something her parents used to play on Sunday mornings while they cooked, the kitchen filled with the smell of fresh garlic and the sounds of Motown on the radio. Benny loved dancing, had since she was too little to even know what she was doing. But partner dancing was somewhat new for her, the true kind— not the sweaty, dive bar kind from her undergrad days. She'd never had a partner to dance with.

It was a funny role to play, in this heist they planned.

But she trusted Gideon.

She just wasn't sure what to expect as he led her to the dance floor, and it seemed her apprehension was obvious because a shy smile spread across his face. The expression was so unlike him that it left her a little breathless, the way that curve of his lips seemed to reshape his face. She was certain she'd never tire of all these little versions of himself he gave her.

Gideon wrapped his hand around her waist and pulled her close, his other hand clutching hers as he brushed his lips against the side of her cheek. She could feel her body tingle at the sensation. Butterflies and nerves all wrapped into one.

"I'm not gonna step on your toes, Russo," he said, voice hovering by her ear.

"I'm not very good at this," she told him as their bodies began to sway to the music.

"This is one of those moments where you're gonna have to relinquish some of that control," he told her, before he helped them fall into the rhythm of the beat. "Do you trust me?"

She looked up, finding his hazel eyes staring down at her, warm and steady.

"Yes."

And with a little flourish, he used his hand to twirl her in his arms, the skirt of her dress twirling along with her. She landed back in his arms, a little gasp passing through her lips. She laughed in spite of herself.

"That was perfect," he whispered in her ear.

She felt her skin warm at his praise. But she liked the feeling it gave her, the way Gideon had seemed to work his way under her skin. She liked him there. He pulled her in tighter against him, holding her hand to his chest as the beat of the music slowed, and Benny rested her head against his shoulder.

9:26pm

"Are you *kidding* me?"

Imani's voice was dripping with disdain, her finger pointing at Olivia and the blonde.

"Oh— no, hi, baby," Olivia said, her martini glass sloshing as she spun to face her, a sheer panic-stricken look on her freckled face. It was a really good touch, the liquid flying. "There you are!"

"Don't you *baby* me," she snapped. "I have been looking for you all night and of course I find you here with some blonde Barbie doll."

"Excuse me?" the woman said, rearing back. "What is happening here?"

"I'll tell you what's happening," Imani continued, lowering her voice. "My wonderful girlfriend here has a fun little habit of leaving me *alone* at parties to flirt with any pretty girl who comes her way and you just happen to be the next basic b—"

"Whoa, hey," Olivia said, stepping forward, her hand gripping at Imani's wrist. "Let's not get ahead of ourselves, huh, baby?"

"Look, I had no idea she was—" the blonde waved her hands. "I don't want to get in the middle of anything, I'm, you know, I'm actually working right now so I'm going to just—" And without waiting for Imani or Olivia to say anything, the blonde barreled through them both and back toward the displays on the other side of the ballroom.

Imani watched, trying to withhold the laughter bubbling in the back of her throat.

It wasn't until Olivia gripped her hand again that she turned to look at her friend, her eyes wide as she tried not to betray their little performance.

9:28pm

"Oh my God, oh my God, I am so so so so so sorry—"

"Jesus Christ, what the hell—"

"Will somebody get me a towel?"

It all happened so quickly, Harker had to admit he was incredibly impressed by the prowess put on display by Cleo. One moment she was gliding through the crowd with a tray of drinks balanced on one hand, the next she was bumping directly into the poor woman tasked with watching over the jewels for the evening, Maggie something, the one Olivia had chatted up at the bar. She was on her way back to resume her duties, and it was all just the perfect amount of disaster.

The display case holding the Heart of Fire was toppled over on its side, the door just cracked open, the necklace nearly hanging out while Cleo and Maggie tried to clean up the mess that was six glasses of champagne and a stained pink suit. Harker gestured for another security guard as he did his best to help assist in cleaning up the mess, stacking empty champagne glasses onto the tray.

"This has been a nightmare of a night," Maggie huffed, dragging herself to her feet.

"I feel so bad," Cleo began, her eyes beginning to water. "I'm so sorry. Did I ruin it? Oh God, I did. I totally ruined your suit—"

The ensuing sobs were an incredible touch. Enough to draw a few curious and startled guests over to the display area. It was beginning to be hard to keep track of just who was near the cases.

"Whoa, be careful," Maggie shouted at the other security guard who was picking up the display case. "If anything happens to that necklace, we are all going to be far worse than fired, do you understand?"

The offending security guard widened his eyes as he exchanged a glance with Harker before he slowly backed away from the case. "It's all you, lady."

9:28pm

One song played into the next, this one a little bit more upbeat, and Gideon was quick to lead Benny back toward the stage, moving their bodies through the other couples with practiced ease. It was the first time since they met that she seemed to give him complete control, her body moving with his wherever he led her. Like she really trusted him. That thought alone made him tug her just a little bit closer as he spun them both.

Though he'd be lying if he said he didn't like their little battles.

"Who taught you how to dance?" she asked, disbelief still lingering behind her eyes.

He shook his head. He wasn't sure he could answer that question truthfully, so he stepped back and twirled her in his arms instead. But no dice, because the moment she was back facing him, her eyes narrowed at him playfully.

"People are watching us, Crawford."

"They're supposed to, Russo," he said, matching her tone.

"Oh, come on," she said, her bottom lip jutting out just slightly.

He tilted his head back with a sigh. That bottom lip could get him to do whatever she wanted. And he wondered if she was beginning to learn that.

"Patrick Swayze," he muttered, hoping the music would drown him out.

But it didn't because Benny's smile went wide.

"Wow," she said, letting the word drag out. "I would have pegged you more as a *Roadhouse* guy than a *Dirty Dancing* guy. But I guess now I know where you got your style from."

He scoffed.

"I mean, listen, I can respect ripping a guy's throat out when you have to, but Johnny Castle is just as much of a badass," he said before he pressed his hand to her lower back and took her in a slight dip.

She closed her eyes, a serene look taking over her face as he held her there. He wanted to kiss her so badly. And then, he laughed because why couldn't he? They had a role to play, after all. So he brushed his lips against hers lightly before he brought her back to her feet, his hand curved around the back of her neck, fingers tangling in her hair.

"I'm gonna make you lift me in a lake," she said suddenly, a wicked smile on her face.

"I wouldn't mind getting you wet in a white shirt," he mused.

She rolled her eyes. "Like you haven't already seen me naked."

"Benny," he said, voice rough, "I like you in clothes and outta clothes. Do you know how incredible you look in this dress? I'm doing my goddamn best not to let you distract me tonight."

Her eyes widened, a little breath passing through her lips and he wondered if the blush working its way across her cheeks was happening anywhere else.

"If we get through this—" She paused, her bottom lip catching between her teeth. "I am going to find a million ways to distract you when we get home."

Home.

"I hope you do, princess."

Out of the corner of his eye he could see Cleo working her way across the ballroom and he knew the song was coming to its end. This was it.

"Alright, you ready for the big finish?" he asked.

Benny nodded.

She hadn't been lying when she said the other couples on the dance floor were watching them. He had been flashy enough to garner that attention on purpose. And now, as the song was reaching its big crescendo, he spun Benny in one, two twirls before guiding her back into his arms. They hovered there for a moment, their eyes locked on one another, and when he gave her a small nod, she repeated the gesture, and he dropped her into a dramatic dip just as a clang of silver and a crashing of glasses came from just beyond the stage.

But it was enough to draw applause from the others on the dance floor.

And create a perfect distraction from the disaster happening behind them.

9:30pm

Tefi watched the ballroom like a hawk.

Four hundred bodies swarming around like little rats, moving from one table to the other, downing expensive champagne while writing their names and bids on the auction sheets. It was such a curious human concept, charity. All these groups and organizations that were built to support issues that were really only problems due to the negligence of some of the very people standing in the room with her. But she supposed the tax break was a bit more appealing than dealing with the issue firsthand.

She traced her fingertip along the edge of the table as she walked the length of it, noticing each of the big sheets filled with messy penmanship and numbers in the thousands. When she reached the end, she stilled, the last item the one she was most concerned about. A meeting with someone very special. It had been the sole purpose for her trip here. That was until she learned that her very favorite child resided in town.

Learning he would be at the very same event had been a delightful surprise.

Even if he had been hard-pressed to share that information with her, Tefi always knew just the right way to get under Lucas Crawford's skin. She knew each and every single one of his secrets. Each and every tell. As was her right as his sire. His blood was her blood, after all. How could he say "no" when she asked so nicely?

The band stilled as the hosts from earlier appeared back on the stage, the woman clearing her throat before taking the microphone off the stand.

Tefi truly hoped this announcement would be less brutal than the welcome.

"Well, ladies and gentlemen," the woman started. "We've officially reached the end of our silent auction! We will announce the winners after we tally the final numbers. If you were the winning bid, please ready your payment method as we will be coming around at the end of the night to collect!"

Tefi smiled, the corner of her mouth hitching just slightly. By the time the night ended, Tefi would be gone, her prize along with her, and she had no intention of paying. Not at the absurd price she'd written down on the bid. Every third line on the form was a different fake name Tefi designed, every third line a bid inching higher and higher in order to stave off other potential winners. And when she stole a glance at the bid sheet nearest her prize, she was pleased to see her handwriting still at the top.

9:34pm

Cleo was certain she'd smell like champagne even after she showered off the sticky and sweet residue. She had at least two bottles worth drenched on her person. But as she wiped the tears away from her skin, she couldn't help but feel just a little bit proud of the absolute meltdown she had bestowed upon the good charitable folk who spent far too much money this evening to watch a waitress lose her shit. Frankly, it felt good to let it all out.

The heavy weight of the ruby in the pocket of her apron was an added bonus.

THIRTY-FIVE

THE HEIST - WRAP UP

9:38pm

THE WOMEN'S BATHROOM WAS quiet as Benny slipped inside, her heels clicking against the shiny porcelain tile. She did a quick check under each stall, making sure she was alone just as the door swung open and Olivia walked inside, her navy-blue jumpsuit highlighting all of her best friend's curves. Neither of them said anything until Benny checked the last stall. When she didn't see a pair of feet underneath, she turned back to her friend and let out an exhilarated sigh.

"You know I was *thisclose* to getting that woman's number," Olivia groaned.

"The night is still young, Liv."

"No, feels too weird now," Olivia said, shaking her head.

Olivia walked over toward the sink, her eyes settling on her reflection in the mirror as she washed her hands. Benny let her body lean against the counter, giving her feet a bit of a break just as the door opened again and Imani walked inside, the train of her copper colored gown sweeping across the tile floor. She took up the sink on the farthest side of the bathroom, Benny right in the middle.

"Anything?" Olivia asked.

"Nothing," Imani said. "Not a whiff of magic."

Benny's brow furrowed.

"Maybe the coven didn't make the cut," she said.

"Maybe." Imani refreshed her lipstick with a quick swipe. "How long will the spell last?"

"Twenty-four hours."

She had passed by the display cases on her way to the bathroom and found herself feeling just a tinge of pride in how difficult it was to decipher between the real ruby and the fake. The transfiguration spell would last them until the blood moon, which was all that mattered. With no Benny and no ruby, the ritual couldn't take place.

They just had to get back to the loft.

9:45pm

"You can't be serious! You're firing me?"

Cleo's voice was shrill, the sound of it echoing off the walls of the kitchen. The catering manager's face contorted into a guilty grimace as her feet shuffled backward. Luke hovered near the swinging door that led back out into the ballroom, his one hand carrying his weight as he leaned against one of the metal prepping tables. He did his best to look appropriately scandalized as Cleo started to cry again.

"I'm so sorry," Laura said. "I really don't want to, but there was just such a mess—"

Her face screwed up in horror. It was like the memory of the champagne glasses flying in the air really seemed to haunt her. Luke pressed his lips into a tight line.

"It wasn't even my fault," Cleo argued. "*She* bumped into *me*."

"There's really nothing I can do," the woman said before she held out her hand. "Now I'll need your apron."

Cleo gasped.

Then, in what Luke thought was an incredible touch, she stomped her foot.

"Fine!" she said, untying the black apron from around her waist. "Fine, I'm gone."

She whipped around and narrowed her eyes at Luke. "Are you coming?" she asked, her hands on her hips.

Laura's eyes widened. "Whoa, no, I can't be down two servers right before dessert."

Luke held up his hands as he shrugged his shoulders.

"Sorry, Laura," he said, offering what he hoped was a sheepish smile as he untied his apron. He neatly folded it before dropping it off in Laura's stunned arms. "But she's my ride, so. Good luck."

It wasn't until they were outside in the cool night air that Luke allowed himself to relax. The night had gone exactly as they hoped, and the only surprise hadn't turned out to be much trouble at all. Still, he couldn't help but wonder if it had gone *too* smoothly. Where was their demon wannabe? Or any of the idiots he seemed to have working for him?

If they could make it back to the loft in one piece, then he'd consider it a real success.

He was relieved to see Harker when they reached the agreed-upon meeting spot just outside of City Hall. The demon hunter nodded in silent greeting as they approached. Cleo let out a tiny squeal of excitement, her hand digging in the pocket of her slacks as Harker stepped out from the shadows.

"Jesus Christ, this thing weighs a million pounds." She laughed, letting the gold chain dangle from her fingers, the ruby glittering in the string lights.

"And yet it's smaller than I imagined," Harker mused.

Luke watched her, a smile tugging at his lips as he propped himself up against the stone wall. "You really went full theater major tonight, didn't you?"

"Oh, don't tell me you didn't love it," Cleo retorted.

His smile widened, the scent of champagne invading his senses.

"Every single minute of it, St. James."

But his good mood didn't last long. The quiet crunch of grass rang in his ears, and he could feel the hairs on his arms stand on end. His whole body suddenly buzzing with the presence of the woman he'd done his fucking best to avoid throughout the night.

"Oh no, darling boy, what have you gotten yourself into?"

Luke closed his eyes.

"Tefi."

9:45pm

Gideon was waiting for the ball to drop.

The evening had gone well. Frankly, too well. Even their most successful heists came with the "that was close" moments. The "we almost got caught" moments. Or the "I thought there was gonna be more in the vault" moments. But this? It was just too fucking easy. Either the security at the hotel were all green as hell, or there was something else going on. His instincts weren't usually wrong. But he hated to think it as he watched Benny cross the lobby. With the way her eyes lit up when she spotted him, Gideon wanted to hope that maybe luck was on their side.

That he would be able to keep Benny safe like he promised.

"What do you think?" she asked hesitantly as she approached him. "Are we good?"

He glanced at his watch.

Everyone should be waiting for them at City Hall.

"So far," he said, but he just wasn't convinced.

Which didn't seem to convince Benny all that much either. She reached for his hand, a soft smile tugging at the corners of her mouth. He watched as she brought his knuckles to her lips and pressed a light kiss against them, the sensation hitting him square in his chest.

"Then maybe we should get out of here while we still can."

She was right.

He nodded. "Let's go home." His hand worked its way through the hair at the nape of her neck, his lips pressing a kiss against her forehead. "And get you out of those shoes."

"Oh my God, please," Benny groaned, sinking against him.

The lobby was fairly empty, most of the party still in the ballroom as the prize proceedings wrapped up and the band started their final set of the evening. If he hadn't been laser-focused on each step of the plan, he might have thought the night wasn't half bad from a party standpoint. Hell, just having Benny there with him made it more enjoyable than a charity dinner had any right being.

Once this was all over, he was going to take her on a proper fucking date.

"Come on."

He led her past the front desk and toward a back hallway that would take them to the South Penn Square exit. He had spent so much time with the floorplans of the hotel, he knew the layout backwards and forwards. This section of the hotel housed the gym along with the entrance to the spa. It was the quietest area of the hotel at this point in the evening with everything closed off to guests.

"You two really put on a show out there—"

Gideon sighed. They were so close to a clean exit.

"Frank," he said, turning to greet his old mentor. "You have a good night?"

"Oh, it's been alright. Slow start, but I'm hoping for a strong finish," the other man replied casually. His eyes turned to Benny, and there was a flash of something behind them that made Gideon think about what Cleo said the other night. "Who's your friend?"

"Oh, this is—"

But there was a sudden change in Benny's demeanor that forced Gideon to stop. She had pulled her hand from his, and her entire body seemed to buzz as sparks began to emit from her fingertips. He could see her jaw tighten.

"I think you already know who I am."

Gideon stepped forward, his eyes traveling from Benny to Frank and back again.

"Your voice," she said. "I remember it so clearly."

No. No fucking way. Frank Markos was a lot of things, but he wasn't—

"Yeah, I sure do," Frank said brightly. "You clean up real good."

Gideon pulled his gun from his holster and pulled back the safety, aiming it directly at Frank's forehead. "Are you fucking kidding me?" he exclaimed, exasperated.

"Put that away, Gideon," Frank said with a wave of his hand, like he was swatting at a bug. "If you've been doing your homework, and I suspect you have, you'll know that there's nothing that can harm me."

"*Immunis sum*," he said, remembering the words Harker had translated for them.

He nearly shot Frank anyway, not caring if it didn't make a dent. But Benny put her hand on his forearm, and he could feel the heat of her power beneath his suit jacket. They exchanged a terse glance before he blew out a breath and lowered his gun, clicking on the safety.

"Good," Frank said, offering them both a smile. "Now, Miss Russo is going to come with me."

"Fuck you," Gideon spat.

Frank's shoulders shook as he let out a hearty chuckle.

"I know, kid," he said, strolling toward them casually. "It's a tough break. You both seem real sweet on each other. But if you hear me out, you might come around."

"I'm not gonna let you touch her, Frank," Gideon said. "Not so you can turn into some goddamn bogeyman."

"Is that what you think this is?" Frank laughed. "The transformation is so much more than the physical, Gideon. The power I'll be granted—I'll be given a gift that no human can comprehend. Now, I am not asking. You give me the witch without trouble, and I'll promise you can have her back when I'm done with her."

A light flickered overhead, and Gideon felt a heaviness settle into his skin. Benny's head whipped around and back again, her eyes wide and alert. The feeling in the air felt strangely familiar, and when Benny's hand gripped at his forearm, it clicked. It was the same as he felt in the hallway at Harker's. That feeling Benny had explained. It was here suddenly all around them.

"The coven," she murmured, confusion flickering across her face. "But Imani said—"

"A coven? No, sweetheart. That's me you feel," Frank said, his mouth widening into a smile. Two large bodies approached from behind Frank, and Gideon was almost certain one of them was the vampire from the quarry. "No, I've learned from my mistakes. I've been patient long enough. I'm not going to leave empty-handed."

The lights in the corridor went out one by one, and soon enough they were enveloped in darkness, the only light the dim red of the emergency signs. The air began to feel thick, like someone had wrapped something around his neck. Benny held her hands out at her sides, little balls of light sitting in her palms.

"Stop—" she cried.

The light of Benny's powers lit up Frank's face, the shadows dancing across his weathered skin. He looked demonic now, just like this.

"Ben—" Gideon's voice faltered, his hand reaching for his throat.

He couldn't breathe.

"Gideon?" Benny reached for him, fingers curling in the lapel of his suit jacket. She looked back to Frank, her face stricken with panic. "What is this? What are you doing to him?"

"I just want to make it real easy for you," Frank said. "'Cause I'm not the bad guy here, Benny. You come with me now, I'll give you right back after the ritual."

"Bullshit," Gideon croaked out.

"If you bring me the ruby," Frank continued, ignoring as Gideon nearly collapsed, his body falling back against the wall, his lungs struggling for air. Benny's hands were steady on his shoulders, and it hurt to even look at her face, the worry settling so heavily into her features. "If you let me have the Heart of Fire, I will take only the blood I need. Fresh strega blood is the strongest offering I can give. I must have it."

"No—" Benny shook her head, her voice growing thick.

"If he doesn't, you die," Frank said. "Now will you come willingly, little witch? Or would you prefer to watch him suffocate? No hard feelings, Gideon. I mean, I'd rather not watch myself. We've always been close."

Gideon shook his head.

He'd rather die than watch her get taken.

He knew Frank. He knew he'd never give her back.

But when he met Benny's gaze, when he saw the tears welling in her eyes and the resolve on her face, he knew what her decision was going to be. And he wished he had the air to tell her no. To let him go. To beg her to blow up the whole goddamn hotel if she had to in order to get free.

"If I come with you, you can't hurt him," she said, turning back toward Frank.

Frank held his hands up.

"He'll be good as new, as soon as we're gone."

"Okay," she said. "I'll go."

If Gideon could shout, he would have. He tried anyway.

"One condition," Frank said, holding up a hand. "No fucking funny business until then from you and Luke, Gideon. You make one attempt to try and take Benny back, and I will hurt her in ways she won't come back from. Do you understand?"

Gideon grunted, his hand banging back against the wall.

"Good," Frank said. "Let's go."

"I'm sorry," she said, leaving him with one last glance. "I'm so sorry."

9:55pm

"Gid? *Gideon!*"

Luke grabbed roughly at his brother's shoulders, using one hand to tap at his face doing his best to restrain the strength behind it as he tried to wake him up. His pulse was there, steady enough. But there was a nasty red ring around his neck, like he'd had a rope wrapped around it. He cursed under his breath.

Gideon was never late. Ever. When he didn't show up to the meeting spot with Benny in tow, Luke knew something was wrong. His instincts never failed him.

It had been too fucking easy.

"Come on, brother," Luke muttered. "Come on—"

His brother woke up suddenly, his chest heaving as he tried to gasp for breath.

"Frank—" Gideon blinked and coughed, his shoulders shaking. "Fucking *fuck*—"

"What? What happened? Where's Benny?"

"It was *Frank*," Gideon said, his eyes squeezing shut. "This whole fucking time."

Luke sat back, his body sinking to the ground as he stared at his brother. How was that possible? Frank Markos running a team of vampires? Kidnapping teenagers? No. It just didn't track. This was the kind of guy who jacked a horse race, who conned a fucking casino. What did he know about ancient rituals? But Gideon had never lied to him before. And he looked like he was on the verge of a nervous breakdown.

"Where's Benny, Gid?" he asked.

"He has her," Gideon replied, fixing his brother with a steady glare.

Luke nodded.

"What are we gonna do?"

"We're gonna stop that ritual, and we're gonna get my girl back."

Thirty-Six

Gideon

Gideon hesitated just outside the front door.

When he turned that knob, he was going to have to explain to the people inside what happened. He was going to have to explain to them how he'd failed to do the one thing he had promised Benny. He had been reliving the scene in his head over and over and over again until it was burned into his retinas. When he closed his eyes, all he could see was the light dancing off of Frank's features, the dim red filter of the emergency exit signs, Benny's tear-stricken face.

"This isn't over, Gid."

He looked over his shoulder to find Luke closing the doors to the elevator lift. He had driven Gideon back to the loft after sending everyone else ahead. The car ride had been quiet, both of them way too in their heads to really say anything. But he was grateful for Luke's presence all the same.

His baby brother was the one constant in his life.

"You know he's gonna go back on his word."

"Of course he is," Luke scoffed. "But we know him. We can use that."

Gideon's jaw tensed, his throat working over itself.

"I want him dead."

"Don't worry, brother," he replied, his hand gripping tightly at Gideon's shoulder. "This isn't gonna end any other way."

The mood inside the loft was no better than the mood in the hallway. Sullen and somber and heavy as fuck.

Harker was propped up against the window ledge, a glass of whiskey in his hands. Cleo, fresh from a shower, was curled up beside Olivia who, still in her jumpsuit, had tucked herself against the arm of the sofa, her face damp with tears. Imani was standing near the kitchen island, hands crossed against her chest, jaw tense. And now they were all looking up at him, their features a mixture of concern and anger and pity.

The last one was the worst.

Gideon winced as he pulled off his tuxedo jacket, his body still feeling the effects of the spell. His chest thudded with a dull ache, like his lungs were still recovering. His bowtie hung loosely around his neck, but he worked at the buttons on his collar, letting the relief of the cool air hit his skin.

"Fucking hell," Harker grimaced, his eyes narrowing in concern on the raw line around Gideon's throat. "What happened to you?"

Gideon waved his hand.

"Frank."

"Jesus Christ," Cleo murmured as she rose from her spot on the couch.

"You never said your old boss was a sorcerer," Imani said, voice cold.

"He's a *what?*" Cleo asked.

"I scried," Imani said, voice growing thick. "I would have found him had I known."

"None of us knew," Luke said.

"Magic or not, we've got to clean you up," the demon hunter said as he crossed toward him. He tilted Gideon's chin back to inspect the damage like Gideon had nicked his chin on the playground. "He didn't have to leave a mark. He really wanted you to feel this."

"It was a fucking ambush," Luke said darkly. "You should have seen the goddamn hallway. Frank had this planned out perfectly. Every single step."

His brother leaned back against the kitchen counter, his shoulders sagging.

"I thought you were dead," he said.

"Yeah well, not quite," Gideon offered with a half smile.

Olivia wiped at her eyes, her nose sniffling as she stood up.

"You're gonna need a warm compress," she said, tilting her head to look at him. "Not too hot, though. We don't want to do any more damage to the tissue."

"On it, doc," Cleo called from the kitchen.

Gideon hitched a curious brow.

"My last girlfriend was a nurse," she shrugged. "Come on, come sit over here."

Olivia nudged him slightly, directing him over to the arm of the couch where he could sit at her eye level. He hadn't realized how short she was without heels on; she barely reached his shoulder on bare feet. But she had an air of authority as she leaned in to inspect his throat.

"Neither of you can Heal?" Luke asked.

Imani shook her head. "Not our gifts. Not like Benny—"

Gideon mostly wanted to beat the shit out of the punching bag hanging in the back corner of the loft or drown himself in a really nice bottle of whiskey. But right now, he couldn't help the relief he felt that he hadn't walked into an empty house. Even if the one person he wanted there wasn't. Benny had been right the other night when she said it wasn't just him and Luke anymore.

He'd found people he could rely on, who could rely on him. Who made him feel taken care of as they worried over his wounds. Like Gideon and Luke could extend their family beyond just each other. And that felt like a slight silver lining to the rest of this stupid goddamn night. Until Tefi walked into the room with the ruby they had worked so hard to steal dangling from her fingers.

"Oh, what the fuck," Gideon groaned. "Why is she here?"

Tefi's lips curled into a smirk, her eyes bright and amused at his outburst.

"You are still so warm and welcoming, Gideon."

"This was not my idea," Luke said quickly.

"It was mine," Cleo said as she wrung out a damp towel.

He rubbed at his face roughly. "Why?"

"Because she wants to help," Cleo replied.

Gideon tried to stifle his snort of laughter, the sensation of it making his ribs hurt. But that might have been the funniest thing he'd heard all night. Tefi never helped. She usually only swooped in to solve a problem after already creating the trouble in the first place. It was exactly the kind of shit she pulled in Chicago that turned Luke into a vampire. And he would never forgive her for that.

"Well, I don't suppose any of the rest of you have witnessed a transformation ritual?"

Olivia startled, eyes widening at the admission. Which immediately drew Tefi's attention. She loved an eager listener and Gideon could feel Olivia's attention focusing keenly on Tefi. Gideon did not love the way the vampire's lips curved into a smile as they settled on the other woman.

"Really?" Olivia asked. "A successful one? Not successful as in positive, of course. You know I'm not pro-demon, but like, it worked?"

"In so many ways," Tefi replied, her brow furrowing. "We can't let that happen again."

Gideon sighed deeply. As far as he was concerned, Tefi was a monster. She just wasn't the biggest monster on the list at the moment. So maybe, for this one time only, he'd accept her help. Christ knew he was desperate enough to get Benny back safely.

Cleo offered him an apologetic shrug as she handed Olivia the compress.

"Fine," he said, fixing the vampire with a glare. "But no fucking around, Tefi."

She held the ruby up to her eyes, staring at the gem as it spun on its gold chain. The reflection left a red haze against her brown skin, and for a moment, she seemed transfixed. Luke shifted from where he stood, his eyes settling on the vampire with concern.

"We're all in danger if we allow this man to ascend. Even vampires. There is a hierarchy, and vampires are not exactly at the top," she told him. "If we let him open the gate, how many more of him do you think we can handle? There is no room for a creature like Halmanthoran into *this* world. There is a reason that demon has spent the last millennium in hell."

"Sounds like a real fun guy," Olivia muttered. She draped the compress around Gideon's neck. It stung a little, his teeth gritting as she tried to clean up whatever Frank did to his skin. "This doesn't look too bad up close. You'll need some burn cream to soothe the pain."

Harker grimaced.

"Wounds inflicted by magic tend to have a way of sticking around, love."

Olivia wrinkled her nose. "Yeah, I was getting to that."

"It's fine, Olivia," Gideon said, offering her a nod. "Thank you."

"So, are we gonna talk about this?" Cleo asked suddenly. "About Frank?"

Gideon got to his feet, his hand pressed against the compress at his neck. What was there to even say? They got fucked. By someone they'd known and relied on for a good chunk of their lives. He was so angry he could feel it in his bones. He only had one thought in his mind when it came to Frank Markos and it was making sure he never saw the morning after the blood moon.

"What was he, like, your criminal mentor?" Olivia asked.

Luke rolled his eyes. Gideon knew he'd never admit that they had learned just as much from Frank as they had their father. Luke was only fourteen when Eamond died. But it was Frank who opened up the door they needed to make it on their own.

Though they weren't exactly left with much of a choice.

"We worked for Frank," Luke said. "Just like our old man did before he died. But he's no one's mentor. He uses you exactly as he sees fit. He's a heavy hitter, and he's got his hands in everything. Chop shops, the tracks, casinos. He oversees every weapon that comes into this city, legal or not. He's got a hell of a lot of resources. I just never thought that would include vampires."

"And he's a fairly powerful sorcerer based on tonight's events," Harker said.

"What exactly is the difference between a sorcerer and a witch?" Cleo asked as she pushed herself up onto the island counter beside Luke.

"Sorcerers study, witches are magic," Imani said. "He's earned his power, through some kind of nefarious channels. A sacrifice, a bargain… It's not natural born power. It's taken."

Gideon walked toward the bar cart.

He really needed a fucking drink.

"So you know where he is," Olivia said. "Why can't we—can't we just get her back?"

The thought had crossed his mind a million times since he left the hotel. But Frank was ruthless. Every little detail of the past month seemed to click in his head now that Gideon knew who they were up against. Frank wasn't going to let Benny out of his sight until the ritual. If they so much as crossed the threshold of any of his haunts, Gideon knew Frank would keep his word.

"That's not a risk I'm willing to take," he said, shaking his head. "Frank is untouchable until the blood moon, and if we make a move, we're only hurting Benny in the process."

"So we just give him the ruby?" Cleo asked, exasperated.

Gideon poured himself a hefty glass of whiskey. "We follow the rules until we get her back, and then we blow the whole goddamn thing up."

"You've got a plan, love?" Harker asked.

"The workings of one," he replied before taking a sip.

"I think this is where I can be of assistance," Tefi said.

Gideon was half asleep and more than half drunk, his body sprawled out on the sofa in the living room. It was pretty late. Or really early. He couldn't tell. His phone was somewhere in the kitchen and his whole body felt heavy. Too heavy to take the few steps and check. Instead, he sank back into the cushions, his eyes drifting to the window. The moon was glowing, the color vibrant as it approached the eclipse.

They just had to make it a little bit longer.

His fingers skimmed across the worn leather cover of the small book that sat beside him on the sofa. Benny had shared it with him the night before, after they'd made love on the rooftop. It had a necklace tucked inside, a small gold pendant on a thin gold chain. He picked it up, the chain wrapped around his fingers, the woman in the chariot reminding him of Benny.

He clutched it in his hand as he let his eyes close. He was so tired. But every single time he tried to fall asleep, he thought of some new concern or risk—another way they could fail while trying to stop the ritual. Another way to fail Benny.

Fuck.

Just when he thought the risk was worth it, she was taken away from him.

A window rattled, the wind rustling outside. He blinked open an eye with a groan, rubbing a hand over his face. The loft was empty. Everyone had left hours ago, leaving Gideon the freedom to drink a little too much whiskey and fall into a healthy pit of self-loathing. He hadn't even changed, though he had at least unbuttoned his tuxedo shirt, his white undershirt untucked from his tuxedo pants.

The rattle came again, but this time from beneath his feet, the floorboards shaking along with the window jambs. Like the loft was somehow on an earthquake fault line. He jolted upright, nearly tripping over his own two feet as a creature appeared suddenly in the middle of the living room, looming over him in a flash of blinding bright light. He staggered back, the sofa preventing him from flying back.

"Be not afraid, Gideon."

"Jesus *fuck*—"

The winged creature was almost impossible to look at dead on, the more he tried the more his vision would blur. He shielded his eyes with his hand, the intensity of the light surrounding the creature almost too much to bear. But if he looked at it just right, he could see the face of a man with delicate nondescript features, nearly covered by wings—many pairs of wings. And on either shoulder sat three other bodies, three other heads. One belonging to an ox, one to a lion, the last one an eagle. They stood on one set of legs, the soles of their feet like the hooves of the ox floating before him.

Four pairs of wings. Four bodies. Four voices.

"You will not be harmed," they said.

Each head spoke with its own unique voice, the sound amplified and echoed.

"Great, what a relief," Gideon replied, oddly more intrigued than horrified, wondering if he hadn't had too much to drink after all. "So what are you doing in my living room?"

"We are here to deliver a message," they replied. "There is a battle to come, and you must play your role, Gideon Crawford. You must let the witch burn brightly."

Gideon blinked.

"Hold on," he said, waving his hand. "What do you mean, I have a role? What is this? What are you?"

"There is an order," they said. "The heavens have set a path that must be followed."

He shook his head.

"Heaven?" he asked, incredulous. "Oh, fuck off. I can suspend my disbelief for a lot of shit but—"

"We are only the beginning of what you will encounter."

"And what the hell am I encountering currently?"

"We are cherubim," they replied. "Agents of the gods."

"Plural? Gods, plural?" Gideon coughed.

"There are many gods, Gideon Crawford," they said. "Just as there are many devils in this world. Or do you not know of your brother's affliction? Halmanthoran is just the first of what is to come. Seven sinners will bring seven atrocities. The witch of the dawn must die, or there will be no atonement. No forgiveness. Her death is essential."

He felt a little nauseous.

"I have no intention of letting anything happen to Benny."

"Death can be a gift," they said. "Do not fail at this."

And before Gideon could respond, the bright and blinding light seemed to cave in on itself, the creature disappearing into a vortex of wind. He stood there, breathless, the loft left silent with its departure. He rubbed his hand over his face, his eyes blinking as he tried to wrap his head around what the hell just happened. Did it happen?

Had he just imagined it?

But a part of him knew it had been real.

It spoke to every fear Benny had. Every fear he brushed aside.

Her death is essential.

He sat down on the sofa, his elbows resting on his knees as he lay his face in his hands. Tomorrow couldn't come soon enough.

THIRTY-SEVEN

LUKE

"You told me I would never see you again—"

Luke lingered by the door leading into the bedroom, his arm resting against the jamb as Tefi kicked off her heels. She had one of the most expensive suites at the Four Seasons, which didn't surprise him. Tefi was always particular.

She pulled a few pins from her hair, and he watched it cascade around her bare shoulders as she moved toward the dresser. Her things were scattered everywhere, her lipstick, her jewelry, a half-empty bag of blood from Roxborough Memorial Hospital. She was always a little frenzied, a little unorganized. He was constantly cleaning up after her.

She took off her earrings, her eyes meeting his in the reflection of the mirror.

"I didn't expect you to be in town."

"Bullshit," he said. "If there was anywhere I'd be, it would be here."

"Not everything is about you, Lucas."

Tefi reached behind herself to undo the zipper of her gown but couldn't seem to reach. She turned to look at him directly over her shoulder, a smile curving at her lips.

"Could you?"

Just like old times.

Luke pushed off from the door jamb and crossed the room toward her.

He hadn't seen her in months. Not since they parted ways in Memphis. He had missed his life, or what it was before he died. He'd missed Gideon. But relaying those thoughts to Tefi had been a mistake. She didn't understand, or maybe didn't want to. She was more than two hundred years old and had lived a thousand lives in that time. Human lives were meaningless to her—a life source, but nothing more.

That had been what she tried to teach him. In the whirlwind that was his transition to becoming a vampire, Tefi became his teacher. His sire. She showed him things he never knew existed in the world. She showed him how to be the vampire she turned him into.

And in the splendor of the pleasures she had provided for him, he realized he didn't want it.

The life of a vampire was dangerous in how addicting it was. How easy it would be to take whatever he wanted. She had given him that power.

And it scared the shit out of him.

But he never expected that fight to be their last.

His fingers grazed against her skin as he reached for the zipper. The cut of her gown dipped low in the back, and he tried to ignore the realization that there was nothing beneath the black fabric as he undid her zipper. He looked up to find her watching him, something mournful in her face.

"I didn't mean to just disappear."

He stepped back.

"It was better you did."

She frowned as she turned around, her hands resting against the edge of the dresser as she fixed him with a heavy look. Tefi was one of the most beautiful women he'd ever seen. Especially when they'd first met. Before he knew what she was. He had been completely infatuated with her, with the way her eyes held a wickedness he wanted to investigate, the curve of her jaw, the way her skin seemed to glow even at night, even without the kiss of the sun. Their relationship had been exciting and chaotic and seductive in a way he'd never experienced before.

It was blood lust.

It was hard to be here with her like this.

Tefi leaving had been the best thing for both of them.

She stepped toward him, her hand resting against his chest, her fingers teasing between the overlap of his shirt. The straps of her gown were slipping from her shoulders, and Luke inhaled. Would there always be this pull between them?

Would he ever feel free of it?

She reached up and traced the arm of his glasses.

"Why do you still wear these?" she asked. "You know you don't need them."

His lips twitched.

Because they made him feel like himself. Like he always had been.

"Why do you want to help us so badly?" he asked instead.

Her brow furrowed. "Can I not just want to help? Must there be a reason?"

But he knew her better than that. There was *always* an ulterior motive. He walked her backwards until she was pressed against the dresser, his body crowding up against hers. He hated how good she felt, all soft curves, all heat. He reached up to brush a strand of hair behind her ear before tilting her chin up, his thumb tracing the long line of her throat.

"You saw something," he said. "Tell me."

Her eyes darkened into red pools, her skin paling as the vampire took over. A guttural sound passed through her lips as she pressed back against him. That transition would always stir something in him, watching the way the blood lust seeped into the skin. He could feel his body react, each and every shift of her against him bringing his blood to the surface, his cock twitching in his pants.

"I saw destruction," she bit out. "I saw total chaos."

"Tefi," he said as he hooked his finger around the strap of her gown, tugging the fabric down her shoulder. "I need more."

"You know my visions are not exact, Lucas," she said. "I can only tell you what I saw, and what I saw was a mess of death. I was telling the truth when I said this ritual would be terrible for all of us."

"And just how terrible for you?" he asked, raising a brow.

She smiled as she reached for his belt, her fingers working the buckle. He had no intentions of stopping her.

"Am I not allowed to have some self-preservation?" she countered. "Do you think it has been easy to make it this far?"

Tefi undid the fly of his pants, and Luke couldn't help the groan that passed through his lips as her fingers grazed at his cock, the fabric of his boxer briefs hardly a barrier against the cool of her skin.

"You know you're going to outlive us all, Tefi."

A wry little smile tugged at her lips as she tugged him closer.

He pressed his thumb against her throat before he leaned forward, his tongue dragging against the same spot. His fangs nipped at her skin as he trailed his mouth up to meet hers, a small gasp passing between them as he deepened the kiss. Time away from Tefi made things clear, made him understand what about them didn't work.

The kissing? That wasn't one of those things.

He craved it.

His hands were rough against her skin, one still curved around her neck, the other traveling from her waist to her breast, fingers tugging at a pert nipple until she cried out against his mouth. Luke knew her body like he knew his own, every inch of her, and he relished in knowing how to elicit every moan and sigh, like a little game only he knew how to win. She shrugged herself from the other strap of her gown, the fabric pooling at her waist as Luke hoisted her onto the dresser, her legs welcoming him between them.

She raked her fingers through his hair, scratching at his scalp.

"You left me to play human, and I find you fighting demons."

"You moved to Spain," he reminded her as he slid his hand up her thigh, fingers slipping beneath the fabric of her dress.

"You could have come with me," she said, her voice catching as he pressed his thumb into the soft flesh of her inner thigh. "Lucas, we could—"

"I'm right where I want to be," he said firmly.

Whatever proposition she had for him, he didn't want to hear it. It was hard to say no to Tefi. She knew how to weave a very convincing argument. Instead, he spread her legs just a little bit wider, allowing himself to fit against her. His cock ached as he teased his fingers against her folds, smiling at the whimper of pleasure against his ear. He wasn't gentle, not when he could feel how wet she was, how hungry, and he slid in one finger, then a second. She twitched, her legs tightening around his waist, her hips rocking against his hand.

"Lucas," she moaned, her head tilting back.

"Tell me you're not going to fuck us over," he said, his thumb pressing against her clit.

She clutched at the edge of the dresser, her other hand digging into his shoulder.

"I wouldn't," she breathed. "Not with this."

He increased his pace, his eyes settling on hers, as if he could read if she was telling the truth or not. But even if he could, even if she was bullshitting them all, it didn't matter. Because they needed all the help they could get, and Tefi knew that.

She lived for the weak spots.

"Lucas, I'm—" she cried out.

"I know," he replied, his thumb rubbing circles against her clit, the little tremors building in her body the sign. There was a hitch in her breath, her thighs tightening around his wrist. She was clinging to him, and he was going to let her take it from him. Just this one last time. And when she let out a breathtaking moan, when a shiver ran through her body, Luke pressed a rough kiss to her mouth.

"When this is all over," he said, voice low and rough against her skin. "I want you to leave, Tefi. Because I won't do this anymore."

She sank back against the mirror, her chest heaving, her eyes wild and red.

But she didn't say anything.

Luke tucked himself back into his pants and refastened his belt. The sooner he was gone, the better. He could already feel the pull of her. And he didn't want that anymore.

It was when he was at the door to the hotel room that she finally spoke. "Your new friend is going to die, Lucas."

"Where the hell have you been?"

It was nearly dawn when Luke finally returned to the loft. He was exhausted and frustrated and fully planned to take a shower, jerk off, and collapse into his bed face down until the insanity of the ritual began. But Gideon was a mess, clearly running on some kind of adrenaline, still half dressed in his tuxedo and reeking of whiskey.

"Did you sleep?"

"I met a fucking angel tonight, Lucas."

He blinked.

"You what?"

"A fucking goddamn angel," he replied, throwing his hands up in the air.

"How much have you had to drink?"

"Not enough," Gideon muttered.

Luke sighed as he undid the buttons of his dress shirt, pulling it from the waist of his trousers. He sank down onto the sofa and something hit his thigh. He glanced down at the offending object, curious to find a small leather book. He smoothed his hand over the cover before flipping open to the first page. The only thing written was 'Notes' in a delicate script. He hitched a brow. Was this the journal Benny had told them about? But when he looked back up at Gideon, he found his brother pacing back and forth in front of him.

One thing at a time.

"Tell me about the angel," he started. "While standing still, Jesus Christ."

"They said I have a role," Gideon said, rubbing his hand against his jaw. "This whole thing with Frank, I knew it was big but this—"

"A role? A role in the ritual?"

"I don't know!" Gideon snapped. He sighed. "They talked about a battle. They said something is going to happen to Benny. That's she's going to—"

For the first time in a very long time, Luke saw real fear flicker across his brother's features. He shifted forward, his elbow resting on his knee as he thought back to Tefi's vision. She had been given the gift of sight long before she became a vampire. She had told him once in their quieter moments that she hoped the visions would have stopped when she turned, but no such luck. They were flashes, mostly. Nothing consistent. Sometimes bits of the past, sometimes bits of the future.

What Benny had to do with Tefi, he had no idea.

"What else did they say?" Luke asked.

"A lot."

Luke glanced up at Gideon with a questioning glance. There was something Gideon wasn't telling him. But he said nothing as his brother sat down on the edge of the coffee table across from him.

"*Seven sinners bring seven atrocities.*"

"What?"

"Frank is one of them," Gideon said. "But whether he's the sinner or the atrocity, I don't know. It's not clear."

"Seven sinners bring seven atrocities," Luke repeated, intrigued. "Well, in Frank's case, he sounds like both. Was there anything else?"

Gideon stared at him for a moment before shrugging his shoulders.

"It was so fast," he said. "A lot of fucking gibberish. And then poof, over."

He had a few more questions about this angel interaction. But most of them would probably result in Gideon knocking him out. Instead, he reached for the leather book.

"What's this?" Luke asked, holding it up.

"It's her mother's," he said. "Benny's."

He swallowed and then cleared his throat.

"She asked me to read it."

Luke's interest was piqued, and he flipped open to a random page.

"Lucas," Gideon said, reaching for the book.

"What?" he asked. "There could be something important in there."

"She didn't give you permission to," Gideon said.

"And if it saves Benny's life?" Luke countered.

"What do you mean?" his brother asked, his voice cracking. "What does that mean?"

Luke rubbed at his jaw.

"There's something I have to tell you about Tefi."

Thirty-Eight

Benny

Benny found herself trapped in a luxury penthouse.

It was a far cry from the first place they kept her. That room had been cramped and small and stale. The windows had been blacked out and a pile of blankets on the floor was the only thing to give her any kind of grace while she was chained to the radiator. They had been purposeful then in keeping her as drained of energy as possible. They wanted her weak and pliable while drawing her blood. And when they transferred her to the shipping container, they had forced a potion down her throat that reeked of valerian.

She had woken up alone and terrified, and it was only when she heard the voices of the Crawford brothers that she thought she might have a chance at getting out there.

But this was different.

Because she had gone willingly. And no one was coming to save her.

Frank had ensured that.

It felt like he wanted to keep her close this time. Like he could no longer trust his men to do the job for him. It was evident when they left the hotel, Frank grabbing at her arm roughly as he dragged her into his car, forcing her in the backseat with two large vampires on either side of her. The cool demeanor he had in the hotel had vanished when he had her within his grasp.

Like he was hungry for her.

"I should apologize, Benedetta," he said, wiping at his mouth with a cloth napkin. "I had this whole thing all wrong. I should have brought you here from the very beginning."

She was seated across from him at a long dining table, each wrist bound tightly to the arms of the chair, watching as he cut into a steak and took a slow bite. The ropes itched against her skin as she flexed her hands. A tingling feeling was creeping into her fingers, like she was losing circulation.

She glared at him.

"Especially considering how much you've made me recently," he continued casually, as if she wasn't wishing she could burn him alive on the spot with just her eyes. "Do you know how much your blood goes for these days? It's a pretty penny."

She grit her teeth. She knew it.

"Don't you think this is overkill?" she asked. "I'm not going any-where."

He smiled.

"No, you're not, are you?" he asked, a glimmer of something wicked behind his dark eyes as he reached for his wine glass. "Still, I like the look of you all tied up."

Heat flared in her skin, and she grimaced. "Is that what I'm here for?"

Frank chuckled, the glass hovering at his lips.

"You're right," he said, before taking a sip. "You're here for so much more than that, Benedetta. You're going to give me something I've wanted for a very long time."

No, he wasn't hungry. He was ravenous.

Fifteen years.

It had been fifteen years since her mother's death. Since the last time everything seemed to fall in Frank's favor.

"What exactly is your end goal?" she asked. "You won't be invincible for very much longer, and I can't imagine it's gonna be good for business when you grow a tail."

A flicker of amusement flashed across his face.

"Don't you ever think about what you can do?" He fixed her with a steady look, like he was trying to pull the answer from her. "Don't you ever let yourself feel the power you have?"

The last time she had, she'd killed someone.

By the look on his face he seemed to know exactly that. He rose slowly from his seat, and she watched as he crossed the room toward her. She tried to slink back as he approached, but the ropes didn't give her much slack. She could feel her heart start to thump in her chest. The sharpness in his eyes relaxed as he perched himself on the edge of the table, close enough that when he leaned in she could feel his breath on her skin.

"Wasn't it nice?" he asked her. "Didn't it feel good?"

That wasn't a fair question.

She was trying to protect herself. Protect Gideon.

But it did. It had given her a realization of her own body, of her own abilities in ways she had never understood before. But Frank didn't need to know that. She didn't want to fuel whatever this was. She swallowed the words she wanted to say, her jaw clenching.

"*Ahh.*" He reached for her, his finger hooking beneath her chin. "It did feel good."

She jerked her head away from him.

"Do you know why?" he asked. "Do you understand what's actually in your blood?"

She refused to meet his eye.

"It's the demon in you," he said, looking smug. "This little power you have—it's demon blood, Benedetta. That's what gives you the craving."

There was no way that was true.

Demon blood? No. Benny couldn't accept that.

"Fuck you," she snapped.

He leaned back but stayed close, his lips curving into a smile.

"I can see why Gideon likes you so much. You're like two sides of the same coin."

She scowled at him.

"Are you going to keep me out here all night?" she asked, trying to ignore the bait. "Might as well send out the dessert course."

Frank considered her for a moment, his hand reaching out to twirl a tendril of her hair around his finger. A silence passed between them, the whole penthouse feeling eerily silent. She knew they weren't technically alone; Frank's vampire bodyguards were lingering outside the front door. But the quiet was so unnerving.

"We could work together, you know," he said. "We'd be unstoppable."

"I'd rather die."

The words came quickly, but they were no less true.

His mouth widened into a wolfish grin.

"If that's what you want, Benedetta."

She was dreaming.

The room was quiet and dark and endless. No matter where she turned, Benny couldn't quite make out where a door or a window could be. It was all hazy. The walls, the ceilings, everything blended together into black. But she didn't feel the urge to panic or flee. She mostly wandered, waiting until something would come. Because deep down she knew something would. Something always did. She just didn't know what it was going to be.

Until a soft humming caught her attention.

She knew that sound.

She knew that voice.

"Mamma?"

Suddenly her feet were carrying her toward the song, hoping to meet it before it disappeared. It was the same silly tune her mother would sing to her when she was little, when she swore there was something in the closet or under the bed or hovering near the window. Benny was always easily spooked as a kid. She was afraid of the dark until she was twelve. A very silly thing for a witch who could summon light. But her mother had always known how to soothe her. She would tuck Benny back into bed and press a kiss to her forehead and sing until Benny fell back asleep.

She missed that sound so much.

But the more she walked, the farther away it felt.

She hurried her steps, her bare feet cold against the floor, until the room flipped unexpectedly and everything turned into a bright, incandescent white. The sudden change brought a warmth along with it, and Benny's skin seeped it up, thirsty for it. Like the sunlight had found her here to keep her strong.

"Be careful, Benny," a voice came, the sound drawing a rush of tears to her eyes. "You're going to burn yourself."

Her mother appeared as if she was always there, as if she was just waiting for Benny to arrive. The sight of her stopped Benny in her tracks. Like if she stepped too close, she'd disappear. But there she was, and Benny wasn't sure when she would get another chance.

Sofia Russo welcomed her with open arms.

She looked just as Benny had always remembered her. Bright and happy and full of life. The same dark curls, the same strong brow, the same lopsided smile. God, she even smelled the same, the vanilla and sandalwood lingering in her hair. Benny inhaled the scent as she sank into the hug. She felt fourteen all over again.

When was the last time she had been hugged by her mother?

"Oh, my beautiful girl," Sofia said, her hands cradling at the sides of Benny's face, the touch like a light tingle in her skin. "You have so much ahead of you."

"I don't understand," Benny replied. "I've never dreamed about you before."

Not once in the last fifteen years.

She'd never really understood why. But she felt the loss of it all the same.

"You're not dreaming," Sofia said with a faint smile. "But we don't have much time."

"What?" Benny asked. "What do you mean?"

Sofia stepped back, her hands falling from Benny's face and twisting against each other as she considered her daughter. It was when she moved farther away that Benny could see the marks on her neck, the vampire bites and the scars they'd left behind.

"I'm not allowed to interfere," Sofia replied with a wave of her hands. "But you're my daughter. How could they just expect me to sit back like this—"

Her mother stopped herself, her eyes closing briefly as she inhaled.

But Benny was stuck.

"This is real?" she asked softly.

"In some way, yes," Sofia replied ruefully. "A part of me, anyway."

"How?"

"Benny, baby girl, listen to me." Sofia stepped closer, her hands gripping at Benny's shoulders. "The sun is rising, and I could get called back at any moment. I need you to pay attention."

She swallowed and nodded her head.

"The power of our line grows stronger each generation," Sofia said. "You must do everything you can to stop this ritual. Do not let Frank walk out of that church, do you understand? Do not repeat my mistakes and temper your abilities. They are a part of you. They will help to keep you alive."

But she wasn't sure that keeping herself alive was an option. She might have gone with Frank willingly based on his promises, but she knew he wasn't going to just hand her over after he had what he wanted from her. Gideon had known it. She could see it in his eyes at the hotel. But what choice did she have?

She couldn't bear to see anyone else get hurt on her behalf.

Especially not Gideon.

"I don't want to die," she confessed, voice small.

"Oh, honey." Sofia sighed, resting her forehead against Benny's. "Death is a funny thing. It's not always what it seems."

"Frank won't let me go," Benny whispered.

"Frank Markos has no idea what he's unleashed," Sofia said, straightening and fixing her daughter with a stern glance. "But you're not in this alone."

Benny chewed on her bottom lip.

"Let them help," Sofia told her with a knowing smile. "Let him help." She shook her head.

"He is quite fond of you," her mother continued with a warm laugh.

"How do you know that?"

"I'm your mother," Sofia said. "I see everything in life and in death."

Benny blinked back tears. She let out a breath, the words stumbling from her lips before she could stop them. "How are you here? Where have you been? What are you?"

Her mother's smile grew.

"There is so much I want to tell you," Sofia said. "But I'm afraid—"

The light in the room started to darken and the air grew colder.

"Oh, Benny," Sofia said, reaching to cup her face. "I love you so much."

"No," Benny cried. "Please, don't go."

But her mother was fading, the brush of her fingers against Benny's jaw growing lighter and lighter with every moment. She tried to reach for her, to bring her back, but her hand moved through what remained of her body like it was translucent. Like her body had dissolved along with the bright light of the room.

Benny stood there, alone, in the endless room.

She could feel the space begin to shift again.

Was she going back?

"Trust yourself," Sofia's voice came from the darkness. "You can win this."

Thirty-Nine

FRANK

It was time.

Frank Markos adjusted his cuff links as he studied his reflection in the mirror. He wore his best suit, a crisp navy Italian wool blend, completely bespoke to his measurements. There was a part of him that mourned the loss of it already, knowing that the transformation he would undergo would all but destroy it in the process. But if one was to elevate beyond the human form, one should do it in style.

His skin was thrumming with the impending sunset as his eyes traveled to the window of his bedroom, watching as the darkness crept into the sky, muting the bright blue with shades of orange and red. Like flames licking at the ocean. Like the delicious light of a Strega witch.

Frank had spent much of his life searching for a witch to fulfill the ritual. It was a process that pulled at him for as long as he could remember. But his one regret was never giving himself the opportunity to see just what a Strega could do. He had heard of their power. He had read about them, almost obsessively. But it wasn't until Benedetta Russo that he had been given the privilege of seeing it in person. He understood why they were such rare creatures. Why they had been hunted so voraciously.

It was mesmerizing. The sheer force behind such an unassuming creature. Frank found himself fantasizing about their allegiance. What they could do if Benedetta were to join him. How he could commodify her power and shape her into the formidable force he knew she could be. It was a shame he hadn't seen this before when he had her mother in his grasp.

Sofia Russo had been a disappointment.

The vampires he'd hired hadn't been able to control themselves, and she was gone before he knew it. Which had been a pity. Even he didn't bother to stop Angelo Torretta from avenging his wife's death. Their greed cost him another delay, and they had to pay. It was convenient he didn't have to get his own hands dirty.

He spent fifteen years waiting for each gift to align—the stone, the witch. Every time he thought he was close, there was another setback.

But this was it.

This was the night everything would change.

Frank found some of his men congregating in the hallway as he strode from his bedroom, the three of them huddled together and talking quietly. One man was clutching his hand to his chest. There was a curious hum of discontent in the air. Something was wrong.

"What is this?"

His voice startled them, the men scrambling as they moved back from their huddle. One of them stepped toward him. Mack. He was on thin ice, losing Benedetta twice, and he was eager to prove his worth. Eager to earn the gifts Halmanthoran could bestow upon him once the ascension was complete. Frank was still undecided on who would ever be worthy of those.

Mack cleared his throat, gesturing to a door to their left.

The door that led to Benedetta's keeping place.

"She's still inside, Master," he said.

"Why?" Frank asked, hitching his brow.

Mack swallowed.

"She's being difficult," he managed as he rubbed at the nape of his neck. "She keeps threatening to set us on fire."

Frank smiled.

"Go and help the others," he said with a wave of his hand. "I will see to her myself."

The hallway cleared quickly as Frank reached for the doorknob. It was hot to the touch, but it bore no effect on his skin. There were only a few hours left of this invulnerability. It would dissipate the moment the moon was at its fullest in the sky. But it would be worth it. Losing all that he knew would be worth it.

"Cute little trick," he said as he stepped inside.

"Yeah, I know it's wasted on you." She sighed. "But at least one of your guys is definitely feeling it."

Benedetta was sitting in the middle of the bed, her one ankle tied to the footboard. He knew it was pointless. She could burn through the fibers with ease without all the drugs in her system from the last time. But he wasn't lying the other night. Keeping her bound was a personal joy. And he had scared her with his threats of hurting the others. He hadn't expected such an intimate connection, but it proved to work in his favor rather nicely.

"Every moment you stall solidifies Gideon's death sentence."

He pressed his palm flat against the wall as he leaned his body weight on one foot.

"And everyone else's," he said, eyes gleaming. "How many lives do you want on your hands, Benedetta?"

When she did not respond, her petulant face glaring up at him with a set jaw, Frank gestured to the white garment draped over a chair. He was insistent on this ritual following the old ways and that included the proper clothing. If she wanted to act like a child, he would get her dressed himself.

He stepped forward.

"You could retain some dignity and change yourself," he offered. "Or I will do it for you."

Benedetta's lips parted, her cheeks flushing a deep pink.

"We had an agreement," he continued as he reached into the pocket of his suit jacket. The opal felt cool against his skin as he brandished his knife. "You come willingly and I'll let you live. This childish behavior does not make me willing to keep that promise."

He reached for her ankle, and Benedetta flinched at his touch. He pressed his thumb into her bone, fingers grazing against the smooth skin. She watched him, her face a mixture of fear and curiosity, and he did not deny the thrill it gave him. But his lips merely twitched as he brought the knife to the zip tie, freeing her with a clean cut.

"Give me the dress," she said, eyes dark.

"Very good," he replied.

He kept his eyes fixed on her as he reached for the dress. It was a plain ceremonial shift. A thin linen. He had a brief vision of the fabric soaked with her blood, and his smile widened as he handed it to her.

"Gotta love all the baked-in misogyny here," she muttered as she shifted off of the bed. Her ankle was marred with some light bruising, no doubt from the long night, and he liked the way the red marks mingled with her olive skin. "Okay… you can leave now. I'm gonna put on your stupid virginal bullshit dress so we can do this."

"I will leave when you're ready," he said simply.

She stared at him, like they were playing a game of chicken.

But he did not move.

"You forfeited your right to privacy when you injured one of my men, Benedetta."

"Fuck off."

"I'm waiting."

Benedetta huffed a strangled breath as she stepped back and turned around to face the back wall. He watched as she reached behind to unzip her dress, the red silk slipping to the floor. She wore only a pair of underwear, a color that matched her complexion, the cut high on the delicious curve of her hips. Her back was bare, and he watched the shift of her muscle and shoulder blades as she reached for the ceremonial dress.

He could step closer.

He could reach out and touch her. Bait her.

Really see what her true power was.

But Frank had a feeling he would see that soon enough.

Our Lady of Perpetual Help was once a thriving community center with a dedicated parish that committed itself to acts of service. It had been where Frank Markos had spent every single Sunday as an altar boy, playing acolyte to soothe his mother's Catholic guilt. Frank was born just as he was now, hungry and calculating and seeking an answer to something his mother was unsure she'd ever be able to satisfy. She was alone, a single parent who worked sixty-hour weeks to keep her only son fed and clothed and in God's good graces.

But there was a small part of her that knew it might never save him. That Frank was born wrong.

He often wondered if she had known that it was her precious church that fed the insatiable need that drove him. That a tiny little voice from beneath the crypt spoke to him while he let the smoke of the incense filter into his lungs during midnight mass. That it begged him to step below the surface, to save it, to give it life.

Blood.

Sacrifice.

Frank had been all too fervent to give it anything it wanted.

In return, it promised him everything.

Figuring out what lived beneath the church was a driving force in his adult life. It pushed him to follow two parallel paths. He was a con man *and* a sorcerer. A dedicated student of the dark arts who knew how to steal better than anyone. It built him a life in the shadows. And when he discovered the gate, when he finally realized what it was that was calling to him all these years, he knew he had always been meant for this.

He was ready to collect.

But the cathedral that stood before him now felt smaller than he remembered. Dingier. Like it had been slowly shrinking into the earth year after year. He craned his neck back slightly as he took in the building, a once-looming fortress in an otherwise quiet neighborhood. It had been nearly forty years since he'd stepped foot inside. He had been fifteen when it happened. A tragic accident left a young boy dead, and the parish was too poor and the diocese too unwilling to step in, leaving the church without recompense. Rumors swirled about what happened, about a curse that lingered in the stone walls of Our Lady of Perpetual Help.

A theory not entirely incorrect.

It was built to hide the gate, after all.

But Rome was unwilling to lose the tax-free land.

They kept a small rotation of seasoned pastors, no bishop willing to take on the job. They made small attempts at reinvigorating the parish. But the tragedy had left its mark, and only the most devout would cross the threshold. Only the most in need.

Well.

Frank was in need.

Just stepping inside the atrium gave him a delicious little chill, his skin tingling with every step closer. His eyes darted to the ceiling, to the sloping arches and intricate engravings, the skylight that might as well have been ticking with the seconds of the crest of the full moon. He tightened his hold on Benedetta's arm and relished in the wince that passed through her lips.

"Can I help you?"

The voice was soft, tired. The age of it clear in the crush of his tone.

"Just here for a little worship," Frank replied amiably.

An older man stepped from a door to the left, no doubt from a passage that connected to the rectory. He had a shock of white hair and thin-framed glasses. He was no taller than Frank, and he wore a thick shawl over his black shirt and collar even in the dead heat of August. He considered Frank for a moment before his eyes darted to where Benedetta stood, barefoot in a thin linen shift, eyes glaring.

"I'm afraid we no longer schedule evening mass," he said simply.

"S'alright, Father," Frank said with a smile. "We don't need much from you to get this going."

The wide double doors to the church slammed open behind him, and his men came filtering inside, all of them armed. He had every man at the ready. More vampire than human at this stage of the game. Harder to control, but the firepower was unmatched. Two particularly large vampires carrying sledgehammers strode past where Frank and Benedetta stood, the priest watching after them with an expression Frank found he couldn't place.

The priest quickly made the sign of the cross as he closed his eyes.

"Forgive me, Lord," the old man sighed out. "For I am not sure I am up to the task—"

Frank's lips quirked.

"Now, Father," he said. "Tell me you know why we're here."

"Don't," Benedetta said.

"Whatever it is you hope to achieve this evening," the priest said, taking the short few steps toward them, "I am certain I cannot let you pass through this atrium."

"Is that so?" Frank asked, delighted. "Are you all that Rome has to offer, old man?"

"It is my duty," the priest replied, "to protect these grounds with my life."

"How convenient for me," Frank grinned.

Then suddenly the whole room went dark as Frank's men cut the power.

FORTY

GIDEON

THE LAST TIME GIDEON had found himself in a church was his father's funeral. It was at a small chapel on the outskirts of Cheltenham, and it was packed to the brim. All of his father's associates, Gideon's baseball team, even men who Gideon now recognized as members of the Caruso crime family. It had been an uncomfortable goddamn day. He had spent most of the service half in a daze, half hoping his mother would show up. That even though she had run off without a word, she'd somehow learn what happened and come back to take care of them, that Gideon wouldn't have to drop out of college and they could rely on an actual adult to handle things. But he had only set himself up for disappointment with that one. She hadn't been much of a mother even when she was around.

The one saving grace at the time had been Frank. The man had paid for the entire funeral. Even the casket and the grave marker. He had ensured that the boys didn't have to do much more than show up. Gideon had been so fucking grateful. Like he had been a goddamn guardian angel.

Strange how shit worked out.

How quickly those allegiances could change.

How bitter the disappointment and betrayal felt.

Because when he and Luke crossed into the atrium of Our Lady of Perpetual Help and found Benny tied up in the center of the altar surrounded by lit candles like they were in some fucking pulp horror movie, his grip on his gun tightened with a fury he hadn't felt in a long time. And it wasn't just about his feelings for Benny, as big and all-encompassing as they had become in the last month. It was realizing he had trusted a man whose true nature was beyond anything Gideon could comprehend. And he knew then that he wasn't leaving the church until Frank Markos was dead.

Frank stepped from behind the altar table with a smug smile on his face. "About time you showed up."

"You oughta be a bit more grateful we're here at all, don't you think?" Luke replied.

"Where are the rest of your friends?"

"None of your goddamn business, Frank," Gideon said, stepping forward as he adjusted his hold on the leather duffle in his hands. "Can we get this little event over with, or are you gonna just showboat some more?"

Benny shifted against her bindings, her eyes dark as she met Gideon's gaze. He couldn't help but look her over, inspect her, hoping he didn't see one hair out of place. But they had changed her into some flimsy white thing, the fabric might as well be see-through it was so thin. His jaw set as he looked back at her face, watching as she shook her head. There was an anger flaring behind her eyes that seemed to match his own.

He only hoped he'd be able to help her unleash it.

"Do you have what I need?" Frank asked.

Luke reached into the inner pocket of his suit jacket and pulled out the ruby.

"You'll get it," Luke said. "As long as you keep up your end of the agreement."

Frank chuckled. "You know my offer still stands, Lucas."

Gideon glanced sideways at his brother.

"What offer?" he asked under his breath.

"A bullshit one, brother," Luke soothed, with a wave of his hand.

"I thought he might want to come back and work for me," Frank said as he stepped down from the altar, his hands in the pockets of his suit pants. "Both of you could. Everything is going to change from this moment on, boys. It'll be a much smoother transition if I didn't have to worry about you two suddenly trying to become heroes."

Frank gestured back toward Benny.

"I tried with this one," he continued with a casual shrug. "But she didn't bite the way I wanted her to."

Gideon was pointing his gun at Frank before he even realized it was happening.

"Have you tested out bullets yet?" he asked. "With your dwindling immortality?"

Frank's eyes gleamed. "Your father tried to play the hero too, you know."

Luke stiffened beside him.

"He didn't like what I was up to," Frank continued. "I expected better loyalty than that from Eamond."

Gideon's jaw tensed.

"You told us it was a job gone bad."

"Well, I needed a replacement," he said simply. "And my little story earned me *both* Crawford boys. It was simply good business."

All this time, all they thought they owed Frank. And he had just set them up. *Everything* about this has been a goddamn setup. He glanced at Luke out of the corner of his eyes, his brother's skin pale, his eyes red. Luke was barely holding it together.

But before either of them could say anything else, a rumble deep within the cathedral shook through the walls around them. His eyes flickered to the stained-glass windows. The only light aside from the candles trickled in from the moon as it reached its peak in the sky, shades of orange and pink filtering in with the colored glass, leaving a kaleidoscope of color on the stone walls. A bell rang in the tower.

Gideon and Luke exchanged another look.

Harker had made it clear that everything began at the witching hour.

Gideon looked at his watch. It was three a.m.

"It's time, Master," a disembodied voice came from beyond the altar stage.

"Indeed it is," Frank replied, turning on his heel to revisit the altar. "Ready the sacrifice. Lucas, give the priest the ruby."

The church suddenly sprang to life, with men and vampires coming from the shadows. Dozens. Two vampires with sledgehammers settled in the center of the aisle, while an older man was carried inside from the atrium behind them. Gideon curled one hand into a fist as the priest was dragged by both arms, his lip split and his face bloodied and bruised.

Another victim they hadn't accounted for.

He was running out of patience, and the ritual hadn't even begun. He didn't know how much longer he could stand here and let this bullshit continue. But he had to hope the window to get Benny back safely was still available to them.

One of the men handling the priest reached for the ruby.

Luke bared his fangs with a hiss before parting with it.

"This better fucking work," he muttered under his breath as the men dragged the priest to the altar. "Because I'm ready to rip out some throats."

"You and me both," Gideon responded.

A sledgehammer slamming against the concrete floors caught their attention.

A low humming noise filled the church as Frank removed his suit jacket and hung it gingerly on the crucifix behind him just as Benny was pulled to her feet by one of Frank's minions. Gideon remembered him from the quarry. Mack. All those years working with Frank, and Gideon had never seen him before. So much had been hidden from him.

With her hands tied behind her back, Benny wobbled, which made Mack roughly tighten his hold on her arm. Gideon almost took a step forward, but Luke touched his wrist. *Right.* Play the game. Keep cool. He wasn't sure how either of them were going to manage that.

Not after what they just found out.

Benny hissed something at Mack that Gideon couldn't make out, but it was enough to make the man flinch. He couldn't help the swell of pride. He loved the feral side of her.

The humming was growing stronger as Frank unbuttoned his dress shirt, revealing an intricate tattoo on his chest. It looked similar to the symbols Benny had drawn on her arms that night in the quarry. A language he couldn't decipher. But it was another startling reminder of how little they'd really known about him.

He began to chant in a language Gideon didn't know, the sledgehammers somehow punctuating each word as the ground seemed to crumble with every hit.

The priest was dropped at Frank's feet.

Another rumble shook the cathedral. This time from the floor beneath them, the sledgehammers creating a sizable break in the stone in the center of the aisle. Gideon's brow furrowed as he saw the light streaming through the rubble, the way it seemed to glow amber.

"Untouched blood to begin," Frank continued in English as he reached for his knife on the altar table. The opal hilt glittered in the light of the moon as he crouched down to where the priest lay, half dead, half muttering whatever prayer would give him the most peace. Frank grabbed the man by his collar, a vicious gleam behind his eyes. "You gave it your best shot, Father."

Without hesitation, he dragged the knife across the man's throat.

The rumbling beneath them increased, the light growing stronger.

"The sacrifice of the Strega to appease Hell," he carried on as he moved to where Benny stood. He tipped her chin up with the point of his knife, the blood from the priest leaving a mark on her skin. "How much blood should I take, Benedetta? How much will make Him happy?"

"Frank—" Gideon bit out before he could stop himself.

The older man pulled her arm from the bindings, and held it out straight. He let the knife trail from her chin to her throat as he moved around her body like he wanted to consume her. He pressed against her, his one hand holding her tightly while he gingerly traced the point of the knife from her inner arm to her wrist. Gideon's whole body tensed, his fingernails biting into the palm of his hand. She was shaking. Her fingers were twitching. She looked terrified. But her eyes were steady, her lips parting as if she were about to say something, her gaze focused on Gideon.

But whatever it was Gideon would never know because Frank's knife sliced through the flesh of her palm and she bit down hard on her lip as he clenched down on her hand to roughly squeeze the blood from the cut, pools of red dripping from their conjoined hands.

"Should I take more?" Frank said, his mouth hovering near Benny's ear.

"It's never going to be enough," Benny said.

"You requested this fate, Benedetta," he said, bringing his knife to her throat.

The gunshot echoed through the cathedral.

Benny staggered sideways as the knife clattered to the floor and Frank sank back against the altar, a neat bullet hole in his shoulder staining his dress shirt red.

"Benny, *run*—"

FORTY-ONE

LUKE

SHOOTING FRANK MARKOS WAS not part of the plan.

At least, not before the ritual was over.

Gideon was the planner.

He was the one who was always thinking twelve steps ahead. He found the holes in Luke's grand ideas and packaged them up as something achievable. He could navigate every possible outcome, every possible roadblock. When they were kids dealing with overdue bills and homework. When they worked as errand boys for Frank. When they made the move to work on their own. Even when Luke was in the throes of his rebirth as a vampire, Gideon always had the answers.

But from the moment Benedetta Russo entered their lives, Gideon had been working off-book.

"Are we improvising?" Luke asked as he ducked a swing from a sledgehammer.

"We're improvising," Gideon grunted as he punched a vampire coming his way.

The cathedral had devolved into mayhem.

Every single one of Frank's men was descending upon the two of them, and Luke was weighing his options between dodging and shooting as a particularly brawny vampire came hurtling toward him. But he didn't have much time to decide as another rumble shook through the church. Like it was hungry for the ritual that had yet to be completed.

Tough fucking break, Lucifer.

He took the distraction to land a clean shot to the vampire's chest, the wooden bullet immolating him from the inside out. The ash almost made him sneeze. He wrinkled his nose as he rubbed at his face.

He could see that Gideon was a man on a mission, moving down what was left of the aisle at a surprising pace amidst the flying fists and bullets. But he hesitated, his head twisting back to look at Luke with a furrowed brow. "Are you gonna be okay?"

"Oh, please," Luke replied. "Like I need your help."

"About Dad—"

"Later," Luke said, trying not to think too closely about it.

He couldn't afford the distraction.

Still, his brother hovered.

"Gideon, go get your girl."

"Luke," he started, but Luke shook his head.

"I'm the one with the superhuman strength, remember?"

"Fucking egotistical pain in my ass," Gideon muttered with a begrudging smile before darting down the pew to the other side of the church.

Luke chuckled just before he took a surprise punch to the face. His head whipped back as his jaw cracked a little under the force of another vampire's fist. He growled, his skin growing hot as he settled a heavy stare on the offending party. He wasn't much bigger than Luke, maybe a little bit bulkier, and he was ready for the fight. Luke loosened the collar of his dress shirt as his eyes turned red, his tongue running across his fangs.

"Fucking traitor," the vampire muttered. "You're not a human anymore, Crawford."

Luke rolled his eyes.

"This old argument? You're literally working for a human."

"Not for long."

He stifled a laugh as he landed his fist on the vampire's cheekbone. The doors to the cathedral banged open. He didn't have to turn around to know that the others had arrived. He could feel Tefi's presence, could feel the adrenaline rushing through her veins just like his own. He still didn't trust her. He wasn't sure he ever would.

But she was here, as promised.

"You're never going to be one of them again," the vampire taunted as he landed a heavy blow to Luke's stomach.

Luke was quick to rebound. He snarled as he grabbed the man's shoulders and drew his knee into his gut. The vampire doubled over, and he smashed his elbow into the side of his head, causing the vampire to stagger back into the nearest pew. Luke wasted no time in brandishing his gun again, firing another wooden bullet.

"And you're nothing at all," he said with a smirk.

"Wow, about damn time someone shot Frank—"

Luke wiped the blood from his split lip. He couldn't help his smile as he found Cleo staring up at the altar with an impressed nod of her head, watching as Frank struggled to stand up, his palm pressed flat against the gunshot wound. She readied the shotgun in her hands, taking careful aim for one of Frank's men approaching from the side. She tossed Luke a bright smile, and it nearly dazzled him, as she landed a shot in the man's leg, taking him down to the ground.

"Where's my crossbow?" he asked her, adjusting the lapel of his jacket.

"Right here."

Tefi gingerly stepped over one of Frank's men, leveled out by Gideon on his quest to find Benny, with a crossbow in one hand and a mace in the other. Luke shook his head. She always had a flair for the dramatic. He pitied anyone who got in her way.

Tefi would always be a force.

He grabbed for the automatic crossbow with a nod.

"We're not out of the woods yet," he said. "Frank isn't going to stop the ritual."

"He will if we just keep shooting him," Cleo offered.

"Be my guest," Luke said as he took in the room around them.

Harker was trading blows with two vampires near a large shrine to the Virgin Mary, his long locs swinging behind him as he took out one of them by the knee.

Angelo Torretta had arrived with more than a dozen of his own men, all of them taking ground within the cathedral, guns firing. Gideon had made the call late last night after Luke sobered him up after that little visit with the angel, plying him with enough water to make the phone call understandable. Torretta deserved to know. And they needed the firepower.

Luke was grateful the man had come through as quickly as he did.

His eyes scanned the cathedral again.

He had lost track of his brother.

But he had to hope that Gideon was getting Benny to safety.

His ears were ringing with the blows of Cleo's shotgun on his left, strands of her red hair falling loose from her ponytail with every recoil. But she was intent on plowing through what she could, her eyes focused on Frank Markos.

Maybe she was serious about shooting him again.

Tefi let out a hell of a battle cry as she swung her mace into the face of a vampire to his right. There was a sickening crack as it knocked him back, his body flipping over the wooden pew. She peeked over to glance down at him, a proud little smirk tracing her lips.

"It's been a long time since I've fought," she said.

"Well, I'm definitely glad you're on our side." Cleo grimaced as she caught sight of the vampire's face. "Because yikes."

Another of Frank's nameless men joined Luke's current sparring partner, the two of them taking turns trying to land a punch. Some of them hit. Some of them missed. Luke landed as many as he could while still trying to keep an eye on the women fighting on either side of him. But it was proving to be a fucking complicated task.

A gunshot narrowly missed Cleo's shoulder, the redhead twisting to the right to avoid the bullet. It landed her right in a vampire's line of sight, and Luke cursed under his breath as he knocked out one of the men lunging for him in order to get to her. But it was too late because the vampire grabbed at Cleo's shotgun and used the weapon to toss her to the ground.

She landed with a rough thud on the concrete.

"Why don't you try me next?" Tefi asked, her mace swinging deftly from her fingers, a wild look on her face.

The vampire took the bait and stalked across the aisle toward Tefi, tossing the shotgun to the ground casually. It went off with a loud bang, a wooden pew thankfully the only target. But it was too fucking close, and Luke's patience was running thin. His remaining assailant took advantage of the distraction and burst forward with a wooden stake clutched in his hand. Luke grabbed at his wrist, squeezing the man's arm tightly, forcing the stake from his grip. It clattered lamely to the floor at his feet.

He hissed before he twisted the man's arm behind his back, drawing his back to Luke's front. Even among the noises of the shooting and fighting, he could hear the man's whimpers and apologies as Luke sank his teeth into his neck. But his blood tasted bitter and salty, nothing worth enjoying, and he only held on long enough to render him unconscious. He needed to get to Cleo, to see if she was alright. Once the man went limp, Luke dropped him to the ground, nudging him out of the way with his foot.

He wiped his hand across his mouth, his eyes meeting Tefi's briefly. An unspoken questioned passed between them, sire to child. She was leading the other vampire back toward the atrium, baiting him with the mace. When she gave Luke a nod, he darted past them and came to his knees where Cleo had tucked herself behind a pew. She was clutching her right arm, teeth grit harshly, and he could see the awkward angle in which it hung from her T-shirt sleeve. He grimaced as he reached for her, brushing a stray lock of hair off of her face, trying to get a read on her pain levels.

"What happened?"

"It's dislocated," she bit out.

A sudden and aggravated roar came from the altar.

Frank was back on his feet.

"The stone heart of the sun" came the man's gruff voice, booming over the gunshots, doing his best to continue the ritual as the church went to shit around him.

Frank was leaning against the table, his body putting all of its weight on the marble, his knife in one hand and the ruby necklace in the other. The gem seemed to radiate with some kind of energy, the red glowing in the same pulsing pattern as the light beneath the rubble of the cathedral floor. Frank yanked the ruby from the chain, letting the gold fall to the floor at his feet.

"Luke, put it back," Cleo said, drawing his attention back to her.

"What?" he exclaimed, not sure he heard her correctly.

"I need you to put it back," she said, propping herself up against the pew.

"Are you sure?" Luke asked, his eyes searching hers.

"We don't have time for you to be precious with me," she told him, exasperated. "It's fine. This has happened before, just snap it back into place."

Her eyes, usually so bright and clear, were dark and urgent. He swallowed, nodding his head as he grabbed her arm. Cleo braced herself against him, fingers digging into his skin. A million questions were burning in his brain but he didn't have the time to dwell. Instead he did just what she asked, popping the bone back into the socket without giving her much warning.

A little whimper passed through her lips as he held her for a moment, keeping her steady as she got her bearings. It did something to Luke to hear that noise, his chest tightening at the sound.

"You good?"

"I'm good," she said, nodding her head. She managed a wonky smile. "Thanks."

He pulled her to her feet using her good arm, handing her back her shotgun. He pressed his lips together as he studied her, suppressing the sudden urge to smooth the wrinkle from between her brows. *Was* he precious with her?

Another rumble worked its way through the cathedral floor, startling them both, and they turned their attention to the altar as Frank drew his knife into his own chest, dragging a shallow line down through the rune tattoo. A heavy hiss escaped from the back of his throat and he staggered slightly. The line was only a few inches long. But Luke began to understand then what he was doing. Before any of them could stop him, Frank pressed the ruby into the center of his chest, directly in the fresh wound, the light at the center of the gem glowing brighter and brighter until it seemed to illuminate the man from the inside out.

And then the floor began to cave in.

It was slow at first, bits of the stone floor falling through the hole the vampires had broken up with their sledgehammers. Then a deep crack worked its way through the ground until it reached the altar, continuing to where Frank stood. His skin was glowing a deep red hue and he was laughing, his arms outstretched and his head tossed back. It was a relentless, hysterical sound.

And it did not cease even as the ground cracked completely open.

Frank sank beneath the floor of the church, leaving nearly everyone stunned.

Luke wasn't sure what the fuck was happening. Had the ritual worked?

The amber light that had been glowing since the start of the ascension went dark. Luke and Cleo exchanged another glance before he leaned just a little forward, his eyes taking in the sight of what was beneath the rubble. Part of him was wondering if the cathedral was going to collapse in on them all, the foundation utterly wrecked. But to his surprise, there was an entire basement beneath their feet. And although it was now dark, he could make out two very large doors, a hint of light peeking from beneath them.

It was like time stood still.

Luke could feel all the hearts rapidly beating from the humans around him. He rubbed at his chest as if it were his own giving him grief. Then, he heard a slow, high-pitched creak.

It grew louder, the doors beneath them pulsing.

"Master, Master," came quiet chanting.

Luke and Cleo exchanged a heavy glance. All of Frank's men had worked their way toward the hole in the floor near the altar, the chanting increasing in volume as they got closer. Luke's jaw clenched as he tried to prepare himself. Then, suddenly, the doors burst open and a heavy step ricocheted off of the stone walls.

"How bad is this gonna be?" Cleo asked.

"You got enough ammo?"

"You should know better than to ask me that."

Something shifted within the rubble, chunks of stone tumbling over themselves as a large hand reached out from below. Not a hand. A claw. The skin was dark and scaled with webbing between each finger and long, sharp claws instead of fingernails. Another followed, and Luke grimaced as he saw two very large horns slowly rise from the basement.

It worked.

Halmanthoran was pulling himself from the carnage, climbing from the pit beneath their feet. If Luke thought the demon in the Codex was hard to look at, it had nothing on the creature Frank had become. He stood nearly nine, maybe ten feet tall if Luke counted the horns, and well, shouldn't he? The horns glimmered in the moonlight that slipped through the stained-glass windows, and there was a weird sheen to his skin, like the scales were slick with something wet. They covered nearly his entire body, save for a thick patch of fur from the knees down which led to hooved hind legs like that of a bull. He was lean and broad, a tail whipping around his legs as he seemed to gather his bearings, large batlike wings fluttering behind him. Luke could see hints of Frank's face in the demon's, maybe, if he tried hard enough. It was hard to see beyond the bright gold eyes and long sharp teeth, the way his forehead jut out in a hard ridge.

But when it spoke, it was all Frank Markos.

"I AM RESURRECTION," he boomed, voice deeper but familiar. "I AM LIFE—"

His declaration was cut short as another rogue gunshot rang through the church, this time hitting the demon in the other shoulder. The impact forced him back for just a moment, and Luke wasn't sure if it had breached the skin or not. But the demon let out a deep laugh and brushed at the wound as if he had just been stung by a bug. Luke whipped his head around to see where it had come from and found Torretta standing there with a rifle in his hands, his face set and his jaw clenched as he fired off another shot.

"No man-made weapon can truly harm me," Frank replied, gold eyes glowing.

"But it'll keep you busy," Torretta snapped.

The demon stepped down from the altar, his footsteps heavy on the stone. "Kill them," he called out to his remaining men. "Kill them all. I must find our little witch so I can bring all of Hell's delights here on Earth."

And the men that had crowded at their master's feet were on their mission once again, leaving Luke wondering how their own numbers looked. It had been hard to keep track. To know where Harker was. Where Tefi was. If any of Torretta's men were still standing.

"Shit, it looks like Harker could use a hand," Cleo said, her hand curving around Luke's wrist for a moment. A moment they didn't have lingered between them, her eyes boring into his. "Stay alive, will you?"

He looked just past her to where the demon hunter was suddenly surrounded, and he nodded. "Go. I'll find Gideon and Benny."

Cleo turned on her heels and readied her shotgun once more, cocking it with one arm as she approached the opposite side of the church, managing to take out one of Harker's attackers. Luke watched after her with a frown for a brief moment before he turned to look for his brother. If Frank was going after them, Luke was going to be there.

He was the one who got them into this mess to begin with.

But then, suddenly, Luke felt something warm and hot pierce his middle. One of Frank's men took the opportunity to lodge a bullet directly in the pit of his stomach, the force of which knocked him off his feet, like an iron spike had wedged itself within him. He sank back against the column, his hands clutching at the wound, his blood spilling over his fingers.

He cursed, gritting his teeth as he felt the pressure of the bullet, knowing that he didn't have the fucking time to heal through this. But without fresh blood he was going to have to deal with the slow regrowth and the utter fucking agonizing pain working its way through his body.

Luke sank back, his head thudding against the wall.

He just hoped they could do this without him.

FORTY-TWO

BENNY

"Benny, *RUN*—"

She was surprised by her own reflexes but grateful her body had better fight-or-flight instincts than her brain as she lurched away from Frank and the subsequent gunshot that pierced through his shoulder. She had been too stuck in her own fear, too consumed by the ritual and by Frank's promise to hurt the people who had so quickly become important to her to do much more than let him take what he needed from her. Would she be complicit in her own end?

After all the fighting, would she give up this easily?

But Gideon had given her an out, the ache in his voice snapping her out of an unforgiving nightmare, and she was going to take it. Even if she wasn't sure what was going to happen next. She owed them all that much.

She stumbled to her feet, pushing past both Frank and Mack as she tried to find an exit. Or any kind of escape from these men and their hunger for her blood. Her power.

"Where do you think you're going?"

A vampire came from the wings of the nave, a gleaming glow in his eyes as he approached her. He was big and bulky, and his eyes were a deep blood red as he bared his fangs. Her hands went up instinctively, her fingers tingling with her magic, until she heard a distinct click right in her ear. It was the unmistakable sound of the safety on a gun, and it was close.

Too close.

She blinked her eyes shut as she felt the pressure of it press against the base of her skull.

"Oh, she's not going anywhere," Mack said snidely. "Right, witch?"

Benny stood still, her chest heaving as she tried to steady her breath. Mack wasn't going to shoot her. He couldn't. Frank wanted her alive. As much as he tried to scare her, Benny knew that he was intent on using her. That he was going to figure out a way to make her his own. Whether it was her still beating heart in sacrifice, or as his own personal witch.

But that didn't mean Mack couldn't hurt her.

It was hard to think with a gun pointed to her head.

"That's what I thought." Mack chuckled, taking her silence for acceptance. "Jax, let's get her tied back up until the boss is ready for her again."

The vampire's wicked smile brought a heavy feeling to the pit of her stomach as Mack pushed her toward him. At the same time another rumble rippled through the cathedral and she tripped, falling heavily to her knees on the floor. She winced at the impact, the hand that Frank sliced open raw and tender as she tried to catch her fall. She could hear the vampire laughing and Mack cursing under his breath as she fumbled to regain her footing.

"Get up," Mack growled. "Get up, or I will shoot you."

Now or never, Benny.

She flattened her palms against the stone, ignoring the sting of the wound, her hands glowing with the heat that had been begging to come to the surface. The floor grew warm under her touch, a quiet thundering working its way through the floor as she pushed herself to her feet. She could make it look like she was just steadying herself. She lurched forward, grabbing at the vampire for purchase, her good hand wrapping around his wrist.

"What the—"

Benny caught the surprise dawning in the vampire's eyes as her grip tightened. The red began to fade from the whites of his eyes as he struggled against her hold, but her magic was already seeping its way through his skin, the spot where she held him starting to bubble, his flesh turning blotchy and deformed. It happened so quickly, neither he nor Mack could do anything before the vampire burst into a cloud of black ash.

"Fuckin' Christ—"

Mack's voice cracked as Benny turned, her eyes blazing with the same heat she now held in her hands. She inched closer toward him even as he aimed his gun directly at her. Was he shaking?

Good. She hoped he was.

She wasn't going to be afraid anymore.

She reached for the gun, the only distance between them now mere inches. Benny could feel her heart beating, moving in rapid time, but she couldn't stop now. She wrapped her hand around the barrel and let her magic work through the metal, turning it hotter and hotter until Mack was hissing in pain.

"Not so tough now, are you?"

He tried to hang on, but she could smell the burning flesh, could see his eyes watering. With a gasp, he released his hold on the gun, and Benny was quick to turn it back on him, her finger hovering at the trigger.

Mack stumbled backwards with his hands up in defense, and she could see the burn marks on his palm, his skin bright red and blistered. She grimaced, knowing that inflicting this kind of pain came with a price in her craft. But she would have to worry about that later.

"*Run,*" she told him.

His head was nodding yes as he backed away from her just as the doors leading to the cathedral slammed open. But she was too deep into the church to see what was happening, hidden away in the back of the nave. The unmistakable sound of bullets flying suddenly filled the space. She could see the confusion working through Mack's face as he turned on his heel, running back toward the altar.

Would she regret letting him go?

Maybe.

But killing him didn't feel right.

"Benny?"

The sound of Gideon's voice nearly brought a sob to her chest. She turned to find him rushing toward her, and the sheer relief she felt to be this close to him was overwhelming. He was drawing her into his arms and holding her tightly, hands smoothing over her hair. Her body sank into his, her arms wrapping around his shoulders, and she didn't want to let him go.

But the gunshots going off around them were impossible to ignore. A reminder of where they were and what they had to do.

"I'm so sorry about your dad," she said.

He held her tightly. "I know. Me too."

"You came," she breathed.

"Always," he said, pulling back, his hands settling on her shoulders. His eyes were warm and searching. "Are you okay? Let me see your hand."

"I'm fine," she told him, although it didn't matter. Gideon was reaching for her, gentle as he turned over her palm, his thumb grazing along the jagged line Frank marked into her skin. Even now, he was so soft with her. "You know I'll heal."

"That doesn't matter," he said. "Fuck, Benny, I'm sorry."

"For what?" she asked. "I did this. I made this choice."

"You never should have had to in the first place."

"I'd make it again," she said softly, when she noticed the faint red ring around his throat, barely hidden by the collar of his shirt. "Oh, Gideon, what did he do to you?"

He shook his head with a wave of his hand. "It's fine."

"Is that what we're doing?"

"It works for you, doesn't it?" he countered as he reached into the pocket of his suit jacket and brandished a handkerchief. "Come here. We don't have much time."

Benny couldn't help her smile as she watched him, studying the worry lines at his brow, the way his jaw tightened as he wrapped the cloth around her hand tightly. She could love him if he continued like this. She might already, the realization sudden and sweeping. She pressed a soft kiss against his cheek, then another at his lips. She didn't know what tonight would bring, and she couldn't fathom not kissing him one more time. He sighed against her lips, his hand tucking around her waist as he drew her close.

"I have your shoes," he said, his mouth against hers.

She drew back in surprise as Gideon's skin flushed.

"You were wearing heels the last time we were together and I—"

But she was kissing him again, her hands cupping at the sides of his face. "Thank you."

A boyish grin spread across his mouth as he dropped his duffle bag to the ground and pulled out her worn trainers before tossing the bag aside. She had never been so thankful to see a pair of shoes in her life.

Frank's whole barefoot, virginal thing was just an added blow to this whole ritual sacrifice bullshit.

"So, what's the plan?" she asked as she pulled them on her feet.

"We're gonna fight," he told her. "A gunshot isn't going to slow Frank down. So we're gonna throw everything we can at him. Take out his resources, leave him alone. Demon or not, he's not invincible anymore."

"And the others?" she questioned. She had a surprising amount of faith in Gideon and Luke but Frank had come armed with dozens of men.

"They're here," he said with a nod of his head, his eyes catching sight of something just beyond her shoulder. "And they're not the only ones."

She turned, unsure of what Gideon meant, only to see her father bounding toward her. The vampire attempting to get in his way hardly had time to attack before Angelo took him out, the ash barely hitting the floor as he reached Benny. She felt a swell of something in her chest, an ache knowing the risks everyone was taking to be here, the danger they were placing themselves in.

"Benedetta," Angelo breathed as he looked her over. The rage and worry behind his eyes was so clear. "You're okay?"

"I'm okay, babbo," she said.

He seemed to not believe her, his face twisting up into concern. And maybe she wasn't actually okay. But she was good enough. She had to be.

"Good, alright, we can take you out the back entrance. I have a car waiting."

"What?" Benny felt her body stiffen. She was not going to let them force her out of here. Not now. Not when she could finally make a difference. "No. Absolutely not. I'm not going anywhere."

"Markos isn't going to let you go without a fight," Angelo replied.

"So that's what he gets," Benny replied hotly. "I'm not going to run off while the people I care about fight my battle."

Gideon shifted behind her, his hand curving around her shoulder. She almost leaned into his touch, marveling at the way he could ground her with even the slightest pressure.

"Benny, please." Her father's voice was pleading.

"Dad, I can do this," she said firmly. "I've been working hard and Mom— I've had her help, too."

Angelo's brow furrowed and his mouth opened but—

"You know what to do!" a voice called out from the other side of the nave and suddenly half a dozen vampires were coming towards them. "Master wants the witch in one piece."

"Give me the gun, Benny." Gideon's voice was quiet against her ear.

Benny was surprised to see the vampire from the quarry leading the pack. And he seemed eager to finish what they had started. Although she knew her father wanted to argue more, they were all distracted by the men coming to attack them. She passed Gideon the gun, more than happy to be done with it before stepping forward, her hands up in front of her, her magic tingling her skin.

"Be careful," was all her father said before he took a shot at one of the men.

It pierced his shoulder, but it wasn't enough to stop him, the vampire hissing as he lunged at her father. She had never seen him in action before, although she had imagined it too many times to count. But it was amazing now to see him, taking on the vampire with surprising agility.

Gideon had guns in both hands, firing off shots at the men approaching, some of them vampire, some of them human. Mack's gun wasn't loaded with wooden bullets, and the vampire from the quarry slipped through the gunfire. He was fully fanged out and looked incredibly pissed off. Like this was personal.

A strangled roar came from the altar, startling Benny.

Frank was pushing himself up onto his feet, his hand clutching at the gunshot wound Gideon left in his shoulder. He was losing a lot of blood, but it wasn't enough to keep him down, his voice ragged as he continued with his spell. He was brandishing the ruby, ripping the stone from the chain and reaching for his knife.

It was all happening so quickly.

"What the hell is he doing?" Gideon muttered as he landed another punch.

"We can't let him finish—" she started.

But one of the vampires grabbed at her arm, drawing her back. She knew what was coming next. And no one seemed capable of doing anything about it. The floor rumbled beneath their feet, and she feared they had run out of time.

"Come with me, witch," the vampire said. "We'll make sure you have a good seat to the transformation."

But Benny couldn't keep her eyes off the jewel, even as she struggled against the vampire's hold. The stone was glowing brighter and brighter and seemed to light Frank up from the inside out as he carefully tucked it into the open slice in his skin. Knowing the step in the Codex wasn't enough to prepare her for seeing it in person.

"*Benny!*"

Gideon's voice was enough to snap her out of her trance, and she yanked against the vampire more roughly, using her body to try and give herself enough leverage to escape from his grasp. The floor was shaking, bits of stone falling into itself. She used the brief distraction to get the upper hand. She sucked in a breath. If he wasn't going to let her go, she was going to use that. She twisted, both of her hands wrapping around his forearm, and she let the heat of her magic work its way into his skin.

He yelped and let her go, stumbling back as his skin started to bubble. "You bitch," he growled.

But she didn't let him get closer, her hands flaring out with the energy simmering under the surface, a bright flash of light engulfing the vampire and turning him to ash.

In the time she had killed one, Gideon and her father had dispatched the rest.

But the ritual was calling to her. Like her blood was singing for some kind of release.

She needed to focus.

Suddenly a high-pitched noise filled the cathedral. It was slow and eerie and made Benny's brain feel like it was about to split open. She swayed in her spot as she pressed her hands to her temples, her eyes squeezing shut. This was it. She could feel the transformation happening like it was her own body, as if her blood was forever tied to Frank and his new demon form.

She could feel warm hands on her shoulders keeping her steady.

"What's wrong?" Gideon's voice was quiet, concerned.

"Benny?" her father asked.

"The ascension," she gasped through the pain, her hand scrambling for Gideon, fingers curling in the lapel of his jacket. "I can feel it."

The chanting was dull at first, Frank's men reaching the destruction of the church grounds and crowding at its edges. But it grew louder, their voices mingling with the pulsing from beneath them. She could hardly tell which was which until a heavy lurch shook them where they stood and Benny's head began to clear. She blinked her eyes open with a strangled gasp.

Halmanthoran had come to greet them.

"He's here," she whispered.

Angelo quickly reloaded the chamber of his rifle.

"Whatever it is you gotta do," he said, fixing her with a heavy stare, "I'm gonna buy you as much time as I can. We'll run him down, okay?"

She nodded, her nerves starting to work through her system.

"Crawford," Angelo continued. "Remember what I told you."

She watched as something she couldn't decipher flickered across Gideon's features and then he reached out to shake her father's hand. Her face screwed up in curiosity as she watched them, and then her father was off, rejoining the fray within the cathedral.

"What was—"

"I'll tell you later," Gideon said, reaching for her good hand. "Come on."

She followed him, her hand clinging to his as they moved down the right side of the cathedral, crouching low and trying to keep out of sight as the demon pulled himself up from the rubble. He was horrifying to witness in person, the Codex incapable of really capturing all of his features. The sheer size of him, the texture of his scales, the sharpness of his teeth, the wings that spanned maybe thirty feet.

His eyes were gold and gleaming and vicious.

"Jesus," Gideon muttered.

A bullet hit the wall above their heads, and Gideon grabbed for her, tucking her against him as bits of stone fell to the ground. She brushed debris from out of her eyes and squinted as she caught sight of a body a few pews ahead of them, propped up against a large column, nearly hidden among the prayer candles tucked in the back corner, the altar rails untouched by the fighting so far. Her skin grew cold when she recognized his face, the unmistakable wire frames, the way his hair fell into his eyes.

"Luke," she gasped.

"What?" Gideon said, twisting to follow her gaze. "Fuck. *Luke*—"

They scrambled toward him, keeping low, trying to dodge any outside attention as Frank tested out his new abilities on a few pews in his way. She flinched as she heard the crack of wood splintering and a bloodcurdling scream. The blood on her hands would be enough to haunt her the rest of her life, she knew.

But not Luke. Not him, too.

He was pale, clammy, and a little dazed when they finally reached him. His hand was clutching at his stomach, his shirt and his fingers stained with blood. He offered them a small smile and a little finger wave with his other hand. A crossbow lay at his side.

"Sorry, brother," he said with a dark chuckle. "I'm out of commission."

"Hey, okay, you're good," Gideon said, reassuring him as he crouched down, his hand brushing back his brother's hair. "What happened?"

"Shotgun wound," Luke replied. "Fucking sneak attack bullshit."

"Damnit," Gideon sighed. "How long, do you think?"

"Without blood, I don't know," Luke said, trying to straighten his posture. He grunted and sank back down. "But I'm sure as shit no use to anyone right now."

Gideon nodded as he started to shrug out of his jacket.

But Benny found she had a much different idea as she sank to her knees beside them both. It was a risk. A hell of a risk, really. But she didn't think they had a better option.

"If you need blood, take mine."

FORTY-THREE

GIDEON

GIDEON WASN'T SURE HE'D ever been in love before.

Real love. The kind that made a heart ache with need and want and hope.

It had always felt too dangerous in their line of work. He was a professional thief. There was no white picket fence. No two-and-a-half kids and a dog. He knew firsthand after dealing with the tumultuous bullshit between his parents that hoping for anything like real love would just bite him in the ass. His mother walking out and never coming back. His father throwing himself into his work in order to avoid coming home to a house without a wife.

He had learned not to set himself up for disappointment.

Gideon prioritized the work. He prioritized Luke.

They had been through too much together. Taken on the burden of adulthood when they were both too young. When the bills were piling up. When homework had to get done and dinner needed to be made. When someone had to argue with the electric company about late bills or fix a broken pipe in the kitchen.

Gideon and Luke against the world.

He'd do anything to protect his brother. He always would.

Which was exactly why he had been so quick to shrug off his jacket and roll up his sleeve. If anyone was going to help his brother heal, it was going to be Gideon. That was just what they did for each other.

He never expected Benny to offer herself up.

This was the same woman who once calmly threatened to set his brother on fire, and now here she was, stepping in so easily, willing to give him blood they all knew was like fucking catnip to vampires. Could she possibly know what that would mean to Gideon?

Could he let her go through with it?

And as that argument played out in his head, he realized what all of these emotions and feelings he had for Benny had been building into. The thing he had been hesitant to name. In these last few weeks, in these countless hours spent together, in sharing the same walls, his feelings for Benny had seemed as natural as breathing, sleeping, eating. Like they were just intrinsically a part of him.

He'd never known love could feel like this.

What the aching, twisting feeling in his chest had been hinting at.

"Are you sure?" Gideon asked.

He needed to hear her say it again.

"Yes," she said, as if it was nothing. "Honestly, it makes the most sense—"

"No. No way, Benny," Luke said quickly, shaking his head, a wince passing through his lips as he pressed his hand to the floor to better prop himself up. "You said that I could never—"

"Luke," she cut in, her voice a little frazzled. "I know what I said. Consider this an exception to the rule."

"I don't think I can," he replied, avoiding her gaze, and Gideon couldn't remember the last time he saw his brother this torn. "I don't want to hurt you."

Benny reached out, her fingers grazing against Luke's jaw.

"You won't," she said gently.

"What if I can't stop?" Luke asked, finally turning back to look at her. Gideon huffed out a breath.

"You'll stop," he said with a pointed look. "Or I'll shoot you, too."

Benny fixed Gideon with a roll of her eyes, but there was something affectionate about the gesture.

"You've been battling with blood lust this whole time," she told Luke. "Believe me, I can see it now. I trust you. Besides, I'm not sure we can do this without you."

"No, you probably can't," he said, smug despite his injury.

Gideon narrowed his eyes, "Okay, Lucas, let's get this over with."

He tried to maneuver Luke more firmly out of sight, letting the rows and rows of prayer candles behind them work as cover. Benny inched forward before resting back on her heels as she held out her left arm for Luke. Gideon could see the hesitation in Luke's features, the way his brow furrowed as he reached for her arm. He was nervous. Gideon could tell that much. But he was hungry, too.

Gideon felt like a fucking idiot.

Blood lust.

He hadn't considered what the reality of that would look like for either of them.

His brother's face shifted, and he tried to pluck out the features that still felt like Luke, that reminded him that his brother was still in there. There was a moment that hung between the three of them, the silence so loud it drowned out the rest of the chaos in the cathedral. And then Luke sank his fangs into her skin.

A small gasp passed through her lips and she reached for Gideon, her hand brushing against his chest, fingers curling in the fabric of his shirt. He couldn't bring himself to watch what was happening so he focused on her face. On the tremble in her touch. On the way her lips parted as Luke continued to drink. There was a hum in her skin as his fingers curved around her wrist. Like a thrumming of electricity.

He held her hand to his chest, right over his heart, and she looked up. There was a softness behind her eyes, like a little glimmer of that hope he never thought could apply to him. And it scared the shit out of him.

"God, you know you two are ridiculous, right?" Luke muttered as he pulled back, wiping at his mouth. "Like goddamn teenagers."

Gideon scowled as he shook his head. Benny pulled her arm back, little beads of blood pooling at the fang marks in her forearm. Gideon could see the way her skin flushed pink against the stark white of the dress she was wearing and he hoped to all the gods he didn't believe in that they'd make it out of this alive.

A heavy thud came from deeper within the cathedral, like a bleak reminder of what was still left for them beyond the pillars they were hidden behind.

"You good?" Gideon asked his brother.

"Brand-fucking-new." Luke grinned. "Jesus Christ, Benny, this feels fucking great."

The corner of Benny's lips twitched.

"Don't get used to it," she warned as she moved to get up.

Gideon was quick to steady her, rising first before helping her stand. She looked up at him even as she reached her full height and he noticed she was a little wobbly on her feet. He frowned. "Are *you* good?"

"As ever," she replied.

"I feel like I can lift a fucking tractor trailer," Luke exclaimed as he sprang to his feet.

"Great, you might have to," Gideon said as they discovered Frank or Halmanthoran or whatever the fuck he was grabbing a man by his shoulders like he was an action figure and tossing him over the side of a pew. "Because I think we've only just gotten to the hard shit."

"Just now?" Benny asked wearily.

He shrugged. "Relatively."

Luke clapped his hands together. "Well, let's fuck some shit up, folks."

Almost as if he summoned it, a stray bullet whizzed past Gideon's ear, and he whipped to the left to see Harker in the throes of battle with a particularly grizzled-looking vampire. The demon hunter landed a heavy elbow into the vampire's stomach and knocked her back before driving a stake through her heart. He looked up with a sheepish grin as the ash pooled at his feet.

"Sorry, love," he called out with a wave. "I tried to stop her."

"We've already dealt with one bullet wound, Harker," Luke called back.

"You look fine to me, darling," the demon hunter retorted as he swung his staff around his shoulders, knocking back two more vampires. "Plan to join back in the fray?"

"Like I'd let you get all the glory."

"Benny," Gideon said. "What do you need from us?"

"Time," she said, hands wringing against her chest. "Right now his only focus is finding me. Whatever his use is, I don't know but—"

"Your heart—" Gideon felt his whole body tense.

"If he can't have me as his own personal witch," she said with a shrug.

"We've really gotta kill that sonofabitch," Luke growled.

"How much time?" Gideon asked.

"As close to sunrise as possible."

In the absolute fucking mayhem that was Our Lady of Perpetual Help's current state, Gideon found himself back-to-back-to-back with Harker and Luke as they all brawled against a handful of vampires. Gideon wiped at his face with the back of his hand, brushing away the beads of sweat that pooled at his forehead. There was a thick heat within the cathedral. From the sticky warm September air or the fucking gate that led to Hell beneath their feet, he wasn't sure. But the atrium was stifling.

"So, tell me about your angel," Harker said in between punches.

"You told him?" Gideon grunted, tossing his brother a look.

"Oh, I told him." Luke laughed. "Of course I told him."

"Well, I'm glad one of you did," Harker snapped as he drove his wooden staff into the center of a vampire's chest. "That's not exactly an everyday kind of event."

"Because the rest of this is," he retorted dryly.

"Knowing that the heavens have a stake in this changes everything."

Harker was bleeding from the lip, his staff resting against his shoulder.

"Were they hot?" Luke asked.

"*What?*"

Gideon dodged a swing of a fist, spinning around him and ramming his heel into the back of a man's knee. The men at Frank's disposal seemed endless. For every one they killed, two more seemed to pop up in their place. It was an exhausting onslaught. But it meant they had time, whatever time Benny needed.

"Were they hot?" Luke repeated slowly as the vampire he was fighting gave him a funny look. He narrowed his eyes as he staked him in the middle of his chest, the ash hovering in the air for a moment before sinking to the ground. "It's an honest question!"

"No, they weren't hot, Lucas," Gideon said as he fired a wooden bullet into the chest of a vampire. "They had like four heads, and only one of them was human."

Harker fixed him with a concerned glance.

"They came to you in their true form?"

"Was there another option?" Gideon asked, grateful for the breather.

The demon hunter chuckled, his head shaking.

"Oh, love," he said. "How do you attract such trouble?"

Gideon wished he had an answer to that question.

"What did they say?" the demon hunter asked.

"What did who say?" Cleo asked as she ducked behind a nearby pillar to reload.

"Gideon was visited by an angel last night," Luke said.

"Jesus Christ," Gideon muttered with a roll of his eyes. "Just tell everyone."

"Holy shit," Cleo said, blowing out a breath. "Like a whole-ass angel?"

"Four heads and everything," Luke offered.

Cleo seemed to consider that visual, her head nodding just slightly.

"Well, I can see how opening up the gates of Hell would probably piss them off," she said as she rested her head back against the pillar.

"They said something about atoning," Gideon said, though it felt difficult to recall the exact wording. Like their interaction was purposefully fading from his memory. "Like maybe we were the sinners and not that sack of shit out there."

"Typical," Harker muttered. "What else?"

Gideon scrubbed a hand across his face, his fingers coming away with blood.

"That was it," he said, his eyes falling to Luke.

His brother said nothing.

Only Luke knew what the angel said about Benny.

Tefi came sweeping into the atrium, her mace dragging on the floor beside her as she licked at her fingertips. She had a splattering of blood across her face and chest, and she looked feral, her eyes still glowing red as she approached.

"We're running out of time," she announced.

"You're certain?" Harker asked.

Tefi nodded, wisps of her long, dark hair slipping from her ponytail. A part of him couldn't believe she was here. Messy hair, a tear in her sleeve from what Gideon assumed was an earlier fight, and actually helping.

Another part of him wondered what they'd pay in return.

"It's only a matter of time before what's down there comes up to join us here," she said as she gestured toward the floor. "And we do *not* want that."

Gideon remembered what she said about the hierarchy of Hell. He had never seen fear in her before. He wasn't sure she was capable of it. But the picture she painted, of dozens of demons like Halmanthoran roaming the earth, the gates of Hell wide open—he understood that fear.

Completely.

"Just think of Cinderella's castle," Harker said.

"What do you mean?" Cleo asked as she rubbed her shoulder, her fair skin a little red and flushed, a trickle of blood at her cheek bone.

"If one door is open…" Harker started hesitantly.

"Then they're all open," Tefi concluded.

"And you waited until just now to tell us?" Luke scoffed, rubbing absently at the healed wound in his gut. He had lost his suit jacket somewhere in the fray, and the red splash of blood on his shirt was starting to darken as it dried.

"I had hoped it wouldn't get to this," Harker sighed. "And why make things worse?"

"This must be our only priority," Tefi said impatiently. "We must close them."

"Gonna be a little hard with Godzilla and his men over there," Gideon said.

"Not for much longer."

Benny's voice was clear as she reached the group.

She had been doing her best to keep out of Frank's sight. Fighting just out of Frank's reach. A game of cat and mouse that had Gideon rattled with nerves. But so far, it was working. At the expense of nearly everyone's energy and a few unfortunate casualties in the Caruso family as they took the brunt of distracting the demon. They threw every bit of firepower they had at the demon. Trying to keep him contained to just one part of the cathedral. The size of the church was their only real advantage until Benny felt like it was time.

But they were getting closer and closer to sunrise.

"How?" Cleo asked, exasperated. "There's not a single weapon here that's been able to put a dent in him. We've tried."

"Not every weapon," Benny replied darkly.

Gideon's whole body tensed. He could feel the heat coming off her skin.

The nuclear option.

"Benny," Gideon said, his voice gruff. "Are you sure? Do you even know how this will work?"

But her face was resolute.

"It doesn't matter," she said. "I won't let him win. I won't let him walk out those doors."

He reached for her, his hand grazing hers, ash staining his skin.

"I promise we'll be okay," she said.

He nodded. It was all he could do.

"Tefi, what do you need to close the gate?" Harker asked.

"A life," the other vampire replied. "I was thinking one of Frank's men would do rather nicely."

Gideon glanced back down at his watch as a plan began to whir in his mind.

"I think I know how we can swing this."

FORTY-FOUR

BENNY

"WHERE ARE YOU HIDING, Benedetta?"

Frank's voice was a booming sound, the effect ringing throughout the cathedral as his heavy footsteps worked their way down the center aisle. Or what was left of it. Pews were damaged and destroyed, tossed aside and shattered in the bedlam of the battle. The desecration of Our Lady of Perpetual Help was evident.

Benny closed her eyes, her head resting back against the pillar she hid behind. She pressed her hand against her chest, her heart beating so rapidly it felt like it was ready to burst. She increased the pressure, almost as if she was trying to hold her own heart in her hand to steady it. Benny took a deep breath. She was giving the others time.

Giving herself time.

She still wasn't sure this was going to work.

Benny only had a couple of days with her mother's journal.

She'd hardly had the time to put her mother's hypothesis into action.

She wasn't sure she was strong enough. Brave enough.

"If you insist on playing the coward," Frank hissed over what sounded like the muffled sounds of a man struggling, "I will be forced to find an alternative solution. If I cannot have your heart, perhaps I will just kill everyone here you love instead."

"No," she whispered, the realization of his words making her stomach flip.

There was a sudden and brutal crash, a choked grunt of pain that forced Benny to turn, keeping her profile low as she stole a glance from behind the pillar. She watched in horror as her father rolled onto his side in the rubble of a freshly broken pew, wood and bibles strewn across the floor. He was bleeding, bright red pooling in one ear as he clutched his arm to his chest.

"I am tired of these games, Benedetta." Frank sighed. "My patience is wearing very thin, and we have only just begun to test the limits of my new body."

She could hear the chilling sound of wings beating.

Her jaw clenched as her fingers flexed at her side.

Her patience was wearing thin too. And her rage was beginning to itch.

A door in the second level slammed shut. Then another.

Frank looked up into the rafters.

"Come out, come out, little witch," he growled. "Do you think I can't feel you nearby? Do you think the blood we share won't bind us forever?"

The thought made her sick.

Frank's footsteps went bounding back down the aisle as his shouted commands to reach the second floor sent the rest of his men scattering.

Just a few more minutes.

"Hey, princess—"

Gideon's voice was deep and warm, yet barely above a whisper as he came from the back corner of the atrium. She could feel the sudden relief working its way through her muscles, his presence easing her as he stepped out from the shadows. But she frowned when she noticed the fresh cut above his eyebrow and the scrap against his cheekbone. She reached out for him almost as soon as he reached her, her fingers hovering along the cut.

"This is new," she said softly.

"Yeah, well, the other guy's dead, so." She watched as his throat worked over itself, his eyes studying her intently. Something she couldn't name flashed behind them, something pained. "You ready?"

She nodded. It was time to toss her the baton. The others had done so much already.

"It has to end."

A moment passed between them, Gideon's features softening as he looked at her.

"But I can be scared, right?" she whispered, the words a confession.

"Fear and bravery don't seem all that much different to me at this point in the game, Benny," he said. "But I think if anyone's gotta be scared right now, it's Frank."

She huffed a breath as she shook her head. "Gideon—"

"You are the only person here who can hurt him," he said, his hands curving at her shoulders as he fixed her with a steady gaze. "You're a fucking marvel, do you know that?"

She blinked her eyes shut. She wanted to believe him. She really did.

"Baby, look at me," he said, tilting her chin with the crook of his finger. "Please."

She opened her eyes as his hand curved at the nape of her neck.

"I know you can do this," he told her, voice tender. "You're incredible, Benny. Everything about you. Don't let him win."

She chewed on her bottom lip.

"Do you think maybe you went into the wrong profession?" she asked.

He stifled his laughter as he pressed a kiss to her forehead.

"You're up," he said, rolling his eyes at her as a smile crept across his lips.

"Right," she said, her heart fluttering rapidly once again. "This is it. This is—*shit*—"

Benny surged forward and pressed her mouth against his, both hands cupping at the sides of his face. Her kiss was deep and urgent. A little voice in her head whispered *mine* as his hands pressed into her hips, and it only grew louder as his fingers tangled in the fabric of her dress. If this was the last instance of pleasure in her life, it would be worth it.

It would be so fucking worth it.

She stepped back, her fingers pressing at her lips.

A thunderous roar bounced off of the walls of the cathedral. Frank was losing it.

Which meant this really was it.

"I think I love you," she breathed. "I have to say it now because I'm not sure what's next. And I don't want to walk out there without telling you that you— God, Gideon, you make me feel more alive than I've ever felt in my whole life."

Gideon opened his mouth to speak, but she powered through. She felt this dizzying mixture of lightness and strength all at the same time and there was more she needed to say. It was too important. And they were running out of time.

"I need you to take cover," she continued. "And to keep Luke as far away from me as possible. Harker too. I don't want to hurt them. And my dad—just, keep him safe, okay? Whatever happens. Please don't let him be alone."

"Benny," Gideon started.

"Promise me, Gideon," she urged.

He looked stricken. "I promise."

"Now go," she said, offering him a smile, her heart feeling like it was going to explode out of her chest. "Please."

There was a moment where she thought he would say something, but he just nodded before breaking off into a jog to reach the others.

It was Benny's turn to step out into the light.

Her footsteps were slow and steady as she reached the edge of the aisle. Bodies lay at her feet, men she knew and men she didn't. The fighting had all but slowed. Too many men dead, too many vampires gone. Out of the corner of her eye she could see Gideon reach her father, Jimmy already trying to carry him toward the entrance of the church. She could see Cleo hidden in the balcony of the second floor, her shotgun propped up on the railing. Benny tried to keep her head up and her shoulders square, her eyes steady. But it was impossible not to think of the cost or of the blood that surely rested on her already black hands. All the lives that were lost.

Because of her.

No.

She had to stop shouldering the blame.

This was because of Frank Markos. Because of countless men just like him throughout history, leaving behind the instructions to their mayhem for other pathetic men to find. Well, that was going to end. It had to.

"There you are, my little witch."

He stepped down from the altar, his hooves heavy on the marble, his eyes gleaming with a certain kind of want. Like she was a toy or a trophy. A thing to play with. It made her skin prickle with gooseflesh as she stepped toward him. He was eager to meet her, eager to rip her heart from her chest. Like he could have ever wanted anything more than to just use up her body, to pull out the pieces he needed most from her without a second thought.

"Are you finally ready, Benedetta?" he asked.

Her eyes flickered to the stained glass, to the burgeoning light beyond the windowpanes. She could hear her mother's voice in her head. She could feel her strength, could feel her support, and her love. Benny flexed her hands at her sides, letting the magic seep into her fingertips.

"Yes, I am."

Frank snarled as he bounded across the hole in the stone floor with ease, as if he were merely skipping over a crack in the sidewalk. The floor reverberated with the impact as he landed and it took everything she had in her not to stumble backwards. She steadied herself as she tilted her head back to meet his gaze.

He was so close.

His body mere inches away from her own.

"I am going to enjoy ripping your heart from your chest," he said as he looked down at her. "And I'm not going to be neat about it."

"You've already taken enough from me," she said. "You're not getting anymore."

"Is that so?" he cooed. "Are you the weapon come to kill?"

"I am," she said. "I am not man-made. I am witch born of generations of Stregas, and all their power flows through me. I am the weapon."

With a ferocious growl, he grabbed for her, his marled, clawed hand wrapping around her waist roughly. She could feel the tips of his claws digging into her skin, cutting through the linen he forced her to wear. A cry spilled from her lips and she could have sworn she heard someone call out her name. But she needed to focus. She needed to draw on her pain, to channel it into her magic.

She held out her hands, her skin tingling with raw power.

Benny closed her eyes, willing the rage and anger and fear she felt into something more. Something that could save the people she loved. She could feel it swirling through her body, bubbling beneath the surface of her skin just waiting to break through. She welcomed it, willing the heat and power to consume her in a way she never had before, and her skin crackled with electricity.

She could see her mother's handwriting, the notes she had scrawled across numerous pages. Sophia had this fear that if she wasn't careful, her power could swallow her whole. That she would become a blitz, a weapon, something more dangerous than anyone had ever seen.

That was exactly what Benny wanted.

She called on the goddess who gifted her these powers. She called on the witches she had lost over the years, the family taken from her. All the Stregas that were killed for their abilities, for their blood.

She was not going to do this alone.

The light within her was growing more and more intense until it was breaking through her skin, illuminating her from the inside out.

"A cute little party trick," Frank mused.

But his hold on her was loosening, the energy radiating through her skin becoming unbearable to touch. She could feel it tremoring through her, every inch of her body feeling like it was trembling with power. Like she was merely a beacon for it.

"No—" Frank stumbled from the intensity of the light, dropping her back down as he sank to his knees. "*No—*"

But her feet never touched the ground.

Benny was floating.

With her head tilted back and her arms splayed out at her sides, her body became a balefire of light and power and electricity. Like a bomb ready to burst. It kept her steady, floating, the power drawing her up into the air and cradling her.

A gunshot ripped through the room, crashing into the stained-glass window and allowing the sun's morning rays to seep into the cathedral, all of the light channeling through Benny's body like it was starved for it.

A small gasp passed through her lips.

She *was* sunlight.

She became Aurora, goddess of the dawn.

A blinding flash of light filled the church, illuminating the entire space before it seemed to centralize into one single unfortunate figure.

It was not with a roar that Frank died, but a strangled cry.

In one moment his body was there, and in another, it was gone. Benny could feel his loss innately; she could feel it in her blood. Would she always feel the ghost of him? The realization brought a dull ache to her chest, her heart feeling tight, as dizziness settled in.

And then, everything went black.

GIDEON

SOMETHING WAS WRONG.

Gideon could feel it in his bones as his vision went white, his eyes stinging from the bright light that overtook the cathedral. The brightness that was Benny. He squeezed his eyes shut for relief as a chilling cry rang through the cathedral, the sound lingering in the air as if it was burrowing its way into the walls. Only a few of Frank's men remained, and he could hear them scramble, cursing and looking for an exit. But when the light dimmed and the haze cleared, there was nothing there. The vampires that had remained had turned to ash, the men had scattered.

Frank was gone. In both forms.

But the only thing he really cared about at that moment was that he couldn't see Benny. From his vantage point near the back, the woman who was only just recently floating in mid-fucking-air was nowhere to be found. Gideon scrambled to his feet as he tried to quell the rising panic he knew was working its way into his body. He climbed over the rubble and the destruction to reach the center aisle, his eyes blinking as he tried to adjust to the natural light, bright sunspots still nagging at his pupils.

Like he had just tried to stare directly into the sun.

But wasn't that exactly what he had done?

"Benny?" came Torretta's voice, hoarse and weak. "Ben?"

"Hold on, Ang," Jimmy muttered. "Let me help you up."

Gideon saw her hand first, ash darkening her skin to her elbow. The marks left behind from her magic, a reminder of the pain she inflicted, of the power she wielded. He could feel his heart sink into his stomach when he found her lying there on the floor, her head tilted back, her body twisted just slightly. Blood had trickled from her nostrils. And as he sank to the floor beside her, his knees crashing against the stone, he knew the prophecy had come true.

Benny was dead.

She wasn't moving. She wasn't breathing. When Gideon pressed his trembling hand against her wrist, he couldn't find a fucking pulse.

"Benny," he said urgently as he crouched over her, his hand gently tapping at her cheek. "Hey, come on, princess, you gotta wake up now."

"What's going on?"

Luke was racing down the stairs from the second floor, Cleo on his heels.

"No, please," Angelo cried. "Not you too, Ben."

Gideon pressed his ear to her chest, wondering if the thudding in his head was drowning out the potential sound of her beating heart. But it was quiet. Achingly so. He sat back on his heels, his brain not understanding, not accepting what he was seeing.

Even if he could still hear the cherubim's voice.

The witch of the dawn must die.

Stone scraped against the ground and out of the corner of his eye he could see Harker and Tefi pulling themselves up from the wreckage where they had been working to close the gate. He could feel everyone crowding around them, the whispers between Tefi and Luke, the quiet sobs from Angelo. It all made him want to scream at the top of his lungs.

"Gideon."

Luke hovered beside him, his hand gripping at Gideon's shoulder.

"She's not—"

"I know," Gideon snapped, waving his hand away. His voice faltered. "I know—"

"She's not what?" Cleo asked.

Gideon refused to say it out loud. He wouldn't. He didn't give a fuck what any angel said. Because he didn't believe this was it. It couldn't be. Not when they had made it this far. Not when she told him she loved him and then gave everything she had to keep them all safe, leaving him staring after her like a fucking deer caught in headlights. Not when he wanted to tell her how much he loved her too. How he still couldn't wrap his head around how easily it had happened.

"In one way or another, they always come true," Tefi said.

"Tefi," Luke warned. "Remember what I said—"

"No," Gideon said, shrugging off his jacket. "We're not doing this, Benny."

He refused to let this be it.

He was careful as he moved her, laying her flat on her back, brushing her hair off of her face. He couldn't perform a ritual. He couldn't summon sunlight and send a demon back to hell. But he could try and save her. He had to try.

Prophecy be damned.

She deserved more time.

He had been a lifeguard when he was a kid, an easy way to get the hell out of the house in the summertime and make enough money to buy himself a new baseball mitt when he needed it. They had CPR certifications at the start of every season, learning chest compressions on a foam dummy. He'd never actually done this on a person before.

Well, this was a hell of a time to start.

He pressed his hands together over her chest and began compressions, counting one for every second, putting the full force of his weight behind them. As he inched closer to the half-minute mark, he leaned forward and pressed his mouth to hers, breathing in for two beats before resuming compressions. She wasn't breathing so he would do it for her.

He would give her every breath in his body if it meant bringing her back.

Each second ticked in his head, the silence falling around them deafening.

Her skin was a little clammy, but it was warm, and with each rescue breath he passed between her lips, he hoped it was working, that it was breathing life back into her.

"Please," he whispered, his voice cracking. "We didn't get enough time—"

Another two breaths.

"This is not how this ends," he told her, the heels of his palms pressing hard into her chest. "Not when I finally know what this can feel like—"

Another two breaths.

"Benny, please." He closed his eyes as he counted his compressions again in his head. *One, two*— "Fuck, come on. Come on, baby—I love you. "

Ten, eleven, twelve—

Benny let out a strangled gasp.

Gideon stopped the compressions, his fingers pressing against her throat, searching for her pulse. It was faint, but it was there, and he could see her chest rising and falling with every new breath. He rested back on his heels, his head tilting back as he tried to catch his breath. He rubbed his hand across his face, his fingers brushing back the hot, wet tears that had been threatening to spill.

"Pat, get your son on the phone," Jimmy barked. "Have him meet us in the lobby."

Everyone was scrambling around him as sirens wailed in the distance. Considering the neighborhood they were in, Gideon was surprised anyone had bothered to call at all. But it only meant they had to move fast. How would any of them be able to explain what had happened here?

"Come on, Gid," Luke said, voice soft. "Let's get her home."

· · · · · ·•)) ❭ ● ❰ ((•· · · · · ·

The loft felt like it had become a triage tent, and Gideon watched as Olivia and Imani moved back and forth between the group of them, assessing damage, shoving bandages and painkillers in respective hands, all while trying to piece together the events of the night. Frank was gone. The gate was closed. But what was it all for if Benny never woke up?

Gideon was sitting in the window, one knee drawn up to his chest, his suit jacket gone, his shirt unbuttoned at the collar, his sleeves rolled up. Benny's necklace was dangling in his fingers, the chain wrapped up in his fist. His eyes were trained on his bedroom door. It had been closed for over an hour, Wilder ushering everyone out so that he could work without interference.

But what good was the Healer's magic if Benny's body wouldn't accept it?

The ride back to the loft had been quick, Luke speeding through the empty, early-morning streets downtown while Gideon cradled Benny in his arms in the backseat. It wasn't lost on him how familiar that scene was, but so much had changed since the night they found her. He couldn't stop himself from checking her pulse every few minutes, as if he would lose her again in the time it took them to return home.

"How long was she out?" Olivia asked.

"It couldn't have been more than a couple of minutes," Cleo replied as she ran a cotton ball against a cut on Jimmy's forehead.

She was using her left hand, her other arm in a makeshift sling that Luke fastened for her as soon as they all returned to the loft. Although Cleo had protested, she eventually allowed him with a sort of funny smile on her face. The remaining Caruso men had returned to their own homes or handled cleanup duty. But Torretta, Jimmy, and Pasquale weren't going anywhere until they knew Benny was okay. Pasquale was cooking in the kitchen, the faint smell of garlic and onion filling the space. He had told them they all looked like shit and needed a good meal. Never mind his crooked, probably broken nose. Imani was there to help, chopping and stirring.

The only one he noticed missing was Tefi.

"Which is... good, right?" Imani interjected. "I mean, they say the longer they're out—"

But she cut herself off, as if she didn't want to let that thought out into the universe.

"Do you think—" Olivia paused as she struggled with the plastic wrapping on a fresh bottle of hydrogen peroxide, and Gideon could see her hands were shaking. "Dammit."

He watched as Luke crossed toward her and reached for the bottle. His brother offered her a small smile as he pulled the plastic off and handed the bottle back to her. She stared up at him, her eyes glassy with unshed tears.

"She can heal," she continued, turning back to look at the rest of the group. "I mean, do you think that'll help?"

He'd be lying if he said that thought hadn't crossed his mind. Had he managed to bring her back enough for her abilities to start working? But Gideon was functioning purely off a combination of adrenaline and hope at this point. A dangerous mixture. He sighed as he rested his head back against the window, his fingers tapping anxiously against his knee. All he wanted to do was bust down his bedroom door and find out what the hell was taking Wilder so long.

"Her abilities far transcend anything I ever expected," Harker said, the awe clear in his voice. He leaned back against the kitchen island, his elbows resting against the countertop. "It's certainly possible."

"Angelo, if you don't sit your ass down," Jimmy muttered from the living room. "You got tossed like a fucking bowling ball into those pews."

"I wanna get in that goddamn room," Torretta said, speaking Gideon's thoughts aloud.

"I know," Jimmy said. "We all wanna know how Benny's doing. But you're gonna be no fucking use to her if you don't rest."

"Neither will you," Olivia said, her voice startling Gideon as he realized how close she was to him. She gestured to his face. "You look like shit. And you're bleeding."

"I'm fine," he said with a wave of his hand.

"Yes, of course you are," she said dryly, soaking a cotton ball in hydrogen peroxide. She perched herself against the edge of the window ledge as she leaned in to wipe at whatever scrapes bothered her. He sucked in a breath at the sting. "You did good, you know."

"She knew," Gideon said, exasperated. The thought had been lingering in his mind for the last hour. He should have known. The way she kissed him, the look in her eyes when she told him she loved him. She had known that night on the roof and he'd selfishly used himself to distract her, to stop the thoughts from being spoken aloud. "She walked out there knowing what was going to happen."

"Maybe she knew you'd have her back," Luke said.

"And you did," Olivia agreed as she placed tape across the cut over his eyebrow. "So, thank you, Gideon. You saved her life tonight."

"She saved everyone."

The door to his bedroom swung open.

Wilder, looking frazzled and frustrated, cleared his throat.

Gideon pushed himself up off the window ledge, his heart beginning to thump in his chest. His hand flexed at his side, the other clutched the necklace in his palm.

"She's awake."

The collective relief was palpable throughout the room. But as everyone seemed to turn toward him, Wilder held out his hands.

"She's got a broken rib and some scratches on her abdomen, but they're fairly surface. I can't do much. I can soothe the pain but her body won't allow me to do much more than that. She's going to be in recovery for a couple of weeks at least, depending on how quickly she can heal. She's going to need a lot of rest," he said, eyeing them all with a stern glance. "Maybe just a couple of you at a time."

"Come on, Crawford," Torretta grumbled as he pushed himself up from the sofa.

He hesitated, watching as the older man limped across the living room.

"You saved her life, kid," he said. "Now tell you love her while she's awake, alright?"

He rubbed his hand against his chest.

Yeah, he probably should.

All of the curtains were tossed open in his bedroom, the sunlight coursing through the windows. Benny was propped up with every pillow on his bed, tucked underneath his covers, her hands no longer blackened with ash, her skin no longer so pale. But she had a bruise on her cheek, and she looked exhausted and small. Still, when she saw them both, her whole face lit up, her smile so wide and so bright it took the breath right out of him.

He couldn't believe how close he had been to losing her.

But he hung back, resting his forearm against the door jamb as Torretta moved ahead.

"Hey, kiddo," the older man greeted, perching against the edge of the bed, a soft smile on his weathered face. "You feeling okay?"

"Well, considering I apparently died"—she winced as she pushed herself up to a sitting position—"I feel pretty good, all things considered."

Torretta choked out a laugh that sounded an awful lot like a sob.

"Jesus Christ, I thought I lost you, Ben," he said, reaching for her hand with both of his. "You really scared the shit outta me."

"I know," she said, her throat working over itself. "I pushed it too far. I couldn't stop even if I wanted to. But I just didn't want anyone else to get hurt."

Gideon's fist clenched, his chest feeling tight.

His brave, selfless girl.

"Wilder said you've got a quiet couple of weeks ahead of you," Torretta said. "You wanna come home? We can bring some of your stuff to the house, if you want."

"I appreciate that," she said, before shaking her head. "But I need to go home. As much as I love this bed... I need to be back in my own space, I need to figure out what's next. I need to be here, in Philly."

Torretta nodded.

"Okay, kid," he said, squeezing her hand. "Whatever you want. But I'm instituting a new rule, okay? Dinners. Every Sunday. I'll come by, and we'll squeeze into that tiny-ass kitchen of yours."

"I would love that," she said, tears shimmering in her eyes.

Torretta smiled as he pushed himself up off the bed.

"I'll have some of the men go by your place, make sure you're all set."

"Thank you, babbo."

Torretta's jaw clenched as he turned away from Benny, the discomfort clear in his steps. The older man was definitely in more pain than he was letting on. When he reached Gideon, he held out his hand to shake, his smile grateful.

But as Gideon took his hand, Torretta was pulling him into a tight embrace.

"Thank you," he said, voice barely above a whisper. "For bringing her back."

Torretta cupped his hand around the nape of Gideon's neck, a knowing smile on his face before he left the two of them alone. It was a gesture Gideon hadn't expected. It was… fatherly, almost. And that threw him. But he realized he liked it all the same.

"Gideon?"

Benny was staring up at him, apprehension settling into her features.

"Hey," he said, moving closer into the room.

"Will you come sit with me?"

She shifted over slowly, and Gideon found there was nothing in the world he wanted more than to do just that. He kicked off his shoes and slid into the bed beside her, relief sinking into his skin as she ducked under his arm and burrowed up against him. Just the feel of her this close was a comfort. But he was careful not to hold her too tightly, very aware that he was the reason her rib was cracked to begin with.

"I promise I'll replace these sheets." She picked at the edge of the top sheet, faint marks of blood and ash sticking to the otherwise crisp white. "I'm sorry."

"I don't care about the sheets, Benny," he replied, exasperated. "You're alive."

"Thanks to you," she said, peering up at him.

He pressed a rough kiss to her forehead.

"We've only just started, you and me," he said. "We deserve more time."

"I said something, earlier," she began, apprehension creeping into her gaze. "And I just wanted to tell you that, you know, it doesn't have to be a big deal if you don't feel the same. Because I know it's fast and it's been a pretty crazy couple of weeks and I just—"

"Benedetta Russo," he cut in gently, his fingers brushing through her hair. "It's a huge fucking deal. You telling me you love me is the best goddamn thing I've ever heard in my life. Do you wanna know why?"

"Why?" she asked, gazing up at him, her mouth twitching slightly.

"Because I love you, too."

He kissed her then with a shameless desperation, his mouth pressing against hers as his fingers tangled in her hair. It was an easy thing to get lost in, to forget everything else going on around them. And he wanted to so badly. He had been so close to losing this. To losing her.

She smiled against his lips, her voice breathless when she asked, "So, what now?"

"Now?" he said. "Benny, I am taking you out on a date."

Six Months Later

"They're saying it's a nor'easter—"

Benny turned on the taps of her bathtub, making sure to crank up the hot water. She had barely made it home from campus before the winds started to pick up, the streets already covered in a few inches of snow. She started to peel her half-damp clothing from her body, creating a trail of sneakers, jeans, a sweater as she dug around in the cabinet of her vanity for her bubble bath. She spent the entire day in advisor meetings discussing the status of her thesis, and she was exhausted. All she wanted to do was curl up on the sofa, turn on some mindless television, and heat up that leftover pizza in her fridge.

"That bad, huh?" Gideon asked from the living room.

"I guess so," she called back. She squeezed in a heavy dollop of bubble bath, the lavender scent a sweet inhale. "I wonder if they're gonna close campus tomorrow."

The old cast-iron tub was filling up fast and the bubbles were dangerously close to overflowing, but Benny didn't mind. She was ready to be consumed. With a little snap of her fingers, the candles on the vanity lit themselves as the overhead light dimmed. She pulled her hair off her face with a hair tie from her wrist, gathering it up into a messy bun before stripping herself of her remaining clothing, socks and underwear tossed with the rest of her things. The only thing that remained was her mother's golden pendant hanging between her breasts.

She tested the water with the back of her hand.

Just the perfect level of scalding.

A deep sigh passed through her lips as she sank into the tub.

It was the first week of March, and she was trying not to panic at the precious few months she had left to finalize her thesis. All these years in her doctorate program, and suddenly the last few months were just whizzing by. Though, it didn't help that for the first time in a long time, she'd had a rather welcome distraction.

The last six months had been a whirlwind. Her recovery was painful, but she was grateful. Thanks to her own healing ability, she seemed to heal in half the time expected. Gideon was with her every step of the way, doting on her and treating her with the utmost care. She'd never tire of his gentle touch. Plus there were plenty of two a.m. grilled cheeses at Betty's when she needed a break.

There had been funerals to attend, for the men who helped save her at Our Lady of Perpetual Help, and a lot of work to be done in her father's organization. New tests of loyalty. Benny found herself more involved with her father's work than ever before. Fighting alongside these men had left her feeling a more vested interest.

And perhaps a more grounded one.

She could do this without losing herself, she hoped.

The Crawford brothers were taking a break from their usual criminal activities, thanks in part to her father coming through on his promise to double his original payment. Gideon and Luke had balked initially, telling Angelo they weren't going to accept it. Not after everything that happened. Which was sweet, but stupid. It was a lot of money. And frankly, well earned.

"So, are you telling me we're gonna be snowed in?"

Gideon was leaning against the door jamb, arms crossed against his chest, dressed in a perfectly worn pair of jeans and a soft, faded T-shirt snug against his biceps. She liked him casual. She liked him every which way, but this was especially good.

She rested her forearms on the edge of the tub as she peered up at him.

"I think so," she said, voice solemn.

Gideon stepped further into the bathroom, a smile playing at his lips as he glanced down at the pink vintage tile, tracking each article of clothing as it led to the bathtub.

"What time do you have to go in tomorrow?" he asked.

"The only thing I've got is lunch with the girls," she said, leaning back. Cleo had become a welcome addition to her weekly coven lunch with Olivia and Imani. She lifted one leg out of the water, running her loofah slowly against her skin. "Tomorrow's pretty much a free day."

"No early morning?" he asked casually.

"No early morning."

"Hm" was all he said.

"Gideon," she said, looking up at him with a sweet smile. "Take off your clothes."

A glimmer of something wicked flashed behind his eyes.

"These clothes?" he asked as he crossed toward her. "You sure?"

And before she knew it, he was stepping into the tub fully dressed.

She shrieked his name with laughter, the water splashing over the side as he kneeled between her legs, his body hovering over hers, his clothing creating an unexpectedly delicious sensation against her bare skin. "What are you doing?"

His smile widened into something playful and boyish.

"Come here," he urged, his hand cupping the side of her face.

"You are out of your mind."

"For you," he agreed before he kissed her, his mouth finding hers thoroughly wanting. She leaned into him, her legs spreading open as he fit himself between her, the denim rough against her thighs. He ran his teeth along her bottom lip and she shuddered. "And you love it."

"I do," she sighed, her fingers dragging down his back until she found the hem of his T-shirt. She slipped her hands beneath the wet fabric, her nails digging into his skin. "You know I do."

"Move in with me," he said, his hand smoothing down her throat, his thumb creating just a little bit of pressure at her pulse point. "I don't just want to be snowed in with you. I want this every single day, Benny."

A breath passed between her lips as his touch trailed from her throat to her breast, his palm rough against her skin. He teased at her nipple, squeezing at the hard bud until she was squirming against him, her thighs tightening around him. He somehow knew exactly what she needed. Always.

"Every day," she repeated, the idea so incredibly appealing at this precise moment.

"Luke is moving out," he told her as his other hand curved around her waist, the water splashing as he pulled her close against him.

"What?" she asked, blinking. "Where is he going?"

"That's not pertinent to this conversation," he said, reminding her with his mouth, his teeth dragging against the line of her jaw.

"Hm, right, yes," she murmured. "You want me to move in with you."

"I do," he said as her fingers moved to his belt buckle. "I would like that a lot."

"Can we turn the other bedroom into an office?"

"We can turn it into a goddamn ballet studio if you want," he told her.

She licked at her lips as she undid the fly of his jeans, her hand slipping beneath the heavy fabric. He was hard as she wrapped her hand around him, her strokes drawing a soft moan from his lips, her magic flowing from her to him. She wasn't sure she'd ever get used to the way he reacted to her touch. She loved the way he fell apart with her. She cupped his jaw in her hand, reaching up to press a rough kiss to his mouth.

"Fuck, Benny," he moaned as she increased her pace.

"Yes," she said, watching the way his eyes darkened, his pupils blown wide.

"Yes?" he repeated, a little breathless.

"I want to move in with you."

"I love you," he said, voice rough as his hips twitched. "I love you so fucking much."

"I love you too," she said. "I'm going to paint the bathroom pink."

"Whatever you want, Benny," Gideon said as he lost himself in her hand. "Whatever you want."

Hell wasn't what he expected it to be.

It was dry, open, vaster than he could have ever imagined. And it wasn't nearly as dark as he thought. In fact, it was almost blinding. The sun bearing down so hard it left him with a permanent kind of headache, a constant thudding pain building between his ears. Or what was left of them. Frank wasn't sure if they had grown back yet, the process of rebuilding himself slow and painstaking.

Death was a different kind of adventure.

Even when one's body was blown up into tiny little pieces.

They could find a way back to each other, build themselves over again.

However, his days in the body of Halmanthoran were over. The demon vessel he had been so intent upon was no longer his for the taking. A part of his punishment was to be denied the ability to transform. His curse was to be put back in his human body. Weak. Mortal. Filled with the ability to feel pain.

Over and over again.

He never could have foreseen the extent of the witch's power. It was foolish of him not to explore all avenues, to predict all outcomes. He was better than that. He had spent far too long trying to achieve ascension for him to have made such a reckless mistake.

But in the time it took him to regrow his bones, his sinew, his skin, he found his way back toward the gate. The large and looming doors standing so tall he wasn't sure he'd ever seen them wholly. He had heard rumblings that the passageway back was still open. That in the aftermath of his destruction, the ritual to close the doors had gone wrong.

They had been so close.

But a tiny sliver of an opening remained.

A wicked smile crossed his lips as he wondered what could be done, what could move beyond the veil and back into the world. See, the tricky thing about Hell was that it was hard to leave. Even if the gate was open, there had to be an invitation. No slamming the doors wide open and unleashing the hounds and the devils in the army he had hoped for.

Hell was a trap. An endless, tormenting circle.

But maybe there was still a way to have a little bit of fun.

ACKNOWLEDGEMENTS

When I first started writing *Love At The Gates Of Hell* I was right in the middle of what felt like an endless journey of infertility. I was hanging on by a thread, honestly. Writing has always been my escape. When I was younger and typing away on the family computer in our living room at all hours of the night, or when I was older and sitting in on my first academic critiques with my fellow creative writing majors in college. Diving in to an alternate world where magic and vampires and demons exist was the perfect way to distract myself when every single pregnancy test came back with a big bold NEGATIVE.

But then this book took on a life of its own.

Enough story to drive more than just the one book I was writing and I suddenly really wanted to see it out in the world. I powered through the first couple of drafts, hired an incredible editor (hi Sarah!), and then after multiple rounds of IUI and IVF, I finally got pregnant. With *twins*.

The version of LATGOH that I wrote then was put on an indefinite hold. I was on bed rest the last six weeks of my pregnancy. I gave birth at 38 weeks. I became a mother!! INSANITY. Can you believe they just let you take the babies home with you from the hospital? It doesn't seem right.

But LATGOH was still somewhere, simmering in the back of my mind, itching to come out.

And I just kept thinking, "What do I have to lose?" This book was my baby, too, and it deserves it's time to shine. And although my life has become just absolute constant chaos with two toddlers running around, I want those little gremlins to see that their mom pursued a passion that makes her so incredibly happy (even when I'm self-editing at 3AM trying to understand what my vague notes mean).

I could not have done this without my friend Jenny. My twin soul. My alpha/beta/whatever it is you call it when you can send random paragraphs on Discord at all hours of the day. She has seen every version of this book. She's cheered me on through every moment of doubt. This book and the rest of the Seven Sinners trilogy would not exist without your support.

A huge thank you to Bridgette and Chrissy, my first ever writing friends. The women who have supported me when we were role playing as teenagers on Livejournal to now being the best goddamn beta readers anyone could ever ask for.

To the immensely talented Kate for an absolutely stunning cover design. Working with you has been a dream and I can't wait to get started on the cover for book two in the series!

A deep bow of gratitude to Sarah, my editor. She is a romance genius and has been such a wonderful person to have in my corner as I plot out the rest of this little series.

To the Hippos— the women who came into my life during one of the weirdest job environments ever and are now truly some of my favorite people in the world. They have been so patient as I bemoan every aspect of marketing myself and were the first to pre-order this book when the link went live.

Nora, thank you for hand-binding my book. It is one of the most special things I will ever own.

To every single person on my ARC team, every reader, every person who has ever liked a post on social, I truly appreciate all of your excitement and support. It means the world.

A very delighted thank you to my family— it has to be pretty weird to see all the spicy little posts I share on social. But you're all so happy for me and so supportive and I just love you all so much.

And finally, to my husband Josh for building me up and up and up even when I was hellbent on crumbling down. You gave me the space and time to publish a book while raising twins. You're the best, and I love you.

ABOUT THE AUTHOR

Stella Rossi is a writer of Romance, both paranormal and contemporary. When she isn't writing romance novels, she works in Advertising Strategy for one of your favorite media companies. She lives in New Jersey with her husband, her children, her cats, and her dog (a menagerie of chaos, if you will). She loves reality television, creating new character runs in Baldur's Gate 3, and prefers a crispy Diet Coke to all other beverages.

Stella loves to tell stories about complicated women, feminine rage, and the men who would crawl on their knees for the women they love.

You can find out more about Stella on her website.
http://stellarossiwrites.com

www.ingramcontent.com/pod-product-compliance
Lightning Source LLC
Chambersburg PA
CBHW030223120726
47903CB00005B/1347